FOLLOW ME!

A black beetling shape loomed up out of the rain, casting mounted men aside from either edge of its hull like the coulter of a plow. Smoke and steam billowed from the stack toward the rear; the rain hissed when it struck that metal. More steam jetted from under the rear wheels, a steady *chuff-chuff-chuff*. A light cannon nosed out from the bow through a letterbox-type slit. Small ports for rifles and pistols showed along its sides.

Men were switching their aim to the car. Sparks flew as bullets spanged and flashed off the surface, but even the brass-tipped hardpoints wouldn't punch through.

"Follow me!" Raj shouted, and slapped his heels into Horace's flanks.

Men followed him—no time to check who—and the hound raced forward at a long gallop, belly to the earth. The iron juggernaut grew with frightening swiftness. Raj judged the distance and launched himself—onto the hull of the armored car. His right hand slapped onto a U-bracket riveted to the hull. His waist was at the edge of the turtleback, and his legs dangled perilously near the spinning spokes of the front wheel.

And any second the commander would stick his head out of the hatch and shoot him like a trussed sheep. . . .

THE STEEL

Book IV of THE GENERAL

S.M. STIRLING

DAVID DRAKE

BAEN

The General, Book IV: THE STEEL

Copyright © 1993 by S.M. Stirling & David Drake

A Baen Books Original

Baen Publishing Enterprises
P.O. Box 1403
Riverdale, NY 10471

ISBN: 0-671-72189-5

Cover art by Paul Alexander

First printing, October 1993

Distributed by Simon & Schuster
1230 Avenue of the Americas
New York, NY 10020

Printed in the United States of America

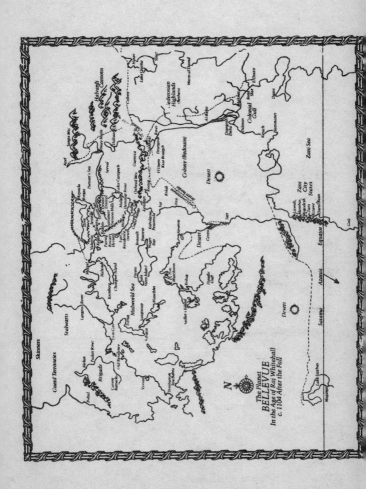

The Planet
BELLEVUE
In the Age of Raj Whitehall
c. 1184 After the Fall

CHAPTER ONE

Thom Poplanich floated through infinity. The monobloc exploded outward, and he *felt* the twisting of space-time in its birth-squall. . . .

I think I understand that now, he thought.

excellent, Center said. **we will return to socio-historical analysis: subject, fall of the federation of man.**

He had been down here in the sanctum of Sector Command and Control Unit AZ12-b14-c000 Mk. XIV for years, now. His body was in stasis, his mind connected with the ancient battle computer on levels far broader than the speechlike linkage of communication. It was no longer necessary for him to see events sequentially. . . .

Images drifted through his consciousness. Earth. The True Earth of the Cannonical Handbooks, not this world of Bellevue. Yet it was not the perfect home of half-angels that the priests talked of, but a world of men. Nations rose and warred with each other, empires grew and fell. Men learned as the cycles swung upward, then forgot, and fur-clad savages dwelt in the ruins of cities, burning their books for winter's warmth. At last one cycle swung further skyward than any before. On a small island northwest of the main continent, engines were built. Ones he recognized at first, clanking steam-engines driving factories to spin cloth, dragging loads across iron rails, powering ships. The machines grew greater, stranger. They took to the air and cities burned beneath them. They spread from one land to the next, springing at last into space.

Earth floated before him, blue and white like the images of Bellevue that Center showed him — blue and white like all worlds that could nourish the seed of Earth. One final war scarred the globe beneath him with flames, pinpoints of fire that consumed whole cities at a blow. Soundless globes of magenta and orange bloomed in airless space.

the last jihad, Center's voice said. **observe.**

A vast construct drifted into view, skeletal and immense beside the tubular ships and dot-tiny suited humans.

the tanaki spatial displacement net. the first model. Energies flowed across it, twisting into dimensions describable only in mathematics that he had not yet mastered. The ships vanished, to reappear far away . . . here, in Bellevue's system. The Colonists, first men to set foot on this world. They landed and raised the green flag of Islam.

even more than the jihad, the net made the federation of man essential, Center said. The empire that rose this time expanded until it covered all the Earth, and leaped outward to nearby stars. A century later, its representatives landed on distant Bellevue, much to the displeasure of the descendants of the refugees. **and the net was its downfall. expansion proceeded faster than integration.** Long strings of formulae followed. **once the tipping point was reached, entropic decay accelerated exponentially.**

The higher they rise, the harder they fall, Thom thought.

true. There was a slight overtone of surprise in Center's dispassionate machine-voice.

More images. War flickering between the stars, mutiny, secession. Bellevue's Net flaring into plasma. The remnants of Federation units turning feral when they were cut off here, bringing civilization down in a welter of thermonuclear fire. Swift decay into barbarism for most areas, a pathetic remnant of ancient knowledge preserved in the Civil Government and the Colony, degenerating into superstition. Now a thousand years and more had passed, and a tentative rebirth stirred.

cycles within cycles, Center said. **the overall trend is still toward maximum entropy. unless my intervention can alter the parameters, fifteen thousand years will pass until the ascendant phase of the next overall historical period.**

An image eerily familiar, for he had seen it with his own eyes as well as through Center's senses. Two young men out exploring the ancient catacombs beneath the Governor's palace in East Residence. Unlikely friends: Thom Poplanich, grandson of the last Poplanich Governor. A slight young man in a patrician's hunting outfit of tweed. Raj Whitehall, tall, with a swordsman's shoulders and wrists. Guard to the reigning Barholm Clerett, and like him from distant Descott County, source of the Civil Government's finest soldiers. Once again he saw them discover the bones outside the centrum, the bones of those Center had considered and rejected as its agents in the world.

Raj will do it, Thom thought. *If any man can reunite the world, he can.*

if any man can, Center agreed. **the probability of success is less than 45% +/-3, even with my assistance.**

He's already beaten back the Colony. The battle of Sandoral had been the greatest victory the Civil Government had won in generations. *Destroyed the Squadron.* The Squadron and its Admirals had held the Southern Territories for more than a century, the most recent of the Military Governments to come down out of the barbarous Base Area. *And he's beating the Brigade.* The 591st Provisional Brigade were the strongest of the barbarians, and they held Old Residence, the original seat of the Civil Government at the western end of the Midworld Sea.

to date, Center acknowledged, **he has taken the crown peninsula and lion city. the more difficult battles remain.**

Men follow Raj, Thom said quietly. *Not only that, he makes them do things beyond themselves.* He paused. *What really worries me is Barholm Clerett. He doesn't deserve a man like Raj serving him! And that nephew he's sent along on this campaign is worse.*

cabot clerett is more able than his uncle, and less a prisoner of his obsessions, Center noted.

That's what worries me.

CHAPTER TWO

The cavalry were singing as they rode; the sound bawled out over the manifold thump of paws from the riding dogs, the creak of harness and squeal of ungreased wheels from the baggage train:

Oh, we Descoteers have hairy ears —
* We goes without our britches*
And pops our cocks with jagged rocks,
* We're hardy sons of bitches!*

"Hope they're as cheerful in a month," Raj Whitehall said, looking down at the map spread over his saddlebow. His hound Horace shifted beneath him from one foot to the other, whining with impatience to be off at a gallop in the crisp fall air. Raj stroked his neck with one gauntleted hand.

The commanders were gathered on a knoll, and it gave a wide view over the broad river valley below. The hoarse male chorus of the cavalry troopers sounded up from the fields. The Expeditionary Force snaked westward through low rolling hills. Wagons and guns on the road, infantry in battalion columns to either side, and five battalions of cavalry off to the flanks. There was very little dust; it had rained yesterday, just enough to lay the ground. The infantry were making good time, rifles over their right shoulders and blanket-rolls looped over the left. In the middle of the convoy the camp-followers spread in a magpie turmoil, one element of chaos in the practiced regularity of the column, but they were keeping up too. It was mild but crisp, perfect weather for outdoor work; the leaves of the oaks and maples that carpeted the higher hills had turned to gold and scarlet hues much like the native vegetation.

The soldiers looked like veterans, now. Even the ones who hadn't fought with him before this campaign; even the former Squadrones, military captives taken into the Civil Government's forces after the conquest of the Southern Territories last year. Their uniforms were dirty and torn, the blue of the tailcoat jackets and the dark maroon of their baggy pants both the color of the soil, but the weapons were clean and the men ready to fight . . . which was all that really mattered.

"Looks like more rain tonight," Ehwardo Poplanich said, shading his eyes and looking north. "Doesn't it *ever* not rain in this bloody country?"

The Companions were veterans now too, his inner circle of commanders. Like a weapon whose hilt is worn with use, shaped to fit the hand that reaches for it in the dark. Ehwardo was much more than a Governor's grandson these days.

"Only in high summer," Jorg Menyez replied. "Rather reminds me of home — there are parts of Kelden County much like this, and the Diva River country up on the northwestern frontier."

He sneezed; the infantry specialist was allergic to dogs, which was why he used a riding steer, and why he'd originally chosen the despised foot-soldiers for his military career, despite high rank and immense wealth. Now he believed in them with a convert's zeal, and they caught his faith and believed in themselves.

"Good-looking farms," Gerrin Staenbridge said, biting into an apple. "My oath, but I wouldn't mind getting my hands on some of this countryside."

And Gerrin's come a long way too. He'd commanded the 5th Descott before Raj made them his own. Back then garrison-duty boredom had left him with nothing to occupy his time but fiddling the battalion accounts and his hobbies, the saber and the opera and good-looking youths.

There were a good many orchards hereabouts; apple and plum and cherry, and vineyards trained high on stakes or to the branches of low mulberry trees. Wheat and corn had been cut and carted, the wheat in thatched ricks in the farmyards, the corn in long rectangular bins still on the cob; dark-brown earth rippled in furrows behind ox-drawn ploughs as the fields were made ready for winter grains. Few laborers fled, even when the army passed close-by; word had spread that the eastern invaders ravaged only where resisted . . . and the earth must be worked, or all would starve next year. Pastures were greener than most of the easterners were used to, grass up to the hocks of the grazing cattle. Half-timbered cottages stood here and there, usually nestled in a grove, with an occasional straggling crossroads village, or a peon settlement next to a blocky stone-built manor house.

Many of the manors were empty; the remaining landlords were mostly civilian, and eager to come in and swear allegiance to the Civil Government. Here and there a mansion stood burnt and empty. Ill-considered resistance, or peasant vengeance on fleeing masters. Some of the peons abandoned their plows to come and gape as the great ordered mass of the Civil Government's army passed, with the Starburst fluttering at its head. It had been more than five hundred years since that holy flag flew in these lands. Raj reflected ironically that the natives probably thought the 7th Descott Rangers' marching-song was a hymn; there was much touching of amulets and kneeling.

We fuck the whores right through their drawers
    We do not care for trifles —
We hangs our balls upon the walls
    And shoots at 'em with rifles.

"Area's too close to the Stalwarts for my liking,"
Kaltin Gruder said. His hand stroked the scars on his
face, legacy of a Colonial shell-burst that had killed his
younger brother. "Speaking of which, any news of the
Brigaderos garrisons up there?"

"The Ministry of Barbarians came through on that
one," Raj said, still not looking up from the map. "The
Stalwarts are raiding the frontier just as we paid them
to, and most of the enemy regulars there are staying.
The rest are pulling back southwest, toward the Padan
River, where they can barge upstream to Carson
Barracks."

Bribing one set of barbarians to attack another had
been a Civil Government specialty for generations.
Cheaper than wars, usually, although there were
dangers as well. The Brigade had come south long ago,
but the Stalwarts were only down from the Base Area a
couple of generations. Fierce, treacherous, numerous,
and still heathen — not even following the heretical
This Earth cult.

"Right," Raj said, rolling up the map. "We'll continue on this line of advance to the Chubut river —" he
used the map to point west "— at Lis Plumhas.
M'Brust reports it's opened its gates to the 1st
Cruisers. Ehwardo, I want you to link up with him
there — push on ahead of the column — with two
batteries and take command. Cross the river, and feint
toward the Padan at Empirhado. It's a good logical
move, and they'll probably believe it. Engage at your
discretion, but screen us in any case."

The Padan drained most of the central part of the
Western Territories, rising in the southern foothills of
the Sangrah Dil Ispirito mountains and running
northeast along the range, then west and southwest
around its northernmost outliers. Empirhado was an
important riverport, and taking it would cut off the
north from the Brigadero capital at Carson Barracks.

"Actually," Raj went on, "we'll cut southeast again

around Zeronique at the head of the Residential Gulf and come straight down on Old Residence. I want them to come to us, and they'll have to fight for that eventually — it *is* the ancient capital of the Civil Government. At the same time, it's accessible by sea up the Blankho River, so we've a secure line of communications to Lion City. Strategic offensive, tactical defensive."

Everyone nodded, some making notes. Lion City was a *very* safe base. Its ruling syndics had tried to resist the Civil Government army, fearful of Brigade retaliation and confident in their city walls. Raj had found an ancient Pre-Fall passageway under them and lead a party to open the gates from within. After the sack, the syndics who'd counselled resistance had been torn to bits — quite literally — by the enraged common folk of the city. The commoners' only hope now was a Civil Government victory; if the Brigade came back they'd slaughter every man, woman and child for treason to the General . . . and for the murder of their betters.

"Meanwhile, I'm going to keep five battalions of cavalry with the main column and send the rest of you out raiding. Round up supplies, liberate the towns and incidentally, knock down the defenses — we don't want Brigaderos occupying them again in our rear. Be alert, messers, there'll probably be more resistance soon. I've furnished a list of objectives of military significance. Grammeck?"

"I don't like these roads," the artilleryman-cum-engineer said.

Like most of his branch of service, Grammeck Dinnalysn was a cityman, from East Residence. Unlike most of the military nobility, Raj Whitehall had never hesitated to use the technical skills that went with that education.

"They're just graded dirt, and it's clay dirt at that. Much more rain, and it's going to turn into soup."

Raj nodded again. "Nevertheless, I intend to make at least twenty klicks per day, minimum."

Jorg Menyez shrugged. "My boys will march it," he said and sneezed, moving a little aside to get upwind of the dogs. "I'm surprised we haven't seen more resistance already," he added. "We're well beyond the zone Major Clerett raided."

Raj grinned. "A little dactosauroid flew in and whispered in my ear," he said, "in the person of the Esteemed Rehvidaro Boyez — he was one of the Ministry talkmongers at Carson Barracks, bribed his way out — that the Brigade has called a Council of War there."

Harsh laughter from the circle of Companions. The Council of War included all male Brigade adults, and decided the great issues of state in huge conclaves at Carson Barracks, the capital the Brigade had built off in the swamps. Or to be more accurate, debated the issues at enormous length. To men used to the omnipotent quasi-divine autocracy of the Civil Government, it was an endless source of amusement.

"No, no — it's actually a good move. They have to decide on their leadership before they can *do* anything. Filip Forker certainly won't." Forker was a mild-tempered scholar, very untypical of the brawling warrior nobility of the Brigade; he was also a defeatist who'd been in secret communication with the Civil Government.

"So they have to get rid of him and elect a fighting man as General. Of course, they have left it a little late."

The troopers below roared out the last verse of their marching song:

> *Much joy we reap by diddlin' sheep*
> *In divers nooks and ditches*
> *Nor give we a damn if they be rams —*
> *We're hardy sons of bitches!*

"Let's get moving, gentlemen. I expect some warm welcomes on the way to Old Residence."

"Compliments to Captain Suharez, and Company C to face left, on this line," Gerrin Staenbridge said. He sketched quickly on his notepad, and tore off the sheet to hand to the dispatch rider. The man tucked it under his jacket to shelter the drawing from the slow drizzle of rain.

Gerrin raised his binoculars. The lancepoints of the Brigaderos cuirassiers were clearly visible behind the ridge there, four thousand meters out and to the west. From the way the pennants whipped backward, they were moving briskly. Bit of a risk to spread his front, but the fire of the other companies should cover it. Better to stop the flanking movement well out than to simply refuse his flank in place.

"And one gun," he added.

The messenger spurred, and the trumpet sounded. Men moved along the sunken lane to his front, where the main line of the two battalions faced north. A company crawled back and stood, then double-timed west in column of fours. Water spurted up from their boots, and squelched away from the gun that followed them, its dogs panting and skidding on the surface of wet earth and yellow leaves as they trundled out of sight to meet the enemy's flanking attack. The remaining men moved west to occupy the vacant space, spreading themselves in response to barked orders.

The paws of the colonel's dog squelched too as he rode down the lane; it was barely nine meters wide, rutted mud flanked on either side by tall maple and whipstick trees. North beyond that was a broad stretch of reaped wheat stubble with alfalfa showing green between the faded gold of the straw. Beyond that was a line of orchard, and the Brigaderos, those whose bodies weren't scattered across the field between from the first failed rush.

"That's right, lads," Staenbridge called out, as he cantered toward the center of the line, where the standards of the 5th Descott and the 1st Residence Life Guards flew together, beside the main battery. "Keep those delectable buttocks close to the earth and pick your targets."

The men were prone or kneeling behind the meter-high ridge that marked the sunken lane's northern edge. The trees and the remains of a rail fence gave more cover still; there were a scatter of brass cartridge cases and the lingering stink of sulphur under the wet mud and rotting leaf smell. Most of them had gray cloaks spread over their backs; Lion City had had a warehouse full of them, woven of raw wool with the lanolin still in them, nearly waterproof. Staenbridge had thoughtfully posted a guard on that when the city fell, and lifted enough for all his men and a margin extra. Raindrops glistened on the wool, sliding aside as the men adjusted sights and reloaded. The breechblock of a gun clanged open and the crew pushed it forward until its barrel jutted in alignment with the muzzles of the riflemens' weapons.

He drew up beside the banner. "Captain Harritch," he went on, "shift a splatgun to the left end of the line, if you please."

The commander of the two batteries shouted, and the light weapon jounced off down the trail, the crew pulling on ropes; there was no need to hitch the dog team for a short move, but it followed obediently, dragging the caisson with the reserve ammunition.

"We could put a mounted company behind the left and countercharge when those lobster-backs are stalled," Cabot Clerett offered.

It was the textbook answer, but Staenbridge shook his head. "Fighting barbs with swords," he said, "is like fighting a pig by getting down on your hands and knees and biting it. I prefer to keep the rifles on our firing-line. We'll see if they come again."

"These're going to," Bartin Foley said emotionlessly.

He was peeling an apple with the sharpened inner curve of his hook; now he sliced off a chunk and offered it. Staenbridge took it, ignoring Cabot Clerett's throttled impatience. It was crisper and more tart than the fruit he was used to. *Probably the longer winters here*, he thought.

Cabot Clerett probably resented the fact that Bartin Foley had started his military career as a protegee — boyfriend, actually — of Staenbridge's. Although the battles that had taken the young man's left hand, and the commands he'd held since, made him considerably more than that.

"Look to your right, Major Clerett," Gerrin said. "They may try something there as well."

Long lines of helmeted soldiers in gray-and-black uniforms were coming out of the orchard three thousand meters to their front. Serried lines, blocks three deep and fifty men broad all along the front, then a gap of several minutes and another wave, but these in company columns.

"Two thousand in the first wave," he said. "A thousand in column behind. Three thousand all up."

"Plus their reserve," Foley noted, peering at the treeline.

Clerett snorted. "If the barbs are keeping one," he said.

"Oh, these are, I should think . . . this is Hereditary High Colonel Eisaku and . . . "

"Hereditary Major Gutfreed," Foley completed. "Thirty-five to forty-five hundred in all, household troops and military vassals."

To the right a battery commander barked an order. The loader for the guns shoved a two-pronged iron tool into the head of a shell and turned, adjusting the fuse to the distance he was given. Within the explosive head a perforated brass tube turned within a solid one, exposing a precise length of beechwood-enclosed powder train. Another man worked the lever that dropped the blocking wedge and swung the breech-block aside, opening the chamber for the loader to push the shell home. The blocks clattered all along the line, five times repeated. The gunner clipped his lanyard to the release toggle and stood to one side; the rest of the crew skipped out of the path of recoil, already preparing to repeat the cycle, in movements better choreographed than most dances. The battery commander swung his sword down.

POUMPF. POUMPF. POUMPF. POUMPF. POUMPF. Five blasts of powder smoke and red light, and the guns bounced backward across the laneway, splattering muddy water to both sides. Crews heaved at their tall wheels to shove them back into battery, as the loaders pulled new shells out of the racks in the caissons.

The *crack* of the shells bursting over the enemy followed almost at once. Men died, scythed down from above. Staenbridge winced slightly in sympathy; over-head shrapnel was any soldier's nightmare, something to which there was no reply. The Brigaderos came on, picking up the pace but keeping their alignment. The columns following the troops deployed in line were edging toward his left; he nodded, confirmation of the opposing commander's design. It was a meeting of minds, as intimate as a saber-duel or dancing. Closer now, it didn't take long to cover a thousand meters at the trot. A thousand seconds, less than ten minutes. The Brigaderos dragoons had fixed their bayonets, and the wet steel glinted dully under the cloudy sky. Their boots were kicking up clots of dark-brown soil, ripping holes in the thin cover of the stubblefield.

POUMPF. POUMPF. POUMPF. POUMPF. POUMPF. More airbursts, and one defective timer that plowed into the dirt and raised a minor mud-volcano as the backup contact fuse set it off.

Nothing like the Squadrones, Staenbridge thought.

The barbarians of the Southern Territories had bunched in a crowded mass, a perfect target. These Brigaderos were much better.

POUMPF. POUMPF. POUMPF. POUMPF. POUMPF. Powder smoke drifted along the firing line, low to the ground and foglike under the drizzle.

At least the Southern Territories were dry, he thought. Descott County got colder than this in midwinter, but it was semi-arid.

"I make it eleven hundred meters," Foley said. Getting on for small-arms range.

"*Ready,*" Staenbridge called. Officers and noncoms went down the firing line, checking that sights were adjusted. "I wonder how the left flank is making out."

"Did ye load hardpoint?" Corporal Robbi M'Telgez hissed.

The rifleman he addressed swallowed nervously. "Think so, corp," he said, looking back over his shoulder at the noncom.

Company C were kneeling in a cornfield, just back from the crest of a swell of ground. The corn had never been harvested, but cattle and pigs had been turned loose into it. Most of the stalks were broken rather than uprooted, slick and brown with decay and the rain; they formed a tangle waist-high in wavering rows across the lumpy field. Just ahead of the line of troopers was the company commander, also down on one knee, with his signallers, and a bannerman holding the furled unit pennant horizontal to the ground. The field gun and its crew were slightly to the rear.

"Work yer lever," M'Telgez said.

The luckless trooper shoved his thumb into the loop behind the handgrip of his rifle and pushed the lever sharply downward. The action clacked and ejected the shell directly to the rear as the bolt swung down and slightly back. The noncom snatched it out of the air with his right hand, as quick and certain as a trout

rising to a fly. There was a hollow drilled back into the
pointed tip of the lead bullet.

"Ye peon-witted dickehead recruity!" the corporal
said. "Why ain't ye in t' fukkin' *infantry*? Ye want one a'
them pigstickers up yer arse?" Hollowpoint loads often
failed to penetrate the body-armor of Brigaderos heavy
cavalry.

He clouted the man alongside the head, under his
helmet. "Load!"

The younger man nodded and reached back to his
bandolier; it was on the broad webbing belt that
cinched his swallowtail uniform coat, just behind the
point of his right hip. The closing flap was buckled
back, exposing the staggered rows of cartridges in
canvas loops — the outer frame of the container was
rigid sauroid hide boiled in wax, but brass corrodes in
contact with leather. This time there was a smooth
pointed cap of brass on the lead of the bullet he
thumbed home down the grooved ramp on the top of
the rifle's bolt. Hunting ammunition for big thick-
skinned sauroids, but it did nicely for armor as well.

"Use yer brain, it'll save yer butt," the corporal went
on more mildly.

He sank back into his place in the ranks, watching
the platoon's lieutenant and the company commander.
The lieutenant was new since Stern Isle, but he
seemed to know his business. The platoon sergeant
thought so, at least. They'd both behaved as well as
anybody else in that *ratfuck* in the tunnel. M'Telgez
smiled, and the young trooper who'd been looking over
to him to ask a question swallowed again and looked
front, convinced that nothing he could see there would
be more frightening than the section-leader's face.
M'Telgez was thinking what he was going to do if —
when — he found out who had started the stampede to
the rear in the close darkness of the pipe tunnel.
There'd been nothing he could do, nothing *anyone*
could do, once it started. Except move back or get

trampled into a pulp and suffocated when the pipe blocked solid with a jam of flesh.

The 2nd Cruisers, jumped-up Squadrone barbs, had gone in instead of the 5th Descott. With Messer Raj. The stain on the 5th's honor had been wiped out by their bloodily successful assault on the gates later that night . . . but M'Telgez intended to find out who'd put the stain there in the first place. The 5th had been with Messer Raj since his first campaign and they'd never run from an enemy.

The gunners were rolling their weapon forward the last few meters to the crest of the slight rise, two men on either wheel and three holding up the trail.

"*On* the word of command," the lieutenant said, watching the captain. A trumpet sounded, five rising notes and a descant.

"Company —"

"Platoon —"

"*Forward!*"

One hundred and twenty men stood and took three paces forward. The lieutenants stopped, their arms and swords outstretched to the side in a T-bar to give their units the alignment.

To the Brigaderos, they appeared over the crest of the dead ground with the suddenness of a jack-in-the-box.

Five hundred meters before them about a quarter of the Brigaderos column was in view, coming over a slight rise. They rode in a column six men broad; expecting action soon, they'd brought the three-meter lances out of the buckets and were resting the butt-ends on the toes of their right boots. The dogs they rode were broad-pawed Newfoundlands, shaggy and massive and black, weighing up to fourteen hundred pounds each. They needed the bulk and bone to carry men wearing back and breastplate, thigh-guards and arm-guards of steel, plus sword and lance and firearms and helmet. Their usual role was to charge home into Stalwart masses already chopped into fragments by their dragoon comrades' rifle fire. Sometimes the savage footmen absorbed the charge and ate it, like a swarm of lethal bees too numerous for the lancers to swat. More often the cavalry scattered the Stalwarts into fugitives who could be hunted down and slaughtered . . . as long as the lancers went in boot to boot without the slightest hesitation.

It was a style of warfare that had ended in the eastern part of the Midworld basin two centuries ago, when breechloading firearms became common. The Brigaderos were about to learn why.

Of course, since there were nearly a thousand of the cuirassiers, the Civil Government troops might not survive the lesson either.

POUMPF.

The field gun recoiled away from the long plume of smoke. The first shell exploded at head-height a dozen yards from the front of the column; pure serendipity, since the fuses weren't sensitive enough to time that closely. It was cannister, a thin-walled head full of lead balls with a small bursting charge at the rear. The charge stripped the casing of the shell off its load and spread the balls out, but the velocity of the shell itself made them lethal. The first three ranks of the lancers went down in kicking, howling confusion. The commander of the cuirassier regiment had been standing in his stirrups and raising the triangular three-bar visor of his helmet to see what had popped up to bar his command's way. Three of the half-ounce balls ripped his head off his torso and threw the body in a backwards somersault over the cantle of his saddle.

Behind him the balls went over the heads of the rear of the column, protected by the dip in the field in which they rode. The projectiles struck the upraised lances instead, the wood of the forward ranks and the foot-long steel heads of those further back and lower down. The sound was like an iron rod being dragged at speed along the largest picket fence in the universe. Lances were smashed out of hands or snapped off like tulips in a hothouse for a dozen ranks back. Men shouted in fear or pain, and dogs barked like muffled thunder.

The cuirassier regiment was divided into ten troops of eighty to ninety men each, commanded by a troop-captain and under-officers. None of them knew what was happening to the head of the column, but they were all Brigade noblemen and anxious to close with the foe. They responded according to their training, the whole mass of lancers halting and each troop turning to right or left to deploy into line. When the Civil Government or Colonial dragoons deployed for a charge under fire they did so at the gallop, but the Brigaderos were used to fighting men equipped with shotguns and throwing-axes. Used to having plenty of time to align their lines neatly.

M'Telgez watched his lieutenant's saber out of the corner of his eye. It swung to the right. He pivoted slightly, taking the general direction from the sword as his squad did from him; a group of lancers opening out around a swallow-tail pennant, borne next to a man whose armor was engraved with silver, wearing a shoulder-cape of lustrous hide from some sauroid that secreted irridescent metal into its scales. The corporal picked a target, a lancer next to the leader — no point in shooting the same man twice, and he *knew* someone wouldn't be able to resist the fancy armor. The rear notch settled behind the bladed foresight, and he lowered his aiming-point another few inches — six hundred meters, the bullet would be coming down from the top of its arch at quite an angle.

"— volley fire —"

He exhaled and let his forefinger curl slightly, taking up the trigger slack. The strap of the rifle was wound round his left hand twice, held taunt with the forestock resting on the knuckles. He might not know who'd fucked up in the tunnel, but at least he was going to get to kill *somebody* today.

"*Fire!*"

Bullets went overhead with an unpleasant *wrack* sound. Down the line from the command group a trooper slumped backward with his helmet spinning free to land in the mud and the top taken off of his head. He'd been holding two rounds in his lips like cigarettes, with the bases out ready to hand; they followed the helmet, a dull glint of brass through the rain.

Gerrin Staenbridge looked back and forth down the sunken lane. Stretcher-bearers — military servants — were hauling men back, crouching to carry them without exposing themselves over the higher northern lip of the laneway. Other bearers and soldiers were carrying forward ammunition boxes, ripping the loosened tops off and distributing handfuls to the troopers on the firing line. Ahead the Brigaderos were advancing again, one line running forward and taking cover while the second fired and stood to charge their clumsy muzzle-loading rifle muskets. He checked; yes, the company and platoon commanders were dividing their fire, keeping both segments under fire and not letting the men waste bullets on prone targets.

"Hot work," Bartin Foley said beside him. He gave the — literal — lie to his words by shaking his head and casting a scatter of cold rain from his helmet and chainmail neck-flap.

"Bloody hell," Staenbridge replied, raising his voice slightly. "Fight in the desert, and you want rain. Fight in the rain and you want the sun. Some people are never satisfied."

He lit two cigarettes and passed one to the young captain. A lot of the enemy rifle-muskets were misfiring; percussion caps were immune to rain, but paper cartridges were not. Another line of the Brigaderos rose to advance, and a crashing stutter of half-platoon volleys met them. At three hundred meters more shots hit than missed, but the remnants came on and stood to fire a return volley of their own. Wounded men screamed and cursed down the lines of the 5th and the Life Guards; but they were protected, all but their heads and shoulders. The enemy were naked. The Civil Government's rifle was a single shot breech-loader; not the least of its blessings was that it could be loaded lying down.

Off to the east the firing line was thinner, where Company C had been detached; the 5th was still overstrength, but not so much so since Lion City. The splatgun there gave its *braaaaak* sound, thirty-five rifle barrels clamped together and fired by a crank. A Brigaderos column was caught six hundred meters out, as it began the ponderous countermarch they used to get from marching column into fighting line. Seconds later two field-gun shells arrived at the same target, contact-fused; they plowed up gouts of mud and toppled men with blast and heavy casing fragments. Staenbridge stepped off his crouching dog and walked down behind the line, the banner by his side. It had a few more bulletholes, but the bannerman kept it aloft in the gathering rain.

"Ser, would ye mind inspirin' ussn where ye won't draw fire?" a sergeant called back to him.

"Inspiration be damned, I'm checking that your leatherwork is polished," Staenbridge said.

A harsh chuckle followed as he strolled back to the center. *Spirit, the things one says under stress*, he thought.

A runner squelched up, a Life Guardsman. "Ser," he said to Cabot Clerett. "Barb movement in t'woods. Mounted loik."

Staenbridge nodded at the Governor's nephew's glance. "We're holding here," he said. "Take a company . . . and the other two splatguns."

"Whitehall's toys," Clerett said.

"Useful toys. Take them, and *use* them."

Clerett nodded and turned, calling out orders. He straddled his dog and the animal rose, dripping; the rain was coming down harder now, a steady drizzle. Water sizzled on the barrels of the splatguns, and the gunners left their breeches locked open as they hitched the trails to the limbers and wheeled. Men on the far right of the 2nd Life Guard's section of the line fired one more volley and fell in behind him, reloading as they jogged. There was a slapping sound, and the 2nd's bannerman gave a deep grunt and slumped in the saddle. Cabot reached out and took the staff, resting the butt on his stirrup-iron as the other man toppled.

"See to him," he said. "You men, follow me." He kept the dog to a steady quick walk as they moved in squelching unison behind him.

"Spread it out there," Foley said sharply. The rightmost company of the 5th and the leftmost of the 2nd shifted to fill in the gap, ducking as they moved to keep under cover.

"He's got nerve," Staenbridge murmured. "Still, I'm happier seeing his back than his glowering face."

"I could resent that remark," Foley said, sotto voce. Aloud: "Lieutenant, they're clumping to your left. Direct the fire, if you please."

"Fire!"

M'Telgez straightened from his crouch and fired. The Armory rifle punished his shoulder, the barrel fouled from all the rounds he'd put through it this afternoon. This was the fifth charge, and looked to be the worst yet. A hundred yards to the front dogs went over and men died; they were close enough that he could hear the flat smacking of bullets hitting flesh and the sharper *ptung* of impacts on armor. He worked the lever and snatched a round he was holding between the fingers of his left hand, thumbing it home.

"Here they come!" he snarled.

The Brigaderos were getting smarter; they'd dismounted some of their men behind the ridge over there to use their rifles for a base of fire. The commander of Company C had backed his troopers half a dozen paces, so that they could load crouching and pop up to fire, but they were still losing men. The enemy were also still trying to charge home; expensive, but although they might win a firefight, they couldn't win it in time to affect the main action half a klick away — and the lancers had been supposed to sweep down on the flank of the 5th's position.

Below in the slight swale between the low ridges the lancers came on in clumps and as stragglers. Their dogs' feet were balls of sticky mud, and the cornstalks there had been trampled into a slippery mass that sent some riders skidding in disastrous flailing tumbles even if the bullets missed them. More came on, though, laboring up the slope.

"Fire!"

The corporal fired again. A ragged volley crashed out around him, the muzzle-blasts deafening — particularly the one from the man behind, whose muzzle was nearly in his ear.

"Watch yer *dressin'*, ye dickead!" he screamed, jerking at his lever, and the man shuffled a few steps right. At least the rifle wasn't jamming; there was *some* benefit to the cold rain that was hissing down into his eyes.

He could see the dogs snarling, and the men behind their visors. Mud flew chest-high on the dogs as they came closer at a lumbering gallop.

"Fire!"

More died and half a dozen turned back, some as their dogs bolted to the rear despite sawing hands on the reins and the pressure of bridle-levers on their cheeks. The rest came on, those who still had lances leveling them. The shafts were tapered and smooth, save for a grapefruit-sized wooden ball just in front of the handgrip; the heads were straight-sided knives a foot long, honed and deadly, with steel lappets another two feet down the shaft on either side. M'Telgez' fingers had to hunt for a second to find a cartridge in his bandolier; the upper rows were empty. He clicked it home just as the straggling charge reached the Civil Government line.

The lieutenant pirouetted aside from a point like a matador in the arena. His saber slashed down on the shaft behind the protective steel splints that ran back from the head, and the razor edges tumbled. He let the motion spin him in place, and shot the rider in the back point-blank with the revolver in his left hand.

M'Telgez had lost interest in any lance but the one pointed at his chest. His lever clicked home when it was only a couple of meters away; the corporal threw himself on his back in blind instinct, falling with a thump as the steel dipped. It passed a hand's breadth over his head and he shot with the butt of his rifle pressed to the earth by his side. The bullet creased the Newfoundland's neck, cutting a red streak through the muddy black fur. The animal reared and then lunged, the huge jaws gaping for his face in a graveyard reek of rotting meat. M'Telgez screamed and flung up his rifle; the dog shrieked too, when its jaws closed on two feet of bayonet. The weapon jerked out of the Descotter's hands and the mud sucked at his back. The Brigadero was standing in his stirrups, shouting as he shortened the lance to stab straight down from his rearing mount.

The young trooper M'Telgez had disciplined for misloading stepped up on the other side and fired with his bayonet touching the Brigadero's armored torso. It didn't matter what he had up the spout at that range. The lancer pitched out of the saddle as the bullet punched in under his short ribs. The armor served only to flatten it before it buzzsawed up through liver, lungs and heart to lodge under his opposite shoulder. Blood shot out of his nose and mouth. He was dead before his corpse hit the ground with a clank of steel.

The dog was very much alive. Its huge paws stamped down on either side of the recumbent Descotter; they were furnished with claws and pads rather than a grazing animal's hoof, but they would still smash his ribs out through his spine if they landed. The great loose-jowled jaws were open as the beast shook its head in agony, splattering rainwater and blood from its cut tongue. The trooper shouted and drove his bayonet toward its neck as the fangs turned toward the man on the ground. The human's attack turned into a stumbling retreat as the dog whirled and snapped, the sound of its jaws like wood slapping on wood.

M'Telgez remembered his pistol. Most of the troopers had strapped the new weapons to holsters at their saddlebows — they were supposed to be for mounted melees. He'd stuffed his down the top of his riding boot when they dismounted, on impulse. Now he snatched it free and blazed away at the furry body above him, into the belly rear of the saddle's girth. The dog hunched up in the middle and ran, its rear paws just missing him as it staggered a dozen paces and fell thrashing.

"Fastardos!" he wheezed, picking up a dead man's rifle and loading as he rolled erect.

The Brigaderos were retreating across the swale, many of them on foot — dogs were bigger targets than men.

"Bastards!" M'Telgez fired, reloaded, fired again. "Bastards!"

Shots crackled out all down Company C's line, then the beginnings of volley-fire. It slammed into the retreating men, killing nearly as many as had died in the attack before they made it back to the dead ground behind their starting-point. The field gun elevated and began dropping shells behind the ridge, the gunners and half a dozen troopers as well slipping and sliding in the muck as they ran it back up the slight rise until the muzzle showed.

Return fire was coming in as well; retreat unmasked the Civil Government line to the Brigaderos across the swale. M'Telgez went back to one knee as the minnie bullets crackled overhead and jerked the trooper beside him by the tail of his jacket.

"Git yer head down, ye fool," he growled, looking around.

Not far away a man writhed with a broken-off lance through his gut, whimpering and pulling at the shaft. It jerked, but the steel was lodged in his pelvis far beyond the strength of blood-slippery hands to extract. Another fumbled at his belt for a cord to make a tourniquet; his arm was off above the elbow. The blood jetted more slowly as the man toppled over. M'Telgez knew there was nothing anyone could do for either of the poor bastards. When it was your time, it was time . . . and he was *very* glad it hadn't been his.

"Kid," he went on, as the young man obediently dropped to one knee and looked at him apprehensively. "Kid, yer all right."

"Will theyuns be back then, corp?" he asked.

M'Telgez wiped rain and blood out of his eyes — none of the blood his, thank the *Spirit*.

"Nao," he rasped.

The low ground ahead of him was thick with corpses of armored men and dogs. Particularly in front of the Company pennant; the Brigaderos had clumped there, driving for the center — and also for the gun, meeting point-blank blasts of case shot.

"Nao, they won't be back." He looked up and down the line. "Dressin'!" he barked sharply. What was left of his section moved to maintain their line.

M'Telgez grinned, an expression much like that the lancer's dog had worn when it lunged for his life. "Hoi, barbs!" he shouted at the distant enemy. "Got any messages fer yer wives? We'll be seein' 'em afore ye do!"

Cabot Clerett caught the bayonet on his sword. It was a socket bayonet, offset from a sleeve around the muzzle so that the musket could be loaded and rammed while it was fixed. Metal grated on metal; he fired into the Brigadero's body beneath their linked arms. The man pitched backward as the H-shaped wadcutter bullet put a small hole in his stomach and a much larger one in his back.

"Forward!" the governor's nephew said. "*Vihtoria O Muwerti!*" The motto of the Life Guards. Or victory *and* death, but nothing came free.

Braaaaap. The splatgun fired from not far behind, to his right. Bullets sprayed down the aisles between the trees; this was a planted oakwood, regular as a chessboard. About sixty or seventy years old, from the size of the trees, and regularly thinned as they grew. Water dripped down from the bare branches. Dim figures in gray-and-black uniforms were running back. A few paused to reload behind trees, but they were only protected from directly ahead. Life Guardsmen strung out to either side picked them off, mostly before they could complete the cumbersome process.

Men flanked him as he walked forward, the new bannerman holding the battalion flag. The company commander was out on the right flank with the other splatgun. He could hear it firing, trundled forward like the one with him to support the advance. Men walked on either side of him, reloading as they dodged the trees. They were cheering as they shot; the platoon commanders turned and flung out arms and swords to remind them to keep their line.

"Runner," Cabot said. "To Colonel Staenbridge; enemy were advancing in column on our right flank. I've driven them back and will shortly take them in enfilade all the way back to their original startline."

The splatguns *were* useful. It took less than ten seconds to replace each iron plate with thirty-five rounds in it, better than three hundred rounds a minute. With them and a hundred-odd riflemen, he would shortly be in a position to rake the front of the Brigaderos firing line from the right side and chop up any reserves they still held in the orchard.

Let that *marhicon* see how a Clerett managed a battle, by the Spirit!

"So we moved forward and caught them on the other side of the orchard as they tried to break contact," Staenbridge said. "Cut them up nicely, then pursued mounted, stopping occasionally to shoot them up again. They retreated to a large fortified manor house, which burned quite spectacularly when we shelled it, rain or no. The outbuildings had some very useful supplies, which will be arriving shortly at ox-wagon pace along with the noncombatants.

"Major Clerett," he went on, "led the right wing with skill and dash."

Raj nodded to the younger officer. "The supplies will be useful," he said. "Difficult to get enough in, when we're moving at speed."

He inclined his head downslope. Most of the troops were trudging by with their rifles slung muzzle-down; their boots had churned the fields on either side of the road into glutinous masses. Some of them were wearing local peasant moccasins; the thick mud rotted the thread out of issue boots and sucked off the soles. Further out the cavalry plodded on, stopping occasionally to scrape balls of mud off their mount's feet; the dogs whined and dragged, wanting to stop and groom. On the roadway itself men — infantry and military servants, with gunners acting as foremen — labored in mud even deeper, laying a corduroy surface of logs and beams. As the officers watched a gun-team came up

with its draught chain looped around a hitch of
fresh-cut logs. They tumbled down the slope to general
curses as men dodged the timber.

"I hope," Raj went on, "that you kept me some
Brigaderos prisoners of rank. We need more information about what's happening at Carson Barracks."

CHAPTER THREE

A hereditary officer from just west of the Waladavir River was speaking:

" . . . a dozen farms and a village burned, my manor looted — only by the grace of the Spirit of Man of This Earth and the intervention of the Merciful Avatars did I and my household escape the devil Whitehall. What does His Mightiness intend to do about it?"

The Hall of Audience was lit by scores of tapers in iron sconces, above the racked battle lasers of antiquity. They cast unrestful shadow across the crowd that packed it, nearly a thousand men. Light glittered restlessly from swordhilts, from the jeweled hairclasp of one lord or the platinum beads on the jacket-fringe of another. The air was cold and dank with the autumn rains that fell outside, but it smelled powerfully of sauroid-fat candles and male sweat. An inarticulate growl rose from the crowd; these were each powerful men in their own right, nobles who commanded broad acres and hundreds of household troops.

Their like crowded Carson Barracks, filling housing blocks that usually echoed emptily at this time of year; the petty-squires and military vassals and freeholders who had come as well camped in the streets. Right now they filled the vast parade square outside the Palace. Crowd-noise came through the stone walls like an angry humm, occasionally breaking into a chant:

"Fight! Fight! Fight!"

General Forker rose from the Seat to reply. The light glittered coldly on the engraved silver of his ceremonial armor, and on the vestments of the Sysups and councilors grouped around his throne.

"We have suffered grievously with the sufferings of our subjects," he began.

A snarl rose from the crowd, and he swallowed nervously as he continued.

"That is why we have summoned you, my lords, to share your council with Us. Our diplomacy at least delayed this attack, and now the rains are upon us, and winter comes on. We will have ample time to prepare —"

Another lord stalked into the speaker's position, on the floor below the Seat and just outside the line of Life Guards.

"We've *had* time; Stern Isle fell five months ago!" he bit out. "All we *did* was to throw High Colonel Strezman and his men into Lion City — just enough to hurt us if they were lost, and not enough to halt the enemy. Now Strezman and his men are dead!

"Lord of Men," he went on, his tone cold, "you may not wish to campaign in winter but the enemy don't seem to share your delicate sensibilities. Whitehall is over the Waladavir, and his men have been sighted not three days' ride from Empirhado."

A roar swelled across the hall; the banners hanging from the rafters quivered.

"Rumors!"

"Truth!" the noble shouted back. "This is no raid, no border war for a province or an indemnity. The Civvies mean to grind us into dust the way they did the Squadron, kill us and take our lands, throw down our holy Church and enslave our women and children. They're coming, and the natives have already risen in half a dozen provinces."

A ripple of horror went through the hall. It was six hundred years since the Brigade came down out of the Base Area and conquered the Spanjol-speaking natives of the Civil Government's western territories, but the peoples were still distinct in blood and language and faith, and the natives were overwhelmingly in the majority. Like the Civil Government, they followed the cult of the Spirit of Man of The Stars, rather than of This Earth as the Brigade and its cousins did.

The nobleman turned his back on the Seat, a breach of protocol that stunned the watchers into silence.

"We need a fighting man to lead us. Not this book-reader who's plotting with the enemy behind our backs. *I move for impeachment.*"

Forker's face was working with rage and a trapped-beast fear. He forced his voice, turning it high and shrill.

"You are out of order. Arrest that man!"

The guards started forward, but a score of nobles grouped around the speaker drew their swords. The edges threw the light back as the heavy blades rose warningly.

"I am not out of order," the noble replied. "As Hereditary High Major, I have the right to call for impeachment before this assembly."

"I, Hereditary Brigade-Colonel Ingreid Manfrond, second the impeachment." Another man stepped into the speaker's circle, thick-set and muscular and griz-zled. "And place my name in nomination for the position of General of the Brigade."

"You!" Forker hissed. "You're not even of the House of Amalson."

"Collateral branch," Ingreid said. "But tomorrow I wed Marie Welf, daughter of General Welf — which makes my claim strong as iron." He turned to the assembly. "And as General, my first act will be to mobilize the host. My second will be to lead it to crush the invaders of our land!"

Forker signed to his guard. There was a pause, one that made the light parade breastplate feel as if it were squeezing his heart up into his mouth. Then they thumped their rifle-butts on the floor. It took a moment for the rumbling to quiet enough for him to speak.

"You lie, Ingreid Manfrond. The hand of Marie *Forker*, my step-daughter, is mine to give or withhold — and she rests content under the guard of *my* household troops."

Another man shouldered forward to stand beside Ingreid. "My name," he shouted in a commander's trained bellow, "is Colonel of Dragoons Howyrd Carstens. Forker lies. My own men guard Marie Welf, and she has agreed to marry our next General, Ingreid Manfrond — worthy heir to the great General Welf. And as bridal gift, she asks for the head of Filip Forker, murderer of her mother. Woman-killer and coward!"

He raised his sword. "Hail General Ingreid!"

"Hail! Hail! Hail!"

"I'd rather rut with a boar and farrow piglets!" Marie Welf shouted through the locked door.

She gripped the pistol more firmly. On either side of the door one of her gentlewomen waited, one with a tall brass candlestick in her grip, the other with a jewel-hilted but perfectly functional stiletto.

"Please, Mistress Fo — ah, Mistress Welf." The house steward's voice quavered, his Spanjol accent stronger than usual. "The soldiers say that you *must* open the door."

"I'll kill the first five men to step through it," Marie said. Nobody listening to her could doubt she would try.

Silence fell. Riding boots clumped on the parquet floors outside, and the strip of light under the door brightened as more lamps were brought.

"Marie, this is Teodore," a man called.

"What are you doing here, cousin?" Marie said.

She was a tall full-figured young woman, with strawberry blond hair in long braids on either side of a face that was beautiful rather than pretty, high cheek-boned and with a straight nose. Spots of anger burned on either cheek now, and she held the pistol with a practiced two-handed grip.

"Talking to you. And I'm not going to do it through a closed door. Watch out."

Shots blasted, and the brass plate of the lock bulged. A man yelled in pain in the corridor outside, and a chilly smile lit Marie's face. The door swung out, and a man stood there; in his mid-twenties, five years older than the woman. His bluntly handsome features were a near-match for hers under the downy blond beard, and he wore a cuirassier officer's armor. The plumed helmet was tucked under one arm, half-hidden by the deinonosauroid cloak that glittered in the lamplight. At the sight of her leveled pistol he spread the other arm away from his body.

"Shoot, cousin, if you want to see one less Welf in the world."

Marie sighed and let the pistol drop to the glowing Kurdish carpet. "Come in, Teodore," she said, and sank down to sit on one corner of the four-poster bed.

The ladies-in-waiting looked at her uncertainly. "Thank you, Dolors, Katrini — but you'd better go to your rooms now."

Teodore set his helmet down on a table and began working off his armored gauntlets. "You wouldn't have any wine, would you?" he asked. "Cursed cold night and wet besides; a coup is hard outdoor work."

She pointed wordlessly to a sideboard, and he smiled as he poured for both.

"You're making a very great deal of fuss about something you'll have to do anyway," he pointed out, handing her the glass and going to sit by the fire.

The velvet of the chair dimpled and stretched under the weight of his rain-streaked armor. The wall beside him held the fireplace, burning with a low coal blaze, and a bookshelf. That carried a respectable two dozen volumes; the Cannonical Handbooks in Wulf Philson's

Namerique translation, lives of the Avatars, and histories and travelogues in Spanjol and Sponglish.

"You'd fuss too if you'd been kept a prisoner since that beast murdered my mother," Marie said. The wine was Sala, strong and sweet. It seemed to coil around the fire in her chest.

"I was fond of Aunt Charlotte myself. 'That beast' is now off the Seat, and running for his life," Teodore pointed out. "Something which I had my hand in."

"Ingreid is a pig. And he supported Forker. I'm certain he was one of the ones who murdered Mother for that *coward*."

"That was never proven. And Ingreid is a *strong* pig," Teodore said, casting a quick look at the door. They were talking quietly, though, and he had told his men to move everyone down the corridor. "The fact that he supported Forker tells in his favor; the alternative was civil war. The alternative *now* is civil war, unless Ingreid Manfrond has an unassailable claim to the Seat. If you don't think that civil war is possible with invaders at the frontiers, then you've read less of our history than I thought." He waved at the bookcase.

"Can Ingreid read at all?" she said bitterly.

"No, probably," Teodore said frankly. "That'll make him all the more popular with the backwoods nobles, and the petty-squires and freeholders. Civvies will keep the accounts as usual, and he's got advisers like Carstens and —" he rapped his breastplate "— for the more complicated things. He can certainly lead a charge, which is more than you can say for that pseudo-scholar Forker."

He leaned forward, a serious expression on his face. "I'm ready to fight and die for him, as General. All you have to do is marry him."

"You aren't expected to go to *bed* with him, Teodore."

"There is that," the young man admitted. "But you'd

have to marry somebody sometime; it's the way things are done at our rank."

"I'm a free woman of the Brigade; the law says I can't be married against my will," Marie said.

Teodore spread his hands. She nodded. "I know . . . but he smells. And he's *fifty*."

"You'll outlive him, then," Teodore said. "Possibly as Regent for an underage heir. And you *will* marry him tomorrow. If necessary, with a trooper standing behind you twisting your arm. That won't be dignified, but it'll work."

"*You* would make a better General, cousin!"

"So I would, if I had the following," Teodore said. "So would you, if you were a man. But I haven't and you aren't. The enemy won't wait for me to acquire a majority, either."

"And how much will *my* life be worth, once I've produced a healthy heir?" Marie said. "Not to mention the question of his own sons, who'll have Regent ambitions of their own."

Teodore went to the door and checked that his cuirassier troopers were holding the servants at the end of the corridor.

"As to the heir," he said, leaning close to Marie's ear, "time will tell. In a year, the war will be over. Once the *grisuh* are back across the sea . . . "

Marie's eyes were cold as she set down the wineglass. "All right, Teodore," she said. "But listen to me and believe what I say: whatever I promise in the cathedron Ingreid Manfrond will get no love or loyalty from *me*. And he'll regret forcing me to this on the day he dies, and that will be soon. Spirit of Man of This Earth be my witness."

Teodore Welf had broken lances with Guard champions on the northwestern frontier, and fought the Stalwarts further east. He had killed two men in duels back home, as well.

At that moment, he was conscious mainly of a vast

thankfulness that it was Ingreid Manfrond and not Teodore Welf who would stand beside Marie in the cathedron tomorrow.

Thunder rippled through the night, and rain streaked the diamond-pane windows of thick bubbled glass. Teodore looked away from his cousin.

"At least," he said, "the enemy won't be making much progress through *this*. We'll have time to get our house in order."

Thunder cracked over the ford. The light stabbed down into a midday darkness, off wet tossing trees and men's faces. Oxen bellowed as they leaned into the traces, trying to budge the gun mired hub-deep in the middle of the rising river; they even ignored the dogs of the regular hitch straining beside them. Dozens of infantrymen heaved at the barrel and wheels, gasping and choking as water broke over them. Others labored at the banks, throwing down loads of brush and gravel to keep the sloping surfaces passable. Wagon-teams bawled protestingly as they were led into the water; men waded through the waist-high brown flood with their rifles and cartridge-boxes held over their heads.

One of the work-crews was relieved, and stumbled upslope to the courtyard of the riverside inn.

"Wat's a name a' dis river?" one asked a noncom.

"Wolturno," the man mumbled, scraping mud off his face. It was a winding stream, meandering back and forth across the flood-plain where the road ran. The Expeditionary Force had already crossed it several times.

"Ever' fukkin' river here is named Wolturno," the soldier said. They slouched into lines before the kettles.

"Thank'ee, miss," the infantryman said, taking his bowl and cup.

He stumbled off a few paces to crouch in the lee of a wagon, spooning up the stew of beans and cubed bacon and taking mouthfuls of the cornbread bannock. More of his squadmates crowded through beneath the awnings to the bubbling cauldrons; like him they were dripping with more than the slashing rain, and so filthy it was hard to see the patches and tears in their uniforms; one was wrapped completely in a shrouding of earth-stained peasant blankets.

Fatima cor Staenbridge — *cor* meant freedwoman, and the name was her former master's — filled the ladle again and swung it out to the outstretched bowl.

"Not much, but it's hot," she said cheerfully. Rain leaked down through the makeshift awning, but most of it ran off the thick wool of the hooded cloak she wore. "Take all you can eat, soldier, eat all you take."

"Bettah dan whut we eaat a' hume," the footsoldier said, in a thick peasant dialect of Sponglish she couldn't place. There were so many. From the looks of his thin young face, the young peon conscript probably hadn't eaten this well before the Army press-gangs swept him up. "Yu an angel, missa."

Mitchi plunked a hunk of cornbread on his bowl, and took his cup to dip it in a vat of hot cider.

"Thank Messa Whitehall, she organized it," she said.

Dozens of the cauldrons were cooking in the courtyard, hauled from the inn kitchens and from houses nearby. Army servants, women — even wives, in a few cases — and miscellaneous clergy carried out fresh loads of ingredients and dumped them in to cook. Rations were issued when there were no markets, but each eight-man squad of soldiers was generally supposed to cook for themselves — that was one of the duties military servants did for the cavalry troopers. Today that would have meant hardtack and cold water for the infantry laboring to keep the ford passable, without Lady Suzette Whitehall rounding up camp-followers and supplies for this. And there would be the usual camp to build at the end of the day's march, with wet firewood and sopping bedding.

Exhausted men forgot to take care for themselves and let sickness in.

"Messer Rahj an' his lady, dey sent by de Spirit," the soldier blurted. His face was pinched and stubbled. "Dey treet de commun sojur right, not jus' dog-boys."

The men were too tired for enthusiasm, but they nodded and muttered agreement as they shuffled forward. Fatima swung the ladle until it was scraping the bottom of the cauldron.

"Take all you can eat, eat all you can — Messer Raj!"

"Thank you, Fatima," he said.

The mud was mainly below the swordbelt, his uniform and boots were sound, and he wore one of the warm rainproof cloaks. Apart from that he looked nearly as exhausted as the infantrymen who'd been shoveling stone and hauling brushwood to the ford. The other officers with him looked no better. A low murmur went through the courtyard as he was recognized, but the men kept to their scraps of shelter at a half-gesture from one hand.

Cabot Clerett looked dubiously at the bowl. The others started shovelling theirs down unconcerned. "I hope there's something better at the end of the day," he said.

Fatima stood aside as more helpers staggered up with pails of well-water, sacks of beans and half a keg of the chopped bacon. The Renunciate leading them tossed in a double handful of salt and some dried chilies. The cauldron hissed slightly as the ingredients went in, and one of the servants dumped more coal on the embers beneath.

"Messa Whitehall said," Fatima put in, "that the headquarters cook had found a lamb, and some fresh bread."

"Something to look forward to." That was Major Peydro Belagez of the Rogor Slashers. "By the Spirit, *mi heneral*, before I met you I spent fifteen uneventful years patrolling the Drangosh border and fighting the

Colonials once every two months. The sun shone, and between patrols I lay beneath orange trees while girls dropped nougat into my mouth. Now look at me! *Mi mahtre* warned me of the consequences of falling into bad company — Malash, she was right."

The major from the southern borders was a slight man in his late thirties, naturally dark and leathery with years of savage desert suns and windstorms, wearing a pointed goatee and a gold ring in one ear. His grin was easy and friendly; Fatima swallowed as she remembered the same pleasant expression last year after Mekkle Thiddo, the Companion who commanded the Slashers, was killed under flag of truce, and Belagez rounded up the men responsible, even in the chaos of the pursuit after the Squadron host was broken. Raj had ordered them crucified, but Belagez had seen to the details, even to having the victims' feet twisted up under their buttocks before they were spiked to the wood. A man lived much longer that way, before asphyxiation and shock killed him.

She had never felt easy around Borderers; the feuds along the frontier between Colony and Civil Government were too old and bitter. Fatima had hated her father, the Caid of El Djem . . . but she remembered too well how he had died, in a huge pool of blood with a Borderer dancing in glee around him, the jiggling sack of the old man's scrotum impaled on the curved knife which slashed it free.

Belagez' smile was innocent as he glanced at her. She was the woman of a friend, and so he would cheerfully face death to defend her.

"Messa Whitehall says she found some good wine, too," Fatima went on.

For that matter, the 5th Descott would fight for her now — and they were the men who'd burned her home and would have gang-raped her, if she hadn't managed to get Gerrin and Bartin Foley to protect her. *Life is strange.* From despised minor concubine's daughter to slave to a freedwoman and mother of the acknowledged son of a wealthy Civil Government nobleman-officer in a year . . . of course, the child could have been Bartin's, just as likely. But Gerrin had adopted it, and he had no other heir. Messer Raj and his lady had stood Starparents.

"If it does not pucker the mouth to drink it," Belagez said. "Spirit, the wine here is even more sour than that dog-piss you northerners like — which I had not believed possible."

Kaltin Gruder grinned. "You mean it's not syrup like that stuff they make south of the Oxheads," he said. "Too sweet to drink and too thick to piss, no wonder you cut it with water."

Raj finished his mug of cider and sighed, wiping his mouth on the back of his hand. "Well, Messers," he said. "No rest for the wicked. I've an uneasy suspicion that some of the Brigaderos at least realize we're not going to curl up somewhere cozy in front of the fire until the rains stop."

"Those who aren't too busy dealing with each other," Bartin Foley said. He handed his bowl back to Fatima with a smile of thanks.

"Even if most are politicking, that leaves an uncomfortable number otherwise employed," Raj said. "Gerrin, you have the main column for the rest of the day. Major Clerett, you and I will —"

Filip Forker, ex-General and no longer Lord of Men, stuck his head out the window of the carriage.

"Faster!" he said, coughing into a handkerchief. *What a time to have a headcold*, he thought.

The road northwest from Carson Barracks had been paved once, very long ago. Even now chunks of ancient concrete made the light travelling coach jounce as it rocked forward through a dense fog. Moisture glittered in the moonlight on the long white fur of the wolfhounds and streaked the carriage windows. There was a spare hitch behind, another carriage with his mistress and the essential baggage, a light two-wheel wagon for the gear, and an escort . . . although the escort was smaller than it had been a few hours ago. Much smaller than it had been when they left the city, although he had promised rich rewards to any who stayed with him until they reached his estates on the Kosta dil Orhenne in the far west.

Some would stay, because they had eaten his salt. There was a bitterness to seeing how few felt bound to him.

"Why aren't you going faster?" he called to the driver.

"It's dark, master, and the road is rough," the man replied.

Even his tone had changed, although he wore an iron collar and Forker had the same power of life and death over him that he'd had before his impeachment. For a moment Forker was tempted to order him shot right now, simply to demonstrate that — but he had few enough servants along. Let a flogging wait until he reached his estates, among the Forker family's military vassals. He would be secure there. . . .

, Men rode across the road a hundred meters ahead. They were wrapped in dark cloaks, but most of them held rifles with the butts resting on their thighs. The clump at their head had naked swords, cold starlight on the edged metal.

Forker swallowed vomit. He mopped at his raw nose and looked wildly about. More were riding out behind him, out of the eerie forest of native whipstick trees that covered the land on either side. The officer of his household troopers barked orders to the handful of guards who'd remained, and they closed in around the carriages, pulling the rifle-muskets from their scabbards. Hammers clicked as thumbs pulled them back, the sound loud and metallic in the insect-murmurous night.

"Halt," the leader of the cloaked men said.

"In . . . " Forker began, hacked, spat, spoke again: "Ingreid Manfrond promised me my life!"

"Oh, General Manfrond didn't send me to kill you," the man said, grinning in his beard. "The Lord of Men just told me where I could find you. Killing you was my own idea. Don't you remember me? Hereditary Captain Otto Witton."

He rode close enough so that the riding lanterns on the coach showed the long white scar that ran up the left side of his face until it vanished under his hairline. It was flushed red with emotion. His dog crouched, and he stepped free.

"Just a little matter of wardship of my cousin's daughter Kathe Mattiwson — and her lands — and she was promised to *me*, and she wanted *me*, you bastard. But *you* assumed the wardship and sold her like a pig at a fair, to that son of a bitch Sliker. Get *out* of there."

Forker found himself climbing down to the roadway without conscious decision. Thin mud sucked at the soles of his gold-topped tasseled boots.

"An, ah, an honorable marriage —"

"*Shut up, you little shit!*" Witton screamed. The scar was white against his red face, and his sword hissed out. "Now you're going to *die*."

The houseguard captain stepped between them. "Over my dead body," he said, calmly enough. The tip of his own sword touched the roadway, but his body was tensed for action the way a cat's does, loose-jointed. There were hammered-out dents in his breastplate, the sort a full-armed sword cut makes.

"If that's how you want it," Witton said.

He looked to the men sitting their dogs around the carriage. "But it'd be a pity, the Brigade needs all the fighting men it can get — this little Civvie-lover will be no loss, though."

"The Brigade doesn't need men who'd let their sworn lord be cut down by thirty enemies on the road," the retainer said. "He may be a cowardly little shit, but we ate his salt."

It said a good deal for the situation that Filip Forker ignored the comment. Instead he squealed: "That's right — my life is your honor! Save me and I'll give you half my lands."

The captain looked over his shoulder at Forker, expressionless. Then he turned back to Witton.

"A man lives as long as he lives, and not a day more," he said. "Sorry to miss the war with the Civvies, though."

"You don't have to," Witton said. This time his grin was sly. "An oath to a man without honor is no oath. We won't overfall your gold-giver with numbers. I'll challenge him here and now; you can be witness to a fair fight."

He stepped closer and spat on Forker's boot. "I call you coward and your father a coward, and your mother a whore," he said. "You've got a sword."

The guard captain stepped back, his face clearing. Both men were wearing blades, neither had armor, and they were close enough in age. If the former monarch was weedy and thin-wristed while Witton looked as if he could bend iron bars between his fingers, that was *Forker's* problem; he should have been in the salle d'armes instead of the library all those years.

Forker looked around; the code said a man could volunteer to fight in his place, but it wasn't an obligation. Some of his men were smiling, others looking away into the night. None of them spoke.

"It's time," Witton said, thick and gloating. He raised the blade. "Draw or die like a steer in a slaughter chute."

"Marcy!" Forker screamed, falling to his knees. There was a sharp ammonia stink as his bladder released. "*Marcy, migo!* Spare me — spare my life and everything I have is yours."

Witton's smile turned into a grimace of hatred.

Forker shrieked and threw up his arms. One of them parted at the elbow on the second stroke of Witton's earnest, clumsy butchery. The stump of the arm flailed about, spurting blood that looked black in the silvery light. That jerked the attacker back to consciousness, and his next blow was directed with skill as well as the strength of shoulders as thick as a blacksmith's.

"Book-reader," the warrior said with contempt, standing back and panting. Thick drops of blood ran down his face and into his beard, speckling the front of his fringed leather jacket.

The dead man's servants came forward to wrap the body; it leaked blood and other fluids through the rug they rolled it in. Forker's mistress looked on from the second carriage; she raised the fur muff that concealed her hands to her lips and stared speculatively over it at the guard captain and the heavy-set assassin.

Witton spoke first. "I hope you don't feel obliged to challenge," he said to the guardsman.

The retainer shrugged. "We were contracted, not vassals. He fell on his own deeds." A wintry smile. "I guess there won't be much trouble finding a new berth for me and my guns."

His expression grew colder. "Although if I catch those pussies who bugged out before we got this far, I don't think they'll ever need another gear-and-maintenance contract as long as they live."

The fog had turned to a light drizzle. Witton lofted a gobbet of spit toward the body the servants were pushing into the carriage. The wolfhounds in the traces whined and twitched at the smells of blood and tension, until the driver flicked his whip over their backs.

"Can't blame them for not wanting to fight for Forker," he said.

"*Fuck* Forker," the guard captain said. "My contract was with him, but theirs was with *me*."

Witton nodded. "You can sign up with my lot," he

said. "I'm down twenty rifles on my assigned war-host tally."

The guardsman shook his head. "Wouldn't look good," he said. Witton grunted agreement; a mercenary's reputation was his livelihood. "We'll head back to Carson Barracks, somebody'll sign us on for the duration, maybe the Regulars. Figure the call-up'll come pretty soon anyway, might as well beat the rush."

He turned and called orders. His men eased back the hammers of their rifles and slid them into the scabbards on the left side of their saddles. There was a moment's pause as one man bent in the saddle and grabbed the bridle of the dogs pulling the baggage wagon, turning it around, and then the fading *plop* of their dogs' paws.

Witton waved the carriage with Forker's body onward. They'd take it back to his ancestral estates for burial, although even in this cool weather it'd be pretty high by then. He had no problem with that, after his second-in-command down the road made a search for the getaway chest with the money and jewels Forker would undoubtedly have been carrying. He looked up at the second carriage. The woman there lowered the fur that hid her face and gave him a long smile. The maid cowering beside her was obviously terrified, but Forker's ex-mistress was a professional too, in her way. Huge violet-colored eyes blinked at him, frosted in the fog-blurred light of the moons.

And quite spectacular. Well, the little bastard *had* been General, no reason he should settle for less than the best. He wiped at his face, smearing the blood, and smiled back while his hands automatically cleaned and sheathed his sword.

"This should be very useful indeed," Raj said.

The estate was well off from the army's line of march, in a district of rolling chalk hills. There was little cultivation, but the ground was mostly covered with dense springy green turf, and grazed by huge herds of sheep and large ones of cattle; pigs fed in the beechwoods on the steeper slopes. Evidently the land hereabouts was held in big ranching estates and yeoman-sized grazing farms rather than let to share-croppers; the manor they'd just taken was surrounded by outbuildings, great woolsheds and corrals and smokehouses, a water-powered scouring mill for clean-ing wool and an odorous tannery off a kilometer or so. The cured bacon and barreled salt beef and mutton would be very welcome. The herds would be even more so, since they could walk back to the main force.

The bolts of woolen cloth woven in the long sheds attached to the peon village would be more welcome still. It wasn't raining right now here, and the soil was free-draining. The air was crisp, though, the breath of men and dogs showing — and a lot of his soldiers were patching their pants with looted bed-curtains. This area would give every man in the army another blanket, which might make the difference between health and pneumonia for many. Enough for jacket-lin-ings too, if there were time and seamstresses.

"I hope everything is satisfactory, sir," Cabot Clerett replied. The *of course it is* and *why are you meddling?* were unspoken.

Cabot Clerett's respect for Raj's abilities as a commander was grudging but real.

"Quite satisfactory," Raj replied. *I'm glad I don't hate anyone that much*, he added to himself.

only partly hatred, Center's pedantic machine-voice said in his mind. **a large element of fear, envy and jealousy as well.**

Tell me, Raj thought.

Cabot envied everything from Raj's military reputa-tion to his wife. Suzette could play him like a violin, of course, and that was probably all that had kept Cabot from goading his uncle into a disastrous recall order for Raj. Not that it would take much goading; Barholm

Clerett's paranoia went well beyond the standard Gubernatorial suspicion of a successful commander.

That doesn't mean I have to like it, Raj thought. Then: *back to the work of the day*.

The lord of the estate had surrendered promptly and been given receipts for the supplies the 1st Life Guards were methodically stripping from the barns and storehouses. Clerett's men seemed to be well in hand; they were helping the estate's serfs load the wagons, and keeping the lined-up manor staff under their guns, but nothing more. Undoubtedly a few small valuables would disappear, not to mention chickens, but nothing in the way of rape, arson or murder was going on. Pickets were posted, keeping the surroundings under observation. . . .

Raj's eyes passed over the lord of the manor, a stout Brigadero in late middle age, standing and ignoring the troopers guarding him with a contemptuous expression. It was mirrored on the hatchet-faced, well-dressed matron at his side. Three younger women with children looked only slightly more apprehensive. One twelve-year-old boy with his tow colored hair just now grown to warrior length and caught with a clasp at his neck glared at the Civil Government commander with open hatred. More Brigadero women and children clustered in the windows of the manor, or in medium-sized cottages separate from the peon huts.

"Right, we'll pull out," Raj said.

It took considerable time to get the wagons and bleating, milling, mooing herds moving down to the road that rolled white through the chalk hills. From the look of the grass, and the iron-gray clouds rolling overhead, there had been as much rain here as in the valley where the army toiled south toward Old Residence. The chalk soil didn't vanish into mud the way bottomland clay did, since it was free-draining, but it would be awkward enough. Many of the Life Guard troopers had been *vakaros* back in Descott or the other inland Counties; they swung whips and lariats and yipped around the fringes of the herds.

"What bothers me is where all the men are," Raj said. "Not just here, but the last couple of manors in this area and the bigger farms."

The two officers rode at the head of a company column of the 1st upslope from the road, out of the milling chaos of the drive and the heavy stink of liquid sheep-feces. Other columns flanked the convoy as it drove downward.

"Well, they've been mobilized," Clerett said.

Raj nodded; that was the first thing Ingreid had done after he took the Seat. The rally-point named was Carson Barracks, in the circulars they'd captured.

"That might be where the nobles' household troops have gone," he said. "I don't think they need big garrisons here to keep the natives in line."

The peons in the manors had looked notably better fed and more hostile to the Civil Government troops than most they'd seen. Herding is less labor-intensive than staple agriculture, and produces more per hand although much less per hectare.

"The problem is," Raj went on, "that this *is* a grazing district."

Clerett looked at him suspiciously. Raj amplified: "It's too thinly peopled to shoot the carnosauroids out," he said.

The younger man nodded impatiently. "Lots of sign," he said.

Strop-marks on trees, where sicklefeet stood on one leg to hone the dewclaw that gave them their name. There had been a ceratosauroid skull nailed over a barn door at the last manor, too: a meter long counting the characteristic nose-horn, and the beast would be two meters at the shoulder, when it ran after prey with head and tail stretched out horizontally over the long striding bipedal legs. Shreds of flesh and red-and-gray pebbled hide had clung to the skull.

"Nice string of sicklefoot dewclaws beneath it," Raj went on. "You're a Descotter too, Major." *More of one than Barholm*, he thought.

The Governor had spent almost his whole life in East Residence, while Cabot stayed home in the hills to keep the Cleretts' relations with the Descott gentry warm. It was no accident that the County which provided a quarter of the elite cavalry also supplied the last two Governors.

Clerett's face changed. "Vakaros," he said. *Cowboys.*

Raj nodded. Ranching meant predator control on Bellevue; and giving rifles and riding-dogs to slaves or peons and sending them out to ride herd was a *bad* idea, generally speaking. Most of the bond-labor at the estate they'd just left had been there for processing work, putting up preserved meats, tanning hides, and weaving, plus gardening and general chores. There had been a number of barracks and cottages and empty stables surplus to peon requirements, and a lot of Brigaderos women of the commoner class. The herdsmen were gone.

"That's why all the estate-owners here seem to be Brigaderos." In most of the country they'd passed through the land was fairly evenly divided between Brigade and civilian. "Brigade law forbids arming civilians. I don't think they enforce it all that strictly, but most of the vakaros — whatever they call them here — would be Brigaderos as well."

And there was no better training for light-cavalry work. Keeping something like a ceratosauroid or a sicklefoot pack off the stock tested alertness, teamwork, riding and marksmanship all at once. Not to mention fieldcraft and stalking.

"Shall I spread the scout-net out wider?" Cabot said.

Raj stood in the stirrups and gave the surroundings a glance. None of the canyons and badlands and gully-sided volcanoes that made much of Descott County a bushwacker's paradise, but the bigger patches of beechwood and the occasional steep-sided coumb in thick native brush would do as well.

"I think that would be a very good idea, Major Clerett," he said.

Marie Welf — Marie Manfrond now — lay silent and motionless as Ingreid rolled off her. The only movement was the rise and fall of her chest, more rapid now with the weight off; she lay on her back with her hands braced against the headboard of the bed and her legs spread. Blood stained the sheet beneath the junction of her thighs, and some of the scented olive oil discreetly left on the nightstand, which had proven to be necessary. The high coffered ceiling of the General's private quarters was covered with gold leaf and the walls with mosaic; they cast the flame of the single coal-oil lamp over the bed back in yellow lambency.

Naked, Ingreid's paunch and graying body-hair were more obvious, but that simply emphasized the troll strength of his blocky shoulders. His body was seamed with scars, particularly down the left side and on the lower arms and legs. Puckered bullet wounds, long white fissures from swords, a deep gouge on one thigh where a lancepoint had taken out a chunk of meat when it hammered through the tasset. Neck and hip and joints were callused where his armor rested, and there was a groove across his forehead from the lining of a helmet. Strong teeth showed yellow as he smiled at her and raised a decanter from the bedside table.

"Drink?" he said. Marie remained silent, staring at the ceiling.

"Well, then I will," he said, splashing the brandy into a glass. The ends of his long hair stuck to his glistening shoulders, and his sweat smelled sourly of wine and beer.

He wiped himself on a corner of the satin sheets and got up, moving about restlessly, picking up objects and

putting them down. After a moment he turned back to
the bed.

"Not so bad, eh? You'll get better when you're used
to it."

Marie's head turned and looked at him silently. The
eyes were as empty of expression as her face. Ingreid
flushed.

"You'd better," he said, gulping down the brandy. "I
was supposed to marry a woman, not a corpse."

Marie spoke, her voice remote. "You got what you
bargained for. That's all you're getting."

"*Is* it, girlie?" Ingreid's flush went deeper, turning
his face red-purple under the weathering. "We'll see
about that."

He threw the glass aside to bounce and roll on the
carpets, then jerked her head up by her hair. His hand
went *crack* against her face, the palm hard as a board.
She jerked and rolled to the edge of the bed, her long
blond hair hiding her face. Then her head came up,
the green eyes holding the same flat expression despite
the red handmark blazing on her cheek.

"I've got better things to do than teach you manners,
bitch," Ingreid snarled. "For now. When the war's won,
I'll have time."

He threw on a robe. Marie waited until he had
slammed out the door until she stood as well, moving
carefully against the pain of pulled muscles and the
pain between her legs. A servant would come if she
pulled one of the cords, but right now even such a
faceless nonentity would be more than she could face.
She walked into the bathroom and turned up the lamp
by the door, looking at herself in the full-length mirror
without blinking, then opened the taps to fill the
seashell-shaped bath of marble and gold. Hot water
steamed; the General's quarters had all the luxuries. It
wasn't until the bath was full and foaming with scented
bubble soap that she realized it was the same tub that
her mother had been drowned in.

She managed to make it to the toilet before she started vomiting. When her stomach was empty she wiped her face and stepped into the bath anyway. She would need all her strength in the days ahead.

"That was too easy," Raj said, resting his helmet on his saddlebow. *And for once, it isn't raining.* The breath of men and dogs showed in frosty clouds, but the sun was bright in a morning sky.

The little town of Pozadas lay at the junction of the chalk downs and the lower clay plain; it had no wall, although the church and a few of the larger houses would have done as refuges against bandits or raiders. So would some of the mills along the river. They were built of soft gold-colored limestone; napping and scutching mills and dye-works for woolen cloth, mostly. The town had many cottages where weavers worked hand-looms and leatherworkers made boots and harness. Wisely, the citizens had offered no resistance, but they were sullen even though the Civil Government had paid in looted gold for most of what it took.

It was a prosperous town for its size; the town hall was new and quite modern, with large glass windows below and an open balcony on the second story, overlooking the roofs of the other buildings.

"Glum-looking bastards," Cabot said, rising in the saddle to look over Raj's shoulder.

Few were on the streets — the troops and the huge herds of livestock they were driving through the main road took up too much room — but there were scowls on the faces peering from windows and doorways.

"Not surprising," Raj said.

He nodded to a vast bleating mat of gray-and-white sheep churning up the chalky flint-studded dirt of the street; it moved like a shaggy blanket, with an occasional individual popping up, struggling for a few steps across its neighbors' backs, and then dropping back into the press. There was a heavy barnyard odor, overwhelming the usual outhouse and chemical reek of a cloth-making town.

"We're taking their livelihood," the general went on. "It'll take years for the herds back there —" he inclined his head back toward the downland they'd just finished sweeping "— to breed back up again. That's assuming that things don't get so disrupted the carnosauroids finish off the breeding stock we left. In the meantime, what'll they do for wool and hides?"

A large army was like a moving suction-machine; his was travelling fast enough that it wouldn't leave famine in its wake, but nobody else would be able to move troops along the same route anytime soon.

"I still wonder where all those men went," Raj said meditatively.

Cabot drew his pistol and pointed it. Raj threw himself flat in the saddle, and the bullet cracked where he had been.

Horace whirled in less than his own length, paws skidding slightly on the sheep-dung coated mud of the street. The Brigadero who'd been behind him pitched backward with a third hole in line with his eyebrows, his floppy-brimmed hat spinning off. There were a dozen more behind him, some still charging out of the opened doors of the town hall courtyard, and more on foot behind them. Still more on balconies and rooftops, rising to fire. Shots crackled through the streets and men screamed, dogs howled, and the bleating of berserk sheep was even louder as the near-witless animals scattered in all directions into alleys and squares and through open doors and windows.

"*Thanks!*" Raj shouted. *Now I know where the herdsmen went*.

The man behind him had a sword raised for a sweeping overarm cut. Raj dodged under it as Horace bounced forward, his saber up and back along his spine; the swords met with an unmusical crash and skirl, and he uncoiled, slashing a third Brigadero across the face. Then his personal escort had faced about and met the rest, shooting and stabbing in a melee around Raj and Cabot and their bannermen. More Brigaderos were charging out of the mills. Raj scanned the housetops. A couple of hundred enemy, and they'd found the best way to hide the scent of their dogs; in the middle of a textile town, with thousands of livestock jamming through it.

Bloody Starless Dark, he thought disgustedly. Another cock-up because he hadn't enough troops to nail things down.

The problem with relying on speed and intimidation was that some people just didn't intimidate worth a damn.

"Rally south of town," he shouted to Cabot Clerett. "Spread out, don't let them get back into the hills. Pin them against the river as you come in."

"They'll swim the stream and scatter," the younger man replied.

Raj gave a feral grin. "Not for long," he said. "Get moving!"

The major jerked a nod, wheeling his dog and waving his pistol forward. His bannerman fell in beside him, and the trumpeter sounded *retreat-rally* as they pounded south, toward the spot where the Civil Government column had entered the town. Men fought free of the herds and plunder-wagons and joined him in clumps and units. Some fell, but everyone understood the need to break contact until they could rally and unite. If they stood, the prepared enemy would cut them up into penny packets and slaughter them.

"Follow me!" Raj barked.

His escort had taken care of the first Brigaderos to attack, but even as he spoke he saw a man and a dog go down. A bullet cracked by his head with an unpleasant puff of wind against his cheek, which was *entirely* too close. He had a full platoon of the 5th Descott with him, beside messengers and aides. That ought to be enough.

He pointed his saber at the town hall and clapped his heels to Horace's flanks. The hound took off from bunched hindquarters, travelling across the muddy sheep-littered plaza in a series of bounds that put them at chest-height from the ground half a dozen times. As he'd expected, that threw off the marksmen; they'd been expecting the troops they ambushed to mill around, or try to return fire from street level. *Never do what they expect*.

Thirty dogs pounded up the stairs to the arcaded verandah of the hall. A final crackle — too ragged to be a volley — at point-blank range knocked another six down. Smoke puffed into their faces, blinding them for an instant. Then they were scrabbling across the smooth tile of the portico and crashing through tall windows in showers of glass and the yelping of cut dogs. Horace reared and struck the big double doors with his forepaws. A jolt went through Raj's body, and he felt his teeth clack once like castanets; something seemed to snap behind his eyes.

The doors boomed open, crushing bone and tearing men off their feet. Horace's jaws closed over the face of another; the inch-long fangs sank in, and the hound made a rat-killing flip that sent the body pinwheeling back in a spray of blood. There were thirty or forty Brigaderos in the big reception hall that backed the portico; from their looks, he'd found the missing herdsmen. With another twenty-five riding dogs, the place was crowded, too crowded for the enemy to recharge their muzzle-loaders. Some of them clubbed muskets, but most drew swords or fighting-knives. Raj's men emptied their revolvers into the press and swept out their sabers. The dogs stamped on men trying to roll under their bellies and cut, snapped with fangs and hammered with their forepaws.

A Brigadero dodged in and cut at Raj's left thigh, always vulnerable in a mounted man. Horace spun on one leg, and Raj stabbed down over the saddle. The blow was at an awkward angle, but it sank into the bicep of the man's sword-arm. His weapon flew free as Raj jerked his steel free of the ripped muscle; then a Descotter wardog closed its jaws in his back and threw him over its shoulder with a snap. Raj lashed back to his right with a backhand cut across the neck of a man trying to come in on his bannerman's rear. The man with the flag had a revolver in his right hand; he was keeping his mount stock-still with a toe-to-foreleg signal and picking his targets carefully.

A last shot barked out. Powder-smoke was drifting to the ceiling; a few more men in blue jackets and maroon pants ran in, troopers whose dogs had been hit outside. As always, the melee was over with shocking suddenness. One instant there were shots and screams and the blacksmith chorus of steel on steel, the next only the moans of the wounded and the quick butcher's-cleaver sounds of troopers finishing off the enemy fallen.

"Dismount!" Raj barked. "Dogs on guard."

Horace pricked up his floppy ears at the word. So did the other mounts as the men slid to the ground, drawing their rifles from the saddle scabbards. Anyone trying to get into the ground floor was going to have a very nasty surprise.

"Walking wounded cover the front entrance," Raj went on. They could bandage themselves and the more severely hurt as well. "The rest of you, fix bayonets and follow me."

He switched his saber for an instant, juggled weapons to put his revolver in his left hand, and led the rush up his half of the curving double staircase with the lieutenant of the escort platoon on the other. Marksmen dropped out halfway up to cover the top of the stairs, firing over their comrades' heads. Hobnails and heel-plates clamored and sparked on the limestone. Center's aiming-grid dropped over his sight . . . which was a bad sign, because that only happened in desperate situations. No time for thought, only a quick, fluid feeling of total awareness. Everyone crouched as they neared the top of the stairs; he signed right and left to the men whose bayonet-tips he could see on either side.

"Now!"

The bannerman dropped flat two steps down, jerking the flag erect and waving it back and forth. The Brigaderos waiting in the upper hallway behind an improvised barricade of tables reacted exactly the way Raj had expected. The pole jumped in the bannerman's hands as a bullet took a piece out of the ebony staff and others plucked through the heavy silk of the banner itself. Raj and the leading riflemen crouched below the lip of the stairs as minié bullets and pistol rounds blasted at the top step. Time seemed to slow as he raised his head and left hand.

Green light strobed around a man with a revolver, aiming between the slats of a chair. Maximum priority. *Crack.* He pitched backward with a bullet through the neck, his scrabbling spraying body fouling several others. Raj fired as quickly as his wrist could move the dot of the aimpoint to the next glowing target, emptying the five-shot cylinder in less time than it took to take a deep breath. Much more of this and he'd get a reputation as a pistol-expert on top of everything else. As he dropped back under the topmost step four men levelled their rifles over it and fired. The heavy 11mm bullets hammered right through the barricade; the four ducked back down to reload, and another set a few steps lower down stood to fire over their heads. The sound echoed back off the close stone walls, thunder-loud.

Not a maneuver in the drill-book, but these were veterans. He shook the spent brass out of the revolver and reloaded, judging the volume of return fire.

"Once more and at 'em," he said. *"Now."*

They stood to charge. A man beside Raj took a bullet through the belly, folding over with an *oof* and falling backward to tumble and cartwheel down the stairs. Troopers behind him shouldered forward; all the Brigaderos behind the improvised barricade were badly wounded, but that didn't mean none of them could fight. There was a brief scurry of point-blank shots and bayonet thrusts.

Raj stood thinking as the soldiers searched the rooms on either side of the corridor, swift but cautious. No more shots . . . except from outside, where the steady crackle was building up again. His eyes fell on an unlit lamp. It was one of a series in brackets along the wall. Much like one back home; a globular glass reservoir below for the coal-oil, and a coiled flat-woven wick of cotton inside adjusted by a small brass screw, with a blown-glass chimney above.

"Sergeant," Raj called, stepping over a dead Brigadero.

The blood pooled around the enemy fallen stained his bootsoles, so that he left tacky footprints on the parquet of the hallway. Light fell in from rose-shaped windows at either end of the hallway.

"Get those lamps, all of them," he said.

"Ser?" The noncom gaped.

"All of them, and there should be more in a storage cupboard somewhere near. Distribute them to the windows. Quickly!" The trooper dashed off; the order made no sense, but he'd see it was obeyed, quickly and efficiently.

"Lieutenant," Raj went on. The young man looked up from tying off a rough bandage around his calf.

"Mi heneral?"

"A squad to each of the main windows, if you please. Send someone for extra ammunition from the saddlebags."

"Sir."

"And check how many men able to shoot there are below. Send some troopers to help them barricade the doors and windows."

"Ci, mi heneral."

He led his own small group of messengers and bannerman through the room opposite the staircase. It looked to be some sort of meeting chamber, with a long table and chairs, and crossed banners on the wall. One was the crimson-and-black double thunderbolt of the Brigade, the other a local blazon.

"Get the table," he said. "Follow me out."

The balcony outside ran the length of the front of the building, wrought-iron work on a stone base. The signallers came out grunting under the weight of the heavy oak table, and dropped it with a crash on its side and up against the railings. They dropped behind it with grateful speed, as riflemen in windows and rooftops across from them opened fire. Luckily, nothing overlooked the town hall except the tower of the church, and it was too open to make a good marksman's stand. Other squads were bringing out furniture of their own, some from the Brigaderos' own barricade at the head of the stairs.

"Keep them busy, lads," Raj said.

A steady crackle of aimed shots broke out; along the balcony, from the windows at either end of the hallway behind, and from the smaller windows on the rear side of the town hall. Raj took out his binoculars. A cold smile bent his lips; the enemy seemed to be coming out into the streets and milling around in surprise, mostly — even a few townspeople joining them.

Amateurs, he thought.

Tough ones, good individual fighters, but whoever was commanding them didn't have the organization to switch plans quickly when the first one went sour. That was the problem with a good plan — and it had been a cunningly conceived ambush — it tended to

hypnotize you. If you didn't have anything ready for
its miscarriage, you lost time. And time was the most
precious thing of all.

South of the town the Life Guards were deploying,
just out of rifle range. Dogs to the rear, extended
double line, one company in the saddle for quick
reaction; right out of the manuals. Also the guns. Four
of them, and the first was getting ready to —

POUMPF. The shell went overhead with a whirring
moan and crashed into one of the mills. Black smoke
and bits of tile and roofing-timber flew up. More
smoke followed; there must have been something like
tallow or lanolin stored there.

"Sir." It was the lieutenant and his platoon-sergeant.
The latter carried a dozen of the coal-oil lamps and
led men carrying more, with still others piled high on a
janitor's wheeled wooden cart.

"Sir," the young officer went on, "there's ten men
downstairs fit to fight, if they don't have to move much.
We've barred the back entrance; it's strong, and they
won't get through without a ram. The front's another
story, we've done what we can, but . . . "

Raj nodded and took a package of cigarettes out of
his jacket, handing two to the other men.

"Right," he began, and spoke over his shoulder.
"Signaller, two red rockets." Turning his attention back
to the other men:

"In about five minutes," he said, waving the tip of his
saber at the town, "the barbs are going to realize that
with us sitting here they can't even defend the town
against the Life Guards — we can suppress their
rooftop snipers too effectively from here.

"So they'll try rushing us. There's only two ways they
can come; in the back, and in the front the same way
we did. We don't have enough guns to stop them, not
and keep the snipers down too. And once they're close
to the walls, we won't be able to rise and fire down
from up here without exposing ourselves."

They nodded. Raj took one of the lamps and turned the wick high, lighting it with his cigarette. The flame was pale and wavering in the bright morning sunlight, but it burned steadily.

"They'll have to bunch under the walls — by the doors, for example." Raj tossed the lamp up and down. "I really don't think they'll like it when we chuck these over on them."

The two officers and the noncom smiled at each other. "What about the front?" the sergeant asked. "There's this —" he stamped a heel on the balcony's deck "— over the portico."

"That," Raj went on, "is where you'll take the keg." He nodded at the clay barrel of coal-oil on the cart, with a dozen lamps clinking against it. "And hang it like a *pihnyata* from one of the brackets."

"Roit ye are, ser," the sergeant said, grinning like a shark. "Roit where she'll shower 'em wit coal-juice as they come chargin' up t' steps, loik."

He took the heavy container and heaved it onto his shoulder with a lift-and-jerk. "Ye, Belgez, foller me."

"A hundred thousand men?" Ingreid asked.

Teodore Welf nodded encouragingly. "That's counting all the regular garrisons we've been able to withdraw, Your Mightiness, and the levies of the first class — all organized, and all between eighteen and forty."

Ingreid's lips moved and he looked at his fingers. "How many is that in regiments?"

Howyrd Carstens looked around the council chamber. It was fairly large, but plain; whitewashed walls, and tall narrow windows. The three of them were alone except for servants and civilian accountants — nonentities. Good. He liked Ingreid, and respected him, but there was no denying that large numbers were just not *real* to the older nobleman. For that matter, a hundred thousand men was a difficult number for him to grasp, and he was a modern-minded man who could both read and write and do arithmetic, including long division. He had enough scars, and enough duelling kills, that nobody would call it unmanly.

Teodore spoke first. "Standard regiments?" A thousand to twelve hundred men each. "A hundred, hundred and ten regiments. Not counting followers and so forth, of course."

Ingreid grunted and knocked back the last of his kave, snapping his fingers for more.

"And the enemy?"

Carstens shrugged. "Twenty thousand men — but more than half of those are infantry."

The Military Governments didn't have foot infantry in their armies, and he wondered why the Civil Government bothered.

"Of mounted troops, real fighting men? Seven, perhaps eight regiments. They have a lot of field artillery, though — and from what I've heard, it's effective."

Ingreid shook his head. "Seven regiments against a hundred. Madness! What does Whitehall think he can accomplish?"

"I don't know, Your Mightiness," Teodore Welf said. The older men looked up at the note in his voice. "And that's what worries me."

Burning men scrambled back from the portico of the town hall. A few of them had caught a full splash of the fuel, and they dropped and rolled in the wet dirt of the square. More leaped and howled and beat at the flames that singed their boots and trousers. The bullets that tore at them from the windows were much more deadly — but every man has his fear, and for many that fear is fire. The smell of scorched stone and burning wool and hair billowed up from the portico, up in front of the overhanging balcony in a billow of heat and smoke. From the ground floor the dogs howled and

barked, loud enough to make the floor shiver slightly
under his feet. The men along the balcony above shot
and reloaded and shot, their attention drawn by the
helpless targets.

"Watch the bloody *roofs*," Raj snapped, hearing the
command echoed by the non-coms.

The Brigaderos began to clump for another rush at
the portico, as the flames died down a little . . .
although there was an ominous crackle below the
balcony floor, from the roof-beams that ran from the
arches to the building wall and supported it. Another
shower of glass lanterns full of coal-oil set puddles of
fire on the ground and broke the rush, sending them
running back across the plaza to shelter in the other
buildings.

Raj looked left and south. Cabot's Life Guards were
advancing, with the battery of field guns firing over
their heads. The gunners had the range, and the
buildings edging the town there were coming apart
under the hammer of their five-kilo shells.

"Messer Raj." The platoon sergeant duckwalked up
to Raj's position, keeping the heaped wooden furniture
along the balustrade between him and any Brigadero
rifleman's sights.

"We singed 'em good, ser," the noncom said. His
own eyebrows looked as if they'd taken combat
damage as well. "Only t' damned roof is burnin', loik.
We'nz gonna have t'move soon."

"The barbs will move before we roast, sergeant," Raj
said. *I hope*, he thought. He also hoped the warmth in
the floor-tiles under his hand was an illusion.

The enemy *should* run. Pozadas had helped set up
the ambush — something its citizens were going to
regret — but the Brigaderos were countrymen.
Caught between two fires, their instinct would be to
head for open ground, out of the buildings that were
protection but felt like traps.

He wiped his eyes on the sleeve of his jacket and

brought the binoculars up. *Yes*. Groups of men pouring out of the houses, pouring out of the mills — most of those were burning now, from the shellfire. On foot and dogback they streamed north to the river, crowding the single narrow stone bridge or swimming their dogs across. The battery commander was alert; he raised his muzzles immediately. The ripping-sail sound of shells passed overhead. One landed beyond the bridge; the next fell short, pounding a hole in the roadway leading to it — and scattering men and dogs and parts of both up with the gout of whitish-gray dirt. The next one clipped the side of the bridge itself, and the whole battery opened up. Shells airburst over the river, dimpling circles into the water, like dishes pockmarked with the splash-marks of shrapnel.

"Out, everybody out," Raj said.

The Life Guards were charging, cheering as they came. The mounted company rocked into a gallop ahead of them.

"Check every room," he went on. Someone might be wounded in one of them, unable to move. "Move it!"

The lieutenant came in from the back, hobbling on his ripped leg and grinning like a sicklefoot. "Bugged out," he said. "All but the ones we burned or shot while they tried to open the back door with a treetrunk."

"Good work," Raj said.

He threw an arm around the young officer's waist to support his weight and they went down the stairs quickly; the lower story was already emptying out. The dogs wuffled and danced nervously as they crossed the hot tile of the portico. Puddles of flame still burned on the cracked flooring, and the thick beams of the ceiling above were covered in tongues of scarlet.

Guess I didn't imagine the floor was getting hot after all, Raj thought. The coal-oil had been an effective solution to the problem of Brigaderos storming the building . . . but it might have presented some serious long-term problems.

Of course, you had to survive the short term for the long term to be very important.

Horace snuffed him over carefully in the plaza, then sneezed when he was satisfied Raj hadn't been injured. The mounted company of the Life Guards streamed through, already drawing their rifles. Two guns followed them, limbered up and at the trot. Raj looked south: the dismounted companies were fanning out to surround the town and close in from three sides.

Cabot Clerett pulled up before the general, swinging his saber up to salute. Raj returned the gesture fist-to-chest.

The younger man stood in the saddle. "*Damn* it, a lot of them are going to get away," he said. The measured crash of volley-fire was coming from the direction of the bridge, and the slightly dulled sound of cannon firing case-shot at point-blank range.

Beside Raj, his bannerman stiffened slightly at the younger officer's tone. Clerett grew conscious of the stares.

"Sir," he added.

Raj was looking in the same direction. The land on the other side of the river was flat drained fields for a thousand meters or so. Brigaderos were running all across it, those with the fastest dogs who'd been closest to the river. Bodies were floating down with the current, now. Not many who'd still been in the water or on the bridge when the troops arrived would make it over; as he watched a clump toppled back from the far bank.

"Oh, I don't think so, Major Clerett," he said calmly. Horace crouched and he straddled the saddle.

Beyond the cleared fields was a forest of coppiced poplar trees, probably maintained as a fuel-source for the handicrafts and fireplaces of Pozadas. The glint of metal was just perceptible as men rode out of the woods, pausing to dress ranks. The trumpets were unheard at this distance, but the way the swords flashed free in unison and the men swept forward was unmistakable.

Clerett looked at him blank-faced. A murmur went through the men nearest, and whispers as they repeated the conversation to those further away.

"You expected the ambush, sir?" he said carefully.

"Not specifically. I thought we could use some help with all that livestock . . . and that everything had been too easy."

"If you'd told me, sir, we might have arranged a more . . . elegant solution without extra troops."

Raj sighed, looking around. The civilians were still indoors, apart from a few who'd tried to follow the Brigaderos over the river, and died with them. The fires were burning sullenly, smoke pillaring straight up in the calm chill air. He reached into a saddle bag and pulled out a walnut, one of a bag Suzette had tucked in for him.

"Major," he said, "*this* is an elegant way to crack a walnut."

He squeezed one carefully between thumb and forefinger of his sword hand. The shells parted, and he extracted the meat and flicked it into his mouth.

"And it can work. However." He put another in the palm of his left hand, raised his right fist and smashed it down. The nut shattered, and he shook the pieces to the ground. "This way *always* works. Very few operations have ever failed because too many troops were used. Use whatever you've got."

Cabot nodded thoughtfully. "What are your orders, sir?" he asked. "Concerning the town, that is."

The wounded were being laid out on the ground before the town hall. Raj nodded toward them.

"We'll bivouac here tonight, your battalion and the Slashers," he said. "Get the fires out or under control — roust out the civilians to help with that. Round up the stock we were driving. Send out scouting parties to see none of the enemy escaped or are lying up around here; no prisoners, by the way."

"The town and the civilians?" Clerett asked.

Raj looked around; Pozadas had yielded on terms and then violated them.

"We'll loot it bare of everything useful, and burn it down when we leave tomorrow. Shoot all the adult males, turn the women over to the troops, then march them and the children back to the column for sale."

Clerett nodded. "Altogether a small but tidy victory, sir," he said.

"Is it, Major?" Raj asked somberly. "We lost what . . . twenty men today?"

The Governor's nephew raised his brows. "We killed hundreds," he said. "And we hold the field."

"Major, the Brigade can *replace* hundreds more easily than I can replace twenty veteran cavalry troopers. If all the barbarians stood in a line for my men to cut their throats, they could slash until their arms fell off with weariness and there would still be Brigaderos. Yes, we hold the field — until we leave. With less than twenty thousand men, I'd be hard-pressed to garrison a single district, much less the Western Territories as a whole. We can only conquer if men obey us *without* a detachment pointing guns every moment."

Raj tapped his knuckles thoughtfully on the pommel of his saddle. "It isn't enough to *defeat* them in battle. I have to *shatter* them — break their will to resist, make them give up. They won't surrender to a few battalions of cavalry. So we have to find something they can surrender to."

He gathered his reins. "I'm heading back to the main column. Follow as quickly as possible."

Abdullah al'-Aziz spread the carpet with a flourish.

"Finest Al Kebir work, my lady," he said, in Spanjol with a careful leavening of Arabic accent — it was his native tongue, but he could speak half a dozen with faultless purity. He was a slight olive-skinned man, like millions around the Midworld Sea, or further east in the Colonial dominions. Dress and more subtle clues both marked him as a well-to-do Muslim trader of Al Kebir, and he could change the motions of hands and face and body as easily as the long tunic, baggy pantaloons and turban.

This morning room of the General's palace was warm with hangings and the log fire in one hearth, but the everlasting dank chill of a Carson Barracks winter still lingered in the mind, if nowhere else. Abdullah was dispelling a little of it with his goods. Bright carpets of thousand-knot silk and gold thread, velvets and torofib, spices and chocolate and lapis lazuli. Since the Zanj Wars, when Tewfik of Al Kebir broke the monopoly of the southern city-states, a few daring Colonial traders had made the year-long voyage around the Southern Continent to the Brigade-held ports of Tembarton and Rohka. If you survived the sea monsters and storms and the savages it could be very profitable. The Civil Government lay athwart the overland routes from the Colony, and its tariffs quintupled prices.

Marie Manfrond straightened in her chair. "This is beautiful work," she said, running a hand down a length of torofib embroidered with peacocks and prancing Afghan wolfhounds carrying men in turbans to the hunt.

"All of you," she went on, "leave me. Except you, Katrini."

Several of the court matrons sniffed resentfully as they swept out; attendance on the General's Lady was a hereditary right of the spouses of certain high officers of state. Marie's cold gray gaze hurried them past the door. Men in Guard uniforms stood outside, ceremonial guards and real jailers. Abdullah looked aside at Katrini. She went to stand beside the door, in a position to give them a few seconds if someone burst through.

"Katrini's been with me since we were girls," Marie said. "I trust her with my life."

Abdullah shrugged. "Inshallah. You know, then, from whom I come?"

His long silk coat and jewel-clasped turban were perfectly authentic, made in Al Kebir as their appearance suggested.

"Raj Whitehall," Marie said flatly. "The Colonial traders don't come to Tembarton this time of year; the winds are wrong."

"Ah, my lady is observant," Abdullah said. Marie nodded; not one Brigade noble in a thousand would have known that.

"But I do not come from General Whitehall . . . not directly. Rather from his wife, Lady Suzette. If Messer Raj's sword is the Companions who fight for him, she is his dagger, just as deadly."

"What difference does it make?" Marie asked. "Why shouldn't I turn you over to my husband's men immediately?"

Abdullah smiled at the implied threat, that he would be turned over *later* if not now. The subtlety was pleasing. He owed Suzette Whitehall his freedom and life and that of his family, but he served her most of all because it gave him full scope for his talents. He could retire on his savings if he wished, but life would be as savorless as meat without salt.

"Forgive me if I presume, my lady, but my lady Suzette has told me that your interests and those of General Ingreid are not . . . how shall I say . . . not always exactly the same."

"That's no secret even in Carson Barracks," Marie said. Not a month after the wedding, with a fading black eye imperfectly disguised with cosmetics. "But Ingreid Manfrond is General, and my people are at war. Do you think I would betray the 591st Provisional Brigade and its heritage for my own spite?"

"Ah, no, by no means," Abdullah said soothingly,

spreading his hands with a charming gesture.

"Lady Suzette is moved by sisterly compassion — and the conviction that General Ingreid will do the Brigade all the harm a traitor could, through his incompetence. Also the Spirit of Man — I would say the Hand of God — is stretched over her lord. He is invincible. Lady Suzette's concern is that you yourself might suffer needlessly from Ingreid's anger."

"And I can believe as much or as little of that as I choose," Marie said.

Silence weighed the warm air of the room for a moment; outside fog and soft raindrops clung to the walls and covered the swamps.

"Is it true," the young woman went on in a neutral voice, "that she rides by his side?"

Abdullah bowed again, a hand pressed to his breast. "She rides with his military household," he said. "And sits in all his councils. At El Djem her carbine brought down a Colonial whose sword was raised above Messer Raj's head."

Marie rested an elbow on the carved arm of her chair and her chin on her fist. "What help can she be to me?"

"Has not General Ingreid said, in public for all to hear, that as soon as you are delivered of an heir he has no use for you?"

The words had been rather more blunt than that. Marie nodded. Once Ingreid had an heir of her undoubted Amalson blood, he would not need their marriage to make his eligibility for the Seat incontestable. She had been throwing up regularly for a week, now.

Abdullah opened a small rosewood case. "Here are *ayzed* and *beyam*," he said, smiling with hooded eyes. "The one for the problem I see my lady has now. The other in case she comes to see that General Ingreid is no shield for the Brigade, but rather a millstone dragging it down to doom."

He explained the uses of the Zanj drugs. Katrini gasped by the door; Marie signed her to silence and nodded thoughtfully.

"Ingreid hasn't the brains of a sauroid," she said thoughtfully. "Go on."

"My lady has partisans of her own," Abdullah said. "Those loyal to her family. Your mother is well-remembered, your father more so."

"Few real vassals. The Seat controls my family estates, so I can't reward followers. Fighting men have to follow a lord who can give gold and gear and land with both hands. And I'm held here without easy access to anyone but Ingreid's clients and sworn men."

Abdullah spread his hands. "Funds may be advanced," he said. "Also messages carried. Not for any treasonous purpose, but is it not your right? By Brigade law does not a *brazaz* lady of your rank have a right to her own household, her own retainers?"

Marie nodded slowly. "We'll have to talk more of this," she said.

CHAPTER FOUR

"Right up ahead, ser," the Scout said. "Turn right off t'road, up to the *kasgrane*, loik."

The Expeditionary Force was winding its way through a countryside of low rolling hills, mostly covered with vineyards and olive trees and orchards; pretty to look at, even with the leaves all down, but awkward to march through. Villages grew more frequent as they approached Old Residence, and the *kasgrane* —manor-houses — were unfortified and often lavishly built with gardens and ornamental waterworks, the country-residences of the city magnates. The light airy construction showed that most of them would have been empty in winter anyway, but many of the villagers had headed for the security of city walls as well. There hadn't been any serious war here in generations, but peasants knew down in their bones that there was usually not much to choose between armies on the march. Either side might loot and rape, perhaps kill and burn. Better to hide in a city, where only one side was likely to come and where commanders were more watchful.

Raj nodded and tapped Horace's ribs with his heels. His escort trotted behind him, along the cleared space beyond the roadside ditch. Past infantry swinging along, their uniforms patched but glad to be out of the mud of the river bottoms, past guns and ox-wagons and more infantry and the hospital carts with the tooth-grating sounds of wounded men jolting over ruts in the crude gravel pavement of the road. Better than two hundred men down with lungfever, too; there'd be more, unless he got them under shelter soon. The nights were uniformly chilly now, the days raw at best, and it rained every second day or so. They'd come more than four hundred kilometers in only a month. The men were worn out and the dogs were sore-pawed.

And I've got the second-biggest city in the Midworld to take at the end of it, Raj thought grimly. Old Residence was only a shadow of what it had been in its glory days six hundred years ago, when it was the seat of the Governors and capital of the whole Midworld basin. There were still four hundred thousand residents, and it was the center of most of the trade and manufacture in the Western Territories.

They passed the head of the column; beyond that were only the scouting detachments, combing the hills ahead and around the main force to make sure there weren't any surprises in wait. A platoon of the 5th Descott waited at the turn-off.

The private laneway was narrow, but better-kept than the public road, smooth crushed limestone and bordered by tall cypress trees. It wound upward through vineyards whose pruning had been left half-finished, some vinestocks cut back to their gnarled winter shapes and some with the season's growth still showing in long bare finger-shoots. Untended sheep grazed between them on the sprouting cover crop of wild mustard. The kasgrane at the heart of the *finca*, the estate, was two stories of whitewashed stone and tile roof. The tall glass-paned doors on both stories showed it to be a summer residence; so did the hilltop location, placed to catch the breeze. The windows were shut now, and smoke wafted from the chimneys.

More came from the elaborate tents pitched in the gardens. Wagons and carriages and the humbler dosses of servants and attendants crowded about, and a heavy smell of many dogs. A resplendent figure in sparkling white silk jumpsuit and cloth-of-gold robe waited at the main entrance to the manor. A jeweled headset rested on his thin white hair, and the staff in his hand was topped by an ancient circuit board encased in a net of platinum and diamonds. It was the Key Chip of the Priest of the Residential Parish, symbol of his authority to Code the Uploading of souls to the Orbit of Fulfillment and the ROM banks of the Spirit. The vestments of the archsysups, sysups and priests around him made a dazzling corona in the bright noonday sun.

The pontiff raised staff and hand in blessing from the steps as Raj drew up. A bellows-lunged annunciator stepped forward:

"Let all children of Holy Federation Church bow before *Paratier*, the seventeenth of that name, Priest of the Residential Parish, servant of the servants of the Spirit of Man of the Stars, in whose hands is the opening and closing of the data gates."

Raj and his officers dismounted. They and Suzette touched one knee to the ground briefly; Raj had the platinum-inlaid mace of his proconsular authority in the crook of his left elbow. That meant he was the personal representative of the Governor — and in the Civil Government the ruler was supreme in spiritual as well as temporal matters. Instead of kneeling, he bowed to kiss the prelate's outstretched ring-hand. The ring too held a relic of priceless antiquity, a complete processing chip set among rubies and sapphires.

a FC-77b6 unit, Center remarked. **generally used to control home entertainment modules.**

"Your Holiness," Raj said as he straightened.

The Priest was an elderly man with a face like pale wrinkled parchment, carrying a faint scent of lavender water with him. His eyes were brown and as cold as rocks polished by a glacial stream.

"*Heneralissimo Supremo* Whitehall," he replied, in accentless Sponglish. "I and these holy representatives of the Church —"

The assembled clerics were watching Raj and his

followers much as a monohorn watched a carnosauroid; not afraid, exactly, but wary. Few of them
looked full of enthusiasm for a return to Civil
Government rule. The Church had been the prime
authority in Old Residence under the slack overlord-
ship of the Brigade Generals. None of them had any
illusions that the Civil Government would be so lax.
And the Governors were also unlikely to allow the
Priest as much autonomy; the Chair believed in
keeping the ecclesiastical authorities under firm control.

"— and of the Governor's Council —"

The civilian magnates. The Council had been
important half a millenium ago, when the Governors
ruled from Old Residence. There was still a Council in
East Residence, although membership was an empty
title. Evidently the locals had kept up the forms as a
sort of municipal government.

"— are here to offer you the keys of Old Residence."
Literally: a page was coming forward, with a huge iron
key on a velvet cushion.

"My profound thanks, Your Holiness," Raj said.

Quite sincerely; the last thing he wanted to do was
try to take a place ten times the size of Lion City by
storm. He turned an eye on the assembled magnates.

"I'm pleasantly surprised at the presence of you
gentlemen," he went on. "Especially since I'd heard
the barbarian General had extorted hostages and oaths
from you."

Paratier smiled. "Oaths sworn under duress are void;
doubly so, since they were sworn to a heretic. These
excellent sirs were absolved of the oaths by Our order."

Raj nodded. *And I know exactly how much* your
word's worth, he thought. Aloud: "However, the
heretic garrison?"

Paratier looked around. He seemed a little surprised
that Raj was speaking openly before his officers; a bit
more surprised that Suzette was at his side.

"Ah —" he coughed into a handkerchief. "Ah, they have been persuaded . . ."

Lion City, Raj thought, *did some good after all*.

"Sir, *please* get on the train!"

Hereditary High Colonel Lou Derison shook his head. "The General appointed me commandant of Old Residence. Here I stay."

"Lou," the other man said, stepping closer. "We lost Strezman and four thousand men in Lion City. We can't *afford* another loss of trained regulars like that. There are only five thousand men in the garrison; that isn't enough to hold down a hostile city *and* defend the walls. But in the field, it may be the difference between victory and defeat. Once we've beaten the *grisuh* in battle, Old Residence will open its gates to us again — it's a whore of a city, and spreads its legs for the strongest."

Behind the junior officer a locomotive whistle let out a screech, startling Derison's dog into a protesting whine behind him. The little engine wheezed, its upright boiler showing red spots around the base, where the thrall shoveled coal into the brick arch of the furnace. Ten cars were hitched by simple chain links to the engine, much like ox-wagons with flanged wheels and board sides marked *8 dogs/40 men*. These were all crowded with soldiers, the last of the Old Residence garrison. Most had left during the day and the night before. The tracks ran westward though tumbledown warehouses and then through the equally decrepit city wall. The driver yelled something incoherent back toward the clump of officers.

Derison shook his head again. "No, no — you do what you must, Torens, and I'll do what *I* must. Goodbye, and the Spirit of Man of This Earth go with you."

Major Torens blinked, gripped the hand held out to

him and then turned to jump aboard the last and already moving car. The wheels of the locomotive spun on the wood-and-iron rails, and the whole train moved off into the misty rain with a creaking, clanging din that faded gradually into echoes and the last mournful wail of the whistle.

Derison sighed and put on his helmet, adjusting the cheek-guards with care. His armor was burnished and there was a red silk sash beneath his swordbelt, but the weapons and plate had seen hard service in their day.

"Come, gentlemen," he said. "We ride to the west gate."

A dozen men accompanied him, his sons and a few personal retainers. One spoke:

"Is that wise, sir? The natives are out of order."

Derison straddled his crouching dog, and it rose with a *huff* of effort. "A man lives as long as he lives, and not a day more. We'll greet this Raj Whitehall like fighting men, under an open sky, not hiding in a building like women."

Massed trumpets played in the entrance to Old Residence. Horace skittered sideways a few steps, and threw up his long muzzle in annoyance. Army dogs expected trumpets to *say* something, and these were just being sounded for the noise. The walls were tall but thin, and some of the crenelations had fallen long ago. There were two towers on either side of the gate, but no proper blockhouse or thickening of the wall. There had been kilometers of ruins first, before they came to the defenses. Some pre-Fall work; most of what the unFallen built with decayed rapidly, but the rest did not decay at all. Rather more of ordinary stone and brick, heavily mined for building material. Those would date from the third or fourth post-Fall centuries, when the Civil Government had been ruled from here and included the whole Midworld basin.

The wall itself had come later, a century or two —

when the population of the city had shrunk and the situation had gotten worse. Old Residence fell to the Brigade about two generations after that.

There was no portcullis, just thick timber and iron doors. The roadway opened out into a plaza beyond, thick with a crowd whose noise rolled over the head of the Civil Government column like heavy surf. This was still a *big* city. The street led south towards the White River, but hills blocked its way, covered with buildings. The giant marble-and-gilt pile of the Priest's Palace off to his left; not just the residence, but home for the ecclesiastical bureaucracy. Further to the right the rooftop domes of the Old Governor's Palace showed, with only a little gold leaf still on the concrete, and the cathedron and Governor's Council likewise — they were all on hilltops, and the filled-in area between them would be the main plaza of the city. The rest was a sea of roofs and a spiderweb of roads, and the familiar coalsmoke-sweat-sewage-dog scent of a big city. There were even cast-iron lampstands by the side of the main road for gaslights, looking as if they'd been copied from the three-globe model used in East Residence. Which they probably had been.

Delegations lined the street on either side; from the Church, from the great houses of the magnates, from the merchant guilds and religious cofraternities. Holy water, incense and dried flower-petals streamed out toward the color-party around Raj; with music clashing horribly, and organized shouts of *Conquer! Conquer!* That was a Governor's salute and highly untactful, because Barholm would have kittens when he heard about it — as he assuredly would, and soon.

Also waiting were a group of Brigaderos nobles, looking slightly battered and extremely angry. Raj and his bannerman and guards swung out of the procession and cantered over to the square of white-uniformed Priest's Guards who ringed them. The soldiers had

shaven skulls themselves, which meant they were
ordained priests.

"Who are these men?" Raj barked to their officer,
pitching his voice slightly higher to carry through the
crowd-roar.

"The heretic garrison commander. Thought he'd left
with the rest, but they were heading this way. We have
them in custody — "

"Where are their swords?" Raj asked.

"Well, we couldn't let prisoners go armed, could
we?" the man said.

"Give them back," Raj said.

He turned his head to look at the white-uniformed
officer when the man started to object. The weapons
came quickly, the usual single-edged, basket-hilted
broadswords of the barbarians. The Brigaderos seemed
to grow a few inches as they retrieved them and
sheathed the blades. Most of them looked as if they'd
rather use them on the priest-soldiers around them.

"High Colonel Derison?" Raj asked, moving Horace
forward a few paces.

"General Whitehall?" the man asked in turn.

Raj nodded curtly. The Brigadero drew his sword
again and offered it hilt-first across his left forearm; the
younger man by his side did likewise. Raj took the
elder's sword, and Gerrin Staenbridge the younger;
they flourished them over their heads and returned the
blades. By Brigade custom that put the owners under
honorable parole. He hoped they wouldn't make an
issue of their empty pistol-holsters, because he didn't
have any intention of returning *those*.

"My congratulations on a wise decision," he said.

Actually, staying on here was either a pointless
gesture or cowardice. He didn't think the High
Colonel was a coward, but it was a pity he'd decided to
stay if he was merely stupid. Raj wanted all the
unimaginative Brigade officers possible active in their
command structure.

Derison inclined his head. "Your orders, sir?" he said.

"*My* orders are to convey you to East Residence," Raj replied. Derison senior seemed taken aback, but a flash of interest marked his son's face. "You'll be given honorable treatment and allowed to take your household and receive the revenues of your remaining estates."

He'd also probably be shunted off to a manor in a remote province after Barholm had shown him around to put some burnish on the victory celebrations, and his sons and younger retainers politely inducted into the Civil Government's armies, but there were worse fates for the defeated. All Brigaderos nobles who surrendered were being allowed to keep their freedom and one-third of their lands. Those who fought faced death and their families were sold as slaves.

"In fact," he went on, "I'd be obliged if you'd do something for me at the same time."

Derison bowed again. Raj reached into his jacket. "Here's the key to Old Residence," he said. "Please present it to the Sovereign Mighty Lord with my complements, and say I decided to send it to him in the keeping of a man of honor."

The Brigadero looked down at the key — which was usually, for ceremonial purposes, left in the keeping of the Priest — and fought down a grin.

"Colonel Staenbridge," Raj went on formally.

"*Mi heneral?*"

"See that these nobles are conveyed to suitable quarters in the Old Palace, and guarded by our own men with all respect."

"As you order, *mi heneral*."

Courtesy to the defeated cost nothing, and it encouraged men to surrender.

And now to work, he thought.

❖   ❖   ❖

"Have any of you ever heard the story of Marthinez the Lawman?" Raj asked.

He stood looking out of the Old Palace windows down to the docks. The gaslights were coming on along the main avenues, and the softer yellow glow of lamps from thousands of windows; both moons were up, the fist-sized disks half hidden by flying cloud. The picture was blurred by the rain that had started along with sundown, but he could just make out the long shark shapes of the Civil Government steam rams coming up the river, each towing a cargo ship against the current.

No complaints about the Navy this time, he thought. *Have to look up their commander.* The room was warm with underfloor hot-air pipes, and it smelled of wet uniforms and boots and tobacco.

Raj turned back to the men around the semicircular table. All the Companions, some of the other battalion commanders, and Cabot Clerett, who couldn't be safely excluded.

"Ah, Marthinez," Ehwardo Poplanich said. Suzette nodded. Her features had the subtle refinement of sixteen generations of East Residence court nobility, able to show amusement with the slightest narrowing of her hazel-green eyes. The rest of the Companions looked blank.

"Marthinez," Raj went on, pacing like a leashed cat beside the windows, "was a Lawman of East Residence." The capital had a standing police force, rather an unusual thing even in the Civil Government.

Someone laughed. "No," Raj went on, "he was a very *odd* Lawman. Completely honest."

"Damned unnatural," Kaltin said.

"Possibly. That's what got him into trouble; he blew the whistle on one of his superiors who'd taken a hefty bribe to cover up a nasty murder by a . . . very important person's son."

Nods all around the table.

"Well, it would have been embarrassing to bring him to trial, so he was thrown in the Subiculum."

That was the holding gaol for the worst sort of criminal. Usually the magistrates eventually got around to having the inmates given a short trial and then crucifixion or hanging or fried at the stake, depending on which crime had been the last before their capture. On the other hand, sometimes they just lost the name in the shuffle. A lifetime in the Subiculum was considerably worse than death, in most men's opinion. Sometimes the loss was deliberate.

"As you can imagine, he wasn't very popular there. Four soul-catchers" — kidnappers who stole free children for sale as slaves — "decided they'd beat him to death the very first night, since he'd put them in there.

"But," Raj went on with a carnivore grin, "Marthinez was, as I said, a fairly unusual sort of man. When the guards came in in the morning, the soul-catchers mostly had their heads facing backward or their ribs stove in. Marthinez had some bruises. So they took him away to the solitary hole for a week, that's the standard punishment for fighting in the cells . . .

"And as they were dragging him off through the corridors, he shouted: *You don't understand! I'm not trapped in here with* you. *You're all trapped in here with* me!"

"He made," Raj concluded, "quite a swath through the inmates until Ehwardo's grandfather pardoned him and made him Chief Lawman."

Raj halted before the central window, tapping one gauntleted fist into a palm. "General Ingreid thinks he has me trapped." He turned. "Just like Lawman Marthinez, eh?"

Kaltin nodded. "I don't like losing our mobility, though," he said. Which was natural enough for a cavalry officer.

Raj went on: "Kaltin, it's not enough to *beat* the

Brigade. Believe me, you can have a good commander and fine troops and win battle after battle and still lose the war."

hannibal, Center said. Raj acknowledged it silently. He was still a little vague on precisely when Hannibal had fought his war — it didn't seem like pre-Fall times at all — but Center's outline of the campaign had been very instructive. Cannae was a jewel of a battle, as decisive as you could want. Even more decisive than the two massacres Raj had inflicted on the Squadron last year — except that Hannibal's enemies hadn't given up afterwards.

"To win this war, we have to do two things. We have to get the civilian population here to actively support us."

There were snorts; Raj acknowledged them. "Yes, I know they've got no more fight than so many sheep, most of them — six centuries under the Brigade. But there are a *lot* of them.

"Second and most important, we've got to make the Brigade *believe* that they're defeated. To do that, we have to get as many of them as we can in one spot; all the principal nobles and their followers, at least. And then we have to kill so many of them that the remainder are convinced right down in their bones that fighting us and death are one and the same thing.

"The best way I can think of doing that is persuading them to make head-on attacks into fortified positions."

Gerrin raised a brow. "That assumes they will," he said. "I wouldn't. I'd entrench a large blocking force and send a mobile field army to attack our forward base in the Crown and mop up the areas we marched through."

Raj snorted. "Yes, but Gerrin — you're not a barb." He jerked a thumb out the window. "According to the latest intelligence, Ingreid has about a hundred thousand men rallying to his banner; that's most of the regular army of the Brigade, and all of their first-line reserves.

"First, remember that the Brigade are a minority here. They're going to be worried about native and peasant uprisings, the more so since we've occupied Old Residence — which doesn't mean anything of military importance by itself, but the *people* don't know that. They'll be impressed.

"Second, they're stripping their northern frontier. The Stalwarts and the Guard will be raiding, even in winter. Especially since the Ministry of Barbarians is subsidizing them to do exactly that."

He went to the frame and ran his hand across the map of the Western Territories at the latitude of Carson Barracks, a little south of Old Residence.

"Most of the Brigaderos live north of here; it was the first area they overran, back when, and it's where most of them settled. The southern part of the peninsula was conquered more gradually, and the barbs are very thin on the ground there. So they'll be anxious about their homes and families in the north, looking over their shoulders, eager to get it over with and go home. The Brigade doesn't have the sort of command structure which can ignore that type of sentiment.

"Third, one hundred thousand men are going to be camping here, in the middle of a countryside which we shall systematically strip of every ounce of food we can. You know the Brigade; they could no more organize a supply system from the rear on that scale than they could fly to Miniluna by flapping their arms."

"There's the railroad to Carson Barracks," Gerrin Staenbridge said thoughtfully. "With that, they can draw on the whole Padan Valley." He turned to whisper to Bartin for a moment. "Yes, I thought so. *Just* capable of handling the necessary tonnage, but without much margin."

Raj nodded. "Something will be done about that. So they're going to be cold, and wet, and hungry, and after a while a lot of them will be sick, too. They'll be thinking of their nice warm manors and snug farmhouses and hot soup by the fire.

"They'll *have* to attack. And we have to be *ready*. Now, gentlemen, here's how we're going to do that. First, since we're not blessed with a contingent from the Administrative Service, I'm appointing Lady Whitehall legate for civil affairs. Next —"

CHAPTER FIVE

"Most should recover," the Renunciate Sister said.

Suzette nodded, stopping for a moment by one man's bedside. His face glistened with sweat, more than the mild warmth of the commandeered mansion's underfloor heating system could account for. He gave her a weak smile as a helper propped him up and lifted the bowl of broth to his lips. The air was full of a medicinal smell, mostly from the pots of water laced with mint and eucalyptus leaves boiling on braziers in every room and corridor. A low chorus of racking coughs sounded under the brisker sounds of orders and soup-carts.

"Lungfever is most serious when the body is debilitated," the Renunciate went on, as they walked out of the room. "Cold, exhaustion, or bad food. With warmth, rest, careful feeding and plenty of liquids, most of these men should be fit for light duty in Holy Church's cause within a month."

Which would give the equivalent of a whole battalion back to Raj. Suzette nodded, smiling.

"You've done wonderful work," she said.

The Renunciate sniffed. "The Spirit was with us, Lady Whitehall," she said tartly.

Church healers accompanied any Civil Government army; these had been with Raj for going on three years now.

"But please tell the *heneralissimo* that men who sleep in cold mud while they're too tired to eat properly *will* get sick."

❖   ❖   ❖

"What is the meaning of this?" the merchant demanded. "Out of my way, you peasants!"

He tried to push past the infantrymen standing in the doorway of his warehouse. The peon soldiers spoke no Spanjol and would have ignored him in any case. He walked into the crossed rifles as if into a stone wall, rebounding backward with a squawk. The morning sun glinted brightly on the honed edges of their bayonets as they swung up to *present*, the points inches from his chest. There was a four-dog carriage behind him, and two mounted servants armed with swords and pistols, as well as a crowd of his clerks and storesmen. None of them seemed likely to get him through into his place of business this day.

"Messer Enrike," a soothing voice said.

Enrike turned; Muzzaf Kerpatik was coming around the corner of the tall building with an officer in Civil Government uniform.

"Messer Kerpatik, am I to be robbed, after all your assurances?" the merchant demanded.

Rumor had it that Kerpatik was Raj's factotum for purchasing, an enviable post. It was plain to see he at least was no Descotter — small and slim, dressed in dazzling white linen with the odd fore-and-aft peaked cap of the southern border cities of the Civil Government, along the frontier with the Colony. His Sponglish had the sing-song accent of Komar.

"Of course not," the Komarite soothed. "Just some precautions."

"Precautions against *what*?" Enrike demanded.

Muzzaf whispered in the officer's ear. The man barked an order in Sponglish, and the squad sloped arms and wheeled away from the door. The others guarding the big wagon-gates of the warehouse remained, but the employees filed into the front section of the building.

Enrike snorted as he settled into the big leather armchair behind his desk. One of the clerks scuttled in to throw a scoopful of coal into the cast-iron stove in one corner, and a maidservant brought in kave and rolls.

"Precautions against unauthorized sales," Muzzaf said. "You'll find that all bulk-stored wheat, barley, maize, flour, rice, beans, preserved meats and so forth have been placed under seal. First sale priority goes to the authorized purchasing agents of each battalion, at list prices." He pulled a paper out of his jacket and slid it across the desk. "Soldiers are free to buy additional supplies retail, of course."

"Outrageous!" Enrike said, scanning the list. "These prices are robbery!"

"Reasonable for bulk sales," Muzzaf replied. "And payable in gold or sight-drafts on Felaskez and Sons of East Residence." The latter were as good as specie anywhere on the Midworld.

"Not reasonable in the least, given the situation," Enrike said. "I hope your General Whitehall doesn't think he can repeal the laws of supply and demand."

He gave a tight smile; the Brigade's nobles were mostly economic illiterates as well as actual ones. Enrike and his peers had done very well out of that ignorance, although it caused no end of problems when the Brigade tried to set policy.

"Oh, no," Muzzaf said amiably. "And in any case, he has in myself and others advisors who can tell him exactly how to *manipulate* supply and demand. Marvelous are the ways of the Spirit, placing to hand the tools that Its Sword has need of. Incidentally, Lady Whitehall has been appointed civic legate. Any complaints will be addressed to her."

Enrike's face fell. Muzzaf went on: "You'll note that after military requirements are met, each household is to be allowed to purchase a set amount once weekly. Also at list price."

"How do you expect to enforce *that*?"

"Without great difficulty," Muzzaf said. "Considering

that we *know* how much each of you has on hand."
Enrike's face fell again as Muzzaf reeled off figures. "And
what normal consumption is. Incidentally, ships will be
coming in from Lion City with additional supplies of
grain from the Colonial merchants' stocks which were
forfeited to the State . . . we wouldn't want anything like
that to happen here, would we?"

"No," Enrike whispered. The news of the massacre
of the Lion City syndics had spread widely.

He had dealt with those men regularly; much of Old
Residence's grain supplies were shipped in from the
Crown in normal years. This fall the city's grain
wholesalers had gone to huge expense to bring in more
from the southern ports, or by railway from the Padan
valley to the west. Everyone knew what the Skinner
mercenaries had done to the Colonials of Lion City,
and the unleashed common people to the wealthy.

"What the Army doesn't need, we'll hand out at the
list prices in retail lots," Muzzaf went on. "Just to
prevent baseless speculation and hoarding, you understand."

"I understand," Enrike said, between clenched
teeth.

He would make a fair profit this year — but nothing
like the killing he'd anticipated. Not even as much as
he'd have made off the shortages caused by the fall of
the Crown and Lion City.

Damn this easterner general and his minions! The
Brigade were far easier to deal with. Grovel a little and
you could steal them blind. Small chance that that
would work with Raj Whitehall. He might pass for a
simple honest soldier in East Residence, that pit of
vipers, but a simpleton from the Governor's court
could give lessons in intrigue to Carson Barracks.

As for fooling Suzette Whitehall . . . he shuddered,
and covertly made the Sign of the Horns with his left
hand against witchcraft.

❖   ❖   ❖

"*Watch* that," Colonel Grammeck Dinnalsyn said.

The officer in charge of the detail nodded nervously and stepped closer to inspect the bracing at the top of the wall. Twin timber-and-iron booms ran out on either side, with counterweighted wood-framed buckets on cables running over common block and tackle arrangements. The whole mass creaked and groaned alarmingly as the full bucket of dirt and rubble from outside the wall rose. Inside the wall ox-teams heaved at the cables, digging their hooves into the dirt as the long stock-whips cracked over their shoulders. The ton-weight of wet soil and rock groaned up to wall-level, then down to the stone as men hauled it in with hooked poles. Others sprang to the top of the load and unhooked the support cables, fastening them to the set running over the inner braces.

"Lock down the pulleys!" the officer Dinnalsyn had warned said. "Chocks. Take up the strain and *sheet her home.*"

Iron wheels squealed against their brake-drums as the bucket lurched up and out over the inner side of the wall. It went down the inner side in jerks as the men at the levers let cable pay out from the winches. When it thumped down the ox-teams heaved again, to tip it over. Hundreds of laborers jumped forward with shovels and mattocks and wheelbarrows, clearing it out and beginning to spread it as a base-layer along the inside of the stone wall. More cranes were operating up and down the length of it, and laborers by the thousands. A step-sided earth ramp was growing against the ancient ashlar blocks of the fortification. Just in from it more work-gangs demolished buildings and hammered rubble and stone into smooth pavement; still more were resurfacing and widening the radial roads further in. Masons labored all along the wall, replacing the top courses of stones and repairing the parapets.

That would enable men and guns to shift quickly

from one section of the outer walls to another, and let troops from a central reserve move swiftly. It was amazing what you could do in a few weeks, with enough hands and some organization.

The building contractor beside the officer shook his head; looking at the ant-hive of activity inside the wall, and the scarcely smaller swarm outside digging a deep moat.

"Amazing," he said, in slow Sponglish with a strong Spanjol accent. The eastern and western tongues were closely related but not really mutually comprehensible. "How you get . . . what you say, organized so quick? Your Messer Raj —"

Cold glances stopped him. The troops referred to their commander that way, but it was not a privilege widely granted.

"— *excuzo*, your General Whitehall, he must understand such thing."

Dinnalsyn shrugged. "He understands what needs to be done, and who can do it," he said.

The contractor nodded enviously. *He* spent most of his time dealing with clients who thought they knew his job better than he did because they could afford to hire him. Working for someone who didn't try to second-guess you was a luxury he coveted.

"How you get those riff-raff to *work* so hard?" he went on, looking at the laborers.

Soldiers were doing the overseeing and technical work; artillerymen, from the blue pants with the red stripes down the legs. His own skilled men were shoring and buttressing and timber-framing. The work-gangs who dug and lifted were townsmen also, but *dezpohblado* factory-hands and day-laborers, mostly.

"Bonus to the best teams, plus standard wages. We're paying a tenth silver FedCred a day," Dinnalsyn said.

The contractor's lips shaped a silent whistle. "You paying *cash*?" he said.

Dinnalsyn nodded. The wage-workers of Old Residence were not peon serfs like the peasants of the countryside, precisely — but their employers mostly paid them in script good only at stores the bosses owned. That let them set prices as they pleased, which meant the workers were usually short by next payday and had to borrow against their wages . . . also from their employers, and at interest.

"You going to get a lot of complaints about that," the contractor said with the voice of experience. Most of his business was with the same magnates.

"No," Dinnalsyn said. His smile made the contractor swallow nervously. "I don't think we'll get many complaints at all."

"What's that?" Lieutenant Hanio Pinya said.

His patrol of the 24th Valencia Foot were dog-weary with an uneventful night of walking the streets. Restless, too. They'd gotten used to thinking of themselves as real fighting men, after Sandoral and the Southern Territories and the campaign in the Crown. A month of warm barracks and good food and new uniforms had put a burnish on the horrors of the forced march down from Lion City. Messer Raj himself had complemented the infantry battalions on their soldierly endurance. Nothing had happened since except wall-duty, unless you counted drunk soldiers asking *Guardia* patrols directions to the nearest knocking-shop or bar . . . and after real soldiering, even an infantry officer got tired of being a pimp in uniform.

"Prob'ly some bitch havin' a fight with 'er old man, sir," the platoon sergeant said hopefully. Their bivouac wasn't very far away.

The screams were louder, more than one voice, and there was a hoarse deep-toned shouting beneath them. It all sounded as if it was coming from indoors, not far down the brick-paved street.

"*Come* on," Pinya snapped. "Messer Raj said we're to keep strict order here."

The patrol lumbered into a trot behind him, their hobnails clashing in the darkened street.

Dorya Minatili screamed with despair and faltered a step as she fled out the door of her home. The soldiers outside had the same uniform as the ones inside. Out of the corner of her eye she could see a long sword swing up, and a hand grabbed at her braid.

The men in the street moved past her. The hand released her hair, and she heard an odd wet *thunk* sound behind her. More soldiers pounded up the steps and through into the house. She turned, trembling. The one who'd been chasing her was lying on the steps, pinned to the stone by a long bayonet. His sword clattered down into the street, spinning. The soldier who had killed him twisted the rifle and pulled the blade out, long and red-wet in the moonlight, blood gushing from the wound and the twitching corpse's mouth and nose. All the other houses on the street were barred and shuttered, and this neighborhood wasn't quite affluent enough to afford gaslights. The girl began to tremble again as she noticed that the uniforms were not quite the same. These soldiers didn't have the chainmail neck-flaps on their helmets, and they wore armbands with a large red letter *G*. They were short dark clean-shaven men, not tall and fair like the others. An officer with a drawn sword led them; he held a bullseye lantern in the other hand.

Lieutenant Pinya shouldered the girl aside and pushed into the room. The 1st Cruisers trooper inside had been standing behind an older woman he'd bent over a table, getting ready to mount her; as the *guardia* burst in he tried to pull up his pants and go for his sword simultaneously. One man buttstroked him in the gut; another chopped his rifle stock down on the man's neck. He grunted and collapsed, while the woman scuttled away to a civilian lying groaning in a corner. Someone had been screaming rhythmically upstairs; the sound broke off in male shouts and heavy thumping.

A man came tumbling down the stairs, another 1st Cruisers trooper. Still alive and conscious, but from the way he moaned and flopped as he tried to crawl, not in very good shape.

Behind him two infantrymen carried a wounded civilian; young, with a deep cut in one leg. The men had twisted a pressure-bandage over it, but blood leaked through it already. Behind the wounded man came a girl, younger than the one who'd run out into the street. This one had a thrall collar on her neck and was buck-naked; in her mid-teens and not bad looking, probably the housemaid. More soldiers prodded another Cruiser ahead of them with their bayonets, and a corporal brought up the rear with a sack and a big ceramic jug, the type the local white lightning came in.

"Oh, *shit*," the lieutenant said.

Garrison duty back in the Southern Territories hadn't been *that* bad. A little boring, maybe. Now he'd be up all night explaining things to everyone, right up to Major Felaskez or even higher. Sober, the 1st Cruisers were pretty good soldiers and disciplined enough you could forget they were Squadrones barbarians. Three weeks on *Guardia* duty had taught him that with a few drinks under their belts they tended to revert to type; also that when drunk they couldn't tell a sow from their sisters, and either would do as well.

The corporal waved the bottle and sack, which clinked like silverware. "Guess these fuckin' barbs figured they'd get drunk and laid and get paid for it too, El-T," he said cheerfully. A chance to beat up on cavalrymen was a rare treat in a footsoldier's life. "Nobody else upstairs. Looks like they were just gettin' started, but this might not be the first house."

A voice called from the rear of the house. "Door to the alley's broke in, sir."

"Toryez, go get the medic, fast," the officer said. "Sergeant, patch the civilians. *Get* these shits trussed."

Soldiers pulled lengths of cord out of their belts and tied the prisoners' hands before them, then immobilized them by shoving the scabbards of their swords through the crooks of their elbows behind their backs. One of the prisoners began mumbling in Namerique at increasing volume, but the sergeant silenced him with a swift kick between the legs.

"Outside," Pinya said, jerking a thumb. "Roust out the neighbors, show 'em the dead barb and the prisoners so they'll sound the alarm next time."

Proclamations were one thing, but example was the best way of demonstrating that the Civil Government commanders really were ready to defend the locals against their own men.

He turned to the civilians. Both the men looked as if they would live, although it was touch-and-go for the younger man if the medic didn't arrive soon. The middle-aged woman looked dazed, and the housemaid suddenly conscious of her nakedness; she snatched up a towel and tried to make it do far too much.

"*Hablai usti Sponglishi?*" Pinya said. Blank looks rewarded him. Then the girl stuck her head around the open front door and spoke:

"I do," she said. "A little."

Her accent was heavy, but the words were understandable. "What will happen to those men?" she asked.

"Crucifixion," Pinya said bluntly. "We'll need your statements. And I want you to translate for me to your neighbors."

The girl looked at him with glowing eyes. He straightened and sheathed the sword. "Names?" he began.

✧   ✧   ✧

"*Heneralissimo Supremo*, we yielded our great city to save it, not to see it destroyed!" the head of the Governor's Council said.

He was standing. All the petitioners were, except for the Priest Paratier, who'd been given a chair at the foot of the table. Raj sat at its head, watching them over steepled fingers with his elbows propped on the arms of his armchair. Motionless troopers of the 5th Descott lined two walls of the long chamber; the fireplace on the inner wall was burning low, hissing less loudly than the mingled rain and sleet on the outer windows. Suzette sat at his right, with clerks taking down the conversation.

"You yielded," Raj said softly, "because you knew what happened to the last city that tried to resist the army of the Sovereign Mighty Lord Barholm. The army also of the Spirit of Man."

A cleric leaned forward; he was red-faced with anger, but throttled his voice back when Paratier laid a restraining finger on his sleeve.

"*Heneralissimo*, you implied that you would be moving on to fight the Brigade, not staying here and making us the focus of their counter-attack."

Raj smiled, a cold feral expression. "No, Reverend Arch-Sysup, your own wishes were father to that thought. I said nothing of the kind."

"Peace, my son," Paratier said. His voice had faded with age, but he adjusted his style to suit rather than trying to force it. The whisper was more compelling than a shout. "Yet would not the Spirit of Man grieve if the priceless treasures within these walls, the relics and records of ancient times, were destroyed by the fury of the heretic and the barbarian?"

Raj inclined his head. "Precisely why I don't intend to allow the barbarians within the walls, Your Holiness," he said briskly. "As you may have noticed, we've been making energetic preparations to receive them."

"Throwing the city into chaos, you mean, *Heneral-issimo* Whitehall," a civilian magnate said. "Overthrowing good order and discipline and encouraging all sorts of riot and tumult."

The cost of his rings and the diamond stickpin in his cravat would have kept a company of cavalry for a month, and the jewelled buckles of his shoes were the purchase-price of remounting them.

Raj smiled openly. "Messer Fedherikos, I think you'll admit that my troops are quite disciplined. So I presume you mean we've been employing the common people of the city on necessary works of defense, and worse still paying them in cash and on time. They've shown great zeal in the cause of the Civil Government of Holy Federation."

His eyes raked the petitioners. Few of them met his gaze; Paratier's eyes did; they were as calm and innocent as a child's — or a carnosauroid's.

"Do you gentlemen suppose your own commons might react to attempted treachery the way those of Lion City did after their community returned to the Civil Government?"

The naked threat clanged to the ground between them like a roundshot.

Raj's voice continued like a metronome. "Of course, there's no possibility of treachery here. We're all loyal sons of Holy Federation Church." Well, one of the Sysups was a *daughter* of Holy Church, but no matter. "And since nobody is considering treachery, I'm showing my trust for the citizens of Old Residence by declaring a general mobilization of the populace. For labor service, or for the militia which I'm forming — to include all private armed forces in the city."

There was a shocked intake of breath. That would leave the Church and the magnates helpless . . . helpless, among other things, against a popular uprising unless Raj's troops guarded them. Also helpless to deliver the city to Ingreid the way they'd delivered it to Raj.

these persons will follow instructions until situation changes drastically, Center said. Outlines glowed around most of the petitioners — most importantly, around Paratier. Red highlights marked others. **these individuals will resist necessary measures, probability 94% +/-3.**

Which of them are truly loyal? Raj enquired.

probability of any of indicated subjects remaining loyal to the civil government unless under threat or directly coerced is too low to be meaningfully calculated.

Exactly what I expected. The only difference is that some have enough guts to be actively treasonous and some don't.

you learn quickly, raj whitehall.

No, I've lived in East Residence, he thought sourly.

Raj noted those marked as most dangerous; best detain those immediately. One or two flinched as his eye stopped at their faces.

"My son, my son," Paratier intoned. "I shall pray for you. Avoid the sin of rashly assuming that your program is debugged. The Spirit has given you great power; do not in your pride refuse to copy to your system the wisdom others have been granted by long experience."

Raj stood, leaning forward on his palms. "Your holiness, messers. I am the Sword of the Spirit of Man. The Spirit has chosen me for Its military business, not as a priest. In spiritual matters, I will of course be advised by His Holiness. In military affairs, I expect you *all* to do the will of the Spirit — Who speaks through me.

"And now," he went on, "if you'll excuse me. General Ingreid is heading this way with the whole home-levy of the Brigade, and I'm preparing for his reception."

CHAPTER SIX

The countryside outside Old Residence had a ghostly look. Colors were the gray-brown of deep winter, leafless trees and bare vines. Nothing moved but an occasional bird, or a scuttling rabbit-sized sauroid. Raj had ordered every scrap of food and every animal within two days' hard riding brought in to Old Residence or destroyed, and every house and possible shelter torn down or burned. The broken snags of a village showed at the crossroads ahead, tumbled brick and charred timbers, looking even more forlorn than usual under the slash of the rain. The two battalions rode through silently, the hoods of their raw-wool cloaks over their heads. Bridles jingled occasionally as dogs shook their heads in a spray of cold water.

Raj reined in to one side with the two battalion-commanders. The two hundred Skinners with him were jauntily unconcerned with the weather; compared to their native steppes, this was balmy spring. Many of them were bare-chested, not even bothering with their quilt-lined winter jackets of waterproof sauroid hide. The regulars looked stolidly indifferent to the discomfort. Anxious for action, if anything; men who don't like to fight rarely take up the profession of arms, and these troopers hadn't lost a battle in a long time. He had Poplanich's Own with him, and two batteries — eight guns. The other unit was the 2nd Cruisers. No artillery accompanied them, but each man had a train of three remounts, and the dogs carried pack-saddles with loads of ammunition and spare gear. The mounts were sleek and glossy-coated.

Fed up to top condition with the offal from Old Residence's slaughterhouses, where the meat from the confiscated livestock was being salted and smoked.

The trumpet sounded and Poplanich's Own swung to a halt. The Skinners straggled to a stop, more or less, which was something of a concession with them. The 2nd Cruisers peeled off to the north, taking a road that straggled off into the hills.

Spirit, but I hate war, Raj thought, looking at the ruined village. It would be a generation or more before this area recovered. If somebody cut down the olive trees and vineyards for firewood, which they probably would, that would be three generations of patient labor gone in an afternoon. Rain dripped from the edge of his cloak's hood. He pushed the wool back, and the drops beat on his helmet like the tears of gods.

Ehwardo was looking after the Cruisers. *"Thought* you had something in mind," he said mildly. "Even if you didn't say."

Raj nodded. "Even the Brigaderos won't neglect to have Old Residence full of spies," he said. "No point in making things easy for them."

"Tear up the railroad before they get here?" Ehwardo asked.

"By no means," Raj chuckled. "Ludwig's men will lie low and scout while the Brigade completes their initial movements. Railroads," he went on, "are wonderful things, no mater how the provincial autonomists squeal about 'em. The whole Civil Government should go down on its knees and thank the Spirit that His Supremacy Governor Barholm has pushed the Central Rail through all the way to the Drangosh frontier — the fact that the Colony has river-transport there has been a ball and chain around our ankles in every war we've ever fought with them."

Ehwardo raised his brows.

Raj went on: "You can do arithmetic, Ehwardo. One hundred thousand Brigaderos. Fifty thousand camp followers, at the least; a lot of them will be bringing their families along. Say, one and a quarter kilos of bread and half a kilo of meat or cheese or beans a day per man, not to mention cooking oil, fuel . . . and preserved vegetables or fruit, if you want to avoid scurvy. Plus feeding nearly a hundred thousand dogs, each of them eating the same type of food as the men but five to ten times as much. Plus twenty or thirty thousand oxen for the wagon trains from railhead to camp, all needing fodder. That's over a thousand tons a *day*, absolute minimum."

"So we wait for them to get here and *then* cut the railway," Ehwardo said. "Still, there are countermeasures. Hmmm . . . I'd station say, twenty or thirty thousand of their cavalry along the line for patrol duty. Easier to feed them, easy to bring them up when needed, and fifty or sixty thousand men would invest the city just as well as a hundred thousand. A hundred thousand's damned unwieldy as a field army anyway."

Raj smiled unpleasantly. "Exactly what I'd do. Ingreid, however, is a Brigadero of the old school; he has to take his boots off to count past ten. And not one of his regimental commanders will want to be anywhere but at the fighting front. Furthermore, all the foundries capable of building new locomotives are in Old Residence, and so are the rolling mills capable of turning out new strap-iron to lay on the rails."

The general turned to the younger commander. Ludwig Bellamy was a barbarian himself, technically — a noble of the Squadron. He looked the part, a finger taller than Raj, yellow-haired and blue-eyed. His father had surrendered to Raj for prudence sake, and because of a grudge against the reigning Admiral of the Squadron. Ludwig had his own reasons for following Raj Whitehall, and he'd managed to turn himself into a very creditable facsimile of a civilized officer.

"Ludwig, this is an important job I'm giving you. Any *warrior* can charge and die; this need's a soldier's touch, and a damned good soldier at that. It's tricky. Some of Ingreid's subordinates are capable men, from the reports." *For which bless Abdullah,* he thought. "Teodore Welf, for example, and Carstens."

He laid a hand on Bellamy's shoulder. "So don't cut the line so badly that it's obviously hopeless. Tease them. Let a trickle get through, enough to keep Ingreid hoping but not enough to feed his army. Step it up gradually, *and don't engage the enemy.* Run like hell if you spot them anywhere near; they can't be everywhere along eight hundred kilometers of rail-line. Keep the peasants on your side and you'll know exactly where the enemy are and they'll be blind."

Ludwig Bellamy drew himself up. "You won't be disappointed in me, Messer Raj," he said proudly.

The three officers leaned towards each other in the saddle and smacked gauntleted fists in a pyramid. Ehwardo shook his head as Bellamy and his banner-man cantered off along the line of the 2nd Cruisers, still snaking away north into the gray rain.

"I don't think you'll be disappointed in him either," he murmured. "You have the ability to bring out abilities in men they didn't seem to have, Whitehall. My great-uncle called it the ruler's gift."

"Only in soldiers," Raj said. "I couldn't get civilians to follow me anywhere but to a free-wine fiesta, except by fear — and fear alone is no basis for anything constructive."

"You're doing quite well in Old Residence," Ehwardo pointed out.

"Under martial law. Which is to civil law as military music is to music. I've gotten obedience in Old Residence, with twenty thousand guns at my back, but I could no more rule it in the long term than General Ingreid could understand logistics." Raj smiled. "Believe me, I know that I'm really not suited to civil administration. I know it as if the Spirit Itself had told me."

correct.

Ehwardo grunted skeptically, but changed the subject. "And now let's get on to that damned railway bridge," he said. "I don't feel easy with nobody there but those Stalwart mercenaries."

Raj nodded. "Agreed, but there was nobody else to spare before the walls were in order," he said.

The rail bridge crossed the White River ten kilometers upstream from Old Residence, the easternmost spot not impossibly deep for bridge pilings. Without it, the Brigade armies would have to go upstream to the fords to cross to the north bank — the south bank of the river held only unwalled suburbs — which would delay them a week or two and complicate their supply situation even further. A strong fort at the bridge could be supplied by river from Old Residence, and would give the Civil Government force a potential sally port to the besiegers' rear.

They heeled their dogs forward, the heavy paws splashing in the mud.

Antin M'lewis whistled silently to himself through his teeth and sang under his breath:

> *When from house t'house yer huntin',*
> *ye must allays work in pairs —*
> *Half t'gain, but twice t'safety ye'll find —*
> *For a single man gits bottled*
> *on them twisty-wisty stairs,*
> *An' a woman comes n' cobs him from be'ind.*
> *Whin ye've turned 'em inside out,*
> *n' it seems beyond a doubt*
> *As there warn't enough to dust a flute,*
> *Befer ye sling yer hook, at t' housetops take a look,*
> *Fer 'tis unnerneath t' tiles they hide t' loot —*

The forest ahead was dripping-wet, and the leaf-mould slippery as only slimy-rotten vegetation could be. M'lewis noted proudly how difficult it was to see his men, and how well the gray cloaks blended in with the vegetation and shattered rock. He made a chittering noise with tongue and teeth — much like the cry of any of the smaller sauroids — and twenty soldiers of the Scout Troop rose and moved forward with him, flitting from trunk to trunk. They halted at his gesture, among broken rocks and wire-like native scrub. Every one of them was a relative or neighbor of his, back in Bufford Parish. Every one of them a bandit, sheep-lifter and dogstealer by hereditary vocation. Following those trades demanded high skill and steady nerves in not-very-lawful Descott County, where every *vakaro* and yeoman-tenant carried a rifle and knew how to use it.

He had no doubt of their abilities. Nor of their obedience. Antin M'lewis had risen from trooper to officer and the Messer class by hitching his star to that of Messer Raj . . . after nearly being flogged for theft at their first meeting. The Scouts — unofficially known as the Forty Thieves — had a superstitious reverence for a man that lucky. They also had a well-founded respect for his garotte and skinning knife.

Visibility was limited; rain, and ground-mist. He could see the railway track disappearing downward toward the river, switching back and forth to the southwest. On the tracks and the road beside them marched mounted men, in columns of fours. Heading toward him, which meant toward Old Residence.

"Message to Messer Raj," he said over his shoulder. "Two . . . make that four hunnert men 'n column approachin'. Will withdraw an' keep 'em unner observation."

"Couldn't tell who theuns wuz, Messer Raj," the messenger said. "Jist they'z marchin' in column, ser."

observe, Center said.

❖   ❖   ❖

The fort on the north side of the railway bridge was a simple earthwork square with a timber palisade. White water foamed just west of it, where the stone pilings of the bridge supported the heavy timberwork arches. Mist filled the surface of the water, turning and writhing with the current beneath. A column of Brigaderos cavalry had ridden onto the southern approaches; more stretched back into the rain, a huge steel-glistening gray column vanishing out of sight. The ironshod wheels of guns thundered on the railway crossties, light brass muzzle-loading fieldpieces.

The Stalwarts within the fort were boiling to the walls; asleep or drunk or huddled in their huts against the chill for far too long. They'd probably had scouts out on the south side of the river, and the scouts had equally probably simply decamped when the Brigade host thundered down on them.

A rocket soared up from the fort. The smoke-trail vanished into the low cloud; the *pop* of the explosion could be heard, but the colored light was invisible even from directly below. As if that had been a signal, hundreds of figures boiled down over the wall and to the skiffs and rowboats tied to a pier below the bridge. They wore the striped tunics of Stalwart warriors under their sheepskin jackets. Equally national were the light one-handed axes they pulled out to chop at the painters tying the light boats to the shore. Chopping at each other as well, as panicked hordes fought for places in the boats. Some of the craft floated downstream empty as would-be passengers hacked and stabbed on the dock, others upside down with men clinging to them, still others crowded nearly to sinking. Arcs of spray rose into the air as those hacked down with oars on the heads of men trying to cling to the gunwales.

Still more Stalwarts tore up the track toward Raj's vantage-point, their eyes and mouths round O's of effort. They scattered into the woods on either side of the track. There were barrels of gunpowder braced under the bridge, with trains of waxed matchcord linking them. Nobody so much as looked at them.

The viewpoint switched to the fort itself. An older man climbed down the wall facing the bridge and began to trudge toward the Brigaderos. His graying hair was shaved behind up to a line drawn between his ears; he had long drooping mustaches, a net of bronze rings sewn to the front of his tunic and cut-down shotguns in holsters along each thigh. Raj recognized him. Clo Reicht, chieftain of the Stalwart mercenaries serving with the Expeditionary force.

"*Marcy, varsh!*" he called, as he came up to the leading enemy, a lancer officer in richly-inlaid armor. *Mercy, brother-warriors,* in Namerique.

Points dropped, jabbing close past the snarling muzzles of the war-dogs. Reicht smiled broadly, his little blue eyes twinkling with friendliness and sincerity. His hands were high and open.

"I know lots about Raj-man," he said. "He tells Clo Reicht all about his plans. Worth a lot. Take me to your leader."

Shit, Raj thought, pounding a fist into the pommel of his saddle.

He'd taken one more gamble with his inadequate forces. This time it hadn't paid off.

Raj blinked back to the outer world, to the weight of wet wool across his shoulders and the smell of wet dog. Ehwardo and M'lewis were staring at him, waiting wide-eyed for the solution. *The Governor shouldn't send us to make bricks without straw,* that's *the solution,* he thought. With enough men . . .

"The Stalwarts bugged out," he said crisply.

He looked from side to side. There were laneways on either side of the low embankment of the railway, and cleared land a little way up the slopes of the hills. The ground grew more rugged ahead, but nowhere

impassible; behind him it opened out into the rolling
plain around the city itself.

"The Brigaderos vanguard is over the bridge and
coming straight at us. Courier to the city, please." A
rider took off rearward in a spatter of mud and gravel.

"Retreat?" Ehwardo asked. M'lewis was nodding in
unconscious agreement.

Raj shook his head. "Too far," he said. "If we run for
it we'll lose cohesion and they can pursue without
deploying, at top speed, and chop us up. Therefore —"

"— we attack, *mi heneral*," Ehwardo said. He took
off his helmet for a second, and the thinning hair on his
pate stuck wetly to the scalp as he scratched it. "If we
can push them back on the bridge . . ."

Raj nodded. He could turn it into a killing zone,
men crammed together with no chance to use their
weapons or deploy.

"Two companies forward, deployed by platoon
columns for movement," he said. Tight formation, but
he'd need all the firepower possible. "Three in reserve,
guns in the middle."

He stood in the saddle and shouted in Paytoiz:
"*Juluk!* You worthless clown, are you drunk or just
afraid?"

The Skinner chief slid his hound down the hillside
out of the forest and pulled up beside Raj. "Long-hairs
come," he said succinctly. "You run away, sojer-man?"

"We fight," he said. "You keep your men to the sides
and forward."

The nomad mercenary gave a huge grin and a nod
and galloped off, screeching orders of his own. Around
Raj, Poplanich's Own split its dense formation into a
looser advance by four columns of platoon strength,
spaced across the open way. A brief snarl of trumpets,
and the men drew the rifles out of the scabbards to rest
the butts on their thighs. Dogs bristled and growled in
the sudden tension, and the pace picked up to a fast
walk. What breeze there was was in their faces, so

there shouldn't be any warning to the enemy from that.

Good scouting meant the five-minute difference between being surprised and doing the surprising.

"Walk-march, *trot*."

They pushed forward, a massed thudding of paws and the rumble of the guns. Over a lip in the ground, and a clear view down through the hills to the white-gray mist along the river, with the bridge rising out of it like magic. The railroad right-of-way between was black with men and dogs, dully gleaming with lanceheads and banners. The double-lightning flash of the Brigade was already flying over the little fort as the host streamed by, together with a personal blazon — a running wardog, red on black, with a huge silver W. The house of Welf; intelligence said Teodore Welf led the enemy vanguard. The Brigadero column was thick, men bunched stirrup to stirrup across all the open space. Young Teodore was risking everything to get forces forward quickly, up out of the hills and onto the plain.

Precisely the right thing to do; unfortunately for the enemy, even a justified risk was still risky.

The trumpet sounded. The platoon columns halted and the dogs crouched. Men stepped free and double-timed forward, spreading out like the wings of a stooping hawk. Before the enemy a few hundred meters ahead had time to do more than begin to recoil and mill, the order rang out:

"Company —"

"Platoon —"

"Front rank, volley fire, *fire*."

BAM. Two hundred men in a single shot, the red muzzle-flashes spearing out into the rain like a horizontal comb.

The rear rank walked through the first. Before the echoes of the initial shout of *fwego* had died, the next rank fired — by half-platoons, eighteen men at a time, in a rapid stuttering crash.

BAM. BAM. BAM. BAM.

The field-guns came up between the units. "If they break — " Ehwardo said. The troopers advanced and fired, advanced and fired. The commanders followed them, leading their dogs.

"If," Raj replied.

The guns fired case-shot, the loads spreading to maximum effect in the confined space. Merciful smoke hid the result for an instant, and then the rain drummed it out of the air. For fifty meters back from the head of the column the Brigaderos and their dogs were a carpet of flesh that heaved and screamed. A man with no face staggered toward the Civil Government line, ululating in a wordless trill of agony. The next volley smashed him backward to rest in the tangled pink-gray intestines of a dog. The animal still whimpered and twitched.

Men have a lot of life in them, Raj thought. Men and dogs. Sometimes they just died, and sometimes they got cut in half and hung on for minutes, even hours.

The advancing force had gotten far enough downslope that the reserve platoon and the second battery of guns could fire over their heads. Shock-waves from the shells passing overhead slapped at the back of their helmets like pillows of displaced air. Most of the head of the Brigaderos column was *trying* to run away, but the railroad right-of-way was too narrow and the press behind them too massive. Men spilled upslope toward the forested hills. Just then the Skinners opened up themselves with their two-meter sauroid-killing rifles. Driving downhill on a level slope, their 15mm bullets went through three or four men at a time. A huge sound came from the locked crowd of enemy troops, half wail and half roar. Some were getting out their rifles and trying to return fire, standing or taking cover behind mounds of dead. Lead slugs went by overhead, and not two paces from him a trooper went *unh!* as if belly-punched, then to his knees and then flat.

The rest of his unit walked past, reloading. Spent brass tinkled down around the body lying on the railroad tracks, bouncing from the black iron strapping on the wooden stringers.

Raj whistled sharply, and Horace came forward and crouched. *Got to see what's going on,* he thought, straddling the saddle and levelling his binoculars as the hound rose.

Then: *damn.*

Hard to see through smoke and mist, but there was activity down by the fort. Men with banners galloping out amid a great whirring of kettledrums. The enemy column had been bulging naturally, where advancing ranks met retreating. The party from the fort was getting them into order, groups of riding dogs being led back and men in dragoon uniforms jogging left and right into the woods. A trio of shells from the second battery ploughed into the knot of Brigaderos, raising plumes of dirt and rock, rail-iron and body-parts. When those cleared the movement continued, and the Welf banner still stood. Raj focused his glasses on the fort's ramparts; Center put a square across his vision and magnified, filling in data from estimation. A man in inlaid lancer armor with a high commander's plumes. Another with a halter around his neck and two men standing behind him, the points of their broadswords hovering near his kidneys. Clo Reicht, pointing . . .

Pointing at me. A man might not be recognized at this distance by unaided eyes, but Horace could.

The press on the bridge behind the fort had halted. Two low turtle-shaped vehicles were coming over it, slowly, men and animals rippling aside to let them pass. Steam and smoke vomited from low smokestacks; the Brigade wasn't up to even the asthmatic gas engines the Colony and Civil Government used for armored cars, but steam would do at a pinch. Another curse drifted through his mind. Someone had had a rush of intelligence to the head. The cars were running on flanged wheels that fitted the tracks. Sections of broader tire were lashed to their decks. A few minutes work to bolt them onto the iron hubs, and they'd be road-capable. Now *that* was clever.

"Ehwardo!" Raj shouted.

"No joy?" the Companion said.

"No. They began to stampede, but whoever's in charge down there is starting to get them sorted out."

A lancer regiment was extracting itself from the tangle and forming up. Guns went *thump* from the fort, and a roundshot came *whirrr*-crash, bouncing up into the air again halfway between the lead spray of enemy dead and the Civil Government's line. More and more riflemen were returning fire, some of them in organized units. The Brigaderos troops were brave men, and mostly trained soldiers. They didn't *want* to panic, and they knew the real slaughter started when one side or the other bugged out. Once somebody started giving orders, they must have been relieved beyond words.

"If that's Teodore Welf, Ingreid Manfrond had better look to his Seat later," Ehwardo said.

"And we'd better look to our collective arse right now," Raj said.

He glanced at the sky, and called up memories of what the terrain was like. More bullets cracked by, and a cannonball hit a tree upslope from him and nearly abreast. The long slender trunk of the whipstick tree exploded in splinters at breast height, then sagged slowly away from the track, held up by its neighbors.

"He's got enough brains to reverse their standard tactic," Raj said. "Those dragoons will try and work around our flanks, and the lancers will charge or threaten to to keep us pinned."

"Rearguard?" Ehwardo asked.

It was obviously impossible to stay. There had been a chance of rushing the bridge if the enemy ran, but if they didn't the brutal arithmetic of combat took over. There were just too many of the other side in this broken ground. Their flanks weren't impassible to men on foot, and the ground there provided plenty of cover.

"I'll do it, with the guns and the Skinners." He held up a hand. "That's an *order*, major. Take them back at a trot, no more, and a company or so saddled up just inside the gate. We'll see what happens. M'lewis, get your dog-robbers together. Courier to Juluk —" the Skinner chieftain "— and tell him I need him now. Captain Harritch!"

The artilleryman in charge of the two batteries heeled his dog over.

"Captain Harritch, put a couple of rounds into the railbed now, if you please" — because he did *not* want those armored cars zipping up at railroad speeds on smooth track — "and then prepare to limber up. Here's what we'll do . . ."

Everyone here looked relieved to hear orders, as well. Now, if only there was someone to tell *him* what to do.

"Now!" the battery-lieutenant said.

Sergeant-Driver Rihardo Terraza — his job was riding the left-hand lead dog in the gun's team — heaved at the trail of the gun. The rest of the crew pushed likewise, or strained against the spokes of the wheels. The field-gun bounced forward over the little rise in the road.

spiritmercifulavatarssaveus, but the barbs were *close* this time. Not four hundred meters away, dragoons and lancers and a couple of their miserable muzzle-loading field-guns pounding up the road in the rain, which was getting worse. They had just time enough to check a little as the black muzzles of the guns rose over the ridge, appearing out of nowhere. There were other Brigaderos crossing the rolling fields, but they were much further back, held up by stone walls and vineyards tripping at their dogs.

The breechblocks clanged. Everyone leapt out of the path of the recoil, opening their mouths to spare their ears.

POUMF. POUMF. POUMF. POUMF.

Instantaneous-fused shells burst in front of the Brigaderos. *Juicy,* Terraza thought with vindictive satisfaction. He'd been with this battery for five years, since the El Djem campaign, when they only brought one gun of four out of the desert. He knew what cannister did to a massed target like that.

"Keep your distance, *fastardos,*" he muttered under his breath as he threw himself at the gun again.

Back into battery; he could feel his thigh-muscles quivering with the strain of repeated effort, of heaving this two-ton weight of wood and iron back again and again. The rain washed and diluted his sweat; he licked at his lips, dry-mouthed. Raw sulfur-smelling smoke made him cough. A bullet went *tunnnggg* off the gun-barrel not an arm's length from his head, flattening into a lead pancake like a miniature frisbee and bouncing wheet-wheet-wheet off into the air.

Their own barbs were opening up, Skinners who stood behind their shooting-sticks and fired with the metronome regularity of jackhammers. Something big blew up over toward the enemy, one of their caissons probably. That might be the Skinners, or the battery's own fire. No time to waste looking and Spirit bless *whatever* had done it, it gave the barbs something to worry about except trying to give Rihardo Terraza an edged-metal enema.

POUMF. POUMF. POUMF. POUMF.

"Limber up!" the lieutenant shouted.

This time the team caught the trail before the gun quite finished recoiling — risking crushed feet and hands, but it was a *lot* easier than hauling the gun by muscle force alone. Faster, too, which was the point right now. They kept the momentum going and the trail up, the muzzle of the gun pointing slightly down, and ran it right back to the limber. That was a two-wheeled cart holding the ready-stored ammunition and the hitch for the team. The steel loop at the end of the trail dropped on the lockbar at the rear of the limber with an iron *clung*.

Terraza ignored it; slapping the lockpin through the bar was somebody else's job. His little brother Halvaro's, in point of fact. It was the lieutenant's job to tell him where to go, and Captain Harritch's to decide where that was, and Messer Raj to look after everything. Rihardo's job was to get this mother where it was supposed to be. He sprinted forward to the head of the six-dog hitch and straddled the saddle of the left-hand lead. The right-hand lead — right-one — wurfled and surged to her feet at the same instant.

"Hadelande, Pochita!" he shouted to her. Pochita was a good bitch, he'd raised her from a pup and trained her to harness himself. She knew how to take direction from the lieutenant's sword as well as he did, and took off at a gallop. The team rocked into unison.

The lieutenant was pointing directions with his saber; off to the right as well as moving rearward, to knock back a flanking party of barbs that were getting too close and frisky. Off they went, a bump and thunder over the roadside ditch, and then up the rocky hillside in a panting wheeze. As soon as they'd moved out of the way the second battery opened up from a thousand meters back; the Skinners saddled up too, moving along with them. All four guns and the two spare caissons with extra ammunition. Which they would need before they saw Old Residence again.

Something hit a rock to his right with a monstrous *crack* and an undertone of metal ringing. Cast-iron roundshot from one of the barb guns, and dead lucky to be this close to a moving target. Fractions of a second later the whole team lurched, and he nearly went over the pommel of his saddle.

Pochita was down. With both her hind legs off at the hocks; the roundshot had trundled through, spinning along the ground and ignoring everything else. She whimpered and floundered; shock was blocking most of the pain, but she couldn't understand why her legs didn't work. She was a Newfoundland-Alsatian cross, a mule-dog, with big amber colored eyes. The huge soft tongue licked at him frantically as he hauled on his reins with his left hand and scrabbled for the release-catch of her harness with his right.

It gave, but he had to draw his saber and slash her free from the right-number-two dog. He clapped his heels to his mount and the team moved forward again, only to lurch to a halt once more.

"Pull up, pull up!" his brother Halvaro shouted.

Rihardo looked back over his shoulder. Pochita had tried to follow the team — she was the best dog he'd ever trained, and the most willing. Even with blood spurting from both her severed rear legs she'd tried, and fouled the limber; the last pair of dogs were almost dancing sideways in their efforts not to trample her. Pochita writhed, her body bent into a bow of agony.

"*Fuck* it!" Rihardo screamed. Rain flicked into his face, like tears. "I wouldn't pull up if it was *you* either, *mi bro*."

He hammered his heels into the ribs of left-one. The ironshod wheel of the limber rolled over Pochita's neck, and the gun-wheel over her skull. The team jerked, and something broke with a noise like crackling timber. Halvaro was standing in his position on the limber, looking back in horror, when the shell exploded. It crumped into the earth right of the moving battery, and a hand-sized fragment of the casing sledged the young gunner forward, tearing open his back to show the bulging pink surface of the lungs through the broken rib.

Halvaro landed in front of the limber's wheels, falling down between the last two dogs of the hitch.

Rihardo turned his face forward with a grunt; he ignored the second set of crackling noises as the wheels went over his brother's back and chest.

"Into battery, rapid fire!" the lieutenant said.

"Right, let's get out of here," Raj said. "They're holding back now they've lost their field guns."

He cased his binoculars; it was two hours past noon, good time for a fighting retreat begun early in the morning. The Brigaderos were scattered over a couple of thousand meters of front to the westward. The ones trying to work through the fields would be slower than Raj's guns trotting home down the road. For the first time that day he noticed the damp chill of soaked clothing; he uncorked an insulated flask and sipped lukewarm kave, sweet and slightly spiked with brandy. *Bless you, my love*, he thought: Suzette had insisted on him taking it, even though he'd planned to be back in Old Residence by noon. He offered the last of it to the artillery captain.

"*Grahzias, mi heneral*," the young man said. He finished it and wiped his eyes, peering westward. "Those brass guns of theirs aren't much," he went on.

The two batteries had limbered up, replacing a few lost dogs from the overstocked teams on the spare caissons. They rumbled into a fast trot. The Skinners lounging about rose, fired a few parting shots and mounted, all except for one who'd decided the roadway was a good spot to empty his bowels.

"True, Captain Harritch," Raj said, as the officers reined about and followed the guns. The dogs broke into a ground-eating lope. "The problem is their determination."

Poplanich's Own seemed to be still bunched around the railway gate into the city.

What can Ehwardo be thinking of? Raj thought irritably.

❖   ❖   ❖

"Open the bloody *gate*, you fools!" Ehwardo Poplanich screamed upward at the wall above him.

Rain spouted out of the gutters on the parapet above, falling down on the troops. He could feel the dogs getting restless behind them, and the men too — retreating was the harshest test of discipline.

A militiaman peered through a tiny iron-grilled opening in the gates at head height. "Go around to the north gate," he said, with an edge of hysteria in his voice. "We *heard* the fighting. We're not going to let the Brigade into our city just to save *your* asses, easterner."

Rifles bristled from the top of the gate. Captured weapons distributed to the city militia, but deadly enough for all that. The rain-gutters could pour boiling olive oil and burning naptha, as well . . . and there was no telling what a mob of terrified civilians would do. They'd put militia on watch in the daytime, when nothing was expected to happen, so that real soldiers could put their time to some use. Another calculated risk because they were shorthanded . . .

Raj pulled up. "*What* is going on here?" he barked. Horace barked literally, a deep angry belling.

Ehwardo made a single, tightly controlled gesture toward the peephole. Raj removed his helmet.

"This is General Whitehall," he said, slowly and distinctly. "Open — the — gate — immediately."

"Whitehall is *dead*," the man quavered. "We heard it from the fugitives. Dead, wiped out with both battalions, *dead*."

That with Raj, a complete cavalry battalion and eight guns waiting in the roadway. All because one or two cowards had bugged out from the retreat, and these street-bred militia had chosen to believe them. Ehwardo was swearing quietly beside him. The whole thing had cost *time*. If Poplanich's Own had been inside he could have rolled the guns and Skinners in with a fair margin of safety. Even if the gates opened right now, it would be chancy; the pursuit was coming in hell-for-leather at a gallop. Bells were ringing in there behind the city walls; the alarm had been given, but it might be fifteen minutes or more until the word got to a real officer.

"Get a runner to headquarters," Raj snapped at the peephole. No time to think about that. No time to think about what he was going to do to the men responsible for this ratfuck.

"Ehwardo, we'll have to see off the ones snapping at our heels before anything else. Deploy into line crossing the axis of the road, with center refused. Captain Harritch, both batteries in support, if you please; two guns in the center and the rest on the flanks. Juluk —"

The rain had died away to a fine drizzle. The land close to the city was mostly flat, and Raj had ordered every scrap of cover cut or demolished out to two kilometers from the walls. He was facing east, down the railway and its flanking road, paved this close to the city. Off to his left was the river, narrowing and turning north about here, with a high bluff in its bend about two kilometers away. Trumpet-calls were spreading out the men of Poplanich's Own, smooth as oil spreading on glass.

Good training, Raj thought. Only a fool wouldn't be nervous in this situation, but the motion was as calm and quick as drill. The column reversed, each dog turning in its own length. Each company slanted out into the fields like the arms of a V, with the platoons doing likewise, then pivoted out into line. Less than eight minutes later the six hundred men of Poplanich's Own were trotting back east in extended open order, a double rank nearly a kilometer long.

A clump of lancers led the Brigaderos' pursuit, about a thousand strong, cantering down the roadway on dogs winded from the uphill chase. The forest of upright lanceheads stirred like a reedbed in a breeze as the thin blue line of Civil Government troopers came toward them at a round trot. Beside Raj, Ehwardo nodded to himself.

"Wait for it," he said quietly to himself.

The distance closed, and the lancers spurred their tired dogs into a lumbering canter forward, charging in a clump.

"Now!"

The trumpet sounded five notes. Company buglers repeated it, and the dogs sank on their haunches to halt, then to the ground. The men ran forward half a dozen paces and sank likewise, front rank prone and second kneeling.

"*Fire!*"

The range was no more than two hundred meters now, close enough to see men's faces if their visors were up. Close enough to hear the bullets striking armor. The flung-forward wings of the Civil Government formation meant that every man could bring his rifle to bear. The two field guns in the center next to the commanders began firing as well, with their barrels level with the ground, firing case shot. The hundreds of lead balls sounded like all the wasps in the world, until they struck the mass of men and dogs. That was more like hailstones on tile. After the third volley the survivors turned to run, but their dogs were tired and fouled by the kicking masses of the dead and dying. Units were coming up the road behind them, dragoons and lancers mixed, rushing to be in at the kill the renewed firing indicated.

The killing went on. From behind a hillock, the Skinners rode out. Some dismounted to shoot; others swooped in, firing their giant rifles point-blank from the saddle and jumping down with knives in either hand, darting out again with choice bits of loot. The Brigaderos at the rear of the pileup began to halt and seep out sideways into the fields again. The Skinners followed, fanning out into the fields. Men ran from the menace of their fire.

"The Brigaderos really need to work on their unit articulation," Raj said coldly. "Those regiments of theirs are too big to react quickly. They get caught up in their own feet when something unexpected happens fast."

Shells went by overhead and burst over the roadway. Shrapnel sleeted down into the mass of enemy troopers caught between the windrows of dead in front of the battalion line and the clumps of riders dribbling in from the rear.

"We can . . . oh, shit," Ehwardo said.

A black beetling shape loomed up out of the rain, casting mounted men aside from either edge of its hull like the coulter of a plow. It was about eight meters long and three wide, and as tall as a tall man in the center of its rounded sheet-iron hull. Smoke and steam billowed from the stack toward the rear; the rain hissed when it struck that metal. More steam jetted from under the rear wheels, a steady *chuff-chuff-chuff*. A light cannon nosed out from the bow, through a letterbox-type slit. Small ports for rifles and pistols showed along its sides.

"*Scramento*," Raj echoed.

Someone back at the bridge had had the car manhandled across the gap they'd torn in the track, then sent it zipping up the undamaged section. A few minutes back behind the last hill to bolt the road wheels over the flanged ones, and it was ready. Now it rattled and wheezed its way forward, and Brigaderos troops followed as if pulled by the twin black lightning-bolts in the red circle on its bow slope.

Only the gun on this side of the railway embankment could bear. The crew were already working on the elevation and traverse wheels of their weapon. It bucked and slid backward; the shell kicked up a gout of dirt from the embankment beside the armored car. The vehicle slewed sideways, skidded, and came back onto the pavement, picking up speed.

"Nothing left but cannister!" the gun-sergeant screamed, as he dashed back to the caisson.

Men were switching their aim to the car. Sparks flew as bullets spanged and flashed off the surface, but even the brass-tipped hardpoints wouldn't punch through. The hatch on top clanged down, leaving the commander only the slots around it. The armored car didn't have the firepower to actually kill all that many troopers. It could break their position, and their cohesion, and that would be all she wrote. The 15mm rounds from the Skinners' sauroid rifles probably would penetrate, but they were out on the flanks . . . and they'd probably consider this his business, even if they were looking this way.

It *was* his business. "Follow me!" he shouted, and slapped his heels into Horace's flanks.

Men followed him — no time to check who — and the hound raced forward at a long gallop, belly to the earth. The iron juggernaut grew with frightening swiftness; it must be travelling at top-dog speed. His shift moved Horace aside, into the ditch. The cannon slewed around, trying to bear on him, then flashed red. Cannister whistled past his left ear, and Horace leaped as if a fly had stung him. A ball had nicked the dog's rump, and then they were inside the shot cone. Behind him a dog bleated in shock, and then he was hauling on the reins. Horace scrabbled, dropping his hindquarters almost to the ground to shed momentum, and whirled. Raj judged distance and launched himself — onto the hull of the armored car, his right hand slapping onto a U-bracket riveted to the hull. It closed like a mechanical grab, and he felt the arm nearly wrenched from its socket as his eighty kilos of mass was jerked out of the saddle and slapped flat against the upper front hull of the armored car.

Rivet-heads hammered into his chest, and the air went out of him with an agonized wheeze. His waist was at the edge of the turtleback, and his legs dangled perilously near the spinning spokes of the front wheel.

And any second the commander would stick his head out of the hatch and shoot him like a trussed sheep, or one of the bullets that were clanging off the hull would hit him.

His left arm came up and clamped onto the next U-bracket. The wool of his cloak tore as his shoulders bunched and hauled him higher. The bucking, heaving passage of the hard-sprung car over the rough roadway flung him up and down on the boilerplate surface of the hull. He scrabbled with his right foot, and got it over the edge of the upper curve of the hull and braced against a handhold. *Now* he could free a hand. The revolver stripped free of the holster with a *pop* as the restraining strap snapped across.

M'lewis was riding alongside the other side of the car — Spirit knew how — leaning far over with his rifle thrust out one-handed into the driver's slit. The sound of the shot was almost lost in the groaning, grating noise of the car's passage. He could feel it lurch under him suddenly, then he was almost flung free as it banged over the roadside ditch and into the field. The cannon slewed, trying to bear on M'lewis as hands inside hauled the body of the driver away from the controls.

That gave Raj a space. Hanging three-quarters on the forward hull, he jammed his revolver through beside the barrel of the cannon and squeezed off all five rounds as fast as his finger could pull the trigger. The minute the hammer clicked on a spent chamber he threw himself back, curling in mid-air as he would have if he'd lost the saddle while jumping a hedge.

Rocky ground pounded at him, ripping and bruising. Something whanged against his helmet hard enough to make the last series of rolls completely limp. He could still see the armored car lurching forward, out of control now as the bullets ricochetted inside its fighting chamber. The prow hit a wall of fieldstone and crumpled, the heavy vehicle bucking up at the back and crashing down again.

What followed seemed quite slow, although it must have taken no more than fifteen seconds in all. The rear third of the car blew apart, the seams of the hull tearing loose in a convulsive puff of escaping steam as the boiler ruptured. That must have sent the fuel tank's kerosine spraying forward into the fighting compartment, because flame gouted yellow through every slit and joint in it. The stored ammunition went off, and probably the last vaporized contents of the fuel tank at the same instant. The car exploded in a ball of white flame. Bits and pieces of iron plating and machinery rose and pattered down all around him.

Something cold and wet thrust into the back of his neck. Horace's nose; Raj grabbed at the stirrup and hauled himself erect, feeling his knees trembling and clutching at his midriff. Skin seemed to be missing from a fair section of his face, but none of the major bones were broken. The Brigaderos were in full retreat. Streaming back east, dog, foot and guns with the Skinners whooping in pursuit. Trumpets played; from his left a battalion of Civil Government cavalry came around the city wall at a gallop and began to deploy into line. He shook his head to clear it — a mistake — and managed to make out the banner of the 5th Descott.

"Ser."

Raj looked up; it was Antin M'lewis, still in the saddle. "Ser, yer all roight, then?"

"I'll live," Raj said, spitting out blood from a cut lip and feeling his teeth with his tongue.

None loose . . . He looked back at the road. Poplanich's Own was moving forward, all except the banner group. They were halted around something in the roadway. Raj walked that way, one arm braced around the pommel of his saddle for support. Ehwardo's dog was lying dead in the roadway, neck broken and skull crushed. Ehwardo lay not far from it. His left side from the floating ribs down was mostly gone, bone showing pinkish-white through the torn flesh, blood flowing past the pressure-bandages his men tried to apply. From the way the other leg flopped his back was broken, which was probably a mercy. The battalion chaplain was kneeling by his side, lifting the Headset from the last touch to the temples.

Raj knelt. The older man's eyes were wandering; not long, then. They passed over Raj, blinked to an instant's recognition. His lips formed a word.

"I will," Raj said loudly, leaning close.

Ehwardo had a wife and four children; including one young boy who would be alone in a world decidedly unfavorable to the Poplanich *gens*.

The eyes rolled up. Raj joined as all present kissed their amulets, then stood.

"Break off," he said harshly to the Senior Captain. "Sound recall. The gate will be open, this time."

Suzette drew up on her palfrey Harbie, beside the banner of the 5th. "Oh, damnation," she said. "He was a good man."

Raj nodded curtly. *He would have made a better Governor than Barholm*, he thought.

no. Center's mental voice fell flat as stone. **he would have been a man of peace. nor would he have had the ruthlessness necessary to break internal resistance to change.**

Don't we need peace? Raj thought. *Can't anyone but a sicklefoot in human form hold the Chair?*

peace can only come through unity. barholm clerett is an able administrator with a strong grip on power, able to cow the bureaucracy and the nobility both. and he will not rest until bellevue is unified. therefore he is the only suitable governor under present circumstances.

And I have to conquer the Earth for him, Raj thought bitterly. *Him and Chancellor Tzetzas.*

bellevue, Center corrected. **earth will come long after your time. otherwise, essentially correct.**

Both units' trumpets sang in a complex interplay. Men wrapped the body of Ehwardo Poplanich and laid him on a gun-caisson; others were collecting loose dogs and the wounded, and enemy weapons.

After a moment, Raj spoke aloud: "I'm bad luck to the Poplanich name," he said.

"It's not your fault, darling," Suzette murmured.

"Didn't say it was," he replied, in a tone like iron. "Didn't say it was."

The gates were open. Regulars lined the roadway, saluting as Raj rode in, and again for Ehwardo's body. The militia stood further back, expressions hang-dog. Troopers of Poplanich's Own spat on them as they rode by, and the townsmen looked down meekly, not even trying to dodge.

Gerrin Staenbridge was waiting just inside the gate; standing orders forbade him to be outside the walls at the same time as Raj.

"The city's on full alert," he said. Then: *"Damn,"* as he saw the commander of Poplanich's Own.

His eyes went back to the milita who'd barred the gate. "What's your orders concerning them, *mi heneral?"*

Raj shrugged. "Decimation," he said flatly.

"Not all of them?"

"Some of them may be of use later," Raj went on. "Although right now, I can't imagine what."

CHAPTER SEVEN

A color party and escort met Teodore Welf at the main north gate of Old Residence. He exchanged salutes with the officer in charge of it, a man younger than himself with a hook in place of his left hand. He was small and dark in the Eastern manner, smelling of lavender soap and clean-shaven, smooth-cheeked — almost a caricature of the sissified *grisuh*. Apart from that hook, and the cut-down shotgun worn holstered over one shoulder, and the flat cold killer's eyes. His Namerique was good but bookishly old-fashioned, with a singsong Sponglish lilt and a trace of a southron roll to the r's, as if he'd spoken it mainly with Squadron folk.

"Enchanted to make your acquaintance, lord Welf," he said. "Blindfolds from here, I'm afraid."

Teodore tore his gaze from the rebuilt ramparts above, and the tantalizing hints of earthworks beyond the gate. He could see that the moat had been dug out; the bottom was full of muddy water, and sharpened stakes. The edge of the cut looked unnaturally neat, as if shaped by a gardener, but the huge heaps of spoil that should have shown from so much digging were entirely missing. The distinctive scent of new-set cement mortar was heavy, and sparks and iron clanging came from the tops of the towers; smiths at work.

The soft cloth covered his eyes, and someone took the reins of his dog. Normal traffic sounds and town-smells came beyond, with a low murmur at the sight of the Brigade banner beside him. An occasional

shout to make way, in accented Spanjol. Once or twice
a member of the escort said something; Teodore had
trouble following it, although he spoke the eastern
tongue well. The men around him pronounced it with
a nasal twang, and many words he'd never read in any
Sponglish book. The feeling of helplessness was oddly
disorienting, like being ill. Mounted troops went by,
and the rumbling of guns passing over irregular
pavement. Minutes passed, even with the dogs at a fast
walk; Old Residence was a *big* city.

By the time the echoes changed to indicate they'd
pulled out into the main plaza, Teodore Welf was getting a little annoyed. Only the thought that he was
supposed to be annoyed kept it within bounds. Someone was drilling men on foot in the plaza, and he
recognized enough Sponglish swearwords to know
that whoever it was was not happy with them. If Raj
Whitehall was trying to make soldiers out of Old Residence militia, then probably all parties concerned
were quite desperately unhappy. The thought
restored some of his cheer as he was helped to dismount and guided up steps with a hand under his
elbow. One of the other emissaries stumbled and
swore.

Cold metal slid between the blindfold and his skin,
light as the touch of a butterfly.

"Be *quite* still, now," the lilting voice said next to his
ear.

The cloth fell away, sliced neatly through. He
blinked as light returned. The faded, shabby-at-the-
edges splendor of the Governor's Council Chamber
was familiar enough. They went through marbled
corridors with high coffered ceilings and tall slim
pillars along the sides, and into the domed council hall
itself. The rising semicircular tiers of benches were
full, with the Councilors in their best; carbide lamps in
the dome above reflected from the white stone and
pale wood. Teodore stiffened in anger to see that the

Brigade banner had been taken down from behind the podium, leaving the gold and silver Starburst once more with pride of place.

There were a few other changes. The guards at the door were in Civil Government uniform of blue swallowtail coat and maroon pants and round bowl-helmets with chainmail neckguards. The Chair of the First Citizen was occupied by a man in an officer's version of the same outfit; on a table beside him was a cushion bearing a steel mace inlaid with precious metals.

Whitehall, the Brigade noble thought. He clicked heels and inclined his head slightly; the easterner nodded. A woman sat on the consort's seat one step below him; even then, Teodore gave her a second glance that had little to do with the splendor of her East Residence court garb. *Woof*, he thought.

Then the general's gray eyes met his. Teodore Welf had fought in a thunderstorm once, with a blue nimbus playing over the lanceheads and armor of his men. The skin-prickling sensation was quite similar to this. He remembered the battle at the railroad bridge and along the road, the eerie feeling of being watched and anticipated and never knowing what was going to hit him next.

He shook it off. His General had given him a task to do.

" . . . and so, Councilors, even now the Lord of Men is willing to forgive you for allowing a foreign inter-loper to seize and man the fortifications which the 591st Provisional Brigade has held against all enemies for so long. Full amnesty, conditional on the eastern troops leaving the city within twenty-four hours. We will even allow the enemy three days' grace before pursuit, or a week if they agree to leave by sea and trouble the Western Territories no more.

"Consider well," the Brigade ambassador concluded,

"how many kilometers of wall surround this great city, and how few, how very few, the foreign troops are. Far too few to hold it against the great host of the Lord of Men, which even now makes camp outside. Take heed and take His Mightiness' mercy, before you feel his anger."

Raj smiled thinly. *Not a bad performance*, he thought. A good many of the Councilors were probably sweating hard right now. This Teodore Welf certainly looked the part, with his sternly handsome young face and long blond locks falling to the shoulderplates of his armor. He'd spoken like an educated man, too — fought like one, in the skirmishes with the vanguard of the Brigadero army. The two other officers beside him were older, scarred veterans in their forties. Their speeches had been shorter, and their Spanjol much more accented.

"Most eloquent," Raj said dryly. "However, lord Welf, *I* speak for this noble Council; as one of their member" — his family were hereditary Councilors in the Civil Government, a minor honor there — "and as duly appointed commander of the armed forces of the Civil Government of Holy Federation, under the orders of the Sole Rightful Autocrat Barholm Clerett. Against which and whom the 591st Provisional Brigade is in a state of unlawful mutiny. You are the foreigner here. General Forker was a rebellious vassal —"

In soi-disant theory the Brigade held the Western Territories as "delegates" of the Chair; a face-saving arrangement dating back to the original invasion, when General Teodore Amalson had been persuaded to move into the Western Territories after harassing East Residence for a generation. Old Residence had already been in the hands of a "garrison" of barbarian mercenaries for a long lifetime before that. Old Amalson had solved *that* problem with blunt pragmatism; he'd killed all their leaders at a banquet and massacred the rank-and-file next day.

"— and your marriage-kinsman Ingreid Manfrond is not even a vassal, being a usurper. Let me further point out that neither you Brigaderos nor any other barbarians built this city or its walls — you couldn't even keep them in repair. It has returned to its rightful rulers, and we intend to keep it. If you think you can take it away from us, you're welcome to try, with hard blows and not with words. Siegecraft is not something the Brigade has ever excelled at, and I predict you'll break your teeth on this nut before you crack it. Meanwhile you'll be camping in the mud and getting sick, while the people rise up behind you and the northern savages burn your undefended homes.

"Go back, lord Welf," Raj went on. "Use your eloquence on your compatriots. Tell them to end their rebellion now, while they have their lives and land, before they're hunted fugitives cowering in caves and woods. Because the Sovereign Mighty Lord has entrusted me with the task of reducing the Western Territories and all in them to obedience. Which I will do by whatever means are necessary."

"So, what's this Whitehall fellow like?" Ingreid Manfrond said.

Ingreid and Teodore and Carstens were alone now. Teodore put his booted feet up on the chest. The servant clucked and began unbuckling the mud-splashed greaves; another handed him a goblet of mulled Sala with spices. The commander's tent was like a small house and lavishly furnished, but it already had a frowsty smell. The young man frowned; Ingreid *was* a pig. *And he doesn't know anything about women*, he thought. *The way he treats Marie is* stupid. Dangerously stupid.

It wouldn't do to underestimate Ingreid, though. There was a boar's cunning in the little eyes.

"Whitehall?" Teodore said. As a relative by marriage to the General, he could leave out the honorifics in private. "About my height, looks to be around thirty. Dark even for an easterner, but his eyes are gray. A real fighting man, I'd say, from the way he's built and from the look of his hands and face — a saddle-and-sword man, not a hilltop commander. Doesn't waste words; told me right out that if we want the city, we can come and fight him for it. And . . . Lord of Men, you've got a real war on your hands. This is a man who warriors will follow."

Ingreid grunted thoughtfully, his hand caressing the hilt of his sword. "They say he has the demon's luck, too."

"I don't know about that, but I saw his wife — and they say she's a witch. I can believe it."

Ingreid shook his head. "We'll break him," he said, with flat conviction. "No amount of luck means a turd when you're outnumbered twenty to one." His shoulders hunched unconsciously, the stance of a man determined to butt his way head-first through a brick wall or die trying.

Carstens and the young officer exchanged a glance. *I had him outnumbered and he killed two thousand of my best men,* Teodore thought. He doubted Whitehall had lost more than a hundred or so. Of course, at that rate the Civil Government army would run out of men before the Brigade did . . . but victory bought at such a price would be indistinguishable from defeat.

"What about the Civvies?" Carstens put in. "He can't hold the city with only twenty thousand men if the natives don't cooperate with him."

"The Council?" Teodore snorted. "They won't crap without asking his permission, most of them. Scared of us, but more scared of him because he's in there with them. We might do something with the Priest, though. Whitehall's been leaning on the Civvie gentry pretty hard, they thought they'd watch the war like spectators at a bullfight and he's not having any of that."

Carstens nodded. "I've got some tame Civvie priests

hanging around," he said. "We can get messages over the wall."

Ingreid flipped a hand. "You handle it then, Howyrd," he said. "Get me an open gate, and you're *Hereditary* Grand Constable." Carstens grinned like a wolf; that would give his sons the title, if not necessarily the office.

"Land?" he said. "I'd need more of an estate, to support that title."

"Those Councilors must have a million or two acres between them. The ones who stick to Whitehall will lose their necks — and you get your pick, after the Seat."

Teodore nodded thoughtfully. "And do I have your authority to oversee the encampment?" he asked.

Both the other officers looked at him. "Sure, if you want it," Ingreid said.

It was routine work. Almost servant's work . . . "We're going to be here a while," Teodore said. "Better to get it right. I don't want us wasting men, we've already lost too many through Forker's negligence."

"Eight camps?" Ingreid Manfrond said, peering at the map the younger man unrolled. "Why eight?"

Teodore Welf cleared his throat. "Less chance of sickness if we spread the troops out, Lord of Men," he said. "Or so the priests say."

It was also what Mihwel Obregon's *Handbook for Siege Operations* said, but Teodore wasn't going to tell his monarch the idea came out of a book, and a Sponglish book at that. He hadn't taken everything in it all that seriously himself, when he read it — but since meeting the Civil Government's army, their methods looked much more credible.

Howyrd Carstens nodded, walking to the tent-flap and using his telescope on the walls of the city two kilometers distant.

"Sounds good," he said. "With twelve regiments in every camp, we'll have enough to block any Civvie thrust out of the city more than long enough for the others to pile in."

"You think they'll dare to come out?" Ingreid said, surprised.

Teodore tossed back his mulled wine and held the goblet out for more. "Let's put it this way, kinsman," he said. "When we've got Whitehall's head on a lance, I'll relax."

"Have you *seen* those handless cows at drill, *mi heneral?*" Jorg Menyez said bitterly. "What're they good for, except getting in the way of a bullet that might hit someone useful?"

Raj chuckled without looking up from the big tripod-mounted binoculars. From the top of the north-gate tower the nearest enemy encampment sprang out at him, the raw reddish-gray earth of the berm around it seeming within arm's reach.

"Others have been known to say the same thing about our infantry, Jorg," he said, stepping back. "Grammeck, tell me what you think of those works."

The artilleryman bent to the eyepiece. The tower-top was crowded; in the center was a sandbagged emplacement for the 200mm mortar, and movable recoil-ramps had been built near the front, timber slides at forty-five degree angles. Field-guns could run up them under recoil and return to battery by their own weight, saving a lot of time in action. A counter-weighted platform at the rear of the tower gave quick access to ground level.

Raj forestalled his infantry commander with a raised hand.

"I know, I know. Still, we have to work with what we've got. I'm going to call for volunteers from the militia; since they'll get full rations and pay —"

"We can afford that?" Jorg said.

"The Priest has agreed to pay a war-levy on ecclesiastical property," Raj said. "I expect about ten thousand men to step forward." They'd been drilling forty thousand or so, and employment was slow in a besieged city.

"We'll take the best five thousand of those. From that, cream off a company's worth for each of your battalions, younger men with no local ties. We'll enlist them, and you can begin full-time training. We've enough spare equipment for that many. At the least, they can stand watch while real soldiers sleep; I suspect we're going to get constant harassing attacks soon."

He grinned. "And just to make you entirely miserable, you can also provide cadre for the rest; that'll be about eight battalions of full-timers, armed with Brigade weapons. Again, they can replace regular infantry on things like *guardia* duty."

Jorg sighed and nodded. Grammeck looked up from the binoculars.

"That looks uncomfortably like one of our camps," he said. "Although they're rather slow about it — a full week, and not finished yet."

"It's straight out of Obregon's *Siege Operations*," Raj said. "Siting, spacing and outer lines — although the street layout inside isn't regular. But digging is servant's work, to Brigaderos. They've got some competent officers, but it isn't institutionalized, with them."

He squinted at the distant earthworks. The air was raw and chill, but the iron-gray clouds were holding off on rain, for once.

"I suspect they'll dig faster soon," he went on.

Junpawl the Skinner moved another half-inch, sliding on his belly through the slick mud. It was deep black, the second hour after midnight with clouds over the stars and both moons down. The Long Hair camp was mostly silent about him, and the nearest light was ten minutes walk away — only the great chiefs had enough firewood to spare for all-night blazes. He drew

the long knife strapped to his bare thigh; he'd stripped
down to his breechclout for this work, and smeared
himself all over with mud, even taking the brass ring
off his scalplock. Cold wind touched his back; good,
the dogs for this tent were upwind ten meters away . . .
and he'd held ox-dung under his armpits, a sure
disguise for man-scent.

The canvas back of the tent parted under the edge
of the knife, a softer sound than the guylines flapping
in the breeze. The Skinner stuck his head through,
flaring his nostrils, letting smell and hearing do the
work of eyes. Four men, two snoring. Fast asleep, as if
they were at home with their women — faster asleep
than any Real Man ever slept, even dead drunk. He
grinned in the darkness, eeling through the meter-long
slit, careful not to let it gape. A breeze could wake a
man, even a Long Hair. Inside, his bare feet touched
pine-boughs; that was why the enemy rustled when
they turned in their sleep.

His fingers moved, feather-light as he touched
bodies to confirm positions. The Long Hairs slept
huddled together for warmth, wrapped in many rich
wool blankets like a chief's women, pinning their own
arms. Their swords and rifles were stacked at the door
of the tent — out of reach. These were indeed men
who ate grass, like sheep. Only Skinners lived as Real
Men should, on the steppe with their families in tents
on wagons, following the herds of grazing sauroids.
Hunting and war were a Real Man's work.

Slowly, moving a fraction of an inch at a time,
Junpawl's left hand crept toward a face. Warm breath
touched his palm. Fingers and thumb clamped down
with brutal suddenness across nose and lips, pinning
them closed; the blackened knife in his right hand
drove down at an angle. It was heavy steel, just sharp
enough — not so sharp that bone would turn the edge.
It made nothing of the muscle and cartilage of the
Long Hair's neck, grating home in the spine. The body

flopped once, and blood poured up his forearms, but the massive wound bled the Long Hair out almost at once. The beardless face went flaccid under his hand; it must be a young man, barely old enough to ride with the war-host.

Junpawl waited, knife poised, ready to slash and dive out of the tent. The man next to the corpse turned over, muttered in his sleep and began to snore again. The nomad mercenary sliced off one of the dead man's ears and tucked it in the pouch at his waist; one silver piece per left ear, that was what the Big Devil Whitehall would pay. Ah, that one was a *frai hum*, a Real Man in his spirit! You could buy a lot of burn-head-water with a silver piece, many fat women, lots of chocolate or ammunition.

He stepped over the sleeping man and squatted down near the second pair, carefully wiping his hands on a corner of the blanket so the next victim wouldn't feel blood dripping on his face.

He'd kill only two of the four in the tent. *Cadaw d'nwit*, a night-gift for the Long Hairs to wake up to. His giggle was utterly soundless.

The joke was worth missing the other two silver pieces. Besides, he'd stop in one more tent tonight on his way out of camp.

Delicate as a maiden's kiss, the Skinner's hand sank toward the sleeping Brigadero's face.

CHAPTER EIGHT

"I suspect we're going to get very sick of this view before spring," Raj said. *It's only a couple of weeks since the Brigaderos arrived and I'm sick of it already.* The strategic arguments for standing on the defensive were strong. He still didn't like it.

He bent to the eyepiece of the brass-and-iron tripod-mounted binoculars. The gun-redoubt the enemy were building — slowly, since they'd gotten reluctant to move outside their walls at night — was mostly complete. Walls of wicker baskets full of earth, loopholed for the heavy siege guns. The guns themselves were rolling out of the nearest of the fortified camps, soda-bottle shaped things on four-wheeled carriages, drawn by multiple yokes of oxen.

The chanting of the morning prayer had barely died; the breaths of the command group on the tower were puffs of white, although there had been no hard frost. Bells rang from the hundreds of cathedrons and churches throughout the city. Silvery fog lay on the surface of the river behind the roof-crowned hills of Old Residence. Steam rose from the kave mugs most of the officers held.

Kaltin Gruder took a bite out of a pastry. "If one has to fight in winter," he said, "this is actually not bad. Clean sheets, hot meals, running water, women. As long as the food holds out, of course."

Muzzaf Kerpatik nodded. "Two ships came in last night under tow," he said. "Eight hundred tons of provisions, and another two hundred thousand rounds of 11mm from Lion City."

Raj glanced up at the black-uniformed naval commander. The sailor cleared his throat:

"Their batteries on the south shore aren't much, at night," he said. "The channel's fairly deep on the north side, we just steam up and they try to hit the sound of our engines. Which is difficult enough if you're *used* to dealing with sound on water."

Tonhio Lopeyz, Raj reminded himself.

"Good work, Messer Commodore Lopeyz," he said, nodding.

Provisions aren't tight yet, he thought. Plenty of beans and bullets, but he needed *men*. What he could do with another five or six thousand veteran cavalry . . .

"What sort of rate of fire do you think they can get with those siege pieces, Grammeck?" he asked.

Dinnalsyn looked up from his plotting table. "Oh, not more than one shot per half hour per gun, *mi heneral*," he said. "Their crews look like amateurs, mostly — I think they keep those guns in storage between wars. Probably only a few real gunners per tube. Still, a day or so and six guns firing those forty-kilo roundshot would bring any hundred meters of wall down, even with the earthwork backing we've put in. Curtain walls like this —" he stamped a foot "— just can't take the racking stress." Which was why they'd been replaced with low earth-backed walls sunk behind moats, in the Civil Government and Colony. The western Midworld was considerably behind the times.

There was a rattling bang from the rear of the tower. The Y-beams creaked as the platform came level with the parapet, and the crew manhandled a 75mm field gun forward onto the flagstones. A gunner waved a flag from beside it, and the platform sank as oxen on the ground below heaved at their traces and compensated for the pull of the counterweights. The timber platform bumped rhythmically against the stones of the tower's inner wall as it went down. The gun-crew trundled the weapon into position on the wooden disk that waited for it. Behind the wheels were long curving ramps; ahead of them rope-buffered blocks. The gunners slid marlinspikes through iron brackets sunk into the circular wooden disk and heaved experimentally. There was a grating sound from the "lubricating" sand beneath the planks, and the weapon pivoted, the muzzle just clearing the crenellations of the parapet.

"Will the structure take it?" Raj asked.

"I think so," Dinnalsyn said cautiously. "We've got the floors below this braced with heavy timbers." He looked at the Brigaderos. "Amateurs. Hasn't it occurred to them to check trajectories? Height *is* distance."

No, Raj thought. *But then, it wouldn't have occurred to* me *unless Center had pointed it out.*

The second gun slid into position. Dinnalsyn looked to the towers left and right of his position; the guns there were ready too.

He touched off a smoke rocket. The little firework sizzled off northward, its plume drifting through the cold morning air. Center looked out through Raj's eyes at the smoke. Glowing lines traced vectors across his vision.

"Colonel," Raj said quietly. "Bring that gun around another two degrees, and you'll make better practice, I think."

Dinnalsyn relayed the order. "We lost a great cannon-cocker when you were born to the nobility, *mi heneral,*" he said cheerfully, bending his eyes to the binoculars. Then: *"Fwego!"*

The gunner jerked his lanyard. The gun slammed backwards, rising up the tracks behind its wheels, paused for a second as mass fought momentum, then slid downward with a rush to clang against the chocks. Bitter smoke drifted with the wind into the eyes of the officers at the side of the tower. They blinked, and a spot of red fire flashed for an instant in the center of a blot of black smoke over the Brigadero redoubt. A second later one of the enemy siege cannon fired, a longer duller *booom* and cloud of smoke. Almost at the same instant there was a splintering crash from far below, and the stone of the tower trembled beneath their feet.

A brass shell casing clanged dully on timber as the crew of the field gun levered open the breech of their weapon.

None of the men on the tower commented on the enemy hit. Dinnalsyn turned to the battery commander at the plotting table. "Triangulate," he said.

The captain moved his parallel setsteels across the paper, consulted a printed table and worked his sliderule. The solution was simple, time-to-target over set ranges to a fixed location. Center could have solved the problem to the limit of the accuracy of the Civil Government guns in a fraction of a second — but that *would* start looking excessively odd. Besides, he didn't want men who needed a crutch. Come to that, neither did Center.

The captain called out elevations and bearing for each gun in the ten tasked with this mission. A heliograph signaller clicked it out in both directions, sunlight on a mirror behind a slotted cover.

"Ranging fire, in succession," Dinnalsyn said.

From east to west along the wall guns spoke, each allowing just enough time to observe the fall of shot. Raj trained his own field glasses. Oxen were bellowing and running in the open center of the Brigadero redoubt, some of them with trails of pink intestine tangling their hooves. Men staggered to the rear, or were dragged by their comrades. More were still heaving at the massive siege guns, hauling in gangs of two dozen or more at the block-and-tackle rigs that moved them into and out of position.

"Five round stonk," Dinnalsyn's voice said, cool and dispassionate. "Shrapnel, fire for effect, rapid fire. Fire."

This time the four towers erupted in smoke and flame, each gun firing as soon as its mate had run back into battery and was being loaded. The rate of fire was much higher than the guns could have achieved firing from level ground; in less than a minute forty shells burst over the enemy position, a continuous rolling flicker. Smoke drifted back from the towers, and covered the target. A rending *clap* and ball of yellow flame marked a secondary explosion as one of the siege-gun caissons went up. Four more explosions followed at half-second intervals, and the huge barrel of one of the siege guns flipped up out of the dust and smoke. When the debris cleared the Brigaderos position looked like a freshly-spaded garden mixed with a wrecker's yard.

Raj bent to the binoculars. Nothing moved in the field of vision for a few long seconds. Then dirt stirred, and a man rose to his feet. He had his hands pressed over his ears, and from the gape of his mouth he was probably screaming. Tears ran down his dirt-caked cheeks, and he blundered out over the mound of earth and into the zone between the bastion — the former bastion — and the city. Still screaming and sobbing as he lurched forward, until a rifle spoke from the wall. Raj could see the puff of dust from the front of his jacket as the bullet struck.

"Five round stonk, contact-fused HE," Dinnalsyn said. "Standard fire, fire."

The guns opened up again, the steady three rounds a minute that preserved barrels and broke armies. Most of the shells tossed up dirt already chewed by the explosion of the stacked ammunition. Several knocked aside the heavy siege guns themselves, ripping them off their iron-framed fortress mounts. Whoops and cheers rang out from the Old Residence wall as troops and militiamen jeered and laughed at every hit. The noise continued until Raj turned his head and bit out an order that sent a courier running down the interior stairs to the wall.

"Nothing to cheer in brave men being butchered by an imbecile's orders," he said.

"Better theirs than ours, *mi heneral*," Kaltin said.

Silence fell. The gunners took the opportunity to swab out the bores of their weapons, clearing the fouling before it bound tightly to the metal. A mounted man with a white pennant on his lance rode out from the central Brigaderos camp. That would be a herald asking permission to remove the dead and wounded, formal admission of defeat in this . . . he couldn't quite decide what to call it. "Battle" was completely inappropriate.

"True, Kaltin," Raj said. "However, remember that every time you fight someone, you teach them something, if they're willing to learn. *Somebody* over there will be willing to learn. Play chess long enough with good players and you get good."

Somebody over there had read Obregon's *Siege Operations*, at least. Not the supreme commander, or they wouldn't have committed this fiasco.

"Our army is already pretty good. We have to work *hard* to improve. All the enemy has to do is learn a few basics and it would double their combat power."

It would be a race between his abilities and the enemy's learning curve.

He remembered Cannae again. The perfect battle . . . but even Hannibal had needed Tarentius Varro commanding on the other side.

"Long may you live and reign, Ingreid Manfrond," Raj whispered.

Some of the other officers looked at him. He explained: "There are four types of commander. Brilliant and energetic; brilliant and lazy; stupid and lazy; and stupid and energetic. With the first three, you can do something. With the last, nothing but disaster can result. I think Ingreid Manfrond has shown us which category he belongs to. Let's just hope he's energetic enough to hang on to power."

❖   ❖   ❖

"I *told* you that would happen!" Howyrd Carstens shouted.

"Watch your mouth!" Ingreid roared back.

"I told you that would happen, *Lord of Men*," Carstens said with heavy sarcasm.

A sharp gasp came from the cot between them. Both men stepped back. Teodore Welf lay on it, a leather strap between his teeth. A priest-doctor with the front-to-back tonsure of a This Earth cleric gripped the end of a long iron splinter with tongs and pulled steadily. The metal stuck out of the young man's thigh at a neat forty-five degree angle. For a second it resisted the doctor's muscles, then came free with a gush of blood.

"Let it bleed for a second," the doctor said. The flow slowed, and he swabbed the wound with a ball of cotton dipped in alcohol, then palped the area and probed for fragments and bits of cloth. "Looks clean, and it all came out," he said. "As long as the bone doesn't mortify, you should be up and around in a while. Stay off it till then or you'll limp for years."

He passed his amulet over the puncture and then cleaned it with blessed iodine. The patient grunted again as it touched him, then stared as the bandage was strapped on.

"This will ease you."

Teodore shook his head. "No poppy. I need my wits." He glared up at the two older men, sweat pouring down his face, but he waited until the doctor was gone before speaking.

"You're both right," he said. "Carstens, we fucked up. You were right. Lord of Men, you're right — we're pressed for time."

"I suppose you've got a suggestion?" Ingreid said, stroking his beard.

The boy was a puppy, but he was brave and had his wits about him — and he was a Welf. That meant a wise General would give him respectful attention, because the Welfs still had many followers. It also meant a sensible General should allow him full rein for his bravery. An honorably dead Welf would be much less inconvenient after the war than a live, heroic one. He scowled, and his hand clenched. *Damn* the wench for miscarrying, just when he was too busy to plow her again. Her hips were good enough and she looked healthy; what had gone wrong? A son of his and hers would unite the branches and be unassailable, an obvious choice for election when he grew too old to hold power. His older sons would be ready to step in to the high offices around the Seat.

"All right," he said. "What's your idea?" He held up a hand. "No more about detaching troops to guard our rear. If I let regiments go, the whole host will start to unravel, screaming for a garrison here and a detachment there. I need them here, under my eye — too many can't understand that this war is more important than raids on the border."

"Lord of Men, the Civvies just showed us that you can throw a rock harder from a hill." Teodore jerked his chin at the map across the tent room. "Here's what I propose —"

An hour or so later, Ingreid nodded slowly. "That sounds like it will work," he said.

"It had *better* work," Howyrd Carstens said. "Unless you like the taste of dog-meat."

Now I know why our ancestors left the Base Area, Ludwig Bellamy thought. *It was that or freeze to death.* They were between Old Residence and Carson Barracks; away from the sea, the winters were harder. Frost every night now, and the rains were half-sleet. His men slept huddled next to their dogs for warmth, dreaming of the orange groves and date-palms of the Southern Territories. And the Base Area up north was even colder than this. No wonder each succeeding wave of invaders was more barbaric — their brains had had longer to freeze in the dark.

He smiled to himself, noticing he'd shaped the thought in Sponglish. When he fought with his own hands or took a woman, or prayed to the Spirit, Namerique still came first to him. For subtle wit or pondering strategy, Sponglish was more natural.

"No prisoners," he said quietly. His voice carried in the cathedron stillness of the oak forest. "No survivors."

Dogs crouched and men squatted by them, united in a tense carnivore eagerness as they heard the mournful whistle of the approaching locomotive. Open fields ran from the forest edge, black soil with cold water and a little dawn-ice in hollows; the winter wheat was a bluish sheen on the surface of it. They were north of the railroad, the embankment sweeping from southwest to northeast a kilometer away. It crossed a small stream on a single stone-piered wooden bridge, and the train and its escorting armored car had stopped there, checking carefully under the piers. He brought up the binoculars, watching the Brigade dragoons splashing through thigh-deep icy water as they poked and prodded and checked below the surface. The smell of cold and wet plowed earth and leaf-mould and dog filled his nostrils as he watched, the scent of the hunt.

They climbed back up, some to the armored car running on flanged wheels, others to the rear car of the fifteen hitched to the locomotive. Black smoke billowed from the stack; he could see the thrall shoveling coal with a will — warmth for himself, as well as power for the engine. The chuff of the vertical cylinders carried across the fields, and a long shower of sparks shot out from under the heavy timber frame as the bell-cranks drove the four coupled wheels of the engine against the strap iron surface of the rails. The locomotive lunged forward, jerked to a halt as the chain came taut, then bumped forward again as the cars slid up in turn and rammed the padded buffer bar at the rear of the coal cart. A ripple of collisions banged each of the cars together, leaving the whole mass coasting forward at less than walking pace. The process repeated itself several times before the train began to move in unison with the linking chains taut.

The armored car slid ahead more smoothly, holding down its speed to match the train it escorted. It took the better part of a kilometer for the train to reach the speed of a galloping dog. Which put it about —

Whump.

The armored car's front wheels crossed the tie he'd selected. The mine was nothing complicated; a cartridge with the bullet pulled, stuck into a five-kilo bag of black powder. A board with a nail in it rested over the bullet, and the whole affair was carefully buried under the crosstie. The car's forward motion carried it squarely over the charge before the gunpowder went off. It flipped off the track and landed upside down, the piston-rods on its underside still spinning the wheels for an instant despite the buckling of the frame. Then orange-white flame shot out of every opening in the hull; the black iron mass bucked and heaved in the center of the fire as ammunition went off in bursts and spurts.

More sparks shot out from under the locomotive's wheels as the panic-stricken driver threw the engine into full reverse. The freight cars had no brakes, however; the whole mass plowed into the rear of the locomotive, sending it plunging off the tracks even before it reached the crater. The middle cars of the train bucked into the air as the sliding weight met the suddenly immobile obstacle ahead. The rear end cracked like a whip, sending the last two cars flicking off the track and crashing to the ground with bone-shattering force.

"Charge!" Ludwig shouted.

The trumpet sounded, and the 2nd Cruisers poured out of the wood with a roar. A few of the Brigade warriors in the caboose staggered free of the wreckage in time to meet the sabers; then the troopers were jumping to the ground and hammering their way into the wrecked train. He looked east and west. The scouts blinked mirror-signals to him. All clear, no other trains in sight.

"Bacon!" a company commander shouted back to Ludwig. "Beans, cornmeal and hardtack, pig-lard."

Shots ran out as his men finished off the last of crew and escort. Ludwig frowned.

"Steel, you fools," he roared.

They needed to conserve ammunition, since the enemy stores were useless to them — although any powder they captured was all to the good. *Good lads, but they still get carried away now and then*, he thought.

The peasants they'd gathered up were edging out of the woods too, several hundred of them. Ludwig grinned to himself; they were welcome to what his men couldn't load on their spare dogs — and they'd hide it much more thoroughly than the raiders could, since they knew the countryside. A squad was down by the bridge, prying stones loose from the central pier with picks and stuffing more linen bags of gunpowder into it.

"Fire in the hole!" one shouted, as they climbed back out of the streambed.

A minute later the dogs all flinched as a pillar of black smoke and water and stone erupted from the gulley. The timber box-trestle that spanned the creek heaved up in the center and collapsed in fragments. Boards and bits of timber rained down across half the distance between the wreck and the bridge. Ludwig noticed that his sword was still out; he sheathed it as a man staggered by under a load of sides of bacon and dropped two for his dog. Loads of food were going on the pack-saddles even as the animals fed. Like most carnivores, war-dogs could gorge on meat and then fast for a considerable time without much harm. Today they'd bolt a man-weight of the rich fatty pig-flesh each.

The first of the peasants arrived, panting. They were ragged men, lumps of tattered cloth and hair, more starved-looking even than usual for peons in midwinter. The Brigade quartermasters had simplified their supply problems by taking as much as possible from areas within wagon-transport distance of the railroad, not waiting for barged loads at the Padan River end of the line.

"Thank you, lord," the peon leader said, bowing low.

His followers went straight for the tumbled cars; some of them stuffed raw cornmeal from ripped sacks into their mouths as they worked, moaning and smacking, the yellow grain staining their beards and smocks.

"The *Gubernio Civil* comes to free you from the Brigade," Ludwig said. "Consider this a beginning. And you don't have to wait for us; you can take more yourselves."

"How, lord?" the serf headman asked. Peasants were already trotting back to the woods, with sacks on their backs. "We have no weapons, no gunpowder. The masters have swords and dogs and guns."

"You don't have to blow up the tracks," Ludwig said. "Come out just before dark. Unspike the rails from the crossties, or saw them through. Wait for the trains to derail. Most of them have only a few soldiers, and few have armored cars for escort. For weapons . . . you have flails and mattocks and scythes. Good enough to kill men dazed by a wreck in the dark. Most of the real Brigade warriors are off fighting at Old Residence, anyway."

And if they got too paranoid to run trains at night, there went half the carrying capacity of the railroad.

The peon headman bowed again, shapeless wool cap clutched to his breast. "Lord, we shall do as you command," he said. The words were humble, but the feral glint in the peasant's black eyes set Ludwig's teeth on edge.

Captain Hortez came up as the peasant slouched off. "Ready to go, sir," the Descotter said. He looked admiringly at the wreck. "That was sneaky, sir, very sneaky."

"I must be learning the ways of civilization; that really sounds like a compliment," Ludwig said. "It did stand to reason the Brigaderos would eventually start checking bridges."

"What next?"

"We'll try this a few more times, then we'll start putting the mine *before* the bridge. Then when they're fixated on looking for mines near bridges, we'll put them nowhere *near* bridges. After, we'll start over with the bridges. And we can just tear up sections of track."

Rip up the iron, pile it on a huge stack of ties, and set a torch to it. Time consuming, but effective.

"And the slower they run the trains so they can check for mines —"

"— and the more carrying capacity they divert to guards —"

"— the better," Ludwig finished.

"A new sport," Hortez said. "Train wrecking." Flames began to rise from the wooden cars as troopers stove in casks of lard and spilled them over the wood. Hortez looked at the line of peons trudging back towards the forest. "The peasants are getting right into the spirit of this, too. Pretty soon they'll be doing more damage than we are. Surprising, I thought the Brigadero reprisals would be more effective."

"As Messer Raj told me, you can only condemn men to death *once*," Ludwig said. "Threats are more effective as threats. Once you've stolen their seed corn and run off their stock and burned down their houses, what else can you do?"

Hortez chuckled. The bannerman of the 2nd Cruisers came up, and Ludwig swung his hand forward. The column formed by platoons, scouts fanning out to their flanks; they rode south, down into the bed of the stream. The brigade call-up had been most complete along the line of rail, too. The local home guards were graybeards or smooth-cheeked youths. Mostly they lost the scent if you took precautions . . . possibly they *really* lost it, although the first few times groups chasing them had barreled into ambush enthusiastically enough.

"I wouldn't like to be a landowner around here for the next couple of years, though," the Descotter officer said.

Ludwig Bellamy remembered the way the serf's face had lit. *Spirit, we'll have to fight another campaign to put the peons back to work after we beat the Brigade.* No landowner liked the idea of the peasantry running loose. A pity that war could not be kept as an affair among gentlemen.

Solve the problems one at a time, he reminded himself. Victory over the Brigade was the problem; Messer Raj had assigned him part of the solution, disrupting their logistics.

Whatever it took.

CHAPTER NINE

"Now that was really quite clever," Raj said. "Not complicated, but clever."

He focused the binoculars. The riverside wall was much lower than the outer defenses, but he could see the suburbs and villas on the south shore of the White River easily enough. Most of it was shallow and silty, here where it ran east past the seaward edge of Old Residence. Once the Midworld had lapped at the city's harbor, but a millenium of silting had pushed the delta several kilometers out to sea. He could also see the ungainly-looking craft that were floating halfway across the four-kilometer breadth of the river.

Both were square boxes with sharply sloping sides. A trio of squat muzzles poked through each flank; in the center of the roof was a man-high conning tower of boiler plate on a timber backing. A flagpole bore the double lightning-flash of the Brigade.

"How did they get them into position?" Raj said. There was no sign of engines or oars.

"Kedging," Commodore Lopeyz said. He pulled at the collar of his uniform jacket. "Sent boats out at night with anchors and cables. Drop the anchors, run the cables back to the raft. Cable to the shore, too. Crew inside to haul in the cables to adjust position."

"Nothing you can do about them?" Raj said.

"Damn-all, general," the naval officer said in frustration. He shut his long brass telescope with a snap.

"They're just *rafts*," he went on. "Even with those battering pieces and a meter and a half of oakwood on the sides, they draw less water than my ships, so I can't get at them. I'd have to ram them a dozen times anyway, break them up. They're floating on log platforms, not a displacement hull. Meanwhile if I try exchanging shots, they'd smash my steamers to matchwood before I made any impression — those are forty-kilo siege guns they mount. *And* they're close enough to close the shipping channel along the north bank."

As if to counterpoint the remark, one of the rafts fired a round. The heavy iron ball carried two kilometers over the water, then skipped a dozen times. Each strike cast a plume of water into the sky, before the roundshot crumpled a fishing wharf on the north bank. The cold wind whipped Raj's cloak against his calves, and stung his freshly shaven cheeks. He closed his eyes meditatively for perhaps thirty seconds, consulting Center. Images clicked into place behind his lids.

"Grammeck," he said, squinting across the river again. "What do you suppose the roofs of those things are?"

The artilleryman scanned them carefully. "Planking and sandbags, I think," he said. "Shrapnel-proof. Why?"

"Well, I don't want to take any cannon off the walls," Raj said thoughtfully. "Here's what we'll do." He took a sketchpad from an aide and drew quickly, weighting the paper against the merlon of the wall with the edge of his cloak.

"Make a raft," Raj said. "We've got half a dozen shipyards, that oughtn't to be any problem. Protect it with railroad strap-iron from one of the foundries here, say fifty millimeters on a backing of two hundred millimeters of oak beam. No loopholes for cannon. Put one of the mortars in the center instead, with a circular lid in segments. Iron segments, hinged. Make three or four rafts. When they're ready, we'll use the same kedging technique to get them in range of those Brigadero cheeseboxes, and see how they like 200mm mortar shells dropping down on them."

"*Ispirito de Persona*," Dinnalsyn said with boyish delight. "Spirit of Man. You know, that'll probably work?"

He looked at the sketch. "*Mi heneral*, these might be useful west of the city too — the river's deep enough for a couple of kilometers, nearly to the bridge for something this shallow-draft. If I took one of those little teakettles they use for locomotives here, and rigged some sort of covered paddle . . . "

Raj nodded. "See to it, but after we deal with the blockading rafts. Muzzaf, in the meanwhile cut the civilian ration by one-quarter, just in case."

"That will be unpopular with the better classes," the Komarite warned.

"I can live with it," Raj said.

The laborers would still be better off than in most winters; a three-quarter ration they had money to buy was considerably more than what they could generally afford in slack times. Of course, the civilian magnates would be even more pissed off with Civil Government rule than before . . . but Barholm had sent him here to conquer the Western Territories. Pacifying it would be somebody else's problem.

"Hmmm. Commodore Lopeyz, do any of your men have small-boat experience?" Two of the rams were tied up by the city docks, upstream of the enemy rafts and unable to move while they blocked the exit to the sea.

"A lot of them were fishermen before the press-gang came by," the sailor said.

"Gerrin, I want a force of picked men from the 5th for some night work. The Brigaderos don't seem to be guarding that boatyard they built the rafts in. Train discreetly with Messer Lopeyz' boatmen, and in about a week — that'll be a two-moons-down night, and probably overcast — we'll have a little raid and some incendiary work."

"General Whitehall, I love you," Gerrin said, smiling like a downdragger about to bite into a victim.

"On to the next problem," Raj said. "Now —"

"Whitehall will get us all *killed*," the landowner said. "We'll *starve*."

His Holiness Paratier nodded graciously, ignoring the man's well-filled paunch. He knew that Vihtorio Azaiglio had gotten the full yield of his estates sent in to warehouses in Old Residence. Whatever else happened, nobody in his household was actually going to go hungry. Azaiglio was stuffing candied figs from a bowl into his mouth as he spoke, at that. The room was large and dark and silent, nobody present but the magnates Paratier had summoned. That itself would be suspicious, and Lady Suzette and Whitehall's Komarite Companion had built a surprisingly effective network of informers in the last two months. They must act quickly, or not at all.

A man further down the table cleared his throat. "What matters," he said, "is that the longer we obey Whitehall, the more likely Ingreid is to cut all our throats when he takes the city. The commons have made their bed by throwing in with the easterner — but *I* don't care to lie in it with them."

"Worse still, he might *win*," a merchant said. Paratier recognized him, Fidelio Enrike.

Everyone looked at him. Azaiglio cleared his throat. "Well, umm. That doesn't seem too likely — but we'd be rid of him then too, yes. He'd go off to some other war."

"He'd go, but the Civil Government wouldn't," Enrike said. "The Brigade are bad enough, but they're stupid and they're lazy, most of them. If they go down, there'll be a swarm of monopolists and charter-companies from East Residence and Hayapalco and Komar moving in here, sucking us dry like leeches — not to mention the tax-farmers Chancellor Tzetzas runs."

Azaiglio sniffed. "Not being concerned with matters of *trade*, I wouldn't know," he said.

It had been essential to invite Azaiglio — he was the largest civilian landowner in the city — but Paratier was glad when one of his fellow noblemen spoke:

"Curse you for a *fool*, Vihtorio, Spirit open your eyes! Carson Barracks always listened to us, because we're *here*. East Residence is a month's sailing time away if the winds are favorable. Why should they pay attention to us? What happens if they decide some other frontier is more important a decade from now when they're fighting the Colony, and pull out their troops and let the Stalwarts pick our bones?"

Everyone shuddered. An Abbess leaned forward slightly, and cleared her throat.

"Seynor, you are correct. No doubt the conquest was a terrible thing, but it is long past. The Brigade *needs* us. It needs our cities —" she nodded to Enrike "— because they have no arts of their own, and would have to squat in log huts like the Stalwarts or the Guard otherwise. They need our nobility because they couldn't administer a pigsty by themselves."

"They *are* heretics," another of the nobles said thoughtfully.

"They may be converted in time," the Abbess said. "East Residence would turn all of Holy Federation Church into a department of state."

There were thoughtful nods. The civilian nobles of the Western Territories in general and the provinces around Old Residence in particular had turned having the second headquarters of the Church among them into a very good thing indeed.

"The Civil Government was a wonderful thing when it was run from here," Enrike said. "As I said, being the outlying province of an empire run from East Residence is another matter altogether. Effectively, *we* run the Western Territories under the Brigade — who provide us with military protection at a price much more reasonable than the Governors charge."

"Not to mention the way Whitehall's stirred up the commons and the petty-guilds against their betters," someone said irritably. "The Brigade always backed us against those scum."

Paratier raised a hand. Silence fell, and he spoke softly into it: "These temporal matters are not our primary concern. Love for Holy Federation Church, the will of the Spirit of Man of the Stars — these are our burden. Raj Whitehall is zealous for the true faith, yet the Handbooks caution us to be prudent. If General Ingreid takes this city by storm, he will not spare the Church."

Needless to say, he wouldn't spare anyone else either.

"However, if he were to receive the city as a gift from us — then, perhaps we might appease him with money. This war will be expensive."

The Brigade troops had to be paid and fed from the General's treasury while they were in the field. It was full right now, Forker had been a miser of memorable proportions and had fought no wars of note, but gold would be flowing out of it like blood from a heart-stabbed man. The conspirators looked at each other uneasily; there was no going back from this point.

"How?" Enrike asked bluntly. "Whitehall's got the militia under his control."

"His officers," the head of the Priest's Guard said. "But not many of them."

"The gates are often held by these battalions of paid militiamen he's raised," the Abbess said thoughtfully.

There were forty thousand of the militia, but most of them were labor-troops at best. Half of them had volunteered when Raj Whitehall called; a thousand of the best had gone into the regular infantry battalions. From the rest he had culled seven battalions of full-time volunteer troops, uniformed and organized

like Civil Government infantry but armed with captured Brigaderos weapons. The training cadre came
from his regulars, but the officers were local men.

Priest's Guard officer snorted. "Every one of the
battalion commanders he appointed is a rabid partisan
of Whitehall's," he said. "I've checked, sounded a few
of them out very cautiously."

Paratier nodded. "Many men of sound judgment,
devoted to Holy Church, were considered for those
positions," he said thoughtfully. "Yet every one ready to
take Our counsel was rejected."

The officer nodded. "It's unnatural. You can't *lie* to
him, to Whitehall. He looks at you and, well, he can
tell." The priest-soldier touched his amulet. "There's a
shimmer in front of his eyes sometimes, have you
noticed? It's not *natural*."

The Priest coughed discretely. "Yet men change.
Moreover, not all of the officers chosen for those
battalions were hand-picked by the *heneralissimo*. He
is but one man, with much to do."

The others leaned forward.

"Fun while it lasted," Grammeck Dinnalsyn said
dismally.

Raj nodded. The first set of Brigaderos gun-rafts
had burned and exploded spectacularly when the
mortar shells dropped on them — and the steamers
had brought in cargo ships unhindered for several
weeks.

Today was a different story. It was a cold bright day,
with thin streamers of cloud high above, cold enough
to dull scent. The waterspouts and explosions across
the river were clear and bright, like miniature images
in an illustrated book. The long *booom* of heavy guns
echoed flatly, and huge flocks of wintering birds surged
up out of the reeds and swamps at the sound. The new
enemy rafts had their sloping sides built up smoothly
into peaked roofs, and the whole surface glinted with

the dull gray of iron. Hexagonal plates of it, like some marble floors, as thick as a man's arm and bolted to the heavy timber wall beneath. A mortar-shell struck one as he watched. It exploded, and the water surged away from that side of the raft in a great semicircle. When the smoke cleared and the spray and mud fell, the iron was polished brighter, but barely scarred.

A port opened in the armored side of the raft, and the black muzzle of a fortress gun poked through. The hole in the center was twice the width of a man's head. Red flame belched through the cloud of smoke. The forty-kilo shot struck the side of the Civil Government mortar-raft only a thousand meters away. White light sparked out from the impact, and a sound like a monstrous dull gong. The smaller mortar raft surged backward under the impact.

More roundshot were striking around the mortar raft, raising plumes of water or bouncing off the armor.

"The son of a whore's keeping his rafts fairly close to the shore batteries, too, in daytime," Dinnalsyn said. "Enough hits and they'll break the timber backing or spall off fragments on ours."

Raj sighed. "Recall them," he said. "This isn't getting us anywhere."

Dinnalsyn nodded jerkily, and signed to his aide. Rockets flared out over the water. After a few minutes, the mortar rafts began to back jerkily, as the crews inside winched in the cables and paid out on the ones attached to the anchors set closer to the southern shore.

"*Losien*," Dinnalsyn said: sorry. Then more thoughtfully: "Although . . . *mi heneral*, if we put a chilled-iron penetrating cap on the mortar shells, maybe a delay fuse . . . or I could . . . hmmm. I know the theory, with a little time I could set up a rifling lathe for some of the big smoothbores we found here. Fire elongated solid shot with lead skirts like the siege guns back home — we use cast steel from the Kolobassian forges, of course, but

I could strengthen the breeches of these cast-iron pieces
with bands. Heat some squared wrought-iron bars
white-hot and then wind them on —"

"Good man," Raj said, clapping him on the shoulder
in comradeship. "Delegate it, though, don't get too
focused on this one aspect. And this sort of move and
counter-move can go on indefinitely."

observe, Center said.

The real world vanished, to be replaced with the
glowing blue-white curved shield of Bellevue seen
from the holy realm of Orbit. Blossoms of eye-searing
fire bloomed against the haze of the upper atmos-
phere. They came from dots that fell downward,
dodging and jinking. Fingers of light touched them
and they died, but others survived, penetrating deeper
and deeper until some went down into the night side
of the planet below. Down to the grids of light that
marked cities, and then sun-fire billowed out in circles,
rising in domes of incandescence toward the strato-
sphere . . .

Raj shook his head. "Muzzaf," he said. "Two-thirds
rations for the populace again. Grammeck, what really
has me worried is the area southeast of the wall. Meet
me in the map room this afternoon, and we'll go over
it."

Sweet incense drifted over the pounded dirt of the
cleared zone between the inner face of the wall and
the buildings of Old Residence. A hundred meters
wide, it stretched on either side of them like a
wavering road. Much of it was as busy as a road; men
marching, or exercising their dogs, or supply wagons
hauling rations and ammunition. This section was the
24th Valencia Foot's, and they were inducting their
recruits, the ones who'd survived probationary training.

The new men stood in ranks, facing the wall and the
rest of the battalion, with the unit standard beside the

commander and Raj. The colors moved out to parade past the files, and the unit saluted them — both arms out rigidly at forty-five degrees with the palms down and parallel to the forearm, the same gesture of reverence that they would have used for a holy relic passing in a religious procession. The banner was commendably shot-riddled and many times repaired; it had *Sandoral* embroidered on it, and *Port Murchison*.

The battalion chaplain gathered up his materials, a tiny star-shaped branding iron and a sharp knife. The unit commander was Major Ferdihando Felasquez, a stocky middle-aged man with a patch over one eye, legacy of a Colonist shell. He had a riding-crop thonged to his wrist.

That was how the oath was administered. *I swear obedience unto death, though I be burned with fire, pierced with steel, lashed with the whip.* A taste of salt, the brand to the base of the thumb, a prick on one cheek with the knife, and a tap on both shoulders with the riding crop. Some officers didn't bother with it personally, but Raj had had the same scar on his thumb since he turned eighteen and took up the sword.

"Captain Hanio Pinya, isn't it?" Raj said, as the men went back to parade rest.

"Ci, mi heneral," the younger man said, stiffening slightly, obviously conscious of the newness of the Captain's two stars on his helmet.

Felasquez spoke: "I'm forming one extra company," he said. "Putting about half recruits and half veterans in it, and splitting the rest of the new men up among the others."

"How are they shaping?" Raj asked.

"Not bad, *seyor*," the newly promoted captain said. "They're all over eighteen and below twenty-five, all over the minimum height, and they can all see a man-sized cutout at five hundred meters and run a couple of klicks without keeling over. Better raw material than we generally get."

They all nodded. Infantry units usually got peons sent by their landlords in lieu of taxes, or whatever the pressgang swept up when a unit was ordered to move and had to make up its roster.

"Odd to have so many townsmen," Felasquez said. "Although some of them are peasants who got in before the enemy arrived. No clerks, shopkeepers or house servants — all farmers or manual laborers."

The three men moved down the ranks. The recruits were all looking serious now — taking the oath did that to a man — and they'd had enough drill already to remain immobile at parade rest. With Old Residence to draw on there had been no problem equipping everyone up to regulation standards, and better than the sleazy junk that garrison units often got stuck with at home. Blanket roll over the left shoulder, wrapped around with the waxed-linen sheet that was part of the squad tent. A short spade or pick-axe stuck through the leather bindings, its head just showing over the shoulder. Spare socks, pants and knitted-wool pullover inside the blanket roll. Bandolier with seventy-five rounds, and twenty-five more in a waxed cardboard box. Three days' allowance of hardtack. Rifle and bayonet; roll of bandages; gun-oil and cleaning gear; cup, bowl and spoon of enameled iron; share of the squad's cooking gear . . .

"And by the way," Raj said, when the officers returned to the standard. "We've managed to get a satisfactory reloading shop set up, so double the usual firing practice and collect all your spent brass. Work them hard."

"They'll sweat, *mi heneral*," Felasquez promised. "Although I'd prefer to get them out under canvas 'til the new men shake down. They'll pick up Sponglish faster with no distractions, too."

"Ingreid might object to maneuvers," Raj replied dryly. "Wall duty will give them some experience of being shot at, at least." The Brigaderos had been infiltrating snipers within range of the wall by night and picking off the odd man.

Felasquez cleared his throat and rested one hand on the pole of the battalion standard.

"Men," he said, in a clear carrying voice. "You are no longer probationers, but members of the 24th Valencia Foot. For two hundred and fifty years, this flag has meant men not afraid of hard work or hard fighting. May the Spirit of Man of the Stars help you be worthy of that tradition. You will now have the honor of an address by our *heneralissimo supremo*, Raj Whitehall."

A brief barking cheer echoed off the surface of the fortification wall. Raj stepped forward, his hands clasped behind his back.

"Fellow soldiers," he said; the cheer was repeated, and he waved for silence. "I've been called the Sword of the Spirit of Man. It's true the Spirit has guided me . . . but if I'm the hilt of the Spirit's sword, my troops are the blade. These veterans —" his stance stayed the same, but he directed their attention to the ranks behind him "— have marched with me from the eastern deserts to the Western Territories, and together we've broken everyone who tried to stop us. Because the Spirit was with us, and because we had training and discipline that nobody could match."

The soldiers made no sound, but Raj could almost feel the pride they radiated. *Poor bastards*, he thought. Every fifth man in the 24th had died in the trenches at Sandoral. Mostly from artillery, with no chance to strike back.

"Victory doesn't come cheap," he went on. "But none of us has been killed running away." Even the 5th's retreat from El Djem hadn't been a bugout. Tewfik's men had been glad enough to break contact. "If you can become worthy comrades of these men — and it won't be easy — then you'll have something to be proud of."

Or you'll be cripples, or bodies in a ditch, he

thought, looking at the young men. Only the knowledge that he shared the danger he sent them into made it tolerable.

"One last thing. Before you enlisted, probably only your mothers loved you." He allowed himself a slight smile.

"Now that you're wearing this —" he touched his own blue jacket "— probably not even your mothers will, any more. And that's no joke. We guard the Civil Government, but damned little gratitude we get for it. Gratitude is nice; so is plunder, when we find it — but that's not what we fight for. There's precious little faith or honor in this Fallen world; what there is, mostly wears our uniform. We fight for Holy Federation, for our oaths . . . and mostly, for each other. The men around you now are your only family, your only friends. Obey your officers, stand by your comrades, and you've nothing to fear from anyone who walks this earth."

"Put your *backs* into it," Howyrd Carstens shouted.

"You put *your* fuckin' back into it," the soldier growled back at him. "I'm a free unit brother, not a goddam peon!"

The Brigade-colonel jumped down from his dog. Sweating, muddy, stripped to the waist despite the chill, the soldier backed a pace. Carstens ignored him. Instead he walked past to the head of the cable and grabbed the thick hemp rope, hitching his shoulder into it.

"Now *pull*, you pussies," he roared.

Men, dogs and oxen strained. The siege gun began to inch forward, over the last steeper section of the hastily-built road. With a groaning shout the teams burst onto the surface of the bluffs. It was full dark, lit only by a few carefully shuttered lanterns. And by the flare of the occasional Civil Government shell, landing in the entrenchments at the eastern face of the hill.

Everyone ducked at the wicked *crack* of the 75mm round going off, but the shrapnel mostly flayed the forward surface of the hill with its earthwork embankments and merlons of wickerwork and timber.

"That's how to do a man's job, boys," Carstens said, panting and facing the others.

Most of the troops on the line had collapsed to the ground once the heavy cannon was on the level hilltop. Their bodies and breath steamed with exertion; the dogs beside them were panting, and the oxen bawled and slobbered. Men ran up to hitch new cables to the iron frame of the gun's mount and lead the animals back down the slope for the next weapon. Winches clanked, dragging the gun across the log pavement laid on the hilltop, an earthquake sound as multiple tons of iron thundered over the corrugations. The soldiers gave Carstens a tired cheer as they looped up the heavy ship's hawser they had used for haulage.

"And keep your jackets on," Carstens called after them. A chill was always a danger when you sweated hard and then stopped in cold weather. There were too many men down sick as it was.

"Yes, mother," a trooper shouted back over his shoulder — the same one who'd challenged his superior to get down in the dirt with them. The men were laughing as they trotted down the uneven surface, dodging around the wagons that followed the gun with loads of ammunition and shot.

His escort brought up his dog, and he took down the cloak strapped to the saddle and flung it around his shoulders. His heart was still beating fast. *Not as young as I was*, he thought.

The area ahead looked like a spaded garden in the dim light. Earth was flying up from it, as thousands of men worked to dig the guns into the edge of the bluff facing the city. A dozen positions faced the wall two kilometers away, each a deep narrow notch cut into the loess soil of the bluff from behind and then roofed over; other teams worked on the cliff-face itself, reinforcing it with wicker baskets of earth and thick timbers driven down vertically. Behind the guns were bunkers with beam and sandbag covers, to hold the ammunition and spare crewmen. As he watched the latest gun was aligned with its tunnellike position and a hundred men began heaving on ropes. Those were reaved through block-and-tackle at the outer lip of the position, in turn fastened to treetrunks driven deep into the soil. The monstrous soda-bottle shape of the gun was two meters high at the breech, and nearly ten meters long. It slid into position with a jerky inevitability, iron wheels squealing on rough-hewn timber.

Carstens followed it, to where Ingreid and Teodore waited under the lip of the forward embankment. Just then an enemy shell plowed into the face beyond. Dirt showered up and fell back, pattering on the thick plank roofing overhead. He bowed to the Brigade's ruler and exchanged wrist-clasps with the younger nobleman.

"Glad to see you on your feet," he said.

Teodore nodded, then waved a hand toward the city. "Our oyster," he said. "A tough one, but we've got the forks for it."

Carstens peered through his telescope. The white-limestone walls were brightly lit by Civvie searchlights, and he squinted against the glare. A globe of red fire bloomed, and a shell screeched through the air to burst a hundred meters to his left. Dirt filtered through between the planks overhead, and he sneezed.

"They're not making much practice against this redoubt," he said.

"Told you," Teodore said with pardonable smugness.

Ingreid barked laughter and thumped him on the back; the glove rang on his backplate with a dull *bong*.

"This time we're the ones pissing on 'em from above," Ingreid said. He took the telescope from his subordinate and adjusted it. "How long will it take?"

"We're at extreme range," Teodore said. "Wouldn't

work at all without —" he stamped a heel "— a hundred meters of hill under us. With a dozen guns, and overcharging the loads — four, five days to bring down a stretch of wall."

"And we've got their supplies cut off, too," Ingreid said happily. His teeth showed yellow in a grin. "Slow-motion fighting, but you two have been doing well. When the wall comes down . . . "

"Don't like to put everything in one basket," Teodore said.

The older men laughed. "We've got another bullet in that revolver," Carstens said. "They'll all be looking this way — the best time to buttfuck 'em."

CHAPTER TEN

"I'll bloody well leave, that's what I'll do," Cabot Clerett snarled, pacing the room. It was small and delicately furnished, lit by a single lamp. The silk hangings stirred slightly as he passed, wafting a scent of jasmine.

"Cabot, you can't leave in the middle of a campaign; not when your career has begun so gloriously!" Suzette said.

"Whitehall obviously won't let me out of his sight again," Cabot said. "He doesn't make mistakes twice. And all he's doing is *sitting* here. I'll go back and tell uncle the truth about him. Then I'll collect reinforcements, ten thousand extra men, and come back here and do it *right*."

"Cabot, you can't mean to leave me here?" Suzette said, her eyes large and shining.

"Only for a few months," he said, sitting beside her on the couch.

She seized his hand and pressed it to her breast. "Not even for a moment. Promise me you won't!"

"Let me out, my son," the priest said shortly.

"I'm no son of yours, you bald pimp in a skirt," the trooper growled. He was from the 1st Cruisers, a tall hulking man with a thick Namerique accent.

Savage, the priest thought. Worse than the Brigade, most of whom were at least minimally polite to the orthodox clergy.

The East Gate had a small postern exit, a narrow door in the huge main portal. A torch stood in a bracket next to it, and the flickering light caught on the rough wood and thick iron of the gate, cast shadows back from the towers on either side. A crackle of rifle-fire came from somewhere, perhaps a kilometer away. Faint shouting followed it; part of the continual cat-and-mouse game between besieger and besieged. Behind him Old Residence was mostly dark, the gasworks closed down for the duration as coal was conserved for heating and cooking. Lamps were few for the same reason, showing mellow gold against the blackness of night. The white puffs of the priest's breath reminded him to slow his breathing.

"I have a valid pass," he said, waving the document under the soldier's nose. There was a trickle of movement in and out of the city, since it was advantageous to both sides.

"Indeed you do," a voice said from behind him.

He whirled. A man stepped out of the shadow into the light of the torch; he was of medium height, broad-shouldered and deep-chested, with a swordsman's thick wrists. Much too dark for an ex-Squadrone, a hard square beak-nosed face with black hair cut in a bowl around his head. Major Tejan M'brust, the Descotter Companion who commanded the 1st Cruisers. The priest swallowed and extended the pass.

"Signed by Messa Whitehall, right enough," the officer said.

More of the 1st Cruiser troopers came out, standing around the cleric in an implacable ring. Their bearded faces were all slabs and angles in the torchlight; most still wore their hair long and knotted on the right side of their heads. He could smell the strong scent of sweat and dog and leather from them, like animals.

Another figure walked up beside M'brust and took the document. "Thank you, Tejan," she said. A small slender woman wrapped in a white wool cloak, her green eyes colder than the winter night. "Yes, I signed it. I *did* wonder why anyone would take the risk of leaving the city just to fetch a copy of the Annotations of the Avatar Sejermo. The man couldn't understand the plain sense of the Handbooks himself and he's been confusing others ever since."

The priest's hand made a darting motion toward his mouth. The troopers piled onto him, one huge callused hand clamping around his jaw and the other hand ripping the paper out of his lips. He gagged helplessly, then froze as a bayonet touched him behind one ear.

Suzette Whitehall took the damp crumpled paper and held it fastidiously between one gloved finger and thumb. "In cipher," she said. "Of course." She held it to the light. The words were gibberish, but they were spaced and sized much like real writing. "A substitution code."

The relentless green gaze settled on him. Her expression was as calm as a statue, but the Descotter officer beside her was grinning like a carnosauroid. He threw back his cloak and held up one hand, with a pair of armorer's pliers in it, and clacked them.

The priest moistened his lips. "My person is inviolate," he said. "Under canon law, a priest —"

"The city is under *martial* law," Suzette said.

"Church law takes precedence!"

"Not in the *Gubernio Civil*, Reverend Father."

"I will curse you!"

The marble mask of Suzette's face gave a slight upward curve of the lips. Tejan M'brust laughed aloud.

"Well, Reverend Father," he said, "that might alarm ordinary soldiers. I really don't think my boys will much mind, seeing as they're all This Earth heretics."

The hands holding him clamped brutally as he struggled. "And," M'brust went on, "I'm just not very pious."

"Raj Whitehall is the Sword of the Spirit," Suzette said. "He *is* a pious man . . . which is why I handle things like this for him." She turned her head to the soldiers. "Sergeant, take him into the guardhouse there. Get the fireplace going, and bring a barrel of water."

"*Ya, mez*," the man said in Namerique: *yes, lady*.

M'brust clacked his pliers once more, turning his wrist in obscene parody of a dancer with castanets. "They say priests have no balls," he said. "Shall we see?"

The priest began to scream as the soldiers pulled him into the stone-lined chamber, heels dragging over the threshold. The thick door clanked shut, muffling the shrieks.

Even when they grew very loud.

"Not much longer," Gerrin Staenbridge said.

The thick fabric of the tower shook under their feet. A section of the stone facing fell into the moat with an earthquake rumble. The rubble core behind the three-meter blocks was brick and stone and dirt, but centuries of trickling water had eaten pockets out of it. The next round gouged deep, and the whole fabric of the wall began to flex. Dust rose in choking clouds, hiding the bluffs two kilometers away. The sun was rising behind them, throwing long shadows over the cleared land ahead. The ragged emplacements along the bluffs were already in sunlight, gilded by it, and it was out of that light that the steady booming rumble of the siege guns sounded.

"Time to go," Raj agreed.

They walked to the rear of the tower and each stepped a foot into a loop of rope. The man at the beam unlocked his windlass.

"I'll play it out slow like," he said. "And watch yor step, sirs."

Gerrin smiled, teeth white in the shadow of the stone. When they had descended a little, he spoke.

"I think he was telling us what he thought of officers who stay too long in a danger zone. Insolent bastard."

The tower shook again, and small chunks of rock fell

past them. Raj grinned back. "True. On the other hand, what do you suggest as punishment?"

"Assign him to the rearguard on the tower," Gerrin said, and they both laughed.

There were dummies propped up all along the section of wall the Brigade guns were battering, but there had to be some real men to move and fire up until the last minute, before they rapelled down on a rope and ran for it. All of them were volunteers, and men who volunteered for that sort of duty weren't the sort whose blood ran cold at an officer's frown.

They reached the bottom and mounted the waiting dogs, trotting in across the cleared zone. Raj stood in his stirrups to survey the whole area inside the threatened stretch of wall. The construction gangs had been busy; for an area a kilometer long and inward in a semicircle eight hundred meters deep, every house had been knocked down. The ruins had been mined for building stone and timbers; what was left was shapeless rubble, no part of it higher than a man's waist. Lining the inner edge of the rubble was a new wall, twice the height of a man. It was not very neat — they had incorporated bits and pieces of houses into it, taking them as they stood — and it was not thick enough to be proof against any sort of artillery. It was bulletproof, and pierced with loopholes along its entire length, on two floors. The ground just in front of it was thick with a barricade of timbers. Thousands of Brigadero swordblades had been hammered into them and then honed to razor sharpness.

The falling-anvil chorus of the bombardment continued behind them. The tower lurched, and a segment of its outer surface broke free and fell, a slow-motion avalanche. Very faintly, they could hear the sound of massed cheering from the enemy assault troops waiting in the lee of the bluffs.

Raj grinned like a shark at the sound. He hated battles . . . in the abstract, and afterwards. During one he felt alive as at no other time; everything was razor-clear, all the ambiguities swept away. It was the pure pleasure of doing something you did very well, and if it said something unfavorable about him that he could only experience that purity in the middle of slaughter, so be it.

"Good morning, messers," he said to the assembled officers, once they were inside the interior wall. The room looked to have been some burgher's parlor, with a rosewood table now dusty and battered. Over his shoulder: "Get the rest of them off the wall. The enemy will be expecting that about now.

"Now," he said, tapping his hands together to firm up the gloves. The juniors were looking at him expectantly.

tell them, Center said. **as i have told you, over the years.**

Raj nodded. "We're receiving a demonstration," he said, "of two things. The advantage of numbers, and the benefits of fortification."

He looked around and settled an eye on Captain Pinya. "What's the primary advantage of superior numbers, Captain?"

The infantryman flushed. "Greater freedom to pursue multiple avenues of attack, sir," he said.

"Correct. Most of the really definitive ways to thrash an enemy in battle involve, when you come right down to it, pinning him with one part of your forces and hitting him elsewhere with another. The greater your numbers, the easier that is to do. If you have enough of an advantage, you can compel the other side to retreat or surrender without fighting at all. Those of you who were with me back in the Southern Territories will remember that the Squadron had a very large advantage in numbers — although they had a substantial disadvantage in combat effectiveness.

"In fact, they could have made us leave by refusing to fight except defensively. Keep a big force hovering some distance from us, and use the rest to cut off our foraging parties. Pretty soon we'd have had to either charge right into them, or starve, or leave. Instead they obligingly charged straight into our guns themselves.

"You have to attack to win, but the defensive is stronger tactically," Raj went on, looking down at the map.

"It's effectively a force magnifier. So is fortification, as long as you don't get too stuck to it. In a firefight, a man standing behind a wall is worth five times one running toward him; one reason why I'm known as the 'King of Spades.' You may note that here we're outnumbered by five to one . . . but the Brigade has to attack. That effectively puts us on an equal footing, and restores the tactical flexibility which the enemy's superior numbers denies us.

"That, gentlemen," he went on, tapping the map, "is the essence of my plans for this action." There was a place marked for every unit on the paper, but nobody's plan survived contact with the enemy. "We use the fortifications to magnify the effect of our blocking forces, which in turn frees up reserves for decisive action elsewhere, with local superiority. I remind you that we're still operating on a very narrow margin here. Our edge is the speed of reaction which our greater flexibility and discipline provide. I expect *intelligent* boldness from all of you."

The meeting broke up as men dispersed to their units. Staenbridge was the last to leave.

"Kick their butts, Gerrin," Raj said.

They slapped fists, wrist to wrist inside and then outside. "My pleasure, Whitehall," the other man said.

"Spirit of *Man*," rifleman Minatelli said.

From the second story firing platform he had an excellent view of the city wall going down. He had lived all his life in Old Residence, working in the

family's stonecutting shop. It was like watching part of
the universe disappear. The quivering at the top of
the wall got worse, the whole edifice buckling like a
reed fence in a high wind. Then the last sway outward
didn't stop; at first it was very slow, a long toppling
motion. Then it was *gone*, leaving only a rumbling
that went on and on until he thought it was an earthquake and the whole city would shake down around
his ears. Dust towered up toward the sun. When it
was over the wall was just a ridge of tumbled stone,
with a few snags standing up from it where the tower
had been.

A cannonball struck with a giant *crack* and fragments of stone blasted around it. The next round came
through the gap, burying itself in the rubble. Minatelli
had never felt so alone, even though there were men
on either side of him, nearly one per meter as far as he
could see. The platoon commander was a little way off,
chewing on the end of an unlit stogie and leaning on
his sheathed saber.

Minatelli swallowed convulsively. The man down on
one knee at the next loophole was a veteran of twice
his age named Gharsia. He was chewing tobacco and
spat brownly out the slit in the stone in front of him
before he turned his head to the recruit.

"Sight yor rif'le yet?" he said.

"Nnn-no," the young man said, straining to understand.

He'd spoken a little Sponglish before he volunteered; the priest in their neighborhood taught letters
and some of the classical tongue to poor children. A
month in the ranks had taught him the words of
command, the names for parts of a rifle and an
immense fund of scatology. He still found most of the
rankers difficult to understand. *Why did I enlist?* he
thought. The pay was no better than a stonecutter's.
The priest had said it was Holy Federation Church's
work, and he'd finally gotten between Melicie

Guyterz's legs the time he got to go back to the home street in uniform. The memory held small consolation. He certainly hadn't been the first one there.

"Gimme." The older man picked up Minatelli's weapon and clicked the grooved ramp forward under the rear sight, raising the notch.

"Das' seven hunnert," Gharsia said. "Aim ad ter feet. An' doan' forget to set it back when dey pass de marks."

He passed the weapon back. "An' wet der foresight," he said, licking his thumb and doing that to his own rifle.

Minatelli tried to do the same, but his mouth was too dry. He fumbled with his canteen for a second and swallowed a mouthful of cold water that tasted of canvas.

"*Gracez*," he said. *Thanks*.

The veteran spat again. "Ever' one you shoot, ain't gonna shoot me," he said. "We stop 'em, er they kill us all."

The young man braced his rifle through the slit and watched the field of rubble and the great plume of dust at the end of it. It occurred to him that if he hadn't enlisted, he'd be at home waiting with his family — completely helpless, instead of mostly so. That made him feel a little better, as he snuggled the chilly stock of his rifle against his cheek.

"Could be worse," he heard the veteran say. "Could be rainin'." The day was overcast, but dry so far. The light was gray and chill around him, making faces look as if they were already dead.

Footsteps sounded on the wood of the parapet behind him. He turned his head, and then froze. Captain Pinya, the company commander — and Major Felasquez, and Messer Raj himself.

"Carry on, son," Messer Raj said. He looked unbelievably calm as he bent to look through the slit. A companionable hand rested on the young soldier's shoulder. "You've got your rifle sights adjusted correctly, I see. Good man."

They walked on, and the tense waiting silence fell again. "Y' owe me a drink, kid," Gharsia said. Some of the other troopers chuckled.

"Up yours," Minatelli replied. It didn't seem so bad now, but he wished something would happen.

"Upyarz!"

The white pennant showed over the edge of the western gate. That was the signal. The Brigade colonel swung his sword forward, and the regiment poured after him. They were very eager; nobody had been told why they were held here, away from the attack everyone knew was coming on the other side of the city. It had to be kept secret, only the colonel and his immediate staff, and they informed by General Ingreid himself and his closest sworn men. Sullenness turned to ardor as he gave them the tale in brief words.

"We're getting a gate opened for us, boys," he said. "Straight in, chop any easterners you see, hold the gate for the rest of the host. Then the city's ours."

"Upyarz!" the men roared, and pounded into a gallop behind him. None of them had enjoyed sitting and eating half-rations or less in the muddy, stinking camps. He didn't envy the citizens of Old Residence when the unit brothers were through with them.

The road stretched out ahead of him, muddy and potholed. The dogs were out of condition, but they'd do for one hard run to the gate. Get in when the Civvie militiamen opened it, hold it and a section of the wall. The following regiments would pour through into the city and the defense would disintegrate like a glass tumbler falling on rock. They'd take Whitehall from behind over to the east, the way the wild dog took the miller's wife.

He was still grinning at the thought when his dog gave a huge yelping bark and twisted into the air in a bucking heave. The Brigade officer flew free, only a lifetime's instinct curling him in midair. He landed with shocking force, and something stabbed into his thigh with excruciating pain. It came free in his hand, a thing of four three-inch nails welded together so that a spike would be uppermost however it lay. A caltrop . . .

"Treachery!" he groaned, trying to get up.

His knee wasn't working, and he slumped back to the roadway. Behind him the regiment was piling up in howling, cursing confusion, men sawing at the reins as dogs yelped off across the fields. Some of them were running three-legged, one paw held up against their chests. Others were down, biting frantically at their paws or flanks. Dismounted men came running forward; riding boots had tough soles, and they had little to fear from the caltrops. Two of them helped him up.

The gates were less than a hundred meters away. They did not open, but two new-cut squares in them did, at about chest height from the ground. The black muzzles that poked through were only 75mm, he knew — but they looked big enough to swallow him whole. He could even see the lands, the spiral grooves curving back into the barrels. Drawing his sword he lurched forward cursing. There was just enough time to see a thousand riflemen rise to the crenelations of the wall before the cannon fired point-blank cannister into the tangled mass of men and dogs halted before them.

"Here dey come," Gharsia said.

Rifleman Minatelli squinted over the sights of his rifle. His mouth was dry again, but he needed to pee. The rubble out where the city wall had been was nearly flat, but the cannonade had lifted. The first line of Brigaderos appeared like magic as they toiled up the ramp the fallen stone made and over the stumps of the wall. His finger tightened on the trigger.

"Wait for it!" the lieutenant barked.

Poles had been planted in the rubble to give the

defenders exact ranges. Minatelli tried to remember everything he'd been told and shown, all at once. Tuck the butt firmly but not too tight into the shoulder. Let the left eye *fall* closed. Pick your target.

He selected a man. The first rank of the Brigaderos were carrying ladders, ladders tall enough to reach his position.

He'd seen the heretics riding through the streets occasionally all his life. Once a child had thrown an apple at one, in the avenue near his parent's street. The big fair man had drawn his sword and sliced it in half before the rotten fruit could strike, booming laughter as the urchin ran. The motion had been two quick to see, a blur of bright metal and a *shuck* as it parted the apple in halves.

When were they going to get the order?

A rocket hissed up into the air. *Pop.*

"Company —"

"Platoon —"

"*Fire!*"

He squeezed the trigger. *BAM.* Loud enough to hurt his ears as two thousand rifles spoke. Smoke erupted all around the semicircle of the inner wall. The rifle whacked him on the shoulder, still painful despite all the firing-range practice he'd had. His hand seemed to be acting on its own as it pushed down the lever and reached back to his bandolier. His eyes were fixed and wide, hurting already from the harsh smoke. It blew back over his head, and the Brigaderos were still coming. The next round clattered against the groove atop the bolt. He thumbed it home and tried to aim again. Another wave of Brigaderos topped the rubble, and another one behind them — they were all wearing breastplates. The muzzle of his rifle shook.

"Pick your targets," the officer said behind him.

He swallowed against a tight throat and picked out a man — bearded and tall, carrying his rifle-musket across his chest. Tiny as a doll at eight hundred meters.

"*Fire.*"

He aimed at the ground just below the little stick-figure and squeezed again. This time the recoil was a surprise. Did the man fall? Impossible to tell, when the smoke hid his vision for a second. Men *were* falling. Dozens — it must be hundreds, the enemy were packed shoulder to shoulder in the breach, running forward, and another line behind them. How many waves was that?

"Keep aiming for the ones coming over the wall," the officer said again. "The men downstairs are firing at the ones closer. Pick your targets."

"*Fire.*"

Again. "Independent fire, rapid fire, *fire.*"

He started shooting as fast as he could, muzzle hopping from target to target. A foot nudged him sharply, bringing him back to himself with a start.

"Slow down, kid," the older man said. He fired himself, levered open the action and blew into the chamber, reloaded, raised the rifle. Without looking around he went on: "Steady, er de cross-eyed ol' bitch'll jam on yu, for shore."

Minatelli copied him, blowing into the breech. The heat of the steel was palpable on his lips, shocking when the air was so cold. He reloaded and braced the forestock against the stone, firing again, and forced himself to load once more in time with the man beside him. It was steady as a metronome; lever, blow, hand back to the bandolier, round in, pick a target — fleeting glimpse through the smoke — fire. Clots of powder-smoke were drifting over the rubble. Fresh puffs came from down among the tumbled stone; some of the barbs were firing back at them. He felt a sudden huge rage at them, stronger than fear.

"Fuckers," he muttered, reaching back again.

His fingers scrabbled; the upper layer of loops was empty. *Twenty-five?* he thought, surprised. How could he have fired twenty-five rounds already? There was

an open crate of ammunition not far from him on the
parapet; when he needed to he could always grab a
handful and dump them into his bandolier loose.

"Fuckers," he said again, snarling this time. His
shoulder *hurt*. "Where are the fucking cavalry?"

He'd spoken in Spanjol, but the men on either side
laughed.

"Who ever see a dead dog-boy?" one asked.

"Dey fukkin' off, as usual," Gharsia said, spitting
out the loophole again. "Dog-boys out ready to get
dere balls shot off chargin', glory-os. I built dis wall,
gonna use it an' that suit me *fine*. Dis de easy life,
boy."

Bullets spattered against the stone near Minatelli's
face. He fought not to jerk back, leaned forward
further instead. Another wave of Brigaderos was
coming through the gap, a banner waving among them.
He aimed at it and shot as it passed a ranging-post. The
banner jerked and fell, the men around it folding up
like puppets. A lot of people must have had the same
idea. He felt just as scared, but not alone any more.

"Come *on*, you fuckers!" he shouted. This time he
pulled out three bullets and put the tips between his
lips.

"Determined buggers," Jorg Menyez said.

Another group of Brigaderos snatched up their
ladders and ran forward. A platoon along the loopholes
to either side of the commanders brought their rifles
up and fired; the volley was almost lost in the
continuous rolling crash of musketry from the wall and
of return fire from the Brigaderos outside. The group
with the ladder staggered. The ladder wavered and fell
as most of the men carrying it were punched down by
the heavy 11mm bullets from the Armory rifles. The
survivors rolled for cover, unlimbering the muskets
slung over their backs.

Raj peered through the smoke. "There must be ten

thousand of them crammed in there," he said.

Bullets from the ground-level loopholes were driving through two and three men. All over the rubble-strewn killing ground, rounds were sparking and ricochetting off the ground where they did not strike flesh. A great wailing roar was rising from the Brigaderos crowded into the D-shaped space, a compound of pain and fear and frustrated rage.

"They're not sending in another wave," Menyez said.

He looked about; the men holding this sector were his own 17th Kelden Foot. They fired with a steady, mechanical regularity. Every minute or so one would lurch backward as the huge but diffuse enemy firepower scored a lucky hit on a firing slit. Stretcher-bearers dragged off the wounded or the dead, and a man from the reserve platoon of that company would step forward to take the place of the fallen. Cartridge-cases rolled and tinkled on the stone, lying in brass snowdrifts about the boots of the fighting men.

Raj nodded slowly. He turned and caught the eye of an artillery lieutenant who stood next to a tall wooden box. An iron crank extended from one side, and copper-cored wires ran from the top into a cellar trapdoor next to it. Raj raised a clenched fist and pumped it down twice. The young gunnery officer grinned and spun the crank on the side of the box. It went slowly at first, then gathered speed with a whine. The corporal beside him waited until he stepped back panting, then threw a scissor-switch on the box's other side. Fat blue sparks leapt from it, and from the clamps on top where the cables rested.

For a moment, rifleman Minatelli thought the wall under him was going to fall as the city's ramparts had. The noise was too loud for his ravaged ears to hear; instead it thudded in his chest and diaphragm. He flung up a hand against the wave of dust and grit that billowed toward his firing slit, and coughed at the thick brickdust stink of it as it billowed over him. The explosions ran from left to right across the D-shaped space before him, earth and rock gouting skyward as the massive gunpowder charges concealed in the cellars of the wrecked houses went off one after another. The Brigaderos on top of the charges simply disappeared — although for a moment he thought his squinting eyes caught a human form silhouetted against the sky.

Silence fell for a second afterwards, ringing with the painful sound that was inside his ears. His mouth gaped open at the massive craters that gaped across the open space, and at the thousands of figures that staggered or crawled or screamed and ran away from them. Then the big barrels of pitch and naphtha and coal-oil buried all around the perimeter went off as well, the small bursting charges beneath them spraying inflammable liquid over hundreds of square meters, vomiting the color of hell. Wood scattered through the rubble of destroyed buildings caught fire. Men burned too, running with their hair and uniforms ablaze. Men were running all over the killing zone, running to the rear.

They're running away! Minatelli thought exultantly. The lords of the Brigade were running away from *him*, the stonecutter's son.

He caught up his rifle and fired, again and again. Then, grinning, he turned to the villainous old sweat who'd been telling him what to do.

The veteran lay on his back, one leg crumpled under him. The bullet that killed him had punched through his breastbone and out through his spine; the body lay in a pool of blood turning sticky at the edges, and more ran out of the older man's mouth and nose. Dry eyeballs looked up at the iron-colored sky; his helmet had fallen off, and the cropped hair beneath was thin and more gray than black.

"But we won," he whispered to himself. His mouth filled with sick spit.

A hand clouted him on the back of his helmet. "Face front, soljer," the corporal snarled.

Minatelli started, as if waking from a deep sleep. "Yessir," he mumbled. His fingers trembled as they worked the lever of his weapon.

"Happens," the corporal went on. He bent and heaved the body closer to the wall, to clear space on the parapet, and leaned the dead man's fallen rifle beside the loophole. "I towt de ol' *fassaro*'d live for'ver, but it happens."

"Yessir."

"I ain't no sir. An' watch watcha shootin', boy."

Rihardo Terraza grinned as he helped manhandle the gun forward. He could see through the firing slit ahead of them; the gun was mounted at the very edge of the new wall, where it met the intact section of the original city fortifications.

The Brigaderos were trying to fall back now, but they weren't doing it in the neat lines in which they attacked. They were all trying to get out at once — all of them who could still walk, and many of them were carrying or dragging wounded comrades with them. That meant a pile-up, as they scrambled over the jagged remains of the city wall. The ones closest were only about fifty meters away, when the muzzle of the gun showed through the letterbox hole in the inner wall. Some of them noticed it.

PAMMM. Firing case-shot. Everyone in the crew skipped out of the way as the gun caromed backward and came to a halt against rope braces.

"One for Pochita, you *fastardos*," Rihardo shouted, leaping back to the wheel.

Four other guns fired down the line; the other battery at the opposite end of the breech in the city wall opened fire at the same moment. The crowds of Brigaderos trying to get out halted as the murderous crossfire slashed into them, while the massed rifles hammered at their backs.

Best bitch I ever trained, Rihardo thought, coughing in the sulfur stink of the gunsmoke. His eyes were stinging from it too.

PAMMM.

"One for Halvaro!"

Gerrin Staenbridge gave Bartin's shoulder a squeeze. They were waiting in the saddle, riding thigh-to-thigh.

The younger man flashed him a smile. Then the massive thudding detonations of the mines came; they could see the pillars of earth and smoke, distant across the intervening rooftops. The gates creaked, the ten-meter-high portals swinging open as men cranked the winches. This was the river gate, the furthest south and west in Old Residence you could get. The bulk of the anchoring redoubt loomed on their left, and beyond it the river wall. Behind them was one of the long radial avenues of the city, stretching in a twisting curve north and east to the great central plaza. It was packed solid with men and dogs, four battalions of cavalry and twenty guns.

The gates boomed against their rests. Gerrin snapped his arm forward and down. Trumpets blared, and the 5th Descott rocked into a gallop at his heels. The gate swept by and they were out in the open, heading west along the river road. Cold wind cuffed at his face, and the sound of thousands of paws striking the gravel road was an endless thudding scuff. The ragged-looking entrenchments of the Brigade siege batteries were model-tiny ahead and to the right. And directly to the right the plain was covered with men, marching or running or riding, a huge clot of them around the gaping wound in the city's wall where the guns had knocked it down. Almost to the railway gate and that was opening too. . . .

He clamped his legs around the barrel of his dog and swung to the bounding rhythm of the gallop; his saber beat an iron counterpoint to it, clanking against the stirrup-iron. Distance . . . *now*. A touch of the rein to the neck and his dog wheeled right and came to a halt, with the bannerman by his side and a score of signallers and runners. The column behind him continued to snake its way out of the gate; the ground shook under their paws, the air sounded with the clank of their harness. Riding eight men deep, each battalion spaced at a hundred yards on either side of two batteries of guns. His head went back and forth.

Smooth, very smooth, he thought. Especially since there hadn't been time or space to drill for this in particular. They'd decided to keep each battalion stationary until the one in front was in full gallop, and that seemed to have worked. . . .

The time it took a dog to run a kilometer and a half passed.

"Now," he said.

Trumpets sang, and the great bar of men and dogs came to a halt — tail-end first, as the last battalion out of the gate stopped with their rear rank barely clear of the portals. Another demanding call, picked up and echoed by every commander's buglers. He turned in his saddle to see it; he was roughly in the middle of the long column, as it snaked and undulated over the uneven surface of the road. It moved and writhed, every man turning in place, with the commanders out in front like a regular finge before a belt. Spaces opened up, and the whole unit was in platoon columns. A third signal, and they started forward at right angles to the road, front-on to the shapeless mass of the Brigaderos force.

It looked as if the enemy had ridden most of the way to the wall, then dismounted for the assault. Now the great herd of riderless dogs was fouling any attempt to get the men who hadn't been committed to face about. More harsh brassy music sounded behind him, discordant, multiplied four times. The platoon columns shook themselves out, sliding forward and sideways to leave the men riding in a double line abreast toward the enemy. And . . . yes, the most difficult part. The men to his right, near the gate, were holding their mounts in check. To his left the outer battalions were swinging in, the whole formation slantwise to the wall with the left wing advanced as they moved north.

Too far to see what Kaltin was doing, as he deployed out of the railway gate to the north of the breach. Presumably the same thing, and that was *his* problem, his and Raj's. He could rely on them to do their parts, just as he could rely on Bartin to keep the left wing moving at precisely the speed they'd planned.

The mass of Brigaderos ahead of him was growing with shocking speed. That was the whole point, hit them before they could recover from the shock of the disaster in the breach — and before the vastly larger bulk of their forces could intervene.

He heeled his dog into a slightly faster canter, to put himself in plain view. "Bannerman, trumpeter," he said, pulling his dog up to a walking pace. "Signal *dismount and advance*."

The long line did not halt exactly in unison — that was neither possible nor necessary with a force this size, and the command lagged unevenly as it relayed down to the companies and platoons — but there wasn't more than thirty seconds difference between the first man stepping off the saddle of his crouching dog and the last. There was a complex ripple down the line as each unit took its dressing from the standard, and the battalion commanders and bannermen adjusted to their preplanned positions. Then the four battalions were walking forward in a staggered double line with rifles at port arms.

The guns stopped and turned to present their muzzles to the enemy a thousand meters away. All except the splatguns; they were out on the left wing, insurance in case the enemy reacted more quickly than anticipated. Metallic clanging and barked orders sounded. A series of *POUMF* sounds thudded down the line, sharpening to *CRACK!* behind him and to the right from the muzzle blast of the nearest guns. The first shells hammered into the enemy. The first fire came from them; he could hear the bullets going by overhead, not much menace even to a mounted man at this range. Unless you were unlucky. The cannon were settling down into a steady rhythm. Dogs milled about ahead of them, some shooting off across the rolling flatland in panic. More and more rifle-muskets thudded from the enemy, tiny puffs of dirty smoke. Here and there a man fell in the Civil Government line, silent or shouting out his pain. The ranks advanced at the same brisk walk, closing to fill in the gaps.

Eight hundred meters. "Sound *advance with volley fire by ranks*," Gerrin said quietly. Kaltin should be in place behind them, anvil to the hammer.

BAM! And nearly fifteen hundred rifles fired in unison. The front rank checked for ten seconds, aim and fire and eject and reload, and the rear rank walked through, on another ten paces, stopped in their turn. *BAM-BAM-BAM-BAM*, an endless stuttering crash. The front rank again. More men falling, but the disciplined rifle fire was stabbing into the Brigaderos like giant hay knives into a pile of fodder. He was closer to the breach in the wall now, close enough to see that it was still jammed with men trying to retreat. The ones outside were trying too, running across from his right to left, but there was nowhere to go. The two sallying forces had met at the westernmost junction, facing about to put the trapped force in a box.

"At the double!"

❖   ❖   ❖

The inside of the mortar-raft was hot, thick with the choking scent of overheated metal and burning coal. The little locomotive engine wheezed and puffed at the rear of the enclosure, shoving the heavy box of iron forward. The chain drive-belt from its flywheels ratcheted against the shaft across the stern, and water from the covered paddle-wheel spattered against the board partition that separated the engine from the gap in the raft's floor.

Commodore Lopeyz stuck his head out of the top hatch, wondering bitterly why he'd volunteered for this. *Because everyone else seemed to be volunteering for* something, he thought dryly.

The cold air flowing over the top of the slope-sided box was shocking after the fetid heat inside. The wind was in his face as he went up the narrowing White River at a walking pace. It carried the long black plume of smoke from the stack behind him, to where the other two rafts followed in his wake. None of them was doing more than four knots . . . but they hadn't far to go, and it was a minor miracle none of them had broken down. The surface of the river was steel-gray, with small whitecaps now and then as the breeze freshened. The land to the right, on the north back, was rising; he could see little over the levee beside the stream, except the three hundred meter tabletop of the bluffs where the Brigaderos siege battery was located.

They were level with it now, turning northwest with the bend in the river. The raft shuddered and slowed under him, fighting the current that grew stronger with every meter upstream. He dropped a few steps down the ladder and signalled to the engineer; no use trying to talk, when the hiss of steam and roar of the furnace blended with the sound of the paddles beating water into froth and made the inside one bath of noise.

The engineer pulled levers; his sweat-glistening attendants hovered over the drive-belts, the improvised part of the arrangement. The right-hand paddle wheel went faster, and the left-hand one slowed. Slowly, clumsily, the mortar raft began to turn its nose in toward the bank. He climbed back up the ladder to judge the water ahead; his hands and feet moved carefully on the greasy iron. The other craft were copying him, and the channel was deeper on the north shore. They moved in further, slowing, until the levee loomed ahead and nearly cut off their view of the bluff a kilometer inland.

He signalled again, waving his arms down the ladder. The engines groaned and hissed to silence. The sudden absence of noise was shocking, like the cool air that funneled down through the hatchway. The black gang leaned wheezing on their shovels, next to the wicker coal-bins; they and the engineers were both stripped to their trousers and bandannas, black as Zanjians with the coal-dust and glistening with heavy sweat. So were the ships' gunners grouped around the mortar. Crewmen swarmed out of the other hatches and the anchors splashed

"Ready?" he called to the gunners.

Their officer nodded. Over the squat muzzle of the mortar was a pie-shape of iron on a hooped frame. The gunner reached up and unfastened a bolt, and one segment of the pie fell down, hinged on the outer curved frame. Gray daylight poured into the gloom of the hold, and a wash of cold air that smelled of water and silty mud.

Lopeyz pushed his head out the hatchway again. The other two rafts were anchored alongside, only ten and thirty meters away. Wedge-shaped gaps showed in their top decks as well.

"Two thousand two hundred," he called, estimating the distance to the enemy gun emplacements.

He levelled his glasses; plenty of activity up there, but only a few of the ant-sized figures were turning towards the river. Lopeyz grinned to himself. The Brigaderos had cleverly dug their guns into the loess soil, presenting impossible targets for the Civil Government artillery in Old Residence. They had also made it impossible to move the big smoothbores in a time of less than hours.

"*Fwego.*" He opened his mouth and jammed his palms against his ears.

SHUMP.

The raft bobbed under him, and ripples floated away from it in a near-perfect circle. Hot air snatched at his three-cornered hat. Smoke billowed through the hold, sending men coughing and gasping. More swept across the upper deck in the wake of the man-high oblong of orange fire that belched out of the mortar's 20cm tube. He blinked against the smoke and watched the blurred dot of the forty-kilo mortar shell rise, hesitate and fall. It plunged into the riverward slope of the bluffs. A second later earth gouted up in a huge plume that drifted and fell in a rain of finely divided dirt. These shells had a hardened tip made by casting them in a water-cooled mould, and the fuses were set for a delay after impact.

"Up three, increase charge one bag," he shouted down past his feet into the hold.

The crew spun the elevating screw and the stubby barrel of the mortar rose. The loader wrapped another donut of powder onto the perforated brass tube at the base of the shell, and three men lifted it into the muzzle.

SHUMP.

This time it arched over the lip of the bluff, into the flat area behind the enemy guns. Lopeyz raised his binoculars and grinned like a downdragger. Men were spilling over the edge of the bluffs, some picking their way down the steep brush-grown slopes, others plunging in their haste. Still more were running eastward, down the gentler slope of the bluff to the rear, where the Brigaderos had shaped the earth into a rough roadway. He could hear shouting; it must be very loud, to carry this far — and his ears were ringing from engine-noise and the firing of the mortar.

"Correct left one," he said. The crew turned the iron traversing screw one full revolution, and the mortar barrel moved slighty to the left. "Fwego."

SHUMP.

Right into the gun positions along the lip of the bluff facing Old Residence.

"Fire for effect!" he barked. The other rafts cut loose as well.

SHUMP. SHUMP. SHUMP. A pause. *SHUMP. SHUMP. SHUMP.* Ragged clouds of smoke drifted upriver with the breeze. The edge of the bluff began to come apart under the hammer of the shells.

The Brigaderos rifles went into the cart with a clatter. Rifleman Minatelli straightened with a groan and rubbed his back; it had been a *long* day. The sun was setting behind the ruined, gutted Brigaderos position on the bluff to the west, tinging it with blood — which was appropriate. The air was getting chilly, but it still smelled the way he was learning went with violent death; like a latrine, mixed with a butcher's shop where the offal hasn't been cleaned away properly. A sour residue of gunpowder mixed with it all. It wasn't quite so bad here in the open fields beyond the breach in the wall, where the wind blew. Some distance off, a company of cavalry sat their saddles, rifles across the pommel and eyes alert.

A wail came up from the field nearby. The Brigade had offered a truce in return for permission to remove their wounded and dead. That had turned out to mean friends and often family coming to look through the bodies when the Civil Government troops had finished stripping them of arms and useable equipment. Or bits of bodies, sometimes. Minatelli swallowed and hitched the bandanna up over his nose. A little further off big four-wheeled farm wagons piled with dead were creaking back to the enemy lines. The priests said dead bodies bred disease; Messer Raj was pious that way, and the word was he was happy to see the Brigaderos taking them off for burial.

One of the women keening over a body looked his way. "Why?" she shouted at him. "What did we ever do to you? Why did you come here?" She spoke accented Spanjol, but probably didn't expect him to understand.

The young private pulled down his bandanna. "I was *born* here, you stupid bitch," he growled, and turned away.

The other members of his squad laughed. There were six all told of the eight who'd started the day; Gharsia dead, and one man with the Sisters, his collarbone broken by a bullet. They moved on, leading the two-ox team, and stopped by another clump of bodies. These had been ripped by cannister, and the smell was stronger. Minatelli let his eyes slide out of focus; it wasn't that he couldn't watch, just that it was better not to. He bent to begin picking up the rifles.

"Fuckin' *Spirit*!" one of his comrades said. It was the squad corporal, Ferhanzo. "Lookit!"

Thumbnail-sized silver coins spilled from a leather wallet the dead Brigadero had had on his waist belt. Whistles and groans sounded.

"Best yet," the corporal said, pouring the money back into the wallet and snapping it shut. "Here."

He tossed it to Minatelli, who stuffed it into a pocket. The young Old Residencer was the best of them at arithmetic, so he was holding the cash for all of them. *They're treating me different*, he thought.

It hit him again. *I got through it!* He'd been scared — terrified — but he hadn't fucked up. *He* was a veteran now.

That made him grin; it also made him more conscious of what was at his feet. That was a mass of cold intestines, coiled like lumpy rope and already turning gray. Insects were walking over it in a disciplined column, carrying bits off to their nest, snapper-ants with eight legs and as long as the first joint of his thumb. He retched and swallowed convulsively.

"Hey, yu shouldda been ad Sandoral," one of the other men said slyly. "Hot nuff tu fry 'n egg. Dem wogs, dey get all black 'n swole up real fast, 'n den dey pops lika grape when yu —"

Minatelli retched again. The corporal scowled. "Yu shut yor arsemout'," he said. "Kid's all right. Nobody tole yu t' stop workin'."

The platoon sergeant came by. "Yor relieved," he said. "Dem pussy militia gonna take over. We all get day's leave."

"'Bout time," the squad corporal said.

The noncom had volunteered his squad for very practical reasons; he finished cutting the thumb-ring off the hand of the corpse at his feet before he straightened.

"C'mon, boys, we'll git a drink 'n a hoor," the corporal said.

"I, uh, just want some sleep," Minatelli said.

The front of his uniform was spattered with blood and other fluids from the bodies he'd been handling. He should be hungry, they'd had only bread and sausage at noon, but right now the thought of food set up queasy tremors in his gut. A drink, though . . . And the thought of a woman had a sudden raw attractiveness. It was powerful enough to mute the memory of the day gone by.

The corporal put an arm around his shoulders. "Nu, best thing for yu," he said. "Wash up first — the workin' girls got their standards."

The Priest of the Residential Parish entered the door at the foot of the long room as if he were walking to the great altar in the cathedron, not answering a summons sent with armed men. His cloth-of-gold robes rustled stiffly, and the staff in his hand thumped with graceful regularity as he walked toward the table at the other end of the chamber. The inner wall was to his left, a huge fireplace with a grate of burning coals; to his right were windows, closed against the chill of night. He halted before the table that spanned the upper end of the room and raised his gloved hand in blessing.

Got to admire his nerve, Raj thought. *He has balls, this one.*

"Why have you brought me here, my daughter?" Paratier said. "A great service of thanksgiving for the victory of the Civil Government and the army of Holy Federation Church is in preparation."

He stood before the middle of the long table. Behind it sat Suzette, flanked by scribes and a herald; Raj was at one corner, his arms crossed. The walls of the room were lined with troopers of the 5th Descott, standing at motionless parade rest with fixed bayonets. Evening had fallen, and the lamps were lit; the fireplace on the interior wall gave their bright kerosine light a smokey coal-ember undertone on the polished black-and-white marble of the floor and the carved plaster of the ceiling. The Priest looked sternly at Suzette, then around for the seat that protocol said should have been waiting for him. Raj admired his calm assumption of innocence.

"The Spirit of Man of the Stars was with us this day," Suzette said softly. "Its will was done — but not yours, Your Holiness."

"*Heneralissimo* Whitehall —" the Priest began, in a voice as smooth as old oiled wood.

"Lady Whitehall is acting in her capacity as civil legate here," Raj said tonelessly. "I am merely a witness. Please address yourself to her."

Spirit, he thought. He had known good priests, holy men — the Hillchapel chaplain when he was a boy, and a goodly number of military clerics since.

Priest-doctors and Renunciates; even some monks of the scholarly orders, in East Residence.

Paratier, however ... there seemed to be something about promotion beyond Sysup that acted as a filter mechanism. Perhaps those with a genuine vocation didn't *want* to rise that high and become ecclesiastical bureaucrats.

"Bring in the first witness," Suzette said.

A door opened, on the table side of the wall beyond the fireplace. A man in the soiled remnant of priestly vestments came through in a wheeled chair, pushed by more soldiers. His head rolled on his shoulders, and he wept silently into the stubble of his beard.

"What is this?" Paratier boomed indignantly. "This is a priest of Holy Federation Church! Who is responsible for this mistreatment, abominable to the Spirit?"

"I and officers under my direction," Suzette said. She lifted a cigarette in a long holder of sauroid ivory. "He was apprehended attempting to leave the city and make contact with the barbarian generals. The ciphered documents he carried and his confession are entered in evidence. Clerk, read the documents."

One of the men sitting beside Suzette cleared his throat, opened a leather-bound folder, and produced the tattered message and several pages of notes in a copperplate hand.

"To His Mightiness, General of the Brigade, Lord of Men, Ingreid Manfrond, from the Priest of the Residential Parish, Paratier, servant of the servants of the Spirit of Man, greetings.

"Lord of Men, we implore you to deliver us from the hand of the tyrant and servant of tyrants Whitehall, and to forgive and spare this city, the crown of your domains.

"In earnest of our good faith and loyalty, we pledge to open to you the east gate of Old Residence and admit your troops, on a day of your choosing to be determined by you and Our representative. This man is in my confidence and bears a signet —"

"Produce the ring," Suzette added.

A box was opened; inside was a ring of plain gold, set with a circuit chip.

"— which is the mark of my intentions. With Us in Our determination to end the suffering and bloodshed of Our people are the following noble lords —"

Paratier thumped his staff on the marble flags. "Silence!" he said, his aged voice putting out an astonishing volume. "How dare you, adultress, accuse —"

"The prisoner will address the court with respect or he will be flogged," Suzette said flatly.

Paratier stopped in mid-sentence, looking into her eyes. After a moment he leaned on his staff. Suzette turned her gaze to the man in the wheeled chair.

"Does the witness confirm the documents?"

"Yes, oh, yes," the priest whispered. "Oh, please . . . don't, oh please."

"Take him away," Suzette said. "Prisoner, do you have anything to say?"

"Canon law forbids the judicial torture of ordained clerics," Paratier snapped. After a moment he added formally: "Most Excellent and Illustrious Lady."

"Treason is tried under the authority of the Chair, and witnesses in such cases may be put to the question," Suzette pointed out.

"This is Old Residence; no law supersedes that of Holy Federation Church within these walls. Certainly not the fiat of the Governors!"

"Let the record show," Suzette said coldly, "that the prisoner is warned that if he speaks treason again — by denying the authority of the Sole Rightful Autocrat and Mighty Sovereign Lord Barholm Clerett, Viceregent of the Spirit of Man of the Stars upon Earth — he will be flogged and his sentence increased."

Paratier opened his mouth and fell silent again. "Does the prisoner deny the charges?"

"I do. The documents are forged. A man under torture will say whatever will spare him pain."

Suzette nodded. "However, torture was not necessary for your other accomplices, Your Holiness. Bring them in."

Seven men filed in through the door, their expressions hangdog. A light sheen of sweat broke out on Paratier's face as he recognized them; Fidelio Enrike, Vihtorio Azaiglio, the commander of the Priest's Guard . . .

"Let the record show the confessions of these men were read," she said. "Prisoner, you are found guilty of treasonable conspiracy with the enemies of the Civil Government of Holy Federation. The punishment is death."

Paratier's lips whitened, and his parchment-skinned hand clenched on the staff. Raj stood and moved to Suzette's side.

"But," she went on, "on the advice of the *Heneralissimo Supremo* this court will temper the law with mercy."

A pair of priests came forward; these were easterners themselves, military chaplains attached to the Expeditionary Force.

One carried a plain robe of white wool. The other bore a copy of the Cannonical Handbooks, a thick book bound in black leather and edged with steel.

"You are to be spared on condition that you immediately take the oath of a brother in the Order of Data Entrists," she said. "From here you will be taken to the mother-house of your Order in East Residence. There you may spend your remaining years in contemplation of your sins."

The Data Entrists were devoted to silent prayer, and under a strict rule of noncommunication.

Paratier threw down his staff violently. "This is Anne Clerett's doing," he hissed.

For the first time since the Priest entered the room, Suzette's face showed an expression; surprise. "The Consort's doing?" she said.

"Of course," the old man said bitterly. "She and her tame Arch-Sysup Hierarch were trying to foist the absurd doctrine of the Unified Code on Holy Federation Church. As opposed to the *true* orthodox position, that the Interface with humanity is an autonomous subroutine only notionally subsumed in the Spirit Itself."

"You are in error, Brother Paratier," Suzette said helplessly, shaking her head. To the priests who stood on either side of him: "Proceed."

When the new-made monk had stalked out between his guards, she turned to the six magnates.

"As agreed, your lives are spared in return for your testimony." She paused. "Your property and persons are forfeit to the State, as are those of your immediate families. Clerk, announce the sentences."

The room filled with silence as the prisoners were herded out; some defiant, others stunned or weeping. When the commander of the detachment had marched his men out, Raj rested one thigh on the table beside his wife and laid a hand on her head, stroking the short black hair, fine as silk.

"Thank you," he said. "Of all my Companions, the best."

Suzette rose to her feet, so suddenly that the heavy chair clattered over behind her. She flung her arms around Raj. Startled, he clasped her in turn, feeling the slight tremors through her shoulders. She spoke in a fierce whisper, her face pressed to his neck:

"Anything for you, my love. *Anything*."

CHAPTER ELEVEN

"Well, now we can see what they've been building," Raj said. "You know, I'd like to get ahold of the man over there who's been coming up with these clever ideas."

"Whh . . . what would you do to him?" the new Alcalle of Old Residence said. He shivered slightly in the breeze; it was another bright cold day, but the wind was still raw from the last week of drizzle.

"Give him a job," Raj replied. "I can use a man that clever."

He bent to look through the tripod-mounted heavy binoculars. The . . . whatever-it-was had just crept out of the Brigade camp, the one that straddled the local railway leading north. In normal times the line carried coal from the mines thirty kilometers to the north. He'd ordered those closed — the pumps disassembled and the shafts flooded — before the enemy arrived, although there had been some coal stacked on the surface. Now the enemy had come up with a completely different use . . .

The railroad battery was mounted on the wheels of several rail cars. They had been bolted together with heavy timbers, and more laid as a deck. On that went three forward-facing smoothbore fortress guns, firing twenty kilo shot. Over the guns in front was a sloping casement; he estimated the iron facing was at least two hundred millimeters, backed by thick beams. The sides and top were covered in hexagonal iron plates, probably taken from the gun-rafts on the south shore of the lake. The whole assemblage was too wide to be

stable on the one and a half meter gauge of the
railroad, so hinged booms extended from either side of
the mass. They rested on wheeled outriggers made
from farm wagons, but reinforced and provided with
iron shields to the front. The battery was pushed by a
single locomotive, itself protected by the mass of wood
and iron ahead of it.

"What do they intend to do with it?" Gerrin
Staenbridge asked.

observe, Center said.

The scene before him jumped, with reality showing
through as a ghostly shadow. At five hundred meters
the battery stopped its slow forward crawl. The slotted
ports on the forward face opened, and the muzzles of
the fortress guns showed through. Flame and smoke
bellowed out, and solid shot hammered into the north
face of the wall, into the gate towers, at point-blank
range.

Then darkness fell across the vision, as the sun
descended. The Brigaderos crew scrambled to
unchock the wheels of the battery, and it crept
laboriously backward as the straining engine tugged it
safely within the gates of the earth-bermed camp.

Raj nodded. "Bring it up to close range," he said.
"Batter the fortifications during the day, withdraw it at
night."

The Brigaderos had gotten very nervous about
leaving their camps during the hours of darkness, with
the Skinners roaming free.

"Hmmm." Grammeck Dinnalsyn considered it.
"Shall I start an interior facing wall?"

"No," Raj said, smiling slightly. "With the guns at
close range, they could cover any assault through a
breach — batter down anything we threw up, and give
close support to the storming party. In fact, with the
outer wall down they'd command the whole city down
to the harbor; it's all downhill from here."

"Sir." Cabot Clerett stepped forward. "Sir, I'll

assemble a forlorn hope. With heavy fire support from the walls, we should be able to reach the casement with satchel charges before it gets to close range."

The young major glanced aside at Suzette. The rest of the officers were glancing at *him*; that was a suicide mission if they'd ever heard one.

"No, Major Clerett," Raj said, his smile broadening. "I don't think I'll give the Sovereign Mighty Lord cause to remove me from my command just yet." *By killing his heir* went unspoken.

His smile grew broader still, then turned into a chuckle. The Companions and dignitaries stared in horrified amazement as it burst into a full-throated guffaw. Cabot Clerett went white around the lips.

"Sir —" he began.

Raj waved him to silence. "Sorry, major — I'm not laughing at you. At the enemy, rather; whoever came up with this idea is really quite clever. But it's a young man, or I miss my guess. Colonel Dinnalsyn, how many field guns do we have within range?"

"Twelve, *mi heneral,*" the artilleryman said. His narrow face began to show a smile of its own, suspecting a pleasant surprise. "But they won't do much good against that armor."

"I don't think so either," Raj said, still chuckling. "So we'll wait . . . yes."

In an eerie replay of Center's vision, the battery halted at five hundred meters from the north gate. Some of the civilians on the tower edged backward unconsciously as the crew edged down behind the shields rigged to the booms and began hammering heavy wedges behind the wheels. Others took out precut beams and used them to brace the casement itself against the surface of the roadbed; that would spread the recoil force and make the battery less likely to derail its wheels. The Brigaderos worked rapidly, shoulders hunched against the knowledge that they were within small-arms range of the defenses — and that while the iron shields on the boom and outrigger might protect them from rifle bullets, they would do nothing if shrapnel burst overhead.

Hammers sounded on wood and iron, then were tossed aside as the soldiers completed their tasks and dove gratefully back into the shelter of the casement. The previous attempts to force a battery near the walls of Old Residence had given the Brigaderos a healthy respect for the artillery of the Expeditionary Force.

Raj tapped Dinnalsyn on the shoulder with his fist. "Now, Colonel, if you'll have your guns concentrate on the roadbed, just behind that Brigadero toy —"

Dinnalsyn began to laugh as well. After a moment, the rest of the Companions joined in, whooping and slapping each other on the back; Suzette's silvery mirth formed a counterpoint to the deep male sound. Only the civilians still stared in bewilderment and fear. Cabot Clerett was not laughing either, although there was an angry comprehension in his eyes.

POUMPF.

The field-gun mounted on the tower strobed a turnip-shaped tongue of flame into the darkness. The *crack* of the shell exploding over the stranded railroad casement was much smaller, a blink of reddish-orange fire. Like a lightning-bolt, it gave an eyeblink vision of what lay below. The casement itself was undamaged save for thousands of bright scratches in the heavy gray iron of its armor. The locomotive was still on the tracks, although a lucky shell had knocked the stack off the vertical boiler. Black smoke still trickled out of the stump, but without the pipe to provide draught over the firebox, there was no way the engine could pull enough air over the firebox to raise steam.

Not that steam would have done any good. For fifty meters back from the locomotive, the tracks were cratered and twisted, the wooden rails and ties smashed to kindling and the embankment churned as if by giant moles.

When the second shell burst over them, the soldiers trying to repair the track under cover of darkness bolted for the rear, throwing down their tools and running for the safety of the camp. Bodies and body-parts showed how well that had worked before, in daylight — and since the guns on the towers of the city wall were already sighted in, the darkness was no shield. No shield to anyone but the Skinners lurking all around; tonight the price of ears had been raised to a *gold* piece each.

A carbide searchlight flicked on from the main gate, bathing the casement and the men around it. A thousand Brigaderos dragoons were grouped there, trying to protect the casement and the gunners within from the savages roaming the night. The only way to do that was to bunch tightly . . . which made them a perfect target now, as the guns opened up with a five-shell stonk and two battalions of infantry volleyed from the towers and wall. The dragoons peeled away from the casement, at first a few men crawling backward from the rear ranks or running crouched over, then whole sections of the regiment throwing down their weapons and pelting for the rear. Fire raked them; it would have been safer to wait in whatever cover they could claw from the ground, but men in panic fear will run straight into the jaws of death. Even though death was the fear that drove them.

By the time the searchlight had been shot out by a Brigadero luckier or more skillful than the rest, only the regiment's commander and a small group around him remained. He turned and began to walk stolidly away, the banner flapping at his side. They disappeared into the darkness; a few seconds later the doors of the casement swung open, and the gunners dropped to the ground in a tight clump. They hesitated for a few seconds, then began running north after the retreating colonel.

Half a minute later firing erupted from the darkness itself, the long muzzle-flashes of Skinner rifles lancing out from positions along the embankment. A screeching followed, like saws biting through rock, a flurry of lighter gunshots from Brigaderos rifle-muskets and pistols. Then only screaming, diminishing until it was a single man sobbing in agony. Silence fell.

"Sir," Cabot Clerett said stiffly, bracing to attention.

Only he and Suzette and Raj remained on the parapet, beside the crews of the two guns and their commander. The parapet was darkened against the risk of enemy snipers, lit by the pale light of a one-quarter Miniluna.

"Sir, I request permission to destroy the enemy casement," Cabot went on, his voice as stiffly mechanical as the compressed-air automatons in the Audience Hall in East Residence.

"By all means, Major Clerett," Raj said.

He had been leaning both elbows on one of the crenelations of the parapet. When he straightened up, the moon turned his face to shadow under the helmet brim, all but the gray eyes that caught a fragment of the light. The younger man could see nothing but cold appraisal in them. Imagination painted a sneer beneath.

"It wouldn't do to let them reoccupy it tomorrow," Raj said. "They did enough damage to the gates as it was."

Suzette moved forward. "I'm sure Cabot will do a splendid job," she said, smiling at him.

Cabot Clerett clicked heels and inclined his head. "Messa."

And nobody will even notice, he thought savagely, as he clattered down the tower stairs to the guardhouse at the base. *It'll be the cherry on the cake of another brilliant Whitehall stratagem. Nobody but Suzette will realize what I did.*

Two Skinners were standing on top of the casement when he arrived at the head of a company of the 2nd Life Guards. They watched silently, leaning on their long rifles, as he lit the rag wrapped around the neck of a wine bottle full of coal oil and tossed it through the open hatch. Another followed, and yellow flame began to lick through the hatchway and the gunports and observation slits.

"Better get out of the way, sir," Senior Captain Fikaros said.

Cabot nodded silently; they rode back to the gate. Men were already at work on it, cutting out the cracked timbers and mortizing in fresh, nailing and hammering. He stood and watched silently as the casement burned; the timbers of its frame were fully involved now, and the iron was beginning to glow a ruddy color around the holes were flame pulsed with a rhythm like a great beast breathing. The munitions must have been stored in metal-clad boxes, probably water-jacketed, because it was fifteen minutes before the first explosion. A few of the iron plates flew free, and the heavy casement jumped as fire jetted out of every opening. Then the whole vehicle disappeared in a globe of orange-red fire that left afterimages blinking across his retinas for minutes. The shock wave pushed at him, sending him staggering against the rough surface of the gate. Men within shouted in alarm as the tall leaves of the doors rattled against their loosened hinges.

"Hope those Skinners had enough sense to get off," Fikaros said. He laughed. "A tidy end to a tidy operation. I wonder how many more siege guns the enemy has?"

"Enough," Cabot Clerett said tonelessly. "Return the men to quarters, Captain."

"Sir. Care for a drink in the mess, Major?"

"For a start, Captain."

❖   ❖   ❖

"Spirit *damn* them," Raj said with quiet viciousness. "I *need* those reinforcements."

The windows were open, to catch the first air of the early spring afternoon. It was still a little chill, but on a sunny day no more than made a jacket comfortable. The air smelled cleaner than usual in a city; coal was running short, even for cooking-fires.

"How many does that make?" Gerrin Staenbridge said. "Landings in the Crown as a whole."

Jorg Menyez shuffled papers. "Five regular infantry battalions," he said. "Ordinary line units, suitable enough for garrison work. And seven battalions of regular cavalry. The 10th Residence, 9th and 11th Descott Dragoons, 27th and 31st Diva Valley Rangers, the 3rd Novy Haifa, and the 14th Komar. Plus about six batteries of artillery, say twenty to twenty-four guns."

"Good troops," Raj said. "And as much use in the Crown as they would be in bloody East Residence — or Al Kebir, for that matter."

"You've got plenary authority as Theatre Commander," Gerrin pointed out.

Raj indicated a pile of letters, his correspondence with the commanding officers of the reinforcements. His teeth showed slightly in a feral smile of tightly-held rage.

"I've got power of life and death over the whole Western Territories — in theory," he said. "Half of them didn't even reply. The other half said they can't get into a city *surrounded* by a hundred thousand troops."

"Odd, since we've no problem getting small shipping in every night," Staenbridge said.

Antin M'lewis nodded. "Ser," he said. "Me boys could git hunnerts in by land, any night ye name. Them barbs is stickin' real close-loik ter their walls."

"The fix is in," Dinnalsyn said.

Raj nodded. "Informally, I've had word from Administrator Historomo. The battalion commanders are under word-of-mouth instruction from the Chair not to place themselves under my orders. They're not under *anyone's* orders, really, although for most purposes they seem to be doing what Historomo says. He's got them split up in penny packets doing garrison work his militia and gendarmes could handle just as well."

He swore again, bitterly. "With another four thousand cavalry I could *end* this bloody war before wheat harvest." That would be in four months. "Without them, it may take *years.*"

"The Brigaderos are in pretty poor shape," Staenbridge said judiciously. "They must have lost twenty thousand men in those attacks over the winter — probably thirty thousand all told, if you count the ones rendered unfit-for-service."

"And they're losing hundreds every week to general wastage," Menyez said. "They've had a visit from Corporal Forbus."

M'lewis nodded, and there was a general slight wince. Cholera in a winter camp was a nightmare. "Them camps is smellin' high," he said. "An' their dogs is in purly pit'ful shape."

"They still outnumber us five to one," Raj said. "We're losing men too, to snipers and harassing attacks. Not as many, but we didn't have as many to start with. Jorg, what about the militia?"

"Limited usefulness only, *mi heneral,*" Menyez said. "The full-time battalions can hold a secure fortified position with no flanks, but I wouldn't ask more of them. The part-timers aren't even up to that. Local recruits in our regular infantry units have settled in splendidly . . . but that's largely because we took only the best and in small numbers."

Raj nodded. "Where's Clerett?" he asked.

"Ah . . . " someone coughed. "He was at luncheon with Lady Whitehall and some of his officers, I think."

"Well, *get* him here,"

He paced like a caged cat until the younger man arrived. When he did, Raj kept his face carefully neutral.

"Sir." Clerett saluted with lazy precision.

"Major," Raj replied. He indicated the map boards with a jerk of his head. "We were going over the general position, now that winter is coming to an end."

Cabot looked at the maps. "Stalemate," he said succinctly.

"Correct," Raj replied. *He's no fool, and he's learned a great deal*, he thought carefully. Judging a man you disliked was a hard task, calling for mental discipline. "We are now considering how to break it. Specifically, we need the four thousand cavalry currently sitting in the Crown."

"With their thumbs up their bums and their wits nowhere," Gerrin Staenbridge added.

Cabot Clerett's face was coolly unreadable. *He has learned*, Raj thought.

"Sir?" the younger man prompted.

Raj returned to his chair and sat, kicking aside the scabbard of his saber with a slight unconscious movement of his left foot. He paused to light a cigarette, drawing the harsh smoke into his lungs, then pulled out a heavy envelope from the same inner pocket that had held the battered platinum case.

"Under my proconsular authority, I'm promoting you to Colonel." He held out the papers; Clerett took them and turned the sealed envelope over in his hands.

A *pro forma* murmur of congratulations went around the table. Cabot Clerett bowed his head slightly in formal acknowledgement. The promotion meant less to the Governor's nephew than to a career officer, of course.

"I'm also detaching you from command of the Life Guards. You will proceed to Lion City immediately, and take command of the forces listed in your orders — essentially, all the cavalry and field-guns in the

Crown. Pull them together, put them through their paces for a week or so, improvise a staff. Then move them out; the Brigade hinterlands have been pretty well stripped of troops, so there shouldn't be much in your way. Use your discretion, but get those men and dogs near here as quickly as possible. Then communicate with me; we'll use the river-barges, slip the troops in at night."

"Sir." Cabot smiled, a slow grin. A major independent command . . . and given because the reinforcing units would obey *him*. Since he was the heir, they'd better. "Sir, do you think it advisable to trap another four thousand men here behind the walls?"

"I do," Raj said dryly.

The militia and the regular infantry between them could hold the city walls against anything but an all-out attack. With fourteen thousand Civil Government cavalry, he could take the mounted units out and use them as a mobile hammer to beat the enemy to dust against the anvil of the fortified city.

Cabot tucked the unopened envelope into the inner pocket of his uniform jacket.

"I'm to proceed to Lion City, mobilize and concentrate the cavalry and guns, form them into a field force, and rejoin the main Expeditionary Force, using my discretion as to the means and place?" he said.

"Correct, colonel."

"Immediately?"

"As soon as possible."

"I believe I'll be able to proceed tonight," Cabot said cheerfully. "If you'll excuse me, sir? I have some goodbyes."

Raj ground out the cigarette savagely as the Governor's nephew left the room.

"Was that altogether wise?" Gerrin murmured.

"Perhaps not," Raj ground out. "But it's the only bloody thing I could think of." He looked around. "Now let's get on with the planning, shall we?"

❖   ❖   ❖

"Glad to see you again, Ludwig," Raj said.

Ludwig Bellamy grinned. The expression was not as boyish as it had been four months ago. His face had thinned down, not starved but drawn closer to the strong bones.

"Glad to be back, *mi heneral*," he said.

They turned their dogs and rode inward from the gate where the last of the 2nd Cruisers was entering; it was pitch-black, overcast and with no moon. Dim light came from the lanterns on the gate towers above, and from shuttered lanterns in the hands of some of the officers. The heavy portals boomed shut behind them, and the locking bars shot home in their brackets with an iron clanking.

"Captain M'lewis did excellent work getting us past the enemy pickets," Ludwig went on.

"Warn't hardly nao problem," M'lewis said. "Them barbs ain't stirrin' by noight."

"We could smell them," Ludwig said. "Although what they've got left to crap, I don't know."

Raj rode in silence for a few moments. An occasional sliver of light gleamed from a second-story window, as some householder cracked a shutter to check what was going by outside. The dogs' paws beat on the pavement, a scud-*thump* sound, in time with the creak of harness among his escort. Bellamy's men had theirs stuffed with rags to muffle noise. A mount sneezed and shook its head with a jingle of bridle irons.

"The railroad's wrecked, then?" he said at last.

"They're repairing segments with plain wood rails," Ludwig said; pride showed in his voice. "And hauling trains with oxen. The whole area's up in arms, peasant revolt and famine, with three or four regiments beating the bush for *insurectos*. We swung north, and they're trying to run wagon trains from the Padan River down to the camps here. Also we saw troops heading north, toward the frontier; the peasants gave us rumors about Guard and Stalwart raiding, and pirates along the coast."

Raj nodded. "Scavengers around a dying bull," he said. "Commodore Lopeyz has sunk three corsairs in the last month, found them hanging about just over the horizon." One hand indicated the delta of the White River to their left. "What with one thing and another, I think the enemy will be forced to make a move soon."

"How's the supply situation, sir?"

"Not bad, but getting worse. We've enough to keep the men and dogs on full rations for now, although the civilians are being shorted. No famine, though."

Apart from the odd body found dead in a doorway in the morning, but that happened in any city, under siege or not.

"What'll they do?"

"I'm not sure . . . but they'll do something. Soon."

"No!" Ingreid Manfrond said, sweeping the map aside.

His eyes were bloodshot as he glared at the other Brigade commanders.

"Lord of Men —" Teodore Welf began.

"Shut up, you puppy!" Ingreid roared. "You lost me twenty thousand men with your last bright idea."

Teodore stepped back from the table, clicked heels — his armor clanked too — and gave a stiff bow before leaving. Ingreid stared after him; it was a breach of protocol to leave the General's presence before permission was granted. Most of the other officers looked elaborately elsewhere; a few looked calculating, wondering if the triumvirate was breaking up. The weak spring sunlight came through the tentflap with a gust of air, ruffling the maps on the table. The sour smell of the camp was worse, men with runny guts and dogs too.

"Your Mightiness," Howyrd Carstens said, "he was

right this time. We've got to deal with this new army."
His thick callused thumb swept over to the Crown,
then up the peninsula from Lion City.

"They're over the Waladavir," he said. "Our arse is
hanging in the breeze like a bumboy's, and if he heads
southwest and cuts us off from the Padan valley we're
fucked — how many men are dismounted already
because we can't bait their dogs?"

"You think I should send Welf off, with his mother's
milk still wet on his lips?" Ingreid said. "Give him
fifteen regiments?"

His voice was no longer a roar, but still hoarse with
anger. He snapped his fingers, and a servant came
forward with wine. It was too early in the day . . . but
he needed it. The raw chill of this damned winter had
gotten into his bones.

I'm not sixty yet, he thought. *I can out-ride and
out-fight any of them.* But the price kept going up
every year.

Carstens shook his head. "Whoever you want," he
said. "Send me, or go yourself. Take twenty thousand
men, the ones with the best dogs and the fewest
troopers down sick. That'll still leave us with seventy
thousand fit for service here, more than enough to
blockade the city. Stamp on this little Civvie column —
there can't be more than four regiments' worth. Then
come back here."

Ingreid shook his head. "I'm not splitting our
forces," he said. "I'm through underestimating Whitehall, Spirit of Man of This Earth curse him. What we'll
do is —"

He began giving his orders, pointing with a stubby
finger now and then.

Carstens hawked and spat on the ground when he
was finished. "Might work," he said. "Anyway, you're
the General."

Ingreid was conscious of their eyes on him. A proper
General led the warriors of the Brigade to victory. So

far he'd lost two-score regiments in battle, and half as many again to sickness. It wasn't a distinguished record . . . and his grip on the Seat was still new and uncertain.

"I *am* the General," he said. "And I'll have White-hall's skull for a drinking cup before the first wheat's reaped this year."

CHAPTER TWELVE

"He's up to *something*," Raj said. The setting sun glittered red on the lancepoints of a regiment of Brigaderos cuirassiers moving at the edge of sight. "Something fairly substantial."

Once more they were gathered on one of the north gate towers; Suzette looking a little pale from the lingering aftermath of influenza and some woman's problem she wouldn't tell him about, curled up under a mound of furs.

"Movin' troops," M'lewis added, nodding. Parties of his Scouts were out every night, collecting information and the ear-bounty. "Looks loik back 'n forth, though."

Gerrin and Ludwig Bellamy bent over the map table. "Well," the older man said thoughtfully, "Ingreid's done bloody silly things before. Hmmm . . . moved about ten thousand men from the south bank of the river to the north, and none of *them* have been moved back."

"Ingreid's trying hard to be clever," Raj said absently, tapping his jaw with a thumb. "He's going to do something — no way of hiding that — but he doesn't want us to know where."

"All-out assault?" Ludwig Bellamy said.

"Possibly. That would cost him, but we can't be strong enough all along scores of kilometers of wall. With his numbers, he could feint quite heavily and then hit us with the rest of it somewhere else."

A crackle of tension went through the officers, like dogs sniffing the spring air and bristling. Raj looked out again at the enemy camps; blocks of men and banners were moving, tiny with the distance.

observe, Center said.

The vision was a map, with counters to represent troops and arrows for their movements.

Are you sure? Raj thought.

probability 82% +/-5, Center replied. **examine the movements of artillery.**

"Ah," Raj said aloud. "He's moving the *men* around, but the *guns* have been going in only one direction."

The other men were silent for an instant. "Foolish of him," Staenbridge said.

Ludwig nodded. "I think he's short of draught oxen," he said. "Probably they've been eating them. Short-sighted."

"Then here's what we'll do," Raj said. "Jorg, select the best eleven battalions of your infantry, and hold them in readiness down by the river docks. You'll command. Move the rest up here to the northern sector. Gerrin, I want you here with me. Ludwig, you'll take the armored cars and all the cavalry except the 5th and 7th —"

When he finished, there was silence for a long moment.

"That's rather risky, isn't it?" Gerrin said carefully. "I think it's fairly certain we could stop Ingreid head-on."

Raj smiled grimly. *What's that toast?* he asked Center: it was something from one of the endless historical scenarios his guardian ran for him.

"A toast, messers," he said, raising his cup. "*He fears his fate too much, and his desserts are small, who will not put it to the touch — to win or lose it all.*"

"Where're we going, Corporal?" rifleman Minatelli murmured.

The 24th Valencia were tramping down the cob-blestoned streets toward the harbor in the late-night chill. They were still blinking with sleepiness, despite a hurried breakfast in their billets. Men with torches or lanterns stood at the streetcorners, directing the flow. It was dark despite the stars and moons, and he moved carefully to avoid treading on the bootheels of the man in front. The cold silty smell of the river estuary was strong, underneath the scent of wool uniforms and men. Occasionally a window would open a crack as the folk inside peered out at the noise below. Trapped and helpless and wondering if their fate was to be decided tonight . . .

"How da fuck should I know?" the corporal snarled. "Jest shut —"

"*Alto!*"

"— up."

Almost as helpless as I am, Minatelli thought.

Although he had his rifle. That was comforting. The Battalion was all around him, which was still better. And Messer Raj always won his battles, which was more comforting still — everyone was sure of that.

Of course, the last battle — his first — had shown him you could get killed very dead indeed in the middle of the most smashing victory. Gharsia's lungs and spine blasted out through his back illustrated quite vividly what could happen to an experienced veteran on the winning end of a one-sided slaughter.

It wasn't worrying him as much as he thought it should, which was cause for concern in itself.

The long column of infantry stumbled to a halt in the crowded darkness.

"Stand easy!" The men relaxed, and a murmur went through the lines. "Silence in the ranks."

Minatelli lowered his rifle-butt to the stones and craned his neck. He was a little taller than average, and the street's angle was downward. The long rows of helmeted heads stretched ahead of him, stirring a little and the dull metal gleaming in the lamplight; the furled Company pennants ahead of each hundred-odd, and the taller twin staffs at the head where the color sergeants held the cased national flag and battalion colors. Another full battalion was passing down the street that crossed the one from the 24th's billet, marching at the quickstep.

"Something big on," he muttered out of the corner of his mouth to the corporal.

Officers walked up and down beside the halted column. Another battalion was marching down behind them, crashing to a halt at a barked order when they saw the 24th blocking their way. Breath steamed under the pale moonlight.

"Doan' matter none," the corporal whispered back, without moving his head. "We jest go where we're —"

The trumpet rang sharply. Men stiffened at the sound.

"Attent-*hun*. Shoulder . . . *arms*."

"— sent."

Minatelli came to and brought the long Armory rifle over his right shoulder, butt resting on his fingers. The trumpet sounded again. He wished the corporal hadn't sounded a little nervous himself.

"Alo sinstra, waymanos!" *By the left, forward.*

His left foot moved forward automatically, without his having to think about it. Hobnails gritted on the cobbles; they were wet and slippery with the dew, although morning was still a few hours off. Marching was easy now, not like at first. The problem with that was that it gave him time to think. Where *were* they sending everyone? Because from the sound, there must be at least four or five battalions on the move, all infantry. They'd been turned out with full kit — but no tents or blanket rolls, only one day's marching rations, and two extra boxes of ammunition each in their haversacks.

They marched through the seagate and onto the road by the wharves. It was a little lighter here, because the warehouses were backed up against the wall and left more open space than the streets. Most of the docks were empty, looking eerie and abandoned with starlight and moonlight glittering on the oily surface of the water. They halted again at the fishing harbor, upstream from the berths where the deep-hulled ocean traders docked.

"Company E, 24th Valencia," a man called softly.

Captain Pinya turned them left from the battalion column onto a rickety board wharf. Boats were waiting alongside the pier, fishing smacks and ship's longboats and some barges with longboats to tow them. Men waited at the oars, in the ragged slops sailors wore; there were others directing the infantry, in Civil Government uniform but with black jackets, and cutlasses by their sides — marines. The company commander stepped down into a long-boat, followed by the trumpeter and bannerman.

The lieutenant of Minatelli's platoon hopped down into a barge. "Sergeant, get the men settled," he said.

"*Come* on, straight-leg," one of the marines snarled at Minatelli. He was holding a painter snubbed around a bollard, anchoring the flat-bottomed grain barge to the wharf. "*Get* your asses in it. I've got to help *row* this bleeding sow."

The corporal clambered down. "About all yu good fur, fishbait," he said. "Yu herd da man, boys. Time fur a joyride."

"Easy, girl," Robbi M'Telgez said. "Easy, Tonita."

His dog wuffled at him sleepily from the straw of her stall. The corporal turned up the kerosine lamp and rolled up his shirtsleeves, taking the currycomb and beginning the grooming at the big animal's head. Tonita's tail thumped at the ground as he worked the stiff brush into the fur of her neck-ruff. It was not time for morning grooming, still hours too early, but the dog didn't mind. Most of the other mounts were still asleep, curled up in their straw. The stable smelled of dog and straw, but clean otherwise; the animals were

all stable-broken, and waited for their trip to the
crapground. It was a regular stable, requisitioned from
a local magnate when the 5th was billeted.

M'Telgez felt the dog's teeth nibble along his
shoulder in a mutual-grooming gesture as he worked
over her ribs. The task had a homey familiarity,
something he'd done all his life — back home on the
farm, too; the M'Telgez family owned five saddle-dogs.
He'd raised one from a pup and taken it to the army
with him; Tonita was his second, bought with the
battalion remount fund as a three-year old, just before
the Southern Territories campaign. War was hard on
dogs, harder than on men. Idly, he wondered what his
family would be doing right now. Pa was dead these
two years; his elder brother Halsandro had the land. It
was a month short of spring for Descott, so the flocks
would be down in the valley pasture.

Probably the women would be up, getting breakfast
for the men; his mind's eye showed them all around
the wooden table, spooning down the porridge and
soured milk.

Ma and Halsandro's wife and his sisters, they'd
spend the day mostly indoors, spinning and weaving
and doing chores around the farmyard. The water
furrow for the garden would need digging out, it
always did this time of year, so Halsandro would be at
that with the two hired men. He'd send Peydro and
Marhinz, the younger M'Telgez boys, down to the
valley pens to guide the sheep and the family's
half-dozen cattle out for the day. They'd be sitting their
dogs, shivering a little in their fleece jackets, with their
rifles across their thighs. Talking about hunting, or
girls, or whether they'd go for a soldier like their
brother Robbi . . .

"Hey, corp," someone called from the stable door.
He looked up. "Turnout, an' double-quick loik, t'El-T
says."

M'Telgez nodded and gave the currycomb a final

swipe before hanging it on the stable partition. Tonita whined and rose as well, sniffing at him and rattling the chain lead that held her bridle to the iron staple driven into the wall.

"Down, girl," M'Telgez said, shrugging into his jacket. He picked up his rifle and turned, away from the plaintive whining. "Nothin' happ'nin'."

You couldn't lie to a dog. They smelled it on you.

"Everything is ready?" Suzette asked.

The Renunciate nodded stiffly. Her face might have been carved from oak, but there was a sheen of sweat on her upper lip. Around them the church bustled; the regular benches had been carried out, and tables brought in instead to fill the great echoing space under the dome. Doctors were setting up, pulling their bundles of instruments out of vats of boiling iodine-water and scrubbing down. The wax-and-dust smell of a church was overlaid with the sharp carbolic stink of blessed water.

"Down to the stretchers and bandages," the nun replied. "For once, there is no shortage."

Suzette nodded and turned away. They'd commandeered a dozen buildings along the streets leading off from the plaza, and all the city's remaining hansom-cabs for ambulances. Plenty of priest-doctors as well, although the Expeditionary Force's own medics would direct everything, having the experience with trauma. Time between injury and treatment was the most crucial single factor, though. More of the wounded would live . . . provided Raj won.

He will, she told herself. A twinge in her belly made her grimace a little. Fatima put a hand under her elbow.

"I'm fine," she said, conscious that she was still pale. The pain was much less, and the hemorrhaging had stopped. Almost stopped.

"You shouldn't have," Fatima whispered in her ear.

"I couldn't take the chance," Suzette said, as softly. "I couldn't be sure whose . . . there will be time."

She straightened and nodded to her escort at the door. They were looking a little uneasy at the preparations. It was odd, even the bravest soldier didn't like looking at an aid station or the bone-saws being set out.

"Back to headquarters," she said.

"Kaltin, you and the 7th Descott are the only reserve on the whole west section of the walls," Raj said.

They stood around the map, watching his finger move and cradling their kave mugs. *I'm trying to fill a dozen holes with six corks*, he thought. Another shoestring operation . . . He went on:

"Ludwig can watch the east with the bulk of the cavalry until it's time. Gerrin and I are up here in the north with the 5th and nine battalions of regular infantry, but you're *it* over there — you and the militia. They're not that steady, and even a fairly light attack will spook them. Keep them facing the right way."

"Count on it," the scar-faced man said, slapping fists. "I am. *Waya con Ispirito de Hom.*"

Raj straightened and sighed as Gruder left. "Well, at least we're getting good fighting weather," he said.

The windows showed the ghostly glimmer of false dawn, but the sky was still bright with stars. Yesterday's rain was gone, although the ground outside the walls would still be muddy. Nothing would limit visibility today, though.

"I hope you messers are all aware how narrow our margins are, here," Raj said. "The blocking force has to *hold*." He nodded at the infantry commanders. "And the rest of you, when the time comes, *move*."

"It seems simple enough," one said.

Raj nodded grimly. "But in war, the simplest things become extremely difficult. Dismissed."

The men filed out, leaving only him and Suzette in

the big room. "You'd be more useful back at the aid station," he said. "Safer, too. This is too cursed close to the walls for comfort."

Suzette shook her head. "East Residence would be safe, my love. I'll be here," she said.

"Mamma, an' ye'll nivver see the loik of *that* comin' down t' road from Blayberry Fair," one of the Descotter troopers on the tower murmured.

The rolling northern horizon was black across an arc five kilometers wide. The Brigade was coming, deployed into fighting formation; the front ten ranks carried ladders and the blocks behind had their muskets on their shoulders and bayonets fixed. The sun was just up, and the light ran like a spark in grass from east to west across the formation as it hove into view, flashing on fifty thousand steel points. They chanted as they marched, a vast burred thunder, timed to the beating of a thousand drums. Between the huge blocks of men came guns, heavy siege models and lighter brass fieldpieces, hauled by oxen and dogs and yet more columns of Brigaderos warriors.

"Now, this isn't particularly clever," Raj said lightly.

To himself he added: *But it just may work.* Brute force often did, although it was also likely to have side-effects. Even if Ingreid won this one, he was going to lose every fifth fighting man in the Brigade's whole population doing it.

"Counter-battery?" Dinnalsyn asked.

"By all means," Raj said.

"Lancers to the fore," Gerrin Staenbridge noted.

The dull sheen of armor marked the forward ranks; they'd left the polearms behind, of course. Muskets were slung over their backs.

"Those lobster-shells will give them some protection," Raj said. "From fragments and glancing shots, at least."

The gunners' signal-lantern clattered. The chanting

of the Brigaderos was much louder, rolling back from walls and hills:

"*Upyarz! Upyarz!*"

Raj swallowed the last of his kave and handed the cup to the orderly; he shook out his shoulders with a slight unconscious gesture, settling himself to the task.

"Since I'm handling the towers," Gerrin said. "I'd appreciate it if you could be ready to move the reserves sharpish, Whitehall," he went on dryly.

"I'll do my best," Raj replied with a slight bow.

They grinned at each other and slapped fists, back of the gauntlet and then wrist to wrist.

"Right, lads," Raj said, raising his voice slightly.

Pillars of smoke were rising into the cold bright dawn air from the towers, stretching right and left in a shallow curve to the edge of sight. Gunsmoke, from the fieldpieces emplaced on them; the infantry on the walls hadn't started shooting yet. The *POUMPF* . . . *POUMPF* of the cannonade was continuous, a thudding rumble in the background. Behind it the sharper *crack* sound of the shells bursting was muffled by the walls. As he spoke a huge *BRACK* and burst of smoke came from one tower far to the west, where a heavy enemy shell had scored a lucky hit. Another came over the wall with a sound like a ship's sails ripping in a storm and gouted up a cone of black dirt from the cleared space inside the walls. The sulphur smell of powder smoke drifted to them, like a foretaste of hell to come.

"The whole Brigade's coming this way," Raj went on. "Most of our infantry went out upriver to take them in the flank. Pretty well all the cavalry's going to go out the west gate and take them in *that* flank.

"The problem is," he went on, rising slightly onto his toes and sinking back, "is that all that's left to hold them while that happens is us . . . and the rest of the infantry on the walls, of course."

He raised one hand and pointed at the north gate towers, his left resting on the hilt of his saber. "Colonel Staenbridge and Captain Foley each hold a side of the gate, with a company of the 5th. The rest of you — and me — have to stop whatever gets over the walls. If we do, it's victory. If we don't . . . "

He paused, hands clasped behind his back, and grinned at the semicircle of hard dark faces. Things were serious enough, but it was also almost like old times . . . five years ago, when he'd commanded the 5th and nothing more.

"You boys ready to do a man's work today?"

The answer was a wordless growl.

"Hell or plunder, dog-brothers."

"Switch to antipersonnel," Bartin Foley said briskly.

The front line of the Brigaderos host was only three thousand meters away. The rolling ground had broken up their alignment a little, but the numbers were stunning; worse than facing the Squadron charge in the Southern Territories, because these barbs were coming on in most unbarbarian good order. The forward line gleamed and flickered; evidently they'd taken the time to polish their armor. It coiled over the low rises like a giant metallic snake. Fifty meters behind it came the dragoons, tramping with their bayonetted rifles sloped. He could make out individual faces and the markings on unit flags now, with the binoculars. Most of the heavy guns were far behind, smashed by the fieldpieces mounted on the towers or stranded when the shelling killed the draught-oxen pulling them. Also further back were columns of mounted men, maybe ten thousand of them — ready to move forward quickly and exploit a breach anywhere along the front of the Brigade attack.

Terrible as a host with banners, he thought — it was a fragment from the Fall Codices, a bit of Old

Namerique rhetoric. The banners of the enemy
flapped out before them in the breeze from the north.
Hundreds of kettledrums beat among them, a thutter-
ing roar like blood hammering in your ears.

POUMPF. The gun on his tower fired again. The
smoke drifted straight back; Foley could see the shell
burst over the forward line of Brigaderos troopers and
hear the sharp spiteful *crack*. Men fell, and more
airbursts slashed at the front of the enemy formation.
Guns fired all along the line, but not as many as there
might have been. Half the 75's had been kept back to
support the cavalry. The duller sound of smoothbores
followed as the brass and cast-iron cannon salvaged
from storage all over Old Residence cut loose, firing
iron roundshot. He turned the glasses and followed
one that landed short, skipped up into the air and then
trundled through the enemy line. Men tried to skip
aside or dodge, but the ranks were too close-packed.
Half a dozen went down, with shattered legs or feet
ripped off at the ankle.

The ranks closed again and came forward without
pause; the fallen ladders were snatched up once more.
The smoothbores were much less effective than the
Civil Government field guns, and slower to load — but
there were several hundred of them on the walls. Their
gunners were the only militiamen in this sector, but
they ought to be reliable enough with the bayonets of
the Regulars near their kidneys . . . The defenders'
artillery fired continuously now, lofting a plume of
dirty white smoke over the wall and back towards the
city. A few of the Brigaderos siege guns had set up and
were firing over the heads of their troops; more of their
light three-kilo brass pieces were wheeling about to
support from close range.

Foley ignored them; he'd had a profound
respect for the Brigade's troopers, but their artillery
was like breaking your neck in the bath — it could
happen, but it wasn't something you worried about.

They must have lost two, three thousand men already, Foley thought.

"Spirit, they really want to make our acquaintance," he said. "I knew I was handsome, but this is ridiculous." The lieutenant beside him laughed a little nervously.

Rifles bristled along the forward edge of the tower. More would be levelling in the chambers below his feet, and along the wall to either side. The city cannon were firing grapeshot now, bundles of heavy iron balls in rope nets. It slashed through the enemy, and they picked up the pace to a ponderous trot. Approaching the outermost marker, a line of waist-high pyramids of whitewashed stones — apparently ranging posts weren't a trick the Brigade was familiar with. One thousand meters.

"Wait for it," he whispered, the sound lost under the rolling thunder of the cannonade.

The Brigaderos broke into a run. Foley forced his teeth to stop grinding; he touched the stock of the cut-down shotgun over his back, and loosened the pistol in his holster. At all costs the Brigade musn't take the gate, that was why there were companies of the 5th in the towers on either side. Gerrin was in overall command of the wall, all he had to worry about was this one tower and the hundred and fifty odd men in it. The troopers were kneeling at the parapets, and boxes of ammunition and hand-bombs waited open at intervals. Nothing else he could do . . .

"UPYARZ! UPYARZ!"

The front rank of dismounted lancers pounded past the whitewashed stone markers. A rocket soared up from the tower on the other side of the gate and popped in a puff of green smoke.

"*Now!*"

Along the wall, hundreds of officers screamed *fwego* in antiphonal chorus. Four thousand rifles fired, a huge echoing *BAAAMMMMM* louder even than the guns. The advancing ranks of armored men wavered, suddenly looking tattered as hundreds fell. Limply dead, or screaming and thrashing, and flags went down as well. Foley caught his breath; if they cracked . . .

"*UPYARZ! UPYARZ!*"

They came on, into the teeth of a continuous slamming of platoon volleys. And behind them, the first line of dragoons halted. The long rifle-muskets came up to their shoulders with a jerk, like a centipede rippling along the line. Their ranks were three deep, and there were thirty thousand of them.

"For what we are about to receive —"

Everyone on the tower top ducked. Foley didn't bother — he was standing directly behind one of the merlons, with only his head showing.

Ten thousand rounds, he thought. The front rank of the dragoons disappeared as each musket vomited a meter-long plume of whitish smoke. *Even so you'd have to be dead lucky —*

Something went *crack* through the air above his head. Something else whanged off the barrel of the cannon as it recoiled up the timber ramp and went *bzzz-bzzz-bzzz* as it sliced through a gunner's upper arm. The man whirled in place, arterial blood spouting.

"Tourniquet," Foley snapped over his shoulder. "Stretcher-bearers."

The next rank of Brigaderos dragoons trotted through the smoke, halted, fired. Then the third. By that time the first rank had reloaded.

"Lieutenant," Foley said, raising his voice slightly — the noise level kept going up, it always did, old soldiers were usually slightly deaf — "see that the men keep their sights on the forward elements."

It's going to be close. I wish Gerrin were here.

❖   ❖   ❖

"Damn," Raj said mildly, reading the heliograph signal.

"Ser?" Antin M'lewis asked.

He was looking a little more furtive than usual, a stand-up fight was not the Forty Thieves' common line of work, but needs must when the demons drove.

"They've put together a real reserve," Raj said meditatively.

Somebody over there had enough authority to control the honor-obsessed hotheads, and enough sense to keep back a strong force to exploit a breakthrough. Gunsmoke drifted back from the walls in clouds. He wished the walls were higher, now — even with the moat, they weren't much more than ten or fifteen meters in most places. Height mattered, in an escalade attack. He grew conscious of M'lewis waiting.

"I can't send Ludwig out until they've committed their reserve," Raj explained. M'lewis wasn't an educated man, but he was far from stupid. "Twenty thousand held back is too many of them, and too mobile by half. Got to get them locked up in action before we can hit them from behind."

M'lewis sucked at his teeth. "Tricky timin', ser," he said.

Raj nodded. "Five minutes is the difference between a hero and a goat," he agreed.

A runner trotted up and leaned over to hand Raj a dispatch.

Current stronger than anticipated, he read. *Infantry attack will be delayed. Will advance as rapidly as possible with forces in bridgehead. Jorg Menyez, Colonel.*

"How truly good," Raj muttered. He tucked the dispatch into his jacket; the last thing the men needed was to see the supreme commander throwing messages to the ground and stamping on them. "How truly wonderful."

❖   ❖   ❖

"We'll proceed as planned," Jorg Menyez said firmly.

"Sir —" one of the infantry battalion commanders began.

"I know, Major Huarez," Jorg said.

He nodded down towards the river. The last of Huarez' battalion was scrambling out of their boats, but that gave them only six battalions ashore — less than five thousand men. The rest were scattered along the river with the sailors and marines laboring at the oars.

"Commodore Lopeyz," Menyez said. "I'm leaving you in command here. Send the steamboats back for the remainder of the force." Rowing had turned out to be less practical than they'd thought from tests conducted with small groups. Speeds were just too uneven. "Assemble them here. As soon as three-quarters are landed, the remainder is to advance at the double to support me. Emphasize to the officers commanding that no excuses will be accepted."

Translation: *anyone who hangs back goes to the wall.* Of course, if the scheme failed they were all dead anyway, but it didn't hurt to be absolutely clear.

He took a deep breath of the cold dawn air. Off a kilometer or so to the east the walls of Old Residence were hidden, but they could hear the massed rifles and cannon-fire well enough. A hazy cloud was lifting, as if the city were already burning. . . . Below him were what he had. A few thousand infantrymen, second-line troops officially. Peons in uniform, commanded by the failed younger sons of very minor gentry. Ahead was better than four score thousand Brigade warriors.

"Fellow soldiers," he said, pitching his voice to carry. Whatever he said would go back through the ranks. With appropriate distortion, so keep it simple.

"Messer Raj and our comrades need us," he said. "If we get there in time, we win. Follow me."

He turned, and his bannermen and signalers formed

up behind him. Normally company-grade officers and above were mounted, but this time it was everyone on their own poor-man's dogs. "Battalion columns, five abreast," he said. "Double quickstep."

The Brigadero emplacements on the bluff above were ruined and empty, but there would be *somebody* there. Somebody to report.

"Hadelande!" he snapped, and started toward the sound of the guns.

"Follow me!" Raj called.

He touched his heel to Horace's flank. The trumpet sang four brassy notes, and the column broke into a jog-trot; he touched the reins lightly, keeping his dog down to the pace of the dismounted men behind him. The fog of black-powder smoke was thick, like running through heavy mist that smelled of burning sulfur. The wall to his right was almost hidden by it despite the bright sun, towers looming up like islands. The noise was a heavy surf, the continuous crackle of rifle-fire under the booming cannon. A louder *crack* sounded as a forty-kilo cannonball struck the ramparts, blasting loose chunks of stone and pieces of men.

Messengers and ambulances were moving in the cleared zone behind the walls. Now they saw men running, unwounded or nearly so. The fugitives shocked to a halt as they saw the Starburst banner and Raj beneath it; everyone recognized Horace, at least.

"You men had better rejoin your unit," Raj said. They wavered, turned and began scrambling back up the earth mound on the inside of the wall.

Raj opened the case at his saddlebow, calming the restless dog with a word as a shell ripped by overhead to burst among the outermost row of houses behind. Through the binoculars he could see the rough pine-log ends of scaling ladders against the merlons of the wall, and infantrymen desperately trying to push them aside with the points of their bayonets. Any defender whose head was above the stonework for more than a second or two toppled backward; there must be forty or fifty blue-clad bodies lying on the earth ramp, most of them shot through the head or neck. The defenders were pulling the tabs of hand-bombs and pitching them over the side; more showered down from the towers a hundred meters to either side, thrown by hand or from pivot-mounted crossbows.

A dozen more scaling ladders went up, even as smoke and flashes of red light above the parapet showed where the bombs were landing among men packed in the mud of the moat, waiting their turn at the assault.

"Deploy," Raj said. The trumpet sang, and the 5th faced right in a double line, one rank kneeling and the one behind standing. A ratcheting click sounded as they loaded their weapons. "And fix bayonets." It would come to that, today.

"Captain, can those splatguns bear from here?"

"Just, sir," the artilleryman said.

The multi-barreled weapons were fifty meters behind the firing line, itself that distance from the wall. The crews spun the elevating screws until the honey-combed muzzles rose to their limit.

Raj drew his sword and raised it. The bullets that had sent sparks and spalls flying all along the parapet under assault halted as Brigaderos helmets showed over the edge, masking their comrades' supporting fire. The Civil Government soldiers rose themselves, firing straight down; but the first wave of Brigaderos were climbing with their pistols drawn. In a short-range firefight single-shot rifles were no match for revolvers. Smoke hid the combatants as dozens of five-shot cylinders were emptied. Seconds later the unmusical crash of steel on steel sounded as scores of the barbarians swarmed over the parapet, sword against bayonet.

"Wait for it."

One moment the firing platform above was a mass of soldiers in blue uniforms and warriors in steel breastplates, stabbing and shooting point-blank and swinging clubbed rifles. The next it held only Brigaderos, the defenders pitching off the verge and into the soft earth of the ramp below, or retreating into the tower doors. A banner with the double lightning flash of the Brigade waved triumphantly.

"*Fwego!*" His sword chopped down.

BAM. Then *BAM-BAM-BAM-BAM*, crisp platoon volleys running down the line. A long *braaaap* four times repeated from the splatguns.

Time shocked to a halt for a second. There were hundreds of Brigaderos jammed onto the fighting platform of the wall, and most of them did not even know where the bullets that killed them came from. Many were looking the other way, waving on comrades below or hauling up the assault ladders to lower down from the wall. The whole line of them shook, dozens falling out and down to crash with bone-shattering force. Some of the Civil Government soldiers who'd jumped down were still moving, it was soft unpacked earth below on the ramp and a grazing impact, but doing it with thirty kilos of steel on you was another matter altogether.

Half the enemy were still up, even with the splatguns punching four-meter swaths through the packed ranks. A few had time to fire revolvers or begin the cumbersome drill of loading their rifle-muskets — both about as futile as spitting, but he admired the spirit — before the next rattle of volleys hit them. The splatguns traversed, snapping out their loads with mechanical precision.

"Cease fire," Raj said. "Marksmen only."

Silence fell as the trumpet snarled; the best shots in each squad stepped forward a pace and began a slow crackle of independent fire at anyone unwise enough to climb the ladders and show his head over the parapet. The Civil Government troops in the towers at each end of the breach were cheering as they fired and lobbed handbombs. That meant the enemy were giving back from the foot of the wall, although the slamming roar of noise continued elsewhere. And incredibly a few of the infantry who'd tumbled down from the fighting platform were up and forming a firing line at the base of the earth ramp. Raj heeled Horace forward; a young officer was limping down the improvised unit of walking wounded, hustling men with the slack faces of battle-shock into line, slapping them across the shoulders with the flat of his saber. Here was someone who also had the right instincts.

"Lieutenant," Raj said.

He had to repeat the command twice before the young man heard; when he turned his eyes were wide and staring, the iris swallowed in the pupil.

"Cease fire, lieutenant."

"*Ci, mi heneral.*"

"Good work, son." The younger man blinked. "Now get them back up there. Anyone who can shoot."

"Back up, sir?" The lieutenant was shivering a little with reaction. He looked at the earth ramp above, littered with enemy bodies, two deep in places. A fair number of bodies in blue-and-maroon uniforms, too. One was crawling down the timber staircase that rose from the flat cleared zone to the ramparts, leaving a glistening trail behind him.

"Back up," Raj said. He scribbled an order on his dispatch-pad and ripped it off. "Get this to your battalion commander."

Telling him to thin his troops out to cover the bare patch; probably unnecessary, but it never hurt to be careful. There were already some riflemen from the towers up above fanning out onto the rampart, firing out at the enemy or pitching bodies down into the moat — the right place for them, let the Brigaderos get an eyeful.

"Hop to it, lad."

A dispatch rider pulled up in a spurt of gravel. "Ser," he said, extending a note from his gauntlet.

Estimate ten thousand mounted enemy reserves moving eastward with artillery, it said. *Remaining ten thousand dismounting and preparing to advance southeast toward wall. Gerrin Staenbridge, Colonel*.

"Well, that's that," Raj muttered. "Verbal acknowledgement, corporal."

Another messenger, this one on foot. "Sir, barbs on the wall, east four towers — Malga Foot's sector. Major Fillipsyn says they'll be over in a minute."

"Lead on," Raj replied.

"Messenger," he went on, as the command group rode back toward the 5th's waiting ranks. "To Major Bellamy. *Now*."

The enemy had ten thousand men in reserve to exploit a breakthrough. He had six hundred-odd to plug the holes.

"Battalions to form square," Jorg Menyez said.

The trumpeters were panting, like all the rest of them — they'd come better than a kilometer at the double quickstep, all the way up from the riverbank, over the railway embankment, looping north and west until they were almost in sight of the eastern gate of Old Residence. They still managed the complex call, repeating it until all the other units had acknowledged. A final prolonged single note meant *execute*.

The 17th Kelden Foot were in the lead; they swung from battalion column to line like an opening fan. So did the 55th Santander Rifles at the rear. The units on either side slid like a pack of cards being stacked, the eight-deep column thinning to a much longer column of twos. Five minutes, and what had been a dense clumping of rectangles eight ranks broad and sixty or so long was an expanding box, shaking out until it covered a rectangle three hundred men long on each side. The fifth battalion stayed in the center as reserve.

Here's where we see if they can do it, Menyez thought, his lips compressed in a tight line.

This sort of thing was supposed to be the cavalry's work. Infantry were for holding bases and lines of communication. He'd said often enough that that was wrongheaded; now he had a chance to prove it . . . or die. Worse, the whole Expeditionary Force would die.

He swept his binoculars across the front of the enemy formation, counting banners. The air was very clear, crisp and cool in his lungs, smelling only of damp earth. The city was a pillar of gunsmoke, rising and drifting south. Sparkling, moving steel was much closer, rippling as the enemy rode over the rolling fields, bending as they swung to avoid an olive grove.

"About ten thousand of them, wouldn't you say?" he said to his second in command.

"Eight to twelve," the man replied. "Three regiments of lancers, the rest dragoons and thirteen . . . no, sixteen guns."

"Runner," Menyez said. "To all battalion commanders. Fire by platoons at any enemy fieldpiece preparing to engage at one thousand meters or less."

That was maximum range for the three-kilo bronze smoothbores the enemy used, and well within range for massed fire from Armory rifles. No artillery here to support *him*, curse it. A few rounds of shrapnel were just the thing to take the impetus out of a Brigade lancer's charge.

"For the rest, standard drill as per *receive cavalry*."

"Los h'esti adala cwik," his second said as the messenger trotted off: *they're in a hurry.* The Brigaderos were coming on at a round trot, and it looked as if the dragoons intended to get quite close before dismounting.

"Ask me for anything but time, as Messer Raj says," Menyez said, clearing his throat.

That was one good thing about an infantry battle. He drew a deep breath, free of wheezes for once. At least there weren't any *dogs* around, not close enough to affect him.

"They'll probably come at a corner first," he went on. That was the most vulnerable part of an infantry square, where the smallest number of rifles could be brought to bear. "They *do* seem to be in a bit of a rush."

Private Minatelli wasn't aware of hearing the trumpet. Nevertheless, his feet were ready for the order when it was relayed down to his platoon; *prone and kneeling.*

The men ahead of him flopped down, angling their bodies like a herringbone comb. He went down on his left knee, conscious of the cold damp earth soaking through the wool fabric of his uniform trousers. This had been a vineyard until someone grubbed up the vines for firewood, and shattered stumps of root still poked out of the stony loam amid the weeds. Now that they were halted he could hear the battle along the city walls, the boom and rattle of it muffled by distance and underlain by a surf-roar of voices.

His own personal Brigaderos were much closer. Hidden by a fold in the ground, but he could see the lancepoints. There looked to be an almighty lot of them. . . .

Omniscient Spirit of Man, he thought as they came over the crest of the rise like a tidal wave. There were *thousands* of them, big men in armor on huge Newfoundlands and St. Bernards. Pounding along in perfect alignment with lances raised, three ranks deep, heading straight for the front right corner of the square. Right at *him.* Fifteen hundred meters away and still far too close, and getting closer every second. His arms seemed to raise his rifle of their own volition, and it took an effort that left his hands shaking to snap it back down to rest on the ground.

"Set sights for four hundred meters."

The order went down the ranks. Minatelli snapped the stepped ramp forward under the rear sight with his thumb, lifting the leaf notch to the second-to-last position; for more than that, it had to be raised vertically and used as a ladder-sight. Four hundred meters still seemed awfully close.

"Fire on the command."

Feet tramped behind him. He looked back for a moment; two companies of the reserve battalion were lining up across the V-angle of the square's corner. Minatelli hoped none of them would fire too low — even standing, the muzzles would be only a half-meter over his head. When he turned his head back the Brigaderos were close enough to turn his mouth even drier. Picking up speed; they were going to start their gallop at extreme rifle range, get through the killing zone as quickly as they could. He could hear the drumbeat sound of the massed paws, feel it vibrating through the ground. The armor was polished blazing-bright, hurting his eyes under the early morning sunlight. Banners and helmet-plumes streamed with the wind of the riders' speed; the long lanceheads glittered as they swung down into position.

"UPYARZ!"

"Wait for it."

The officer sounded inhumanly calm; Minatelli took a long breath and let it out slowly. If he missed, that was one more sauroid-sticker coming at *him*. Another breath.

"Aim."

The rifle came up and the butt snuggled into his shoulder. Let the weight of the bayonet drop it a little, aim at the dog's knees. Ignore the open snarling mouths.

"Fire!"

BAM. A hammer thudding into his shoulder. And *crack* as hundreds of bullets went over his head. Reload. The deadly beauty of the lancers' charge was shredding, dogs falling and men flying in bone-shattering arcs. *BAM* and more of them were down. Adjust the sights. *BAM*. Charge coming forward in blocks and chunks, piling up where galloping dogs didn't have enough time to avoid the dead and wounded — heavy dogs with an armored man on their backs weren't all that nimble. *BAM* and the Brigade standard was down, and a lancer dropped his weapon and bent far over to snatch it off the ground. *BAM* and his body smashed back over the cantle of his saddle; a couple of dozen infantrymens' eyes must have been caught by the movement.

Thank the *Spirit* for a stiff breeze to carry off the powder-smoke, otherwise he'd be firing blind into a fogbank by now.

BAM. The metal of the chamber was hot against the callus on his thumb as he pushed home another round. The kick was worse, the rifle hit you harder when the barrel began to foul. Dogs snarling, a sound like all the fear in the world, fangs as long as daggers coming closer to his face. Lancepoints very close . . .

BAM. BAM. BAM.

"Back and wait for it!" the company commander barked.

Spirit damn it, where are Jorg and Ludwig? Raj thought.

Up the street, the Brigaderos paused as they saw the improvised barricade of overturned wagons and tables. They were a mixed group, dismounted lancers and dragoons . . . Then an officer shouted and they came pounding down the pavement with their rifle-muskets leveled. Probably planning to reserve fire until the last minute. Not a good decision, but there weren't any in their situation.

Nor in his, now that the enemy were over the walls.

"Pick your targets, make it count," the captain said. Rifles bristled over the barricade. "Now!"

The volley slammed out, the noise echoing back from the shuttered buildings on either side. At less than a hundred meters, with the Brigaderos crammed into a street only wide enough for two wagons to pass, nearly every bullet hit home. Men fell, punched off their feet by the heavy bullets. The survivors paused to return fire, hiding the chaos at the head of their column with a mantle of powder-smoke. Into it fired the splatguns in the buildings on either side of the barricade, taking the whole length of the street back to the cleared circuit inside the walls in a murderous X of enfilade fire. The *braaaap* sounded again and again.

Damned if I like those things, Raj thought as the smoke lifted a little. The head of the roadway was covered in bodies, many still moving. The splatguns were certainly effective, but they made the whole business too mechanical for his taste.

you need not worry. Center's voice held a cold irony. **if you fail here, men will hunt each other with chipped flint before the next upward cycle begins.**

Did I say I wouldn't use them? he thought.

"That's that for the moment," he went on aloud. "They'll be back soon."

He ducked into the commandeered house they were using as forward HQ. His spurs rang on the oak boards as he climbed the stairs to the second story.

"Still not spreadin' out, ser," the Master Sergeant there said, pointing without lowering his binoculars.

Raj levelled his own glasses through the window. The Brigaderos were over the wall in three places, and the numbers were enough to make his belly clench. The defenders in the towers were still holding out, keeping up their fire on the enemy-held sections of the wall. Despite that more and more of the barbarians were coming over, and they'd dropped knotted ropes and ladders down to the earth ramp backing the wall. The only good news was that they didn't seem to know what to do once they got down. Most of them were milling around, returning fire at the towers. A thousand or so were pushing directly in at the houses where the 5th had taken refuge, standing and exchanging fire with the riflemen hidden in door and window and garden wall.

They were probably a mix-and-mash from dozens of units, he decided, and no senior officers had made it over the defenses yet. Plenty of aggression — you'd expect that from men who'd kept on coming through the killing zone and the moat and the wall — but nobody directing them.

That changed as he watched. A new banner went up on the wall, and he could hear the roar from the Brigaderos. A running wardog, red on black, over a silver W. Teodore Welf's blazon.

What they should *be doing is enlarging their breach and taking the gate from the rear,* he thought. Once they had a gate, the city was doomed. *Welf's clever. On the other hand, he's also young. . . .*

"Get my personal banner," he snapped over his shoulder. He reached around to take the staff, then blinked as he saw it was Suzette handing it to him.

"I put the bannerman on the firing line," she said.

The carbine slung from her shoulder clacked on the polished wood of the staff. Raj swallowed and nodded, before he braced the pole out the forward window of the parlor and shook the heavy silk free. It slithered and hissed, snapping in the wind and chiming — a flying sauroid picked out in gold scales on the scarlet silk, with a silver Starburst behind it all.

The stiff breeze swung it back and forth, then streamed it out sideways. Raj ducked down and pulled Suzette with him as bullets pocked the limestone ashlars around the window.

"I don't think the Whitehalls are all that popular around here," he said.

"Provincials," Suzette replied, rounding out her vowels with a crisp East Residence tone. "What can one expect?

"I'm a monkey from the wilds myself," Raj answered her grin, pushing away the knowledge of what the heavy bone-smasher bullets from the enemy rifle-muskets could do to a human body. Hers, for example.

Instead he duckwalked below the line of the windows to one in the corner and looked out. The amorphous mob of the Brigade vanguard was turning into something like a formation. Welf's banner was down among them now, and he and his sworn men — probably a cross between a warband and a real staff — were pushing the remnants and individual survivors of the storming party and the 5th's greeting into line and behind what cover there was, even if only the heaped bodies scattered in clumps across the broad C-shaped arc of the cleared zone they held. As soon as that was done they started forward . . . right towards his HQ.

Perils of a reputation, he thought dryly. Teodore had a personal mad on with him; also he was probably apprehensive about leaving Raj in his rear.

"Runner," he said sharply. "Compliments to Captain Heronimo, and shift all splatguns to the front immediately." Suzette handed him a glass and sank down beside him, back to the wall; he drank the water thirstily.

"Young Teodore is a clever lad," he said absently. The fire directed at the houses was thickening up, growing more regular. "But he's making a mistake. He should leave a blocking force and peel back more of the wall, go for the gates."

Suzette touched him lightly on the knee. "Can we stop them?"

"Not for long," he said. "Not for very long at all."

❖   ❖   ❖

"Your Mightiness," the courier said, as he spat the reins out of his teeth.

One hand held a pistol, the other a folded dispatch. His dog stood with trembling legs, head down and washcloth-sized tongue lolling as it panted.

"Report," Ingreid Manfrond said. Howyrd Carstens took the paper.

"Lord of Men," the dispatch rider said, "High Brigadier Asmoto reports we couldn't break their square — it's advancing, slowly. More infantry coming up from the river, marching in square, about as many again but strung out in half a dozen clumps. The High Brigadier requests more troops."

"No!" Manfrond roared. "Tell him to *stop them*. They're only foot soldiers, by the Spirit. Go!"

The man blinked at him out of a dirt-splashed face and hauled his dog's head around, thumping his spurred heels into its ribs. The beast gave a long whine and shambled into a trot.

Another rider galloped up and reined in, his mount sinking down on its haunches to break. "Lord of Men," he said. "From Hereditary Colonel Fleker, at the eastern gate. Sally."

"How many?" Manfrond barked.

"Still coming out, Your Mightiness. Thousands, mounted troops only — and guns, lots of guns. They punched right through us."

The Brigade's ruler sank back in the saddle, grunting as if belly-punched. Beside him Howyrd Carstens unlimbered his telescope and peered to the southeast. They were on a rise a kilometer north of the point where the assault had carried the defenses; the action over to the west was mostly hidden except for the rising palls of powder-smoke, but they could see the northeast corner of the city walls.

"I *told* you the wall was too fucking easy," he rasped. "Here they come, guns and all."

Ingreid snatched the instrument, twisting the focus

with an intensity that dimpled the thin brass under his thick-fingered grip. The first thing he saw was Brigade troops scattering, a thin screen of mounted dragoons. Some of them were firing backward with their revolvers. Then the head of a column of enemy troops came into view, loping along in perfect alignment at a slow gallop. A half-regiment or so came into view — a battalion, they called it — and then a battery of four guns, then more troops . . .

"Get the message off to Teodore to withdraw now," Carstens said. "I'll get the flank organized."

"Withdraw?" The telescope crumpled in his hands, and the weathered red of his face went purple. "Withdraw, when we've *won*?"

"Won *what*?" Carstens roared. "We've got our forces split three ways, thousands of them on the other side of the bloody *wall*, no gate, and eight thousand of the enemy coming out to corn-cob us while we look the other way!"

"Shut up or I'll have you cut down where you stand!" Ingreid roared. "Get down there and hold them off while Welf finishes Whitehall."

Carstens stared at him incredulously, then looked down the hill. The bulk of the Brigade force — sixty or seventy thousand men — was jammed up against the face of the Old Residence northern wall, what he could see of it through the smoke. Most of the men were firing at the walls and the towers, the ones who weren't dying in the moat. Artillery ripped at them, and thousands of rifles. A section of the wall a thousand meters long was quiet, in Brigade hands . . . except that the towers were still mostly holding out. The north gate was a colossal scrimmage, the moat *full* of bodies. He looked over at the enemy force. Already cutting in west, their lead element was north of the main Brigade force under the walls. Carstens could play through what happened next without even trying; the guns — must be fifty of them — pulling

into line and the Civvie cavalry curving in like a
scythe.

"Get Teodore out of there, you fool," he said. "I'll try
and slow down the retreat."

"UPYARZ!"

Raj rose and shot the Brigadero in the face. He
toppled backward off the ladder, but the one below
him raised his musket one-handed through the window, poking up from below the frame. Raj felt time
freeze as he struggled to turn the weapon in his left
hand around. He could see the barbarian's finger
tightening on the trigger, when something burned
along the ribs on his right side. Suzette's carbine, firing
from so close behind him that the powder scorched his
jacket.

The Brigadero screamed; his convulsive recoil sent
the bullet wild, *whtaanngg* off the hard stone of the
wall. Suzette stepped forward, her face calm and set.
She leaned out and fired six times, pumping the lever
of the repeating carbine with smooth economy. Behind
her the Master Sergeant was pulling the friction-fuse
tab on a handbomb; he shouldered her aside without
ceremony as the last shot blasted the helmet off a
dragoon climbing up toward the Whitehall banner.
The bomb arched down and exploded at the base of
the ladder. Men screamed, but the heavy timbers
remained, braced well out from the wall. Raj and the
noncom set the points of their sabers against the
uprights and heaved with a shout of effort. Steel sank
into wood, and the ladder tilted sideways with a
gathering rush.

"Stairs!" someone shouted.

Raj left Suzette thumbing rounds into the tube
magazine of her Colonial weapon and led a rush to the
head of the stairs. There were three rounds left in his
revolver; Center's aiming-grid slid down over his
vision, and he killed the first three men to burst up the

stairwell. The fourth stumbled over their bodies because he refused to release the rifle-musket in his hands. Raj kicked him in the face with a full-force swing of his leg. Bones crumpled under the toe of his riding boot, feeling and sounding like kicking in thin slats in a wooden box. The man after that swung a basket-hilted sword at Raj's knees. Raj hopped over it, stamped on the barbarian's wrist as he landed, and thrust down between neck and collarbone. Muscle clamped on the blade, almost dragging it from his hand; then half a dozen troopers were shooting down the stairway on either side of him, or thrusting with their long bayonets.

"Watch where yer shootin', fer fuck's soik!" a Descotter voice shouted up to them.

Muzzle-flash showed crimson in the murk from below, and the flat crash of steel on steel sounded for an instant.

"Watch who ye lets in t'fuckin' door, ye hoor's son," the Master Sergeant shouted back.

Raj dragged breath back into his lungs; powder-smoke lay in wisps through the shattered furniture of the parlor. *We're not going to stop the next one,* he thought with sudden cold clarity.

"Raj." Suzette's voice was raised just enough to cut through the background roar. "Who are those men?"

He stepped to the side window. Just visible to the left — the west — were troops marching down the cleared zone behind the walls. They wore Civil Government uniforms, but there *weren't* any troops in that direction except the infantry holding the north wall, who had all they could cope with and more right now. And none of the Regulars in his command marched that sloppily. They weren't marching at all, not double-timing, they were *running.* Running like men fleeing a battle, except that they were running straight into one.

Raj was fairly sure Teodore Welf was still alive, from

the speed of the reaction. A block of Brigaderos peeled off from the stream coming over the wall and swung out to confront the —

Militia, Raj realized. *It's the local militia.*

The confused-looking group halted and gave fire; too ragged to be a real volley, a long staccato flurry. The Brigaderos heading for them returned it, but they didn't bother to stop. They charged, while the militiamen fumbled with ramrods and percussion-caps. Raj gave a silent whistle of amazement; the city troops *didn't* disintegrate in panic. Some did, running back along the way they'd come, but most stood to meet the gray-and-black tide. They were going to be slaughtered when it came to hand-to-hand, but they were trying, at least.

"Ser," the Master Sergeant said at his elbow. "Got a bunch've t'locals comin' up behind us, say they wants t'help, loik."

The seamed, scarred face of the noncom looked deeply skeptical.

"Bring them forward, sergeant," Raj said. "By all means. Beggars can't be choosers."

Ludwig Bellamy reined in. "Cease fire!" he shouted, and the trumpets echoed it. The last of the enemy ahead were hoisting reversed weapons, or helmets on the muzzles of their rifles. "Get these men under guard."

Silence fell, comparative silence after the roar he'd grown accustomed to over the last two hours. He waved his bannerman forward, and they rode past the last Brigaderos holdouts within the walls of Old Residence and down the wall toward Messer Raj's command post.

Bellamy looked around. "Spirit of *Man*," he swore.

The carnage around the gate had been bad. Probably more bodies than here. It had taken a fair amount of time to get the way unblocked. But this *looked* every bit as bad; smelled as bad, as far as he could tell through a nose already stunned into oblivion today. The whole two-hundred meter width of cleared ground inside the wall was carpeted with bodies, no matter how far they rode; black-and-gray uniformed Brigaderos dragoons, armored lancers, men in the blue and maroon of the Civil Government. Stretcher-bearers had to step on the dead to get at the wounded, and there were thousands. More bodies hung from the walls, or carpeted the earth ramp where the enemy had tried to retreat when they realized what was happening outside. Occasionally a patch of living Brigaderos sat with their hands behind their heads, or putting field-dressings on their own wounded.

He stopped at a mound of dead gathered more thickly around a banner of a running wardog; the pole still canted up from the earth, but the bodies were two and three deep in a circle around it. Armor rattled.

"Stretcher bearers!" he called sharply, reigning aside. A pair trotted over. "This one's alive."

"Sir. Orders are for our wounded first."

"This is an exception," Ludwig bit out. The man's armor was silver-chased and there had been plumes in his helmet. "Get him to the aide station, *now*." Although from the amount of blood and the number of bullet holes, it might be futile.

The three-barred visor was up, and the face inside it was enough like Ludwig Bellamy's that they might have been brothers. It was something far more practical that prompted his action, though. If that was Teodore Welf, he had two presents for Messer Raj today.

He swore again when they finally pulled up in front of the forward HQ building. The stone facing looked as if it had been *chewed*. Men were sitting in the windows, or leaning against the walls, looking a little lost. Another stood in the main entranceway. A tall man, his face black as a Zanjian's with powder-smoke. Suzette Whitehall stood beside him with her arm around his waist.

Ludwig Bellamy drew rein and saluted. "*Mi heneral*," he said.

Raj grinned, a ghastly expression in the sooty expanse of his face. When he removed his helmet, there was a lighter streak along the upper part of his forehead.

"Took you long enough," he said.

Bellamy motioned a man forward; he dismounted and laid a flag at Raj's feet. "It's the flag of Howyrd Carstens, Grand Constable of the Brigade," he said. "We would have brought the head, but . . . " Ludwig shrugged. A 75mm shell had landed close enough to Carstens that there really wasn't much left besides the signet ring they'd identified him with.

CHAPTER THIRTEEN

"It seems a good deal of trouble to go to, to hang me healthy," Teodore Welf said; his voice was low, because it hurt to breathe deeply.

He was sitting propped up in the big four-poster bed, swathed in bandages from neck to waist, one arm immobilized in splints. A priest-doctor in the ear-to-ear tonsure of a Spirit of Man of This Earth cleric stood by the bedside, glaring at Raj and Suzette and the Companions; he was of the Brigade nobleman's own household, allowed in during the after-battle truce. It was a cold spring night, and rain beat at the diamond-pane windows, but a kerosine lamp and a cheerful fire kept the bedroom warm. The flames lit the inlaid furniture and tapestries; also the hard faces of the fighting men behind Raj.

"I'm a thrifty man," Raj said, in Namerique almost as good as Teodore's Sponglish. "I've no intention of hanging you, or anything else unpleasant."

"Excellent, your excellency: I've had a surfeit of unpleasantness just lately," the young nobleman said. "Did you take Howyrd, too?"

"The Grand Constable? I'm afraid he died holding the rearguard."

Welf sighed. "Spirit have mercy on the Brigade," he said.

"I doubt that the Spirit will, just now, since the Spirit has tasked me with reuniting civilization and you're trying to stop me," Raj said.

The young Brigade noble looked at him; his eyes went a little wider when he saw the flat sincerity in Raj's.

"Particularly since the Spirit has given you Ingreid Manfrond for a ruler," Raj concluded.

Teodore was a young man, and still shaken by the wounds and the drugs the surgeons had given him. His agreement almost slipped out.

Raj nodded. "We'll talk more when you're feeling better," he said, and raised a brow at the priest.

The cleric bowed his head grudgingly. "Lord Welf will live," he said. "Fractured ribs, broken arm and collarbone, and tissue damage. Much blood loss, but he will walk in a month. The arm, longer."

A servant came in with a tray bearing tea and a steaming bowl of broth, dodging with a squeak as she met the high-ranking party going out through the same entranceway. Nothing spilled on the tray despite her skittering sideways, a feat which required considerable dexterity and some risk of dumping the hot liquids on her own head. Raj absently nodded approval as they tramped down the corridor. It wasn't far to his own quarters; Teodore Welf was one ace he intended to keep quite close to his chest.

"I suppose you've got some use for him?" Gerrin Staenbridge said, as they seated themselves around the table. Orderlies set out a cold meal and withdrew. "Apart from making sure that Ingreid doesn't have the use of him, that is."

Raj nodded. "Any number of uses. For one thing, while he's here he can't replace Manfrond — which would be a very bad bargain for us."

Staenbridge laughed, then winced; there was a bandage around his own head. "I imagine he's not too charitably inclined toward the Lord of Men right now," he said. "About as much we were toward our good Colonel Osterville down in the Southern Territories."

Kaltin Gruder drew the edge of his palm across his neck with an appropriate sound. Gerrin nodded.

"I might have *done* that, if we'd had a war down

there after you left," he said to Raj. "He'd have gotten us all killed."

Raj nodded. "Young Teodore probably does feel like that," he said judiciously. "Something we can make use of later, perhaps. Now, to business."

Jorg Menyez opened a file. "Ten percent casualties. Fifteen if you count wounded who'll be unfit-for-service for a month or more. Unevenly distributed, of course — some of the infantry battalions that held the north wall are down to company size or less."

"The 5th's got five hundred effectives," Staenbridge said grimly.

Raj nodded thoughtfully. "Ingreid lost . . . at least twenty-five thousand," he said.

"Plus five thousand prisoners," Ludwig interjected, around a mouthful of sandwich. "From their rear-guard, mostly — they fought long enough to let the rest get back to their camps, but we had them surrounded by then. None of them surrendered until Carstens died, by the way."

"All of which leaves us with about seventeen thousand effectives, and Ingreid with nearly sixty thousand," Raj said. If the Brigade hadn't had fortified camps to retreat to he would have pursued in the hope of harrying them into rout. He certainly wasn't going to throw away a victory by assaulting their earthworks and palisades.

"Still long odds, but their morale can't be very good. What I propose —"

A challenge and response came from the guards outside the door, and then a knock. Raj looked up in surprise.

"Message from Colonel Clerett, *mi heneral*," the lieutenant in charge of the guard detail said.

"Well, bring it in," Raj said. He'd left standing instructions to have anything from Cabot Clerett brought to him at once.

"Ah —" the young officer cleared his throat. "It's addressed to Messa Whitehall."

"Well, then give it to *her*," Raj said calmly. He kept his face under careful control; there was no point in frightening the lieutenant.

The younger man handed the letter to Raj's wife with a bow and left with thankful speed. Suzette turned the square of heavy paper over in her fingers, raising one slim brow. It was a standard dispatch envelope, sealed by folding and winding a thread around two metal studs set in the paper, then dropping hot wax on the junction and stamping it with the sender's seal. Silently she dropped it to the table, put one finger on it and slid it over the mahogany toward Raj.

A bleak smile lit his face as he drew his dagger and flicked the thin edge of Al Kebir steel under the wax. The paper crackled as he opened it. There was nothing relevant in the first paragraphs . . . the others looked up at his grunt of interest.

"Our dashing Cabot fought an action outside Lis Plumhas," he said. A sketch-map accompanied the description. "He's got the four thousand cavalry with him, and twenty-seven guns. Met about ten thousand of the Brigaderos, and thrashed them soundly."

Nice job of work, he thought critically. Got them attacking with a feigned retreat — barbs usually fell for that — and then rolled them up when they stalled against his gun line. *Our boy has been to school.*

"What!"

The roar of anger brought the others bolt upright in surprise; Raj was normally a calm man. His fist crashed down, making the cutlery dance and jingle.

"The little *fastardo*! The clot-brained, arrogant, purblind little *snot*!" Raj's voice choked off; there were no words adequate for his feelings.

Suzette's fingers touched his wrist; the contact was like cool water on the red-hot heat of his anger. He drew a deep breath and continued reading, lips pulled tight over his teeth.

"Our good Colonel Clerett," he said at last, throwing down the paper — Suzette scooped it up and tucked it into a file of her papers — "has decided that it's pointless to join us here. Instead he's going to head straight southwest across the Brigade heartland, wasting the land, and head for Carson Barracks to draw off Ingreid's main force and free up the situation."

The shocked silence held for a full minute. Then Gerrin Staenbridge spoke: "You know, *mi heneral*, that might just work."

Raj gulped water and spoke, his voice hoarse. "It might work if *I* was leading the detachment. I might've told *you* to do that if *you* were leading it. Cabot Clerett —"

observe, Center said.

Reality faded, to be replaced by a battlefield. He had an overhead view, of three hills held by ragged squares of Civil Government soldiers. Columns of smoke rose from each, as rifles and cannon fired down into a surging mass of Brigaderos that lapped around like water around crumbling sandcastles. As he watched the wave surged up over one of the squares, and the neat linear formation dissolved into a melee. That lasted less than a minute before nobody but the barbarians was left alive on the hilltop. Those men turned and slid down the slope in a charge like an avalanche to join the assault on the next formation.

A flick, and he saw Cabot Clerett standing next to his bannerman. A dozen or so men were still on their feet around him. Cabot's face was contorted in a snarl that would have done credit to a carnosauroid. He lunged forward and drove the point of his saber through a barbarian's chest. Six inches of metal poked out through the back of the Brigadero's leather coat. The blade was expertly held, flat parallel to the ground so that it wouldn't stick in the ribs. It still took a moment to withdraw, and a broadsword came down on his wrist. The sword was sharp and heavy, with a strong man behind it. The young noble's hand sprang free; he pivoted screaming, with arterial blood spouting a meter high from the stump. The bannerman behind him drove the ornamental bronze spike on the head of the staff into the chest of the swordsman who'd killed Clerett, then went down under a dozen blades. The Starburst trailed in blood and dirt as it fell.

probability 57% +/-10, Center went on dispassionately.

Raj blinked back to reality, feeling the others staring at him.

"Well," he said calmly, "the way I figure it, there's about an even chance or a little more he'll get himself killed and his force wiped out."

Kaltin filled his wineglass. "You've taken the odd risk yourself, now and then," he pointed out.

Raj shrugged, loosening the tense muscles of his shoulders. "Only when it's justified. We don't *need* to take risks now. With those four thousand men, I can wrap this war up in a year or two. The Western Territories have waited six hundred years for the reconquest, a year won't make any difference."

Kaltin's right, he thought. *A couple of years ago I'd have done the same thing myself.* For a moment he felt Center's icy presence at the back of his mind, wordless.

"Anyway," Ludwig said thoughtfully, "they'll have to detach a pretty big force to deal with Cabot. That should give us an opportunity."

"Expensive if it costs four thousand of the Civil Government's elite troops," Raj said. He shrugged. "Let's deal with the situation as it is. Bartin, bring the map easel over here, would you?"

"Most Excellent mistress, there's been a terrible disaster!"

Marie looked up from the pile of samples the merchant was showing her.

"News from the front?" she said tonelessly.

The steward shook his head and continued in his Spanjol-accented Namerique. "No, the main graineries down by the canal, mistress."

He wrung his hands; Marie stood and swept out of the room, up the grand curving staircase to the rooftop terrace. It was a clear spring night in Carson Barracks, smelling as usual faintly of swamp. Some previous General had bought an astronomical telescope. Marie had ordered it brought out of storage and set up here, on the highest spot in the city; she wasn't allowed out of the palace much, but she could *see* the whole town. When she put her eye to the lense the squat round towers of the grain storage leapt out at her. Smoke was billowing out of their conical rooftops, red-lit by the flames underneath. The warehouses were stone block, but the framing and interior partitions and roofs were timber . . . and grain itself will burn in a hot enough flame.

One of the towers disintegrated in a globe of orange fire that swelled up a hundred meters above the rooftops. Burning debris rained down on the surrounding district, and on the barges and rail-cars in the basins and switching-yards near the end of the causeway.

Flour will not only burn: when mixed with air, as in a half-empty bulk storage bin, it is a fairly effective explosive.

"Manhwel," she said crisply to the steward, standing and drawing her shawl about her bare shoulders against the slight damp chill. The ladies-in-waiting were twittering and pointing about her. "Send all the Palace staff but the most essential down to help fight the flames."

"At once, Most Excellent Mistress," he said.

"The rest of you, back to your work. Don't stand there gaping like peasants."

All of them surged away, except Dolors and Katrini.

And Abdullah, bowing with hand touching brows and lips and heart, a slight smile showing teeth white in his dark beard. He didn't say a word: none was necessary. Thanks to a few gallons of kerosine and a few loyal Welf followers, and the Arab's timing devices, Carson Barracks was now in no state to stand a siege. With harvest four months off, the central provinces around the rail line to Old Residence devastated, and every city short of food as winter stocks dwindled, it would probably be impossible to resupply to any meaningful degree.

"And Manhwel, send my personal condolences immediately to General Manfrond."

There was a fairly good courier service between the capital and the forces in the field. Her lip curled. Good enough for her to learn how that *fool* Ingreid Manfrond was wasting his fighting men. Every second family in the Brigade was in mourning for a father, a son, a husband. With Teodore prisoner and Howyrd Carstens dead, he'd be even worse.

We cannot win this war, she told herself. *And if Manfrond remains General, he will destroy the Brigade trying to.*

The flames were mounting higher, and the red glow was beginning to spread as timbers from the explosion caught elsewhere, for thousands of meters around. Bells clanged and ox-horn trumpets hooted, but Carson Barracks was a city of women and old men and servants now.

Ingreid Manfrond must go . . . and there would be revenge for her mother and for the House of Welf. The servant shivered as he watched her smile.

She motioned Abdullah closer as the steward left. The guards at the corners of the terrace were well out of earshot.

"I suppose you'll be reporting as well," she said. He shrugged expressively. "Those devices you showed us worked well."

"They are of proven worth, my lady," he murmured, bowing again.

"Everything I've done has been my own decision," Marie said after a moment, looking at his bland expression. "Why do I get this feeling that you're behind it?"

"I merely offer advice, my lady," he said.

"We're like children to you, aren't we?" she said slowly.

He must be conscious that the guards would hack him in pieces at her word, but there was a cat's ease in the way he spread his hands.

"There is much to be said for the energy of youth, Lady Welf," he said.

"Send my regards to Teodore," she went on. "Tell him I was right about Manfrond."

"He's definitely pulling out," Raj said.

The windows of the conference room were open to the mild spring day; the air smelled fresh and surprisingly clean for a city. Buds showed on the trees around the main plaza — those that hadn't been cut for firewood during the siege — and a fresh breeze ruffled the broad estuary of the White River, past the rooftops of the city. A three-master was standing downstream, sails shining in billowing curves of white canvas as she heeled and struck wings of foam from her bows. Pillars of smoke marked the Brigade camps on the distant southern shore, where excess supplies and gun-rafts burned.

"Cautiously," Jorg Menyez said. "The troops on the south shore are guarding his line of retreat southwest of here, along the rail line." He traced a finger on the map. "And north of the city he's withdrawing from the eastern encampments first."

Kaltin Gruder rubbed the scarred side of his face. "We could try and snap up moving columns," he said.

Raj shook his head. "No, we want to speed the

parting guest," he said. "From the latest dispatches, Clerett is ripping through everything ahead of him."

A few of the Companions looked embarrassed; the dispatches were all addressed to Lady Whitehall.

Raj cleared his throat. "I'd say our good friend Ingreid 'Blind Bull' Manfrond isn't retreating, to his way of thinking — he's charging in another direction. Right back toward his home pasture at Carson Barracks, against an opponent he thinks he can get at in the open field."

And very well may, if Center's right, Raj thought. It was so tempting . . .

"You plan to let him withdraw scot-free?" Tejan M'Brust looked unhappy, his narrow dark face bent over the map, tapping at choke-points along the Brigade's probable line of retreat.

"Did I say that?" Raj replied, with a carnosaur grin. "Did I? Commodore Lopeyz, here's what I want you to do . . . "

They're holding hard, Raj thought.

The terrain narrowed down here, a sloping wedge where the railway embankment cut through a ridge and down to the river. A kilometer on either side of him hills rose, not very high but rugged, loess soil over rock. Trees covered them, native whipstick with red and yellow spring foliage, oaks and beeches in tender green like the flower-starred grass beneath. The air smelled intensely fresh, beneath the sulfur stink of gunpowder.

Just then the battery to his left cut loose; some of the aides and messengers around him had to quiet their dogs. Horace ignored the sound with a veteran's stolid indifference; in fact, he tried to sit down again.

"Up, you son of a bitch," Raj said, with a warning pressure on the bridle.

Three shells burst over the Brigaderos line ahead of him, two thousand meters away. They were three deep across the open space, with blocks of mounted troops in support and a huge mob of dogs on leading lines further back, their own mounts. He trained his binoculars; the forward line of the enemy fired — by troops, about ninety men at a time — turned, and walked through the ranks behind them. Fifty paces back they halted and began to reload, while the rank revealed by their countermarch fired in turn and then did the same. His own men were in a thinner two-rank formation about a thousand yards closer, giving independent fire from prone-and-kneeling and advancing by companies as the barbarians retreated. It gave their formation a saw-toothed look; once or twice the mounted lancers behind the dragoons had tried to charge, but the guns broke them up.

The enemy were suffering badly, paying for their stubborn courage. Neither side's weapons were very accurate at a thousand meters, but the Civil Government troops didn't have to stand upright and stock-still to reload. Still, a steady trickle of wounded came back, born by stretcher-bearers and then transferred to dog-drawn ambulances. Their moaning could be heard occasionally, from the road that wound by the hillock he'd selected to oversee this phase.

Cost of doing business, he told himself. He'd not have paid this sort of butcher's bill just to hustle the enemy on their way, though.

More firing came from the wooded hills on either side, an irregular crackling rather than the slamming volleys of open-field combat. That was bad country, tangled gullies overgrown with brush, steep hillsides and fallen timber. Jorg's infantry were pressing forward on either flank, but it was slow work. Up close and personal, as the men put it.

Antin M'Lewis pulled up. "Ser," he said. "Barbs gettin' tight-packed back terwards t'bridge. Them fish-eaters is in position."

Raj nodded. An aide puffed on his cigarette and

walked over to touch it to the paper fuse of a signal rocket; quite a large one, as tall as a small man with its supporting stick. The missile lit with a dragon's hiss and a shower of sparks and smoke that sent the aide skipping back and the dogs to wurfling and sneezing in protest. Their eyes followed it, faces turning up like sauroid chicks in a nest when the mother returned. At a thousand meters height it popped into a ball of lesser streamers, a huge dandelion-fluff that held for a moment and then drifted northward with the breeze, losing definition as it went.

"That's it," Lopeyz said, from the conning tower of the first steamboat. "Slip the cables."

The reddish smoke of the rocket drifted away. A wailing screech from the whistle of his craft echoed back from the bluffs, and the three mortar-boats chuffed into the current. Here the river was tending as much north as west, and the water ran faster. Their converted locomotive engines wheezed and clanged; he looked down between his feet and saw the sweat-gleaming bodies of the black gang as they shoveled the coal into the improvised brick hearths around the firedoors. To his right on the north bank of the river he could hear the firefight going on in the woods, and see the drifting smoke of it. A little further on, and the river narrowed. The banks were black with men and dogs, the rail bridge swarming with them like a moving carpet of ants — he could see that even a kilometer away.

Panic broke out at the sight of the Civil Government riverboats, shouts and screams and a vast formless heaving. The bridge locked solid as men tried to stampede to the south bank and safety. Bullets began to sparkle off the wrought-iron armor of the three boats, some of them punching through the thinner metal of the smokestacks with a distinctive *ptunggg* sound. He swung a metal plate across the opening, leaving only a narrow slit for vision, and shouted down the hatchway.

"Reduce speed to two knots!"

The central channel was deep here, but narrow, and there were sandbanks and snag-heads all around. He looked back; the other two craft were following in line, the black coal-smoke pouring from their stacks and the river frothing in the wake of their paddles. Just then a monstrous *tchunggg* made the interior of the gunboat ring like a bell. Lopeyz clutched for a handhold and looked around.

"Four-kilo shot," his first mate shouted over the engine noise. The helmsman hunched his shoulders and kept his eyes firmly ahead.

Lopeyz nodded. Light field piece firing roundshot, no menace to the gunboats . . . unless they got really lucky and took off a smokestack, in which case the furnaces wouldn't draw and he'd lose steam. The danger was less unpleasant than the thought of how it would foul up the mission. *I have been around Raj Whitehall too long*, he thought.

The earthwork fort holding the north end of the bridge came into view. The sides were gullied with the winter rains and poor maintenance, but it was still occupied, and the enemy had moved heavier guns in. Fortress models throwing forty and sixty-kilo solid shot, which *was* a threat to the gunboats.

"Prepare to engage," he called.

The gunners in the forward part of the hull loaded a round into the mortar, one set for delayed explosion. At the same instant a flash of red showed on the ramparts of the fort. About a second later a plume of water five meters high erupted off the port bow as the cannonball struck.

"Range one thousand. Let go the anchors, engines all stop." Silence struck ears accustomed to the groan and clank of the engine, broken by the sounds of water and of venting steam from the safety valve. There was

an iron clank as a wedge-shaped segment of the deck
armor over the muzzle of the mortar was released and
swung down.

"*Fire!*"

"Spirit," Raj murmured to himself.

POUMF. The field-gun fired again, and the crew
cheered as the shell struck just short of the bridge. It
hammered into ground covered with men and dogs,
gouting up a candle-shape of dirt and body-parts. The
crowding down there was so bad that the empty space
filled at once, pressure from the sides forcing men in
like water into a splash-hole. All along the ridge
overlooking the narrow ledge of floodplain Civil
Government troops stood and fired down into the
dense mass, working their levers with the hysterical
exultation that a defenseless target brings. The bulk of
the enemy were far too closely packed to use their
weapons, even if they had the inclination. More guns
came up; they'd been slowed by the press of surren-
dering men and riderless dogs behind.

The fort by the bridge was broken and burning. So
was the center span of the bridge itself, the wooden
trestle licking up flames that were pale in the bright
midmorning sun. The heads of men and dogs showed
in the water. The swift current swept most of them
downstream, toward the tidal estuary and the waiting
downdraggers. More followed them into the water by
the minute. . . .

"Cease fire!" Raj shouted.

There hadn't been much fight in the Brigaderos
since they realized the bridge was under attack behind
them. A splatgun bounced up, unlimbered and cut
loose down the slope into the enemy. A pocket opened
for a second, where the thirty-five rounds punched in
together.

"Cease fire, Spirit-dammit, sound *cease fire!*" Raj
shouted again.

The bugles sang again and again, and the sound began to relay down the other units. The Civil Government soldiers were packed almost shoulder to shoulder above their opponents as well, and the firing began to die away reluctantly. As the noise died, the movement below did as well. Ten minutes later the cries of the wounded were the loudest sound; he could see thousands of faces turning toward him, toward the Starburst banner amid the guns.

"White parley flag," he said to an aide. "Find an officer. Unconditional surrender, immediately, but I guarantee their lives and personal liberty if nothing else." He had better uses for troops this good than sending them to the mines.

"Well, Ingreid's down to what, fifty thousand by now?" Gerrin Staenbridge said.

"Four thousand dead, four thousand surrendered, from their rearguard — roughly," Bartin Foley said, looking at his notepad.

The commanders were sitting around a trestle table. Below them squads of prisoners were picking over the field, collecting the dead and the weapons under the supervision of Civil Government infantry. Wagonloads of enemy wounded and plunder groaned up the switchback road, and packs of captured dogs. Artillerymen and artisans from Old Residence were swarming over the railway bridge and repairing the damage; the sound of sawing and hammering drifted back along with the endless rushing sound of the river against the stone pilings. Still more prisoners were at work repairing the earthworks of the fort. Even the artillery might be salvageable; those cast-iron and cast-bronze pieces were hard to damage.

Raj swallowed a mouthful of bread and sausage and followed it with water. "Grammeck, how long on the bridge?"

"Ready by tomorrow if we push it," the artilleryman said. "No real structural damage."

Raj nodded. "Kaltin, how many dogs did we capture?"

"More than we can use or feed," the Companion said. "Eight, nine thousand, not counting the ones who're better shot. Why?"

He raised a hand. "All right," he said. The others leaned forward. "As you may have guessed, I don't intend to give Ingreid a free passage home. If he gets behind the fortifications of Carson Barracks, we could be here for years — and it'd be cursed hard to cut off its communications, not with the river so close."

Staenbridge rubbed a hand along his jaw, rasping the blueblack stubble. "An open-field encounter?" he said. "Fifty, fifty-five thousand men . . . chancy."

Raj shook his head and smiled, weighing down the corners of a map with plates and cups. "I've no intention of fighting unless he obliges me by attacking a strong position head-on . . . and I think even the Lord of Men has realized *that's* a mistake."

The others chuckled and watched intently as Raj's finger traced the line of the railway between Old Residence and Carson Barracks, four hundred kilometers to the southwest in the valley of the Padan.

"He has to withdraw along this line . . . well, he *could* march straight to the nearest riverport on the Padan, but that's not what he'll do. This stretch of country along the line of rail is bare and the railway is useless for anything substantial, thanks to Ludwig here." The ex-Squadrone blushed. "He'll have to bring in wagon trains from areas with supplies — and at the worst time of year, too."

"Ah, *bwenyo*," Kaltin Gruder said. "A razziah, eh?"

"Hmmm." Gerrin pursed his lips. "Still, we'd have only six thousand men," he pointed out. "Difficult to coordinate and not much if we *do* have to fight."

"Not nearly enough," Raj agreed. "We'll need eleven

thousand rifles and all the field guns as a minimum. Jorg, we'll take nine battalions of your infantry."

The Kelden County nobleman looked up, blinking in surprise. "My boys can march," he said. "But they're bipeds, *mi heneral.*"

"Not on dogback they aren't," Raj said. "That's why I asked how many dogs we captured." He held up his hands against the storm of protest.

"I know, I know; it takes years to train a cavalryman, he practically has to be born at it. I don't expect them to be able to fight mounted, or maneuver, or switch from mounted to dismounted action quickly — I don't expect them to do anything but stay on the beasts, then get off and form up on foot for infantry action. Mounted infantry, not cavalry."

Jorg Menyez closed his mouth on the protest he had been about to make and sat silent for a second. Then he nodded. "Yes, they can do that," he said.

Raj rapped his knuckles on the rough boards. "Spirit willing and the crick don't rise," he said. "Pick the best, leave the units that got hardest-hit during the assault behind. Put a good solid man in charge, he can recruit up to strength locally. Not likely to be any real fighting around here for the rest of the campaign, anyway.

"We'll divide into three columns," he went on. "Gerrin, Kaltin and Ludwig to command, fifteen guns each. Bare minimum supplies, no tents, no camp followers, no wheeled transports except the ammunition limbers for the guns. Put six hundred rounds of 11mm per man on pack dogs, three days' hardtack, and that's about it."

He drew a straight line on the map along the railway. "That's Ingreid." Three X's, one ahead of the Brigade force and two more on the south and left of it. "That's us. Just enough skirmishing to keep them slowed down."

A big army was a slow army anyway, and if they were forced to deploy, they'd be slower still. Every day cross-country increased their supply problems. Raj stretched out a hand with the fingers splayed, then pulled it back toward himself and clenched them.

"We'll stay close enough together to keep in supporting distance," he said. "Cut off all foragers, and retreat sharpish if a substantial force tries to attack. If Ingreid stops and lunges for us, we can all close up and pick our spot. Either he breaks his teeth on us by attacking entrenchments front-on, or he has to resume marching toward Carson Barracks — in which case we resume harassment. With any luck, by the time he gets to his capital he'll be starving."

"What about their right flank?" Gerrin asked, tracing an arc to the north of the railway line.

"Our good and faithful Colonel Clerett's up there, burning and killing," Raj said. "From the reports, I expect him to reach Carson Barracks long before Ingreid does. Also, I'll put the Skinners on that flank. Juluk will enjoy that."

"Spirit help the civilians," Jorg said. Raj shrugged.

"Fortunes of war — and Skinners consider killing civilians poor sport when they've got Long-Hairs at hand," he said. "When we all get where we're going, we can link up with Clerett, which will give us fifteen or sixteen thousand first-rate troops . . . and Ingreid should be considerably weaker by then. Any questions?"

A murmur of assent. "I want to be moving by tomorrow," he went on. "Here's the disposition of units —"

CHAPTER FOURTEEN

The long gentle ridge above the roadway was covered in peach trees, and the whole orchard was in a froth of pink blossom. The scent was overpoweringly sweet, and rain-dewed blossoms fell to star the shoulders and helmets of the troopers sitting their dogs beneath. Grainfields stretched down to the roadway and rolled away beyond, an occasional clump of trees or a cottage interrupting the waist-high corn or thigh-high wheat. Ploughed fallow was reddish-brown, pastureland intensely green. The sun shone bright yellow-orange in a cloudless sky, with both moons transparent slivers near the horizon. A pterosauroid hovered high overhead, its ten-meter span of wings tiny against the cloudless sky; toothed feathered almost-birds chased insects from bough to bough above the soldiers, chirring at the feast stirred up by the paws of the dogs. Occasionally one would flutter to a stop, cling to bark with feet and the clawed fingers on the leading edge of their wings, and hiss defiance at the men below.

"We look like a bunch of damned groomsmen riding to a wedding," Kaltin Grueder said, brushing flowers off his dog's neck. The officer beside him chuckled.

Half a kilometer to the north and a hundred meters below, a train of wagons creaked slowly eastward. Oxen pulled them, twenty big white-coated beasts to the largest vehicles, land-schooners with their canvas-covered hoops; they ranged from there down to the ordinary humble two-wheeled farm carts pulled by a single pair. Kaltin whistled tunelessly through his teeth as he moved his binoculars from east to west. Most of the people with the convoy were obviously natives, peasants in ragged trousers and smocks. More followed, driving a herd of sheep and slaughter-cattle in the fields beside the road — right through young corn and half-grown winter wheat, too.

There were other men on dogback, though, with lobster-tail helmets and black-and-gray uniforms. Riding in columns of twos on either side of the convoy, and throwing out small patrols. One group of four was riding up the open slope below towards the orchard.

"About two hundred dragoons," he said, and began to give brisk orders. That was just enough to make sure that no band of disgruntled peons jumped the supply train. Not enough to do anything useful today.

A bugle sounded; the Brigaderos scouts hauled frantically on their reins as three hundred men rose to their feet and walked in line abreast out of the orchard. Another two companies trotted down and took up position across the road ahead of the convoy, blocking their path back towards the main Brigade army.

"Now —" Kaltin began, then clicked his tongue.

The Brigade kettledrums whirred. The civilians were taking off straight north through the grainfields; if the commander of the convoy escort had any sense, he'd be doing the same. Instead the barbarians fired a volley from the saddle — not a round of which came anywhere near the Civil Government force, although he could hear bullets clipping through the treetops five meters overhead — drew their swords, and charged.

"More balls than brains," the battalion commander said, and called to a subordinate.

Further back on the ridge, guns crashed. Shells ripped by overhead and hammered up ground before the charging Brigaderos. At four hundred meters the riflemen cut loose with volley fire. Thirty seconds later the survivors of the Brigade charge were galloping frantically in the other direction, or holding up reversed weapons. All but their leader; he came on, sword outstretched. At a hundred meters from the Civil Government line his dog stumbled and went down as if it had tripped, legs broken by shots fired low.

"Let's see what we've got," Kaltin said, touching a heel to his dog's flank.

He rode up to the fallen man. *Boy,* he thought. Only a black down on his pale cheeks; on his hands and knees, fumbling after his sword. Kaltin leaned down and swung the point of his saber in front of the boy's eyes.

"Yield," he said.

Blinking back tears of rage, the young man stood and offered his sword across his forearm.

"I am hereditary Captain Evans Durkman," he said, and flushed crimson when his voice broke in mid-sentence.

Down below the troopers of the 7th Descott were proceeding in businesslike fashion. The oxen were unharnessed and driven upslope with whoops and slapping lariats. Men stood in the wagons to load sacks of cornmeal and beans and dried meat and sausages onto strings of dogs with pack-saddles. An even louder whoop told of a wagon filled with kegs of brandy; there were groans as a noncom rode up and ordered the tops of the barrels smashed in and the pale liquor dumped on all the remaining vehicles. Less than five minutes after the action began, the first brandy-fueled flames licked skyward. A few minutes after that, the whole train was burning. Sullen prisoners smashed their own rifles against the iron tyres of the wagon wheels under the muzzles of the Descotter guns.

"You won't get away with this, you bandit," the extremely young Brigadero growled in passable Spong-lish.

Several of the men around Kaltin chuckled. He smiled himself; not an unkindly expression, but the scars made it into something that forced the younger man to flinch a little beneath his bravado.

"If you mean that force of fifteen hundred men who was going to meet you," he began.

Just then a faint booming came from the northeast, echoing off the low hills. It took the Brigadero a few moments to recognize the sound of a distant cannon-ade, and then he went chalk-white under his pale skin.

"— that's them," Kaltin finished. "Now your boots, young messer."

The other man noticed that the prisoners were barefoot; he surrendered his own grudgingly, watching in puzzlement as the footwear were thrown onto the roaring bonfire that had been a wagon a few minutes before.

"We don't have time or troops to guard you," Kaltin said helpfully to the hangdog group of prisoners. "And I doubt Ingreid has mounts, weapons or footwear to spare — to say nothing of food. So if you've got any sense, you'll all start walking home right now. I'm sure your mother will be reassured to see you, Hereditary Captain Durkman."

He sheathed his sword and gathered up his reins. The Brigadero burst into sputtering Namerique; Kaltin spoke a little of that language, mostly learned from his concubine Mitchi. Judging by the terms for body parts, most of what the youngster was saying was obscenities. Several of his older subordinates grabbed him by the arms. *They* probably understood exactly what the alternative to release was for an inconvenient prisoner, and were surprised they were still alive.

Markman shook them off. "When are you going to

stop hiding and skulking?" he said hotly. "When are you going to come out and give battle like honest men?"

Kaltin grinned as he turned his mount eastward. "We are giving battle," he said over his shoulder. "And we're winning."

He turned and chopped a hand forward. "*Waymanos!*"

"Well, this is something new," Bartin Foley said.

The road was a churned-up mass of mud and dung and dogshit; exactly what you would expect after a major army passed by. The litter of discarded baggage was about what he'd become accustomed to, after the first week. One of the main problems had been preventing the men loading themselves down with non-essential loot. Some of it *had* been fairly tempting — even a silver bathtub, for the Spirit's sake! Masses of servants and thralls and camp followers as well, not just whores but families.

This time it was guns, their barrels glistening under the quick spring rain. The bronze glittered more brightly as the clouds split and watery sunlight broke through. Twenty of the guns were light field-pieces; three were heavier, not quite siege guns but nearly . . . and that must be about all of Ingreid's remaining artillery, counting what had bogged down in fords and fallen off bridges and broken its axles before getting this far.

"They're over here, sir," Lieutenant Torridez said.

The ruts didn't stop at the edge of the road; in fact, it was difficult to say just where the road had been, in the swath of trampled and churned devastation cutting southwest through the fields. Only the line of the railway embankment made it certain. There was a good deal of swamp and forest hereabouts, and drainage channels in the cleared fields. The three hundred Brigaderos squatting with their hands behind their heads were in what had probably been a pasture in better days.

"Found them sitting here," Torridez went on. "Didn't give us any trouble at all."

Foley wrinkled his nose slightly at the smell, and made a mental note to make sure the priests were checking on the mens' drinking water. Dysentery like this was the last thing they needed. The two Civil Government officers pulled up beside an older man; he was wearing back-and-breast armor, although the troops in the field were dragoons. He rose, blinking watery gray eyes at the young man with the hook; his head was egg-bald, and his face had probably been strong before fever and hunger left the skin sagging and ash-colored.

"Colonel Otto Witton," he said hoarsely.

"Captain Bartin Foley," the younger man replied in careful Namerique. "This is your regiment?"

Witton laughed, then coughed wrackingly. "What's left of it," he said. "The ones who didn't bug out last night" He laughed again, then coughed until he retched. "We're the rearguard, officially."

Foley touched his lips with his hook. "Colonel, you *may* be in luck," he said. "I'm sending back an escort with our walking wounded." The Brigadero nodded, as aware as he of the other option. "However, there are a few things I'd like to know . . ."

Witton grunted and spat red-flecked spittle into the mud. "Ask away. A brother and a son I've lost because that pig-ignorant sauroid-fucker Manfrond bungled this war into wreck, and Teodore Amalson's whole legacy with it. Outer Dark, *Forker* might have done better."

"The Spirit of Man is with General Whitehall," Foley said. "Now, what we'd like to know is —"

The sound from the edge of the swamp was nearly half a kilometer away, and still loud enough to stun. The form of it was something halfway between a

gobbling shriek and a falcon's cry, but the volume
turned it into a blur in the background, like the stones
in a watermill. The creature charged before the last
notes died. Its body was seven meters long and it had
the rangy lethality of a bullwhip. Half the length was
tail, and most of the rest of it seemed to be head, split
in a gape large enough to engulf half a man's torso. It
was running on its hind legs, massive yet agile, thick
drumsticks pushing the clawed eagle feet forward
three meters for each bounding birdlike stride. The
forelegs were small by comparison, but they each bore
clawed fingers outstretched toward the prey. Mottled
green scales covered the upper part of its body; the
belly was cream, and the wattles under its throat the
angry crimson of a rooster's comb.

The stink of decay had brought it out of the swamps
where it hunted hadrosauroids. The target was the
three hundred disarmed Brigaderos, and it would plow
into them like a steam-powered saw through soft
wood. A big carnosaur like this would kill until
everything around was dead before it started feeding,
then lie up on the kills until the last shred of rotting
meat was engulfed.

"Dismount, rapid fire, *now!*" Foley shouted, his
voice precise and clear and pitched high to carry.

A hundred men reacted smoothly, only the growling
of anxious dogs making it different from a drill. The
first shot rang out less than twenty seconds later. Foley
could see bullets pocking the mud around its feet,
small splashes amid the piledriver explosions of mud
and water each time the three-toed feet hit the
ground. More were striking the outstretched head, but
a sauroid's brain was smaller than a child's fist, in a
large and very boney skull. Then a lucky shot hit the
shoulder girdle and bounced down the animal's flank.
It was far from a serious wound, but it stung enough to
make the carnosaur think — or to trigger one of the
bundles of hardwired reflexes that passed for thought.

It spun in place, tail swinging around to lever it and jaws snapping shut with a sound like a marble statue dropping on flagstones as it sought the thing that had bitten it. That put it broadside-on to Foley's company, and he could *hear* the bullets striking, a sound like hailstones hitting mud. Most of them would be brass-tipped hardpoint sauroid killers. The beast swung around again and roared, breaking into a fresh charge. Foley clamped his legs around the barrel of his dog and drew his pistol, aware as he did so that he might as well kiss the beast on the snout as shoot it with a handgun. Ten meters from the firing line — a body length — the carnosaur's feet stopped working; one slid out in front of it, the other staying behind instead of moving forward for the next stride. The long head nosed down into the soft dirt, plowing a furrow toward them.

The jet-colored eyes stayed open as the three-ton carnivore slid to a halt barely a meter away. The troopers went on shooting, pumping four or five rounds each into the sauroid; that was experience, not nervousness.

Foley quieted his dog, fighting to control his own breathing. He'd done his share of hunting for duty back home in Descott, although he'd never much enjoyed it. But Descott was too arid to support many big carnivores, the more so as the grazing sauroids had all been shot out long ago. A pack of man-high sicklefeet, of which there were plenty, were just as dangerous. But not nearly so nerve-wracking.

"Sorry for the interruption," he said, turning back to Otto Witton. The Brigadero's hands were still making grasping motions, as if reaching for a nonexistent gun.

"They, ah, they usually don't —"

"— come so near men," Foley finished for him. "Except when we make it safe for them by killing each other off."

Which happened fairly often: one reason why it was

so easy for land to slip back into barbarism. Once a tipping-point of reduced population was reached the native wildlife was impossible to keep down. How anyone could think that the Spirit of Man was of *this* Earth was beyond him, when Man was so obviously unsuited to living here. It probably wasn't the time for a theological controversy, though.

"Thank you," the older man said. He inclined his head toward his men, most of them too exhausted even to run when the carnosaur appeared.

"*Danad,*" Foley said in his native tongue: *it's nothing.*

Witton took a deep breath, coughed, and began: "Ingreid's got about —"

"Ser," Antin M'Lewis said. "'Bout six thousand of 'em, workin' ter ourn left, through thet swamp."

Raj nodded, looking southeast. The main force of the Brigade host had shaken itself out into battle formation, although that had taken most of the morning. The countryside here was almost tabletop flat, planted in grain where it wasn't marsh. There were still an intimidating number of the enemy, stretching in regular blocks from one end of sight to another, but they were advancing very slowly. Noon sun cast back eye-hurting flickers from edged metal and banners, but there was a tattered look to the enemy formations even at this distance.

"Is it my imagination," Gerrin said, focusing his binoculars, "or are they even slower than usual?"

"One-third of them aren't mounted any more," Raj replied.

They both grimaced; scouts had found charred dog-bones in the Brigaderos' campfires, the last couple of days. That was not quite cannibalism, but fairly close for a nobleman bred to the saddle. The enemy might be barbarians, but they were gentlemen of a sort. It probably came no easier to them than it would to either of the Descotters, or to any Messer.

"Well, we've cost them a day," Gerrin said.

"Indeed. Grammeck, stand ready to give them a quick three-round stonk when they get in range, then pull out.

"Jorg." Raj raised his voice slightly; Menyez was on his long-legged riding steer, and the beast liked dogs no better than its master. "Get the infantry back, mounted and moving."

"We'll backpedal?" Staenbridge said.

Raj shook his head. "Take the cavalry, loop over and have a slap at that flanking column," he said. "M'Lewis, you and the Forty Thieves accompany. We'll cover your flank. Don't push unless you take them by surprise; if you do, run them into the marsh."

Gerrin nodded, tapping on his gauntlets and watching the Brigade army. "Maybe it's my classical education," he said, "but don't you get a sort of unfulfilled feeling at winding up a campaign without a grand climactic battle?"

"I certainly think Ingreid would like to go out in a blaze of glory rather than lose to runny guts and no rations," Raj said. "Personally, it's my ambition to set a new standard someday by winning an entire war without ever actually fighting. This one, you'll note, is not over yet."

The five thousand Civil Government troops along the gunline stood, turned and marched smartly to the rear as the trumpets blared. They were not exactly on a ridge, this terrain didn't have anything worthy of the name, but there was a very slight swelling. Enough to hide the fact that they'd mounted and ridden off, rather than just countermarching and ready to reappear as they'd done half a dozen times.

"And it's only another week to Carson Barracks," Raj said.

"Ten days, if Ingreid doesn't speed up," Gerrin replied. "See you at sundown, *mi heneral*."

Raj stood for a moment, looking at the advancing army. *Waste*, he thought. *What a bloody waste.*

He didn't hate Ingreid Manfrond for resisting. Raj Whitehall knew that it was absolutely necessary to reunite Bellevue, but the Brigaderos didn't have his information. You couldn't blame the Brigade's ruler for wanting to defend his people and hang onto his position. It was the man's sheer lack of *workmanship* that offended Raj.

CHAPTER FIFTEEN

"General."

Cabot Clerett's salute was precise. Raj returned the gesture.

"Colonel."

They walked into the tent and sat, waiting silently while the orderly set out watered wine.

"A first-class encampment," Raj said.

It was: right at the edge of the causeway that carried road and railway to Carson Barracks, and hence commanding the canal as well. Clerett had dug the usual pentagonal fort with ditch and bastions, but he'd worked a small Brigadero fort into one wall, making the position very strong. It smelled dismally of swamp and the stingbugs were something fierce, but the men and dogs were neatly encamped, drainage ditches and latrines dug, purifying vats set up for drinking water. He'd made it larger than necessary, too; with some outlying breastworks, it would do for the whole force at a pinch and as long as they didn't have to stay too long.

"However, Ingreid should be here in about a day or so," Raj went on.

Cabot leaned forward. The past few months had fined down his face and added wrinkles to it as well; he looked older than his years now, stronger, more certain of himself.

Not without justification, Raj thought grudgingly. It had been a daredevil campaign, but apart from the recklessness of the concept quite skillfully managed. The man could command.

"And we're between him and his capital!" Clerett said, striking the table with his fist. The clay cups skittered on the rough planks of the trestle, which looked as if they'd been salvaged from some local stable. "We've got him trapped."

"Well, that's one way of looking at it," Raj nodded. "Or you might say that he'll have us between his field army and the garrison of Carson Barracks, who together outnumber us by about five to one."

Clerett's hand clenched on the table. "I consider it absolutely essential," he said, his voice a little higher, "to maintain my force in its present position. If Ingreid gets behind the fortifications of Carson Barracks, he can bring supplies in through the swamp channels, or move troops out — it could take years to complete this conquest if we were to allow that."

"Reconquest," Raj said, sipping some of the sour wine and looking out the open flap of the tent. "It's a reconquest."

The sun was setting over the swamps, red light on the clouds along the horizon, shadow on the tall feathery-topped reeds. The milk-white fronds dipped and billowed across the huge marsh, tinged with blood-crimson. Above them the sky was darkening to purple.

"You consider it *absolutely essential*?" he went on. Clerett nodded curtly, and Raj smiled. "Well, then it's fortunate I agree with you, isn't it, Colonel?"

Clerett nodded again, looking away. He still needed to do that, not experienced enough to hide his expression completely. "I've been in correspondence with Marie Manfrond — Marie Welf, she prefers — since I got here last week," he said neutrally.

"Excellent; so have I. Or rather, so has Lady Whitehall."

"Suz— Lady Whitehall is here?" Clerett asked. His hand tightened on the cup.

"Indeed. So we're aware of the supply situation in

Carson Barracks." *And I hope she's not aware of dissension in our ranks,* Raj added to himself. Maintaining psychological dominance over a proud and intelligent barbarian like Ingreid's unwilling wife was difficult enough.

Clerett cleared his throat. "What about Ingreid? I've got about a week's supplies."

"I've got three days. Ingreid doesn't *have* a supply situation . . . but he's a stubborn fellow, and he may be learning. We wouldn't want to have him move north up the Padan and entrench in Empirhado or one of the riverport towns."

Clerett shook his head. "No more sieges," he agreed.

"Well." Raj stood. "I'd better see to settling the main force," he went on. "If you'd care to join us for luncheon tomorrow, we could settle plans."

There was something pathetic in the way Clerett thanked a man he hated for the invitation.

"I hope you're feeling well," Raj said.

Teodore Welf looked from Raj's face to Suzette's, to the Companions grouped around the table. The Expeditionary Force was digging in outside, and this inn at the head of the causeway had been selected as the praetorium at the center of the encampment.

"Thank you, Excellency," he said. "The dog-litter wasn't too uncomfortable, and the ribs are healing fine. The priests say I can ride now." His arm was still in a cast and strapped to his chest, but that was to be expected. "Although at the rate I've been going this past year, my skeleton is going to look like a jigsaw puzzle."

Raj nodded; broken bones were a hazard of their profession. "I've brought you here to discuss a few things," he said. Young Teodore had talked a little with him, rather more with Ludwig Bellamy and some of the Companions, and Suzette had ridden by his litter a good deal.

He nodded at the pile of letters before the Brigadero noble. "You can see your cousin Marie doesn't think much of Ingreid Manfrond's stewardship."

Teodore nodded cautiously, running his good hand through his long strawberry blond hair. "I may have made a mistake supporting Manfrond for General," he admitted. "In which case the marriage was an . . . ah, unnecessary sacrifice."

"Let's put it this way," Raj said. "Ingreid Manfrond came at me with rather more than a hundred thousand fighting men — about half the home-levy of the Brigade, and the better half. Right now, between disease, desertion and battle, in the siege and the retreat, he's down to about forty-five thousand, all starving. While we're stronger than we were when we started."

Teodore nodded, tight-lipped. Raj went on: "Now, let's say Ingreid has the sense to retreat, heading for the north or even the Costa dil Orrehene in the far west. He'd be lucky to have twenty thousand by the time he reached safe territory where I'd have to let him break contact. Personally I think every man with him would die or desert before then. But say he did, and raised another hundred thousand men, stripping your garrisons in the north. That'd be the last of your fighting men this generation. Do you think he'd do any better in a return match?"

Teodore hesitated for a long moment. "No," he said finally.

Center's grid dropped down around the young man's face, showing heat distribution, capillary flow, pupil dilation.

subject teodore welf is sincere, probability 96% +/-2.

"Ingreid Manfrond isn't the only noble of the blood of the Amalsons," Teodore said. Beads of sweat showed on his forehead, although the evening was mild.

Raj nodded again. "There is that," he said. "But honestly now, could any of the likely candidates — could you, for example — do more than prolong the war even more disastrously for the Brigade — given the situation as it now exists?"

The pause was much longer this time. "No, curse you," he said at last, his voice a little thick. "Ingreid's tossed away the flower of our strength and handed you half the Western Territories on a platter. The south and the coastal cities will go over to you like a shot; there are hardly any Unit Brothers down there anyway. We'd end up squeezed between you and the Stalwarts and Guard to the north and ground into dogmeat. It might last one year, maybe two or three, but that's it."

subject teodore welf is sincere, probability 91% +/-3, Center said. **high probability of mental reservations to do with period after your departure.**

Teodore sighed and relaxed in his chair. "Anyway, *I* don't have to worry about it anymore, Excellent Heneralissimo."

Raj grinned, a disquieting expression, and jerked his chin toward the door. "On the contrary," he said. "Outside there is a saddled dog, with that priest of your household on another. This," he slid a paper across the table, "is a safe conduct through our lines."

The blue eyes narrowed in suspicion. "Your terms, Lord Whitehall?"

"No terms," Raj said, spreading his hands. "I make you a gift of your freedom. Do with it what you will."

The Brigadero picked up the paper and examined the seals, gaining a few seconds time. "How do you know I won't advise Ingreid to resist and tell him what I know of your dispositions?" he said.

"I don't," Raj replied. "But I'm fairly sure of your intelligence . . . and your regard for your people." *Also of your hatred of Ingreid and regard for the fortunes of the House of Welf, but let's be polite.*

An orderly came in with Welf's sword-belt. The weapon was in its scabbard, the flap neatly buckled over the butt of the revolver opposite it. Teodore stared at him wonderingly as he stood to let the man buckle it about him. Then his face firmed, and he made a formal bow.

"Messer Heneralissimo, Messa Whitehall, messers," he said, and turned on his heel to walk out into the gathering darkness.

"That was a bit of a risk," Jorg Menyez said soberly.

"About a nine-tenths chance I'm right," Raj said. He looked around at the Companions and his wife. "And now we can expect another guest."

"Ser."

Raj shot upright, hand going to the pistol beneath his pillow. Suzette sat up beside him, a gleam in the darkness of the room. The voice came again from outside the door.

Raj padded over to it, pulling on his uniform trousers. "Yes?" he said, walking out into the ready room.

"Shootin' in t' barb camp," M'Lewis said.

"The Skinners?"

"Barb guns, ser," the ferret-faced scout said. There was burnt cork on his cheeks and a black knit cap over his hair; the testimony was first-hand. "Purty heavy, then dyin' away."

"Shall I beat to arms, *mi heneral*?" Tejan M'Brust asked; he was officer of the night watch.

Raj blinked and looked out the window. Maxiluna three handsbreadths from the horizon, near the Saber. Four hours until dawn.

"No," he said. "Let the men get their sleep." To M'Lewis. "Keep an eye on things, but don't interfere unless they move out of their camp."

Raj waited impassively, seated at the head of the long table. It was an hour short of noon; formalities with safe-conducts and protocol had eaten the hours since dawn. The common room of the inn was severely plain, whitewashed stone walls, hearth, long table, all brightly lit through tall windows flung open to the mild humid air. The inlaid platinum mace of office lay in front of Raj; his personal banner and the Starburst of Holy Federation stood against the wall behind him, but otherwise he hadn't made any effort to fancy it up. Some of the officers standing behind and to either side of him were talking softly. Cabot Clerett was stock-still but fairly quivering with tension. Once or twice Raj thought he was actually going to walk out on the ceremony, and only a word from Suzette in his ear calmed him down a little.

At last a snarl of Brigade kettledrums sounded outside, answered by a lilt of bugles. Boots crashed to earth as the honor guard presented arms. Bartin Foley's clear baritone announced:

"Her Illustriousness, Marie Welf, Provisional Regent of the Brigade. His Formidability, Teodore Welf, Grand Constable of the Brigade."

Foley marched through, saluted, and dropped to parade rest beside the door.

"The *Heneralissimo Supremo*; Sword-Bearing Guard to the Sovereign Mighty Lord and Sole Autocrat Governor Barholm Clerett; possessor of the proconsular authority for the Western Territories; three times hailed Savior of the State, Sword of the Spirit of Man, Raj Ammenda Halgren da Luis Whitehall! The Heneralissimo will receive the Regent and Grand Constable. Enter, please."

The two young Welfs walked in proudly, Marie's hand resting on her cousin's good arm. Raj raised a mental eyebrow as he watched the woman's cold hawk-face; beautiful enough, but Ingreid might as well have taken a sicklefoot to his bed, if it had been against her will. They halted across the table from him; Teodore bowed, and Marie made a formal curtsey.

Silence fell, until breathing and the low tick of a pendulum clock in one corner were the loudest sounds.

Raj took the victor's privilege. "What of General Ingreid Manfrond, who I assumed ruled the Brigade?" He kept his voice carefully neutral.

"Ex-General Ingreid has been deposed by the assembly-in-arms," Teodore said, meeting Raj's eyes levelly. "For treasonous incompetence. Civilian authority has been vested in Marie Welf as nearest in blood to the last legitimate General, and military authority in myself. Ingreid Manfrond was placed under arrest last night. Unfortunately, he killed himself before he could be brought for trial."

Raj nodded; Marie Welf *was* wearing a black ribbon on one arm in formal token of mourning. She was also wearing the ceremonial laser-pistol of the Generals over a gown stiff with gold embroidery and silver lace.

"I take it this embassy is recognition of defeat?" Raj went on.

Two more stiff bows. This time Marie spoke, in a husky contralto. "*Heneralissimo*, as the Brigade's armies are still in the field, I request terms of surrender equivalent to those given the Squadron nobles who surrendered before the final battles in the Southern Territories."

Ah, shrewd, Raj thought. Technically reasonable, and it would preserve two-thirds of the landholdings of individual Brigade members, rather than the one-third he'd been granting up to now.

"I'll certainly recommend those terms to the Sovereign Mighty Lord," Raj said judiciously. Whoever ended up as Vice-Governor out here was going to need the Brigaderos in a not-too-sullen mood. "And I'm sure those of my officers with influence at court will as well."

That was Cabot Clerett's cue. After an embarrassing

pause, he spoke in a tone suggesting that the words were being dragged out of concrete:

"I will certainly recommend that course to the Sole Rightful Autocrat."

Raj resumed: "Unfortunately, pending confirmation from East Residence all I can accept is unconditional surrender."

Marie stiffened, but Teodore leaned over to whisper in her ear. "Very well," she said bleakly, and drew the ancient laser. She stepped forward to lay it on the table before Raj; Teodore followed with his sword.

Raj nodded, smiling. It took several years off his face. "I'll have rations sent to your camp immediately, Grand Constable," he said. "We'll return the men to their homes as rapidly as possible. Please, be seated."

Suzette went round the table to draw Marie Welf to a chair. "I have been looking forward to meeting you in person," she said. "This is Colonel Clerett, nephew to the Governor . . . "

The citizens of Carson Barracks watched in silence as Raj Whitehall rode through the gates, following the Starburst flag of the Civil Government. Their silence seemed more stunned than hostile, as they crowded thickly before the low squat buildings and the barbaric ornament of gilded terracotta; lines of infantry kept them from the pavement. Paws thudded, the ironshod wheels of the guns rumbled over granite paving blocks and the hobnailed boots of marching foot soldiers crashed down. The column was thick with banners, color-parties representing all the units. The cheering started as the color party trotted into the central square; it was packed with the orderly ranks of the Expeditionary Force. Bannermen peeled off to stand before their comrades as Raj rode on to the steps of the palace, beneath the three-story columns shaped in the form of Federation landing boats.

The noise beat at him like surf as he pulled Horace to a halt. Teodore Welf stood to hold his bridle as he swung down; Raj waited until Suzette's fingers rested on his swordarm before he began to climb the steps. The mace of office and symbol of the proconsular power was in the crook of his left elbow, responsibility heavier than worlds. The Companions followed him in a jingle of spurs on marble.

He stopped at the top of the stairs, turned to face the assembled ranks and held up his right hand for silence. It fell slowly.

"Fellow soldiers," he began. Another long swelling roar. "I said when we started this campaign a year ago" — *was it that long since Stern Isle?* — "that you needn't fear to face any troops in the world. You've met an army ten times your numbers, and beaten it utterly. Your discipline, your courage, your endurance have won a victory for the Civil Government that men will remember for ever. I'm proud to have commanded you."

He bowed his head in salute. This time the sound of his name beat back from the high buildings surrounding the square like thunder echoing down a canyon.

"*RAJ! RAJ! RAJ!*" Helmets went up on rifles, bobbing in rhythm to the chant. Yet when he raised his hand again, silence fell as if the sound had been cut off by a knife-blade.

"And the first thing I want you to do with your donative of six months' pay —" he cut off the gathering yell with a gesture "— is drink to our fallen comrades." That sobered the crowd a little.

"The Spirit has uploaded their souls to Its net. For the Spirit's sake, and theirs, and mine, remember that this land and these people are now also subjects of the Civil Government of Holy Federation, not our enemies." He smiled and made a broad gesture. "Remember that, and have fun, lads — you've earned it. Dismissed to quarters!"

He turned through the great bronze doors with an inward sigh of relief. The Spirit knew the men deserved the donative, and congratulations from their commander, but he'd never liked public speaking. Worse, there was always the risk some overenthusiastic imbecile would start hailing him with Gubernatorial honors, which rulers far less suspicious than Barholm Clerett would neither forget nor forgive.

The dying cheers were faint inside the great hall. Here the only soldiers were those who lined the red-carpeted passageway to the high seat of the Generals. They snapped to attention and presented arms as Raj passed by; he was conscious of six hundred years of history looking down from the walls. Six hundred years since Teodore Amalson conquered Old Residence and started this building; nearly that since his grandson finished it. Never in all that time had men in the uniform of the Civil Government entered here armed. That was not the only first today. Star Spirit priests proceeded him, swinging their censers of incense and chanting. Behind the seat the double lightning-flash of the Brigade was hidden by a huge Starburst banner. Other banners lay piled on the steps, Brigade battle-flags.

It was all highly symbolic, and from their stunned expressions the Brigade nobles who made up most of the audience appreciated every nuance. Raj paced up to the Seat, treading banners underfoot. Suzette stopped at the lower Consort's seat; Raj turned at the top of the dais and raised the mace of office. Save for the soldiers braced to attention, every head sank low in bow or curtsey, holding the posture until he sank back to the cushions.

"The Western Territories have returned to the care of Holy Federation, forever," he said. "And now, gentlemen, we have a great deal to do."

CHAPTER SIXTEEN

"Spirit, has it only been a month?" Raj said, looking down the table. The staff meeting had taken several hours, and it was not the only official gathering of his working day. "Middle age and Bureaucrat's Bottom is creeping up on all of us."

"Good work, Muzzaf." He tapped the sheaf of billeting and supply files before him. "Without you, we'd have had to do *all* this ourselves."

The slimly elegant Komarite bowed in his chair. "Willingly I suffer the emplumpment of the civil service in your cause," he said.

The Companions grinned; a few groaned in sympathy.

"One of us should escape," Gerrin Staenbridge said, leaning back and puffing on his cheroot. "Somebody's going to have to deal with the west coast."

Nods of agreement: the Forker family still had many partisans on the Costa Dil Orrehene, beyond the Ispirito mountains. A good many of them had refused to come in and swear allegiance.

"None of you," Raj said. "I'm going to quarter Juluk and his Skinners out there until they see the merits of law, order and submission."

After a moment's silence, Jorg Menyez spoke. "Now that is what they call an *elegant* solution," he said with a slow smile. His infantry were in charge of keeping order in the billeting zone, which was a fair definition of "utter futility" where Skinners were concerned.

"Kaltin, you *will* be getting out of town," Raj went on. "The Stalwarts have been making trouble north of

Lis Plumhas. I want you to take your 7th, the 9th and 11th Descott Dragoons, 27th and 31st Diva Valley Rangers, the 3rd Novy Haifa, and the 14th Komar and go put a stop to it. You'll pick up fifteen thousand Brigade troops from the northern garrisons; don't hesitate to listen to their officers, they've had experience with the savages."

Kaltin nodded eagerly, then paused. "Ah, those are mostly Clerett's troops, aren't they?"

"No, they're the Civil Government's troops," Raj said coldly. "And it's about time they were reminded of it. Since Colonel Clerett prefers to remain in the city" — *and sniff around my wife, damn him* — "I'm sending them with you."

His tone returned to normal. "Incidentally, no prisoners, and you're authorized to counterraid across the frontier once you've disposed of those on our soil. With Stalwarts, you have to speak in a language they understand."

"I'd have to swear eternal brotherhood with them before killing them, to make them really comfortable," Kaltin said. "Actually, I'm fairly glad to get away from my own household right now."

A chuckle ran through the other men. "You really should slow down," someone said. "You'll wear yourself away to a sylph."

Kaltin gave him a look of affronted virtue. "It's Jaine, the little mophead I rescued from the Skinners? It turned out she was some sort of fifth grand-niece of the family I'm billeted with here."

"That's a problem?" Raj asked.

"No, floods of happy tears and she's off to the kinfolk and I'd be a fool to object, wouldn't I? Only Mitchi turns out to have gotten attached to the girl and she's moping and blaming *me*."

"Get her pregnant, man," Tejan M'Brust said.

"She *is* pregnant. Have you ever slept with a woman who pukes every morning?" Gerrin made a *tsk* sound. "Easy for *you* to say. In any event, I'm glad to be on my way back to the field."

"Quickly," Raj said. "And take the Forty Thieves with you."

Antin M'Lewis looked up; his men were enjoying themselves in Carson Barracks, and only a few had been caught as yet.

"The Honorable Fedherko Chivrez is coming to join us," Raj said. "As the Governor's representative in the field." At the others' blank look: "He was Director of Supply in Komar back a couple of years."

Muzzaf Kerpatik swore sharply in a Sponglish whose sing-song Borderer accent was suddenly very strong.

Kaltin frowned. "Not the cheating bastard who tried to stiff us on the supplies just before the El Djem raid?"

"Just the one. And the one you and Evrard ran out a closed window headfirst, then held while Antin here started to flay him from the feet up."

"It worked," Kaltin pointed out.

Raj nodded. "And I still want both of you out of town when he arrives, which could be any time."

"Chivrez is Tzetzas' dog," Muzzaf cut in. "And the Chancellor never forgets an injury."

"Agreed," Raj said. "See to it you're gone by this time tomorrow." The two men left.

"If there's nothing else?"

Ludwig Bellamy coughed politely. "Ah, *mi heneral*, Marie and Teodore would like a word with you this evening. Confidential."

Raj raised a brow, caught by something unusual in the young man's tone. "By all means," he said.

"I thought I might be there," Ludwig said. "And possibly Gerrin?"

Raj leaned back in his chair. "They requested that?" he said, his eyes narrowing slightly.

Ludwig flushed slightly and looked at his fingernails. "No, it was just a thought."

"Then I'll see them alone in my private office in —" he consulted a watch "— twenty minutes. If that's all, messers? Not you, Gerrin."

When they were alone: "What was that in aid of, do you know?"

"Not really," the other man said, taking out a small ivory-handled knife and trimming a fingernail. "Ludwig has been talking to me of late . . . and not for the sake of my winsome charm, worse luck. I think he's worried about this administrator they're sending out; he's convinced it would be a mistake to replace you so soon, if that's what he's going to do."

"I was never much good at overseeing civilians," Raj pointed out.

"These Brigaderos are scarcely that, my friend. They're used to a strong hand. *And* they respect you, which they wouldn't some lard-bottomed penpusher from East Residence. Things need to settle down here. A year as proconsular governor would be a good idea; five would be better."

"A year might be advisable but it's unlikely, and five is neither," Raj replied. It was firm Civil Government policy never to unite military and civil command except in emergencies.

He tapped a thumb against his chin. "Ludwig's also been seeing a good deal of the late Ingreid Manfrond's widow, hasn't he?"

"My delectable young Arab conduit to the gossip pipeline tells me so. Ludwig's been hunting with Teodore a good deal, too. Hadrosauroid heads and deep conversation. I don't think you have to fear conspiracy; Ludwig's still of an age for hero-worship, and you're it."

"Conspiracy against me, no," Raj said. "Hmmm. Ludwig and Marie . . . that might not be a bad thing, in the right circumstances."

Those being a new address in East Residence for Marie Welf . . . or Bellamy, as she would be then.

Teodore would probably be welcomed there also, encouraged to have the revenues of his estates shipped east, given lands and office, and never, never allowed west of the Kelden Straits again.

"In any case, stick around, wouldn't you?"

Raj's private office was fairly small; he'd never felt comfortable working in a room that had to be measured in hectares. It gave off the bedchamber he shared with Suzette, which *was* that sort of place, and he supposed it must have been a maid's on-call room before the Palace changed hands. He'd had the plain walls fitted with bookcases and map-frames, and a solid desk moved in. Right now the overhead lantern and the low coal fire made it seem cozy rather than bleak, and he smiled as he welcomed the two young Welf nobles. The smile was genuine enough. Teodore was a likeable young spark, an educated man in his way, and he had the makings of a first-class soldier. Marie was just as able in her own way, if a bit alarming.

And she'll probably lead poor Ludwig a devil's dance, he thought, but that was — might be — Bellamy's problem.

"Be seated, please," he said. "Now, you had something you wished to discuss with me?"

The two Brigaderos glanced at each other. He nodded. "That door gives on to my bedchamber, and it's bolted from the other side," he said encouragingly. "The other door leads to a corridor with a guard party ten meters away. It's quite private."

Marie gripped the arms of her chair. "*Heneralissimo Supremo,*" she said, in fluent but gutturally accented Sponglish, "we have come to discuss the future of the world . . . starting with the Western Territories."

Raj leaned back in the swivel-mounted seat. "Illustrious Lady, I'd say that particular issue has been settled rather definitely."

"No, it hasn't," Marie replied. "You've said you want to unite the Earth."

"Bellevue," Raj corrected. "I've been *instructed* to unite the planet Bellevue, yes." Exactly by whom he'd been instructed was something they had no need to know.

"We believe — almost all the Brigade now believes — that you've been sent by the Spirit to do just that," Marie said passionately. There was a high flush on her cheeks, and her eyes glowed. "How else could you have defeated the greatest warriors in the world with a force so tiny?"

Teodore coughed discreetly; his sword-arm was out of its cast, although still a little weak. "I think I can speak for the Brigade's fighting men," he said. "That's about their opinion too, although not everyone puts it down to the Spirit. Some of them just think you're the greatest commander in history."

"I'm flattered," Raj said dryly. "The Sovereign Mighty Lord has many able servants, though."

"To the Outer Dark with Barholm Clerett!" Marie burst out. "We've all heard of his ingratitude to you, his suspicion and threats — and we've all heard of his other servants, Chancellor Tzetzas and his ilk who'd skin a ghost for its hide."

Teodore leaned forward. "Barholm didn't conquer the Western Territories," he said. "*You* did. We're offering you the Brigade, as General — and with the Brigade, the *world*. You want to unite it? We'll back you, and with you to lead and train us *nothing* can stop us. Your own troops will follow you to Hell; they already have, many times. That'll give you the cadre you need. In five years you'll march in triumph into East Residence; in ten, into Al Kebir. Your Companions will be greater than kings, and your sons' sons will rule human kind forever!"

Whatever I expected, it wasn't this, Raj thought.

Marie was leaning forward, fists clenched at her

throat and eyes shining. Raj looked from one eager
young face to the other, and temptation plowed a fist
into his belly. The taste was raw and salty at the back of
his throat. He kept most of it off his face, but neither of
the Brigaderos were fools. They exchanged a trium-
phant glance, and would have spoken if he had not
held up a hand.

"If —" he cleared his throat. "If you wouldn't mind
waiting for me in the conference room, messer,
messa?"

"I could do it," he whispered into the hush of the
room. Aloud: "I *could*."

It wouldn't even be all that difficult. The Western
Territories were naturally rich, and they had at least a
smattering of civilized skills among the native
aristocracy and cityfolk. The Brigade hadn't known
how to use them, but he would. Grammeck
Dinnalsyn could have the factories here producing
Armory rifles in a few months. Lopeyz was a better
fleet commander than any Barholm had on the
payroll. They could snap up Stern Isle and the
Southern Territories before winter closed the
sealanes. That would give them sulfur, saltpeter,
copper and zinc enough. Modern artillery would be
more difficult, but not impossible.

In a year he would have a hundred thousand men
trained up to a standard nobody on Bellevue could
match. The Skinners would flock to his standard. With
men like Muzzaf to help organize the logistics and a
fleet built in the shipyards of Old Residence and
Veronique, they could —

observe, Center said.

— and Raj Whitehall rode through the streets of a
ruined East Residence. Crowds cheered his name with
hysterical abandon, even though the harbor was filled
with fire and sunken hulks.

Chancellor Tzetzas spat on the guards who dragged

him before the firing squad. Barholm wept and begged. . . .

Maps appeared before his eyes; blocks and arrows feinting and lunging along the upper Drangosh. The towers of Al Kebir burning, and one-eyed Tewfik kneeling to present his scimitar. Fleets ramming and cannonading on a sea of azure, and the white walls of cities he'd only read of, Zanj and Azanian. The Whitehall banner floated above them.

Raj Whitehall sat on a throne of gold and diamond, and men of races he'd never heard of knelt before him with tribute and gifts . . .

. . . and he lay ancient and white-haired in a vast silken bed. Muffled chanting came from outside the window, and a priest prayed quietly. A few elderly officers wept, but the younger ones eyed each other with undisguised hunger, waiting for the old king to die.

One bent and spoke in his ear. "Who?" he said. "Who do you leave the scepter to?"

The ancient Raj's lips moved. The officer turned and spoke loudly, drowning out the whisper: "He says, *to the strongest*."

Armies clashed, in identical green uniforms and carrying his banner. Cities burned. At last there was a peaceful green mound that only the outline of the land showed had once been the Gubernatorial Palace in East Residence. Two men worked in companionable silence by a campfire, clad only in loincloths of tanned hide. One was chipping a spearpoint from a piece of ancient window, the shaft and binding thongs ready to hand. His fingers moved with sure skill, using a bone anvil and striker to spall long flakes from the green glass. His comrade worked with equal artistry, butchering a carcass with a heavy hammerstone and slivers of flint. It took a moment to realize that the body had once been human.

❖   ❖   ❖

Raj grunted, shaking his head. *Couldn't my sons —* he began.

any children of yourself and lady whitehall will be female, Center said relentlessly. **genetic analysis indicates a high probability of forceful and intelligent personalities, but the probability of any such issue maintaining stability after your death is too low to be meaningfully calculated.**

I could pick a successor, adopt —

irrelevant, Center went on. **the ruling structure of the civil government will never voluntarily submit to rule from outside — and you would represent a regime centered on the western territories. to force submission you would be compelled to smash the only governmental structure capable of ruling bellevue as anything but a collection of feudal domains. this historical cycle would resume its progression toward maximum entropy at an accelerated rate upon your death.**

Better for civilization that I'd never been born, Raj thought dully. The residue of the visions shook him like marsh-fever.

in that scenario, correct. Center's voice was always wholly calm, but he had experience enough to detect a tinge of compassion in its overtones. **i pointed out that your role in my plan would not result in optimization of your world-line from a personal perspective.**

Raj shook his head ruefully. *That you did,* he thought.

Voices sounded from the bedchamber, raised in argument. The bolt shot back and Cabot Clerett came through behind a levelled revolver — one of Raj's own, he noticed in the sudden diamond-bright concentration of adrenaline. The younger man was panting, and his shirt was torn open, but the muzzle drew an unwavering bead on Raj's center of mass.

"Traitor," Clerett barked. His heel pushed the door

closed behind him. "I suspected it and now I can prove it."

Raj forced himself out of a crouch, made his voice soft. "Colonel Cabot, you can scarcely expect to shoot down your superior officer in the middle of his headquarters," he said. "Put the gun down. We'll all be back in East Residence soon, and you can bring any charges you please before the Chair."

Which will believe anything you care to say, he thought. With a competent general as heir, Raj Whitehall became much more expendable.

"Back to East Residence," Cabot laughed. His face was fixed in a snarl, and the smell of his sweat was acrid. "Yes, with a barbarian army at your back. Your henchmen may kill me afterwards, but I'm going to free the Civil Government of your threat, Whitehall — if it *is* the last thing I do."

The door opened behind Clerett and Suzette stepped through; she was dressed in a frilled silk nightgown, but the Colonial repeating-carbine in her hands had a well-oiled deadliness. Clerett caught the widening of Raj's eyes as they stared over his shoulder. The trick is old, but the breeze must have warned him. He took a half-step to the side, to where he could see the doorway out of the corner of his eye and still keep the gun on Raj.

Suzette spoke, her voice sharp and clear. "Put the gun down, Cabot. I don't want to hurt you."

"You don't know — you didn't hear," Cabot shouted. "He's a *traitor*. He's even more unworthy of you than he is of the trust Uncle placed in him. I'll free *both* of you from him."

A sharp rap sounded at the other door. Everyone in the study started, but Cabot brought the gun back around with deadly speed. He was young and fit and well-practiced, and Raj knew there was no way he could leap the space between them without taking at least one of the wadcutter bullets, more likely two or three.

"*Mi heneral*, the Honorable Fedherko Chivrez has arrived." Gerrin's voice was as suave as ever; only someone who knew him well could catch the undertone of strain and fear. "He insists that you grant him audience at once to hear the orders of the Sovereign Mighty Lord."

Cabot's snarl turned to a smile of triumph. His finger tightened on the trigger —

— and the carbine barked. The bullet was fired from less than a meter away, close enough that the muzzle-blast pocked the skin behind his right ear with grains of black powder. The entry-wound was a small round hole, but the bullet was hollowpoint and it blasted a fist-sized opening in his forehead, the splash of hot brain and bone-splinters missing Raj to spatter across his desk. Clerett's eyes bulged with the hydrostatic shock transmitted through his brain tissue, and his lips parted in a single rubbery grimace. Then he fell face down, to lie in a spreading pool of blood.

Strong shoulders crashed into the door. Raj moved with blurring speed, snatching the carbine out of Suzette's hands so swiftly that the friction-burns brought an involuntary cry of pain. He pivoted back towards the outer doorway.

Gerrin and Bartin Foley crowded it; others were behind, Ludwig and the Welfs. Among them was a short plump man in the knee-breeches and long coat and lace sabot that were civilian dress in East Residence. His eyes bulged too, as they settled on Cabot Clerett.

Raj spoke, his voice loud and careful. "There's been a terrible accident," he said. "Colonel Clerett was examining the weapon, and he was unfamiliar with the mechanism. I accept full responsibility for this tragic mishap."

Silence fell in the room, amid the smell of powder-smoke and the stink of blood and wastes voided at death. Everyone stared at the back of the dead man's head, and the neat puncture behind his ear.

"Fetch a priest," Raj went on. "Greetings, Illustrious Chivrez. My deepest apologies that you come among us at such an unhappy time."

Chivrez' shock was short-lived; he hadn't survived a generation of politics in the Civil Government by cowardice, or squeamishness. Now he had to fight to restrain his smile. Raj Whitehall was standing over the body of the Governor's heir and literally holding a smoking gun.

He drew an envelope from inside his jacket. "I bear the summons of the Sovereign Mighty Lord and Sole Autocrat," he said. "Upon whom may the Spirit of Man of the Stars shower Its blessings."

"Endfile," they all murmured.

A chaplain and two troopers came in and rolled the body in a rug. Chivrez cut in sharply:

"The body is to be embalmed for shipment to East Residence." Then he cleared his throat. "You, General Whitehall, are to return to East Residence immediately to account for your exercise of the authority delegated to you. Immediately. All further negotiations with the Brigade will be conducted through me and my staff."

"You won't do it, will you, sir?" Ludwig Bellamy blurted.

Raj looked at the bureaucrat's weasel eyes.

observe, Center said.

He saw those eyes again, staring desperately into the underside of a silk pillow. The stubby limbs thrashed against the bedclothes as the pillow was pressed onto his face. After a few minutes they grew still; Ludwig Bellamy wrapped the body in the sheets and hoisted it. Even masked, Raj recognized Gerrin Staenbridge as the one holding open the door.

The scene shifted, to the swamps outside Carson Barracks. The same men tipped a burlap-wrapped bundle off the deck of a small boat. It vanished with scarcely a splash, weighed down with lengths of chain and a cast-iron roundshot weighing forty kilos.

"Of course I'll go," Raj said aloud. He looked at Chivrez and smiled. "You'll find my officers very cooperative, and dedicated to good government," he said.

Raj's smile grew gentle as he turned to Suzette; she stared at him appalled, her green eyes enormous and her fingers white-knuckled where they gripped each other.

"It's my duty to go," he went on.

observe, Center said.

This time the scene was familiar. Raj lashed naked to an iron chair in a stone-walled room far beneath the Palace in East Residence. The glowing iron came closer to his eyes, and closer . . .

chance of personal survival if recall order is obeyed is less than 27% +/-6, Center said. **chance of reunification of bellevue in this historical cycle is less than 15% +/-2 if order is refused, however.**

"It's my duty to go," Raj repeated. His head lifted, from pride and so that he wouldn't have to see Suzette's eyes fill. "And may I always do my duty to the Spirit of Man."

THE END OF BOOK IV

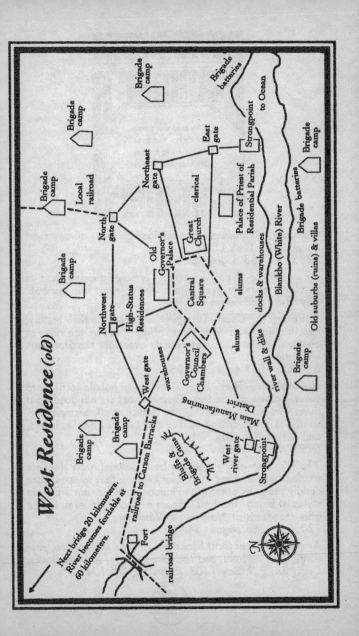

West Residence (old)

Brigade camp

Brigade camp

Brigade batteries

to Ocean

Brigade camp

Strongpoint

East gate

Northeast gate

clerical

Palace of Priest of Residential Parish

Local railroad

North gate

Great Church

Old Governor's Palace

Central Square

slums

Blankho (White) River

Brigade batteries

docks & warehouses

Old suburbs (ruins) & villas

Brigade camp

Northwest gate

High-Status Residences

West gate

warehouses

Governor's Council Chambers

slums

river wall & dike

Main Manufacturing District

Brigade camp

Brigade camp

Bluffs & Brigade Guns

West river gate

Strongpoint

Next bridge 20 kilometers. River becomes fordable at 60 kilometers.

railroad to Carson Barracks

Fort

railroad bridge

JOHN DALMAS

He's done it all!

John Dalmas has just about done it all—parachute infantryman, army medic, stevedore, merchant seaman, logger, smokejumper, administrative forester, farm worker, creamery worker, technical writer, free-lance editor—and his experience is reflected in his writing. His marvelous sense of nature and wilderness combined with his high-tech world view involves the reader with his very real characters. For lovers of fast-paced action-adventures!

THE REGIMENT
The planet Tyss is so poor that it has only one resource: its fighting men. Each year three regiments are sent forth into the galaxy. And once a regiment is constituted, it never recruits again: as casualties mount the regiment becomes a battalion ... a company ... a platoon ... a squad ... and then there are none. But after the last man of *this* regiment has flung himself into battle, the Federation of Worlds will never be the same!

THE WHITE REGIMENT
All the Confederation of Worlds wanted was a little peace. So they applied their personnel selection technology to war and picked the greatest potential warriors out of their planets-wide database of psych profiles. And they hired the finest mercenaries in the galaxy to train the first test regiment—they hired the legendary black warriors of Tyss to create the first ever White Regiment.

THE KALIF'S WAR
The White Regiment had driven back the soldiers of the Kharganik empire, but the Kalif was certain that

he could succeed in bringing the true faith of the Prophet of Kargh to the Confederation—even if he had to bombard the infidels' planets with nuclear weapons to do it! But first he would have to thwart a conspiracy in his own ranks that was planning to replace him with a more tractable figurehead . . .

FANGLITH
Fanglith was a near-mythical world to which criminals and misfits had been exiled long ago. The planet becomes all too real to Larn and Deneen when they track their parents there, and find themselves in the middle of the Age of Chivalry on a world that will one day be known as Earth.

RETURN TO FANGLITH
The oppressive Empire of Human Worlds, temporarily filed in *Fanglith*, has struck back and resubjugated its colony planets. Larn and Deneen must again flee their home. Their final object is to reach a rebel base—but the first stop is Fanglith!

THE LIZARD WAR
A thousand years after World War III and Earth lies supine beneath the heel of a gang of alien sociopaths who like to torture whole populations for sport. But while the 16th century level of technology the aliens found was relatively easy to squelch, the mystic warrior sects that had evolved in the meantime weren't. . . .

THE LANTERN OF GOD
They were pleasure droids, designed for maximum esthetic sensibility and appeal, abandoned on a deserted planet after catastrophic systems failure on their transport ship. After 2000 years undisturbed, "real" humans arrive on the scene—and 2000 thousand years of droid freedom is about to come to a sharp and bloody end.

THE REALITY MATRIX

Is the existence we call life on Earth for real, or is it a game? Might Earth be an artificial construct designed by a group of higher beings? Is everything an illusion? Everything is—except the Reality Matrix. And what if self-appointed "Lords of Chaos" place a chaos generator in the matrix, just to see what will happen? Answer: The slow destruction of our world.

THE GENERAL'S PRESIDENT

The stock market crash of 1994 makes Black Monday of 1929 look like a minor market adjustment—and the fabric of society is torn beyond repair. The Vice President resigns under a cloud of scandal—and when the military hints that they may let the lynch mobs through anyway, the President resigns as well. So the Generals get to pick a President. But the man they choose turns out to be more of a leader than they bargained for....

PRAISE FOR
LOIS MCMASTER BUJOLD

What the critics say:

The Warrior's Apprentice: "Now here's a fun romp through the spaceways—not so much a space opera as space ballet.... it has all the 'right stuff.' A lot of thought and thoughtfulness stand behind the all-too-human characters. Enjoy this one, and look forward to the next." —Dean Lambe, *SF Reviews*

"The pace is breathless, the characterization thoughtful and emotionally powerful, and the author's narrative technique and command of language compelling. Highly recommended." —*Booklist*

Brothers in Arms: "... she gives it a geniune depth of character, while reveling in the wild turnings of her tale.... Bujold is as audacious as her favorite hero, and as brilliantly (if sneakily) successful." —*Locus*

"Miles Vorkosigan is such a great character that I'll read anything Lois wants to write about him.... a book to re-read on cold rainy days." —Robert Coulson, *Comics Buyer's Guide*

Borders of Infinity: "Bujold's series hero Miles Vorkosigan may be a lord by birth and an admiral by rank, but a bone disease that has left him hobbled and in frequent pain has sensitized him to the suffering of outcasts in his very hierarchical era.... Playing off Miles's reserve and cleverness, Bujold draws outrageous and outlandish foils to color her high-minded adventures." —*Publishers Weekly*

Falling Free: "In *Falling Free* Lois McMaster Bujold has written her fourth straight superb novel.... How to break down a talent like Bujold's into analyzable components? Best not to try. Best to say 'Read, or you will be missing something extraordinary.' " —Roland Green, *Chicago Sun-Times*

The Vor Game: "The chronicles of Miles Vorkosigan are far too witty to be literary junk food, but they rouse the kind of craving that makes popcorn magically vanish during a double feature." —Faren Miller, *Locus*

MORE PRAISE FOR
LOIS MCMASTER BUJOLD

What the readers say:

"My copy of *Shards of Honor* is falling apart I've reread it so often.... I'll read whatever you write. You've certainly proved yourself a grand storyteller."
—Liesl Kolbe, Colorado Springs, CO

"I experience the stories of Miles Vorkosigan as almost viscerally uplifting.... But certainly, even the weightiest theme would have less impact than a cinder on snow were it not for a rousing good story, and good storytelling with it. This is the second thing I want to thank you for.... I suppose if you boiled down all I've said to its simplest expression, it would be that I immensely enjoy and admire your work. I submit that, as literature, your work raises the overall level of the science fiction genre, and spiritually, your work cannot avoid positively influencing all who read it."
—Glen Stonebraker, Gaithersburg, MD

" 'The Mountains of Mourning' [in *Borders of Infinity*] was one of the best-crafted, and simply best, works I'd ever read. When I finished it, I immediately turned back to the beginning and read it again, and I can't remember the last time I did that."
—Betsy Bizot, Lisle, IL

"I can only hope that you will continue to write, so that I can continue to read (and of course buy) your books, for they make me laugh and cry and think ... rare indeed."
—Steven Knott, Major, USAF

What do you say?

Send me these books!

Shards of Honor 72087-2 $4.99 _____

The Warrior's Apprentice 72066-X $4.50 _____

Ethan of Athos 65604-X $4.99 _____

Falling Free 65398-9 $4.99 _____

Brothers in Arms 69799-4 $4.99 _____

Borders of Infinity 69841-9 $4.99 _____

The Vor Game 72014-7 $4.99 _____

Barrayar 72083-X $4.99 _____

The Spirit Ring (hardcover) 72142-9 $17.00 _____

Lois McMaster Bujold: Only from Baen Books

If these books are not available at your local bookstore, just check your choices above, fill out this coupon and send a check or money order for the cover price to Baen Books, Dept. BA, P.O. Box 1403, Riverdale, NY 10471.

NAME: _____

ADDRESS: _____

_____

I have enclosed a check or money order in the amount of $ _____.

POUL ANDERSON

Poul Anderson is one of the most honored authors of our time. He has won seven Hugo Awards, three Nebula Awards, and the Gandalf Award for Achievement in Fantasy, among others. His most popular series include the Polesotechnic League/Terran Empire tales and the Time Patrol series. Here are fine books by Poul Anderson available through Baen Books:

THE GAME OF EMPIRE

A *new* novel in Anderson's Polesotechnic League/Terran Empire series! Diana Crowfeather, daughter of Dominic Flandry, proves well capable of following in his adventurous footsteps.

FIRE TIME

Once every thousand years the Deathstar orbits close enough to burn the surface of the planet Ishtar. This is known as the Fire Time, and it is then that the barbarians flee the scorched lands, bringing havoc to the civilized South.

AFTER DOOMSDAY

Earth has been destroyed, and the handful of surviving humans must discover which of three alien races is guilty before it's too late.

THE BROKEN SWORD

It is a time when Christos is new to the land, and the Elder Gods and the Elven Folk still hold sway. In 11th-century Scandinavia Christianity is beginning to replace the old religion, but the Old Gods still have power, and men are still oppressed by the folk of the Faerie. "Pure gold!"—Anthony Boucher.

THE DEVIL'S GAME

Seven people gather on a remote island, each competing for a share in a tax-free fortune. The "contest" is ostensibly sponsored by an eccentric billionaire—but the rich man is in league with an alien masquerading as a demon . . . or is it the other way around?

THE ENEMY STARS

Includes for the first time the sequel to "The Enemy Stars"; "The Ways of Love." Fast-paced adventure science fiction from a master.

SEVEN CONQUESTS

Seven brilliant tales examine the many ways human beings—most dangerous and violent of all species—react under the stress of conflict and high technology.

STRANGERS FROM EARTH

Classic Anderson: A stranded alien spends his life masquerading as a human, hoping to contact his own world. He succeeds, but the result is a bigger problem than before . . . What if our reality is a fiction? Nothing more than a book written by a very powerful Author? Two philosophers stumble on the truth and try to puzzle out the Ending . . .